VESSEL OF KALI

VESSEL OF KALI

RICHARD MILNER

Moz & Callie,

For unremitting love and
support, this book is a small
gesture.
Moz — thank you for making
one dream come perfectly
true.
Callie — you're as wonderful a
friend now as you were when
sleeping on a mattress on our
floor in Japan.

ISBN: 978-0-578-13715-5
eBook ISBN: 978-1-4951-0144-1

richardmilnerauthor.com

facebook.com/richardmilnerauthor
twitter.com/AuthorMilner
authormilner.tumblr.com/

Jacket design: Brandon Blackwell
Author photograph: Tripp Page

For you who've had to fight for the right to your own inborn dignity.

For my wife, in whom I daily see the face of the Great Mistress.

ACKNOWLEDGEMENTS

Thank you to all the individuals who supported me over the years and helped make this book possible:

Melinda, my wife, for listening to my endless monologues and offering clarity in return; Andrew Morris, my editor, whose profound insight into themes and structure finally made me a true believer in my own work – accept the compliment, man!; the members of Sit Down, Shut Up & Write – both the OC and Austin variety – for being the guardrails on an unstable path; Rita Nelson, for wisdom, patient conversations, and unflagging cheerleading; Karen & Larry White, for understanding both mystical and practical concerns; Frank Pray, for timekeeping and spurning me to my first public book reading; Uday Gupta, for unconditional acceptance and a whole lot of crazy ideas; Lisa Bryan, for saving me from the greatest terror of all: formatting; Brandon Blackwell, for making a kick-ass cover in the middle of harsh deadlines; Zachary Turner, Josh Navarro, and Damarcus Holbrook, for creating amazing pieces of book-inspired art; Tyler Cushing, for helping me get a handle on how to present this work to others.

Thank you to the myriad friends, acquaintances and near-strangers who offered an offhand comment of support; you'll never know how strongly you affected me.

All the wordsmiths, alive or deceased, whom I count as influences – Poe, Lovecraft, Conrad, Dick, Herbert, Miéville, to name a few – your prowess and talent continue to humble me and provide bottomless inspiration.

If I've forgotten anyone, the fault is mine.

TABLE OF CONTENTS

PREFACE

When they escape Illusion, they dwell here incarnate. By virtue of being gods, they mimic aspects of their true selves: separate, but seeking contact; seeking to use the lash of power; longing for their old connections. But they never fear death, either the first time or after, for once dead, they know they will remember everything forgotten.

– Transcription from Kali'ka oral tradition (approximate)

PROLOGUE

Deep in catacombs beneath the golden, light-filled streets of New Corinth, sunken within black stone and the crackling, impetuous flickering of torchlight, two figures fought.

They whirled and spun; point, counter-point; charge, shock. One female, one male; she ivory, he blue, both blurred – conjoined in an interwoven contest of sweeping limbs and kinetics. They stabbed, arced, and struck. Seamlessly blended, peerless in form, never once did they collide, never once did their shifting, sliding, hammering limbs impact anything but the dark, enshrouding air.

Arrayed in a circle around the contest, the Kali'ka – disciples of the Goddess Kali – kept the hoods of their gray robes pulled forward and their hands clasped to their chests. Their murmuring mantra throbbed like a heartbeat and rose in the flame-filled darkness like sweet, sweet offerings to Kali, the Goddess of Time.

"In darkness, your eyes shine, oh Kali.
Tilt the wheel to carry us onward,
Over the ocean of birth and death."

Receded in the furthest, blackest corner stood the form of a man-creature – overseer of the rarely seen, arcane rite. Its gray hood was thrown back, revealing a perfectly smooth head of ashen, putty-like flesh tautly bound over a protruding brow and cheekbones. Its two blind, clouded eyes stared without blinking. Nestled in its forehead, a third eye ceaselessly flit and jittered in spastic fits and restless quivers.

The masked woman in their center, wearing Kali's fanged, black-eyed mask, flowed in elliptical eloquence and gyroscopic perfection, while her partner, the blue-painted man, matched her motion for motion. The single-edged blade in her left hand swept out and in, around and through, like a pendulum.

At the apex of rhythm, within the space where the man and woman fought, where the mantra of Kali'ka lips and tongues surged in unison and shifted against a foreground of motion, the Kali'ka crossed an impasse that the millennia-old history of their order would never recover from, never forget, nor ever see again.

A vision flared in the mind of the woman wearing the mask of Kali. It coated her eyes and stamped out the physical realm – the realm of Creation. It saturating her sight and shuddered through her in pounding waves.

...Puckered canyons like earthen wounds spewed gouts of magma across a ruddy horizon of barren mountains and scarlet dunes, sending their fiery rain to engulf the charred and split bodies saturating the desolate sandscape, a tinder of flesh for an oceanic, cascading inferno...

The vision winked away. She stumbled and staggered, snarling and gnashing at the air like a severed marionette. Her sense of self – ego, identity, will – disintegrated. It fled, locking itself away in a discrete, untouchable part of her consciousness, unable to intervene, unable to stop.

Each wrench of her shoulder, kick of her leg, and twitch of her arm sent the earthen room rocking and quaking. A hell-shriek of a host of voices erupted from her throat, muffled behind her mask, blasting the stone of the floor, walls, and ceiling, diffusing gossamer fractures that spit shards of stone and dust.

A spectral fist of blind, remorseless energy squeezed the chamber. Kali'ka dropped to the floor, their screams of terror colliding with their howls of pain, bursting from gurgles of blood lodged in their throats. Those on their knees begged with hands outstretched, blinded by scarlet rivers squeezed from their eyes. Some tried desperately to twist away and flee, but they were welded in place, unable to move, lanced by agony, skin to flesh to bone.

Only the blue-painted man in the center – partner to Kali, the man chosen to embody the god Shiva – stood firm. He braced himself with iron-taut legs. Clear as a pane of frosty glass, he observed his partner as she stood curled around herself, wrapped in miasmic, writhing energy.

The instant her gaze landed on him, the woman playing Kali shrieked and delivered a stone-hard, lunging kick to his chest that sent him sprawling to the ground. She slid over him, explosive, blade lifted to cleave him open.

In that moment, the man playing Shiva took no action to stop her, no movement to save his own life. He stayed propped on his elbows, staring at her with on odd blend of awe and awareness. He accepted her choice … whatever it might be.

At the sight of him and his acceptance – his acknowledgement and repose – she cooled as though plunged in a stream. She lowered her blade as her muscles loosened and her breathing evened. In one smooth motion, she gripped the underside of Kali's mask, yanked it off, and flung it across the room.

The moment the mask left her, the paralyzing grip of pain in the room vanished. Like an exhaled breath, the rumbling ceased. Without the mask, the woman's real, exposed face glared through a mane of auburn hair that fluttered in fiery wisps.

On the ground around her, Kali'ka grasped at their bodies, weeping, crying out, wailing to their Goddess to salvage their spirits from their wrecked forms. The woman who'd worn the mask of Kali, epicenter of chaos and source of bedlam, scanned the diorama of writhing bodies, her hard jade eyes inflamed with fading animal fury.

In a haze of sticky, red wrath, she vaguely remembered what had happened. Comprehension flit through her mind and evaporated. Rational thought melted. Memories blurred and bled together. The vision she'd seen inside – of red-hewn mountains and scarlet dunes – clashed with reality and exploded into fragments.

Never before – never! – had the ancient rite of the Gehana been consumed by this type of nightmare. And now, it happened here, with *her* as the genesis.

Confused, shocked, and dazed, she hurled Kali's blade to the floor in a rebounding clang and sidestepped crumpled Kali'ka who crooked their arms towards the ceiling like claws. Without a single look back, she swept out the doorway, in her wake leaving behind groaning, weeping, bloodied adherents. Many were incapable of even lifting themselves to their feet.

The man with blue-painted skin, whom she'd nearly cut in half, stayed exactly where she'd struck him, seeing nothing but the image of her auburn hair fleeing the room, waving behind like flames caught on the wind.

Meanwhile, in the corner, the third eye of the maggoty-white man-creature had stopped quivering and now tracked the woman's location, even as she raced through stone corridors far from the ritual room.

This was the evidence it needed; proof of its long-held secret.

The turning of the ages crept closer, and neither the Kali'ka under the streets of New Corinth nor the citizens above understood the dark edge they all teetered on.

***

Aboveground in the city of New Corinth, in the center of Advent Square, a lone man prowled from point to point, stabbing his fingers at the air and shouting in a snarling, scathing tone. His gray robe billowed behind him as he strode across the sprawling, marble plaza, cleft into the radiant, creamy-white cityscape. Around him, a ring of figures in the same gray robes stood motionless, their faces lost to the depths of their hoods.

"Your death shroud has come, New Corinth! We, the Kali'ka, are here! We have always been here, watching you, living amongst you! We dwell under the stone and soil of these very streets. We are the truth that paints the scions of Logic and their god Logos as frauds! As liars!"

Corinthians slowed along lanes, skyramps, terraced landings, and suspended causeways, their necks craned, heads tilted, to lift their hands to point at the crazed man roving in their midst. The citizens of New Corinth, holy city of the theocracy of Logic, shuffled to get a better view, gasping and clenching their hands to their mouths at a sight unseen for centuries.

The cultists. The grays. The third eye. The shadow, peeled from their collective unconscious, lifted from their whispering tongues. Living myths in breathing bodies, standing, talking, walking. No longer rumors, dismissed offhandedly, but actual, *physical* beings.

The Kali'ka were real. The disciples of the dark Goddess Kali existed, after all.

"We are the true face of the Goddess! We are the heirs of Earth, the ones most worthy! You once reviled us! You forget us! You, who refuse to cast your third eye on the darkness within! You, who gag on the mind-blighted light of New Corinth! Your statues, your creeds, your wealth, the light you cling to – all of it will die! Nothing will remain but a scar painted across the ground on a once-bright city!"

The roving man, his cohorts and their gray robes were the only spots of darkness in sight. The Eternal Day consumed the city, blanketing the citizens of New Corinth at all hours in a ceaseless brow-beat of shine. Light blazed down from megalithic superstructures around Advent Square, refracted from buildings' creamy synthstone surfaces.

"This beginning is the end. Mark me, supplicants of Logos! From this moment forward, right here, right now – I will leash us to one fate. I will carry us to an era where the Eternal Day has no meaning! The Goddess of Time, Kali, presides over the precession of ages. From the realm of Illusion, She waits and watches and demands your annihilation!"

Through the light of the Eternal Day, Corinthians caught snatches of the man's face, clumped with scar tissue and crisscrossed, torn flesh. His right eye was long-welded shut. The other held a pitiless gaze that never wavered, never faltered.

"I will crack you wide open to us, to *Her*, to what you've tried to ignore for centuries! It is inevitable!"

He slipped a hand up his sleeve and slid out a long, thin, duel-sided dagger that tapered to a fine tip. In the Eternal Day, the flat of the blade flashed like a seizuring beacon.

A hushed silence fell on the onlookers in the square. Never before had the citizens of New Corinth seen such a tool. Never before had their hands held any form of weapon. Yet, they recognized the dagger for what it was. It spoke to an imprint in their collective memory, of times long past where blood and bone collided with the sharp scuff of metal on stone.

The blade was the kindling of a purpose long forgotten: to survive and harm, through fang and blade to *live*.

"Goddess, I see You!! The darkness... I admit it! I embrace it! I hate them! They will never contain me, never control me!"

He pressed the dagger's edge into the softness of his throat.

"Life to death! Death to life!"

Graceful as wind, he yanked the blade in a fine, clean line. A geyser of red burst from his throat in petulant spurts and misting sprays. Seconds later, he teetered forward and his head smacked the white marble of Advent Square.

The crowd erupted, screaming, scrambling, arms flailing and shoving others who could only stare in dumbfounded shock. They dropped purses, shopping bags, and datapads. They lost the hands of their children, forgetting them in a futile attempt to flee unknown and inarticulate sensations.

Several of the gray-robes broke into economized, practiced movement, hoisting their fallen leader at the shoulders and thrusting into his neck a nozzle connected to a sack of pearly gel that, when squeezed, oozed globs into his wound.

A mass of caulk bulged out from the man's throat and solidified before it could drip, hissing and foaming into the exact form of his neck, leaving a crusty, prismatic film that flaked away in a meandering, coruscated dust shower. There was no scar left on his skin.

He lay there, drifting, his conscious mind teetering between worlds, his line of sight glimpsing the undercurrents of Illusion that churned the whitecaps of the physical realm, Creation.

...Crags of fire belched boulders of roiling magma across the rolling red dunes, through the flame-streaked air, screaming, searing over an endless plain of cindered, desiccated corpses...

He gasped awake and sucked in huge gulps of air. As his rattling chest slowed to a sputter, those holding him lowered him to the ground. New Corinth's effusive brilliance engulfed the rim of his unscarred, living eye in a halo of white.

Goddess... One day, I'll join you there in that other place! I and all of those worthy of Your name! We, the true Kali'ka!

All around him, Corinthians raced and scattered in a glorious, intoxicating fever of desperation and fear. The newly resurrected man rubbed his neck and sneered at them in a contorted twist of disgust, gratification, and enmity.

Running was a useless, feeble gesture, like anything else they did. The horror was real, lodged like a barb in their minds, gestating and primed to burst forth in a violent afterbirth of pulsing chaos. All the churning legs, all the jumbled sounds, all the trampled, useless bodies, all the stupid faces frozen in frantic foolery... All would be gone. All would vanish.

Soon, he reminded himself, soon. New Corinth, seat and citadel of Logic, the great operatic god experiment, would be reduced to nothing more than little dramatists and lost giants in a forgotten farce of history. Nothing and no one could deny their own true nature for so long, not without consequences.

Once Logic was placed face to face with the Kali, who dwelled within them all in the realm of Illusion, the city would obliterate itself in a firestorm of blood and death.

"Reconvene in the Veneer. It's time." He spoke like calmly poured water.

With those words, the cluster of gray-robed men and women scattered and sped away, each along a different path.

Their leader vanished behind them, dagger in hand, still fingering his new neck, melting into the motion and mayhem engulfing the streets of New Corinth, indistinguishable, interwoven, entwined.

Behind them on the pristine, white marble of Advent Square, a dark blot of blood stained the unblemished eye of Logic, unable to be scrubbed out.

ACT I

KINDLING

CHAPTER 1
CLOISTER SANGRA

Ascendant Elara Aeve ghosted through the vast, underground catacombs of Cloister Sangra, deep in the earth below the Eternal Day of New Corinth. She stalked over the uneven stone floor, legs piston-like, arms tightly crossed, the hood of her coarse, gray robe pulled forward. The white plume of her breath fumed in the frigid air, and her roving, jade eyes pierced the cold, torchlit darkness with the gaze of a predator.

She let herself be guided by familiarity, voluntarily captive to instincts that guided her down the cold, empty blackness of winding corridors, shoulder-width tunnels, and natural caverns, past spires of stone that climbed into the cavernous darkness overhead to touch their twins hanging in toothy rows.

If she was lucky, she wouldn't come across another Kali'ka until absolutely necessary.

She was late, she knew. Behind. They would be waiting for her, whispering in the dark without her present. Let them. Let them think what they would. Their opinions wouldn't change what had happened, any more than they would control her actions. She had no need to defend herself, least of all from her fellow ascendants. Kali's Eyes, they were nothing but an annoyance. Everyone was.

It was easier without others, without explanations, without having to justify herself. Without dithering platitudes, or cumbersome rituals and mundane precepts. It was far, far easier without the inconvenience of moralizations, or the impediment of consensus. *Her.* Just her, alone. Able to choose and not be hindered.

Besides, how could she explain to her fellow Kali'ka what she herself didn't understand? How could they see what they couldn't imagine and she could barely explain? Would her trembling hands and palpitating heart be enough? The waves of nausea and dizziness? The shifting and warping vision? No, no, it would all sound like rambling insanity.

It hadn't been her fault. She'd had no control over it. She'd never intended to harm those who hadn't earned it. She'd had no choice but to run and hide after the Gehana, to stay out of sight, to try and deal with … *whatever* had happened. That, more than anything, goaded her.

A physical, palpable *presence* had taken residence in her, ever since she donned and mask of Kali and hefted Her blade. It was as though the energy of that night lingered like the weight of peeled gauze, conspiring to change her into an indefinable, ruthless *something,* sculpting the materials of her spirit into a shape of crafted cruelty.

…The ruddy clay horizon of barren mountains and desolate plains. The flame-streaked sky spewing fiery meteors…

The vision wouldn't vanish and wouldn't abate. Her sight touched otherworldly images and impressions of pure, raging madness. Her third eye – the inner eye that faced inward and gazed on the unseen realm of Illusion – delved of its own accord into a world of fire, blood, and death, refusing to relent, refusing to cease.

…The sulfuric taint. The glow of embers. The bodies, endless like the scarlet dunes they saturated…

It never left, that place. It hunted, haunted. At all times it welled up to consume the full volume of her mind and being. Every restless night, every breathless morning, replaying over and over like a compulsive wheel of imagery. Devouring, roiling and gnashing, stalking her, *craving* her, enveloping her until she swore she *lived* there in the hellscape within.

…A titan of the cosmos, released. A living blade. A blood-slaked horror forging a trench of terrible life…

"Kali sees you, Ascendant Aeve."

The voice snapped Elara from her reverie. A gray-robed Kali'ka, hands tucked into her sleeves, approached from the opposite direction, passing through the sphere of a quivering torch's light.

Elara smoothed her face till she resembled a glacial bust. She tuned her voice to the practiced lilt of the greeting, lifting the tips of her fingers to her forehead. "As She sees all, adherent."

Only when the woman slipped into shadow did Elara risk a backwards peak. She stomped down irritation and indignation at being caught off guard. It must have been her hair, that's how. That's how they recognized her, in the dark of the cloister. Reaching into her hood, Elara tucked little escaping wisps of her thick, mahogany mane further behind her neck. Total anonymity was the safest route.

No one should be able to see her in the dark. No one at all. They hadn't earned the right to know her. Her darkness was hers, alone. Darkness was solace, and safety. Safety was solitude. And those three things were the same: darkness, safety and solitude.

Darkness without – fire within. The two worked in tandem. That was the Kali'ka creed, and she believed it utterly. She believed it because she *lived* it. It was a rational choice. There was simply no other way to survive. Separation was the pathway to freedom – the only pathway – she'd discovered growing up in New Corinth, aboveground.

"Come to me, Great Mistress," she whispered from fervent lips, blinking away acrid droplets of sweat that fell on her eyelashes, "Let my fire join with Yours ... Let my face become Your own."

***

Rounding a corner, Elara kept her eyes straight ahead as she passed into the Spine of Dogen. No matter which path she took – through the thin, obsidian columns of the Inner Court, the recursive, spiraling path of Silvia's Curve, or the rises and falls of the Third Manifold – she'd invariable have to pass through this central corridor. Better to get it over with than backtrack through ancillary passages that branched like arteries and diverged again and again only to reconnect in an obscure part of the cloister.

Elara passed Kali'la in twos, threes, clustered groups or straggling loners. They stood aside plumes of throbbing flame from firepots and slipped in and out of murky chambers. They stood tucked into niches and barely lit alcoves. They whispered in subdued hisses, gesturing vehemently, their flickering corneas glinting in the enflamed torchlight of the corridor.

In an open recess on the left, row upon row of adherents knelt facing the same direction, heads to the floor, murmuring the Chant of Ages, constant like the sweep of tides sliding in and out, glazing the shore.

"In darkness, your eyes shine, oh Kali.
Tilt the wheel to carry us onward,
Over the ocean of birth and death."

In a circular clearing on the right, pairs of Kali'ka shifted through sequences of kanas. At a glance, Elara recognized each individual kana: 44 … 45 … 46. Doing the whole cadence of 72, it seemed. The names for each form ticked off in her mind.

Sun Salutation. Moon Declaration. Tickling the Palm. Betwixt Rushes Run. Kissing Antlers. Ghost of Dusk. Clavicle Twain. Sky's Cavity.

She maintained her pace. If she restrained her energy and kept herself feeling small, she might be able to pass through undetected.

The Gehana had made her a celebrity, like one of the scions of Logos aboveground in New Corinth. The unexplainable events of that ritual had stoked the fire of superstition that already engulfed her. Violence had made her an icon.

Her innate reclusiveness didn't help, she knew. Nor did her uncompromising attitude. She didn't fumble over her choices, that was all. Was that such a rare trait? Nothing excused their muttering supplications and crane-necked stares, or their deference clothed in paranoia and dark reverence. They surrounded her in myth because they wanted to *believe*. And they wondered why she kept to herself.

Who were they, really? Amongst the Kali'ka – an order sworn to absolute anonymity – secrets defined everyone. Faces within faces, hidden in the dark – all of them. By what right did they pay any attention to her? By what merit did they presume to know anything – *anything* – about her?

They were blank people whom she didn't care to know, all of them.

Composites of mechanistic features and animated limbs painted into an overbearing pastiche.

The Kali'ka in the Spine of Dogen fell out of sight as Elara passed beyond its bounds and into the Seventh Arteriole, spiraling down in tight whorls, deeper into the bedrock and beating heart of Cloister Sangra.

The tension in her chest vented as she focused on slow, measured exhalations. This was her true home, roaming alone in the corridors of an underground catacomb. The original, mimetic womb-state. Separate, enclosed, with no one and nothing to distract her from a flowing, inner world of impressions and sensations.

She needed time to think, and space. Time, the Goddess's own domain, had turned against them. Their order was under siege. Something needed to be done. Action needed to be taken.

Elara had to convince the rest of her fellow ascendants, leaders of the cloister. They would be waiting, below. Soon, there'd be no escaping unwanted attention. Scrutiny. Complications. She was late. Behind.

In the meantime, she would be content, she decided, to live side by side with the shushing of her two slippered feet, the whisk of her robe, and the pulsing throb of her own hot blood in her ears, storming from the core of a fuming, roiling heart.

It was a better option than being with others – and less alone.

CHAPTER 2
THE COVEN OF ASCENDANTS

In one smooth swish of her robe, Elara lowered herself cross-legged onto the cold, stone floor, the final of five hooded figures sitting around a central firepit. Extending from their five backs, ever-shifting slashes of shadows jittered through the massive cavernous dome of the Chamber of Sarcophagi, deeply cleft into the lowest levels of Cloister Sangra. The blooming orange of the fire warmed Elara's face and hands, and melted some of the cloister's frozen dampness.

To the untrained eye, Elara and her fellow ascendants would appear still as stone statues sitting idle for generations in the lonely dark. Elara, though, caught ripples of seized breath and tense muscles when she sat down. Tiny insinuations of head turns and glances flickered and vanished.

Yes, they'd been waiting for her. She felt her lips curl back. Had they been talking about her before she arrived? She'd left her chambers to help, and what – for this? Gossip and whispers?

She felt her eyes gravitate to the one person in the circle of ascendants who she dreaded seeing more than the others: the man who played the blue-skinned god Shiva during the Gehana, whom she'd nearly split open with the blade of Kali:

Ascendant Inos.

Her eyes prodded for some cue, some key to Inos' thoughts, something she could use to confirm his judgment of her, something indicating that he thought she was blame for what had happened.

Instead, she saw only emptiness in his fire-illuminated face. He gazed into the fire, eyes cold and blue like a frosted sky, the yantra on his temples girding his deep-set eyes like guardians of ink. She frowned at the oddness of matte, waxy scars, all divots and lines, crossing his face and ears.

Encircling their group, the upright shapes of twelve sarcophagi spanned the darkness of the chamber. Blacker than the midnight of a new moon, they looked like portals to a starless plane, carved in the shape of an arched doorway large enough to admit a person.

No features were visible on their upright surfaces. No texture, no contours. They cast no shadows whatsoever. In the Chamber of Sarcophagi, perhaps the first-build part of the cloister – no one was sure – it was said only beings of Creation casted shadows. The sarcophagi were instruments of Kali's will, residing half in Illusion, projecting Her purpose, occupying the non-space between realms.

The twelve Undying Firepyres roared and lashed around the periphery of the chamber, one for each entrance, allowing passage so long as they burned, though the watery tar of the *pores* warding the thresholds of this innermost sanctum. The light from the firepyres lashed and furled from their iron pots, revealing great swaths of hematite glistening along the chamber's single, unbroken wall, etched with the geometric emblems of the now-dead Kali'ka language.

Elara stared out at the keepers of the firepyres, rocking in the darkness, tending their flames, stoking the coals and kindling, oblivious to the heat through their white, ovular masks. Not for the first time, she wondered, and admired, what it took to endure such a devotional, let alone volunteer to be a Kachina.

Inos lifted his hands and clapped twice, sharp like a blade, before lifting his firm baritone. "Hail, Kali!"

All five of them replied as one. "Hail, Great Mistress!"

"Hail, Goddess of Time!" Inos led.

Like a chorus, they raised their echoing voices. "Hail, Shadow Slayer! All hail, You who are dark and powerful! You, who guard the transition of ages! You, who wait on the surface of water!

"Fire destroys the old life. Blood is the path to new life. Shadow is where She dwells. To shadow we must go. To shadow we must go. To shadow we must go."

They placed their palms together, and Inos concluded the invocation. "Let the Coven of Ascendants begin."

In unison, they lowered their hoods and exposed their faces, a gesture left over from times when Kali'ka first hid under the ground beneath New Corinth.

Elara settled her hands, straightened her posture, centered her breathing, and attempted to stay calm and focused on the task at hand.

Then, at the sight of the woman sitting across the fire from her, she felt her anxiety spike.

Ascendant Marin's pinched, severe face looked at each of them in turn. Predictably, deliberately, she passed her eyes straight over Elara. *Of course* the thin, terse woman would take any chance to talk first.

Marin's contralto clipped along, deliberate and crisp. She tilted her chin high. "Our presence has become known. Our way of life is at risk. Rumors spread like disease: shadows stealing people out of homes; gray figures skulking in alleyways; the remains of horrific, bloody rituals; howls of pain from cellars; family members turning violently ill; whispers and paranoia."

"Too bad none of it is true." Ascendant Brae, shifted his great bulk and crossed his arms. His voice boomed. "I remember when discussion of the 'crazy cultists' took the form of tittering laughter over polite dinner conversation. Now that we're *real*, well … they don't know *what* to think, do they?"

Ascendant Oren cleared his throat and raised a weak-limbed hand for attention. "Um, now – not to interrupt, but I was thinking, well, it might be best – that is, we have to assume that His Holiness will respond, somehow. The scions of Logos and their Magistrate will be on the lookout."

Marin spoke in precise tones. "No Kali'ka, not one, can be picked out of a crowd. Not a single one of us doesn't undergo the same rigorous training."

"We have plenty of experience hiding in plain sight." Inos kept his muscular hands and long fingers cradled in his lap. "But not when someone is looking. We could easily give ourselves away, no matter how well trained, no matter how well we act the part of a Corinthian. We've never had anyone actively looking for us."

Brae guffawed. "They're not about to root us out. No offense." Inos raised his hands to say it was alright, and Brae continued. "They know to look, but they don't know what to look *for*. They're blind. Drugged on Levitant. Lost to worshipping Logos whenever they're not at pageants and Penance and so on. We all remember what it was like."

"Brae, that may be the case, but my main concern is…" Marin's eyelids fluttered in what Elara recognized as a sign of annoyance. The older woman hated feeling like her authority was being undermined. "If this man is indeed Kali'ka – the inciter, the one in Advent Square – there have never been dissidents in our order. Never. No sects, no divisions, no schisms."

"But, I just – I don't…" Oren's mouth got ahead of him, as always. He paused to restructure his thoughts. "He's drawing undue attention to our order. In a deliberate way, too. He's misrepresenting us. Violent, aggressive and all that. It's intentional. Why would he want that? What would he get out of it?"

Inos stared into the fire. "There have always been deviants who would warp beliefs or pervert language for their own purpose, to satisfy some internal defect or need. Like Logic and their god."

"He might not mean us direct harm." Marin waggled her hand dismissively. "He ideology could be a sham. More complicated plots have been flawlessly pulled off. Remember Cymbeline the First. He maintained his façade of allegiance to the scions of Logos for decades – as a fundamentalist, no less – simply to deliver false reports to His Holiness and thereby prevent other scions from inviting actual scrutiny into our goings on."

Elara stared at her in disgust. The truth or non-truth of her words didn't matter – she was lecturing. She was using her old, staccato 'teaching' voice. Funny how it sounded just like a Corinthian debutant. Slipping back into old habits in her old age? Repulsive.

"And, well, where do you suppose these…" Oren lowered his voice as though afraid he might be overheard. "…extremists – I suppose we can call them – would be?"

"Some lavish loft in the Uppers, maybe?" Brae was combing his puffy beard with sausage fingers, face contemplative. "His Holiness' Tabernacle? Under the floor in a scion's parish? I think they'd fit in very well strolling down the Path of Gold, actually … gray robes swaying, buying earrings, terrorizing the population. All in all, a pleasant day."

Marin sighed, exasperated. Oren rolled his eyes and kept talking. "My point is – the other cloisters could *be* the enemy, don't you think? Cloister Mors? Cloister Ignis? Some outside location? Some larger conspiracy at work? An ascendant perhaps, like us, you think? Someone with a lot of clout?"

Marin arched a pencil-thin eyebrow. "The Stabat wouldn't raise someone to ascendancy who isn't worthy to represent Kali. They're manifestations of the realm of Illusion. They represent Kali Herself, in this plane, in Creation. These are their sarcophagi, around us. Through them, the Stabat manifest themselves, perceiving the strands of our lives and acting accordingly. They're insentient entities, incapable of making such an error."

"Walking corpses is more like it." Brae winked at Elara. He knew her dislike of them. She suppressed a grin, which only encouraged him to keep going. "Nothing moving but their third eye. Lukewarm to the touch. Can't talk to them, can't argue. No ego. Doesn't matter how many times I see them. Disturbing."

"Have initiations gotten too lax?" Inos redirected things back on track.

Marin answered. "We shadow potentials for months, sometimes years before first contacting them. Even if a Corinthian *did* understand how to get through the pores, they'd never be able to pass as one of us down here."

Oren piped up. "Well, it would be best if we don't overlook practicalities. Food and provisional intakes need to be adjusted to compensate for the recent influx of people."

Brae crossed his thick, elephant arms. "Never thought I'd see so many Kali'ka *volunteering* to be cloistered. We didn't have a choice, at least, did we? Once we ascended. Adherents, though – initiates, even…?

It's too much of a change, too quickly, from their old lives."

"We have to be prepared, regardless." Oren lifted his hands and started finger counting. "Our smugglers – that is, the Kali'ka still living aboveground in New Corinth – have to be notified. Their contacts have to be informed, so on and so on, down the chain of contacts. We have to be careful of comeyes hovering above shops, that sort of thing. Might be best to cut back on more fringe requests. Soap. Paint. Pillows."

"Pillows." Brae chuckled and shook his head.

"Yes, pillows!" Oren mumbled something to himself. "Yes. That sort of thing."

"I'm meeting with one of my covens in a few days." Marin spoke as though no further points needed to be made. "We should receive new information then."

"Aboveground? At a time like this?" Inos spoke softly but firmly.

Silence passed over the group. Marin visibly composed herself, redoubling her efforts at imperiousness. For some reason that Elara couldn't put a finger on, Inos was the only one who could unsettle her.

After several purse-lipped seconds, Marin nodded yes.

Inos said nothing in reply. He just stared at her, calm – overly calm, deliberately so – examining her as though casually deconstructing her most well-hidden thoughts.

"I'm sure I'll be fine, Ascendant I nos. It's completely safe. I'll be extra careful." Marin looked away from him, shifting her weight and smoothing her robes. Her eyes rested on Elara for the first time since the coven began. Her cool gaze peered through the fire separating them.

"Ascendant Elara. Contrary to the norm, you're rather quiet and composed. But uninvolved, as usual. How nice of you to rejoin us after your … self-appointed isolation. As your once-advocate, I assumed I'd come to be able to predict the full breadth of your irresponsibility, but it seems I was wrong."

The tense mass in Elara's chest spiked. Just hearing Marin speak to her in that tone was enough to prime her body for conflict.

She chose her words carefully. "You said it yourself, Marin: *once*-advocate. That label falls off after initiation, let alone seven years later."

"Direct and disrespectful, as always, Ascendant Elara. Why bring further discord into an already tenuous situation?"

"Attack the attacker." Elara glared at her, refusing to blink. "Destroy those who would destroy you, including other Kali'ka. Isn't this what our order teaches? Admit, then accept, then embrace our innermost pain? Tear down our egos? Obliterate our falsities? Know ourselves, truly? That's what we profess to believe. That's what we learn when we practice kanas. That's what we teach. That is, in fact, what *I* teach, as an ascendant. An ascendant – just like you."

She tapped the yantra for Circle Eighteen – the first Circle of Ascendancy – etched into her left temple. It was an emblem of harsh slashes, curved lines, hooks and barbs, resembling the inscriptions they all wore.

Brae and Oren receded into the background. They wanted nothing to do with the clash of wills in front of them. Inos just raised an eyebrow and crossed his arms.

Marin ignored them. "Well then, Elara, as our *newest* ascendant, perhaps you'd have the wisdom to know what happened at the Gehana, a week ago. When you injured nearly thirty of our number. Plastein healed their body, but it can't fix whatever happened to their minds. A preventable waste of our plastein supply, I might add."

Elara caught Inos glance at her. So, he *had* been thinking about the Gehana, after all. She had been an instant from gutting him alive in a primal dream of otherworldly motion, an instant away from losing herself, tearing his body open, and spilling his blood on the black stone underfoot. Now he sat there, unconcerned and unmoved, just like then. Acceptant.

"You know that rituals exist for a reason, don't you, Elara?" Marin pressed. "To carve out safe pathways for us to approach dangerous forces?"

Elara said nothing.

The older woman scoffed. "The Goddess is unpredictable, and we open ourselves to Her every day. This is why we have to be so careful. This is why we can't be *rash*."

Elara faced her squarely. "I thought we were talking about the dissident Kali'ka in Advent Square, Marin."

"Of course. How like you to distract from the issue at hand. You did hear what I said, didn't you?"

Elara's fingernails dug into her clenched fists. "You assume what happened at the Gehana was my fault because I'm not careful? You assume I'm to blame because something *involved* me? I have no idea what happened. The Goddess can't be controlled. You just said as much."

Marin started shaking her head before Elara even finished her sentence. "You flaunted the vision of Kali that the Stabat chose you to wear. You. They chose *you* to embody the Goddess, at the one time – the *one time* – when we allow an image of Kali to be seen with our two physical eyes, when we behold the celestial contest between Kali and her consort, Shiva. You – you even disgraced Her further by tossing Her mask on the floor! And, you almost killed Ascendant Inos!"

"She didn't." Inos' factual enunciation cut in. "That, I think, is the point, Marin."

Marin ignored him. "Would you care to explain yourself, *Ascendant* Elara? Especially because you might vanish for another week when we're done here?"

Elara stared at Marin across the fire, seething, remembering her vision of a flame-scorched earth and blood-red sky. "No, I wouldn't," she whispered.

Several robes rustled as they were resettled.

"But I *would* like to talk about this threat to our order, Marin. I think we should contact the other cloisters, openly. Ask them what they've heard about these dissenters."

Marin fumed. "Out of the question."

"Why not?" Elara challenged.

"No single Kali'ka knows more than a handful of other Kali'ka. Covens know those in their covens. Not even ascendants of any cloister – Sangra, Mors, or Ignis – know more. We know those we advocate for and bring to Kali – no one else. The more Kali'ka who know each other, the more at risk we are. Secrecy keeps us safe. The cloisters are separated for a reason. It keeps us uncorrupted."

"I agree. It's a bad idea," Oren offered. "Selenist is often enough. We see each other every four years. That's it."

Elara scowled at him. "We have to turn our attention towards the man in Advent Square. The leader. A body without a head can't function. They're organized. But us? We're not even a whole, unified group. Look at us! We're sitting here talking in circles.

"We have to find out as much as we can. Not conjecture. *Facts.* There are deeper layers at play, and we can't just look at what's obvious. We can't afford to simply react. We have to be proactive. We have to find out who they are and where they came from, these *others.*"

"And what? Charge off to the other cloisters like an army?" Marin's face contorted in disgust.

"If need be! The Great Mistress is a warrior, isn't She? She single-handedly defended the gods from the daemon Bloodseed, correct? That's not just a story. It's *advice.*"

Marin lifted a hand to interrupt. Elara recognized the tactic: break down momentum to gain control over the discussion.

"I understand your point, Elara, but more importantly, this dissident leader – or extremist, or whoever he is – has exposed Corinthians to their inner selves. They've seen the face of the Goddess. They've been exposed to blood. Their third eye is being pried open. They are more at risk than we are."

"That's what I'm saying, Marin!" Elara wouldn't – couldn't – back down. "We were all once Corinthian. At one point, we all followed the scions and the precedents of Logic. Living dual lives, smiling for family portraits, attending Penance, misting on Levitant. We were all once used by their *doctrine.* But we were ready – ready to move on. The rest of New Corinth isn't, at least not yet. That's their choice. They're limbs that will hack themselves off … but not until they're ready. We can't be their guide if they don't *want* a guide."

"We have to be careful not to rescind on fundamentals, Elara." Marin jabbed the air with a bony finger. "The Kali'ka have no permanence beyond the span of our lives. Oral tradition is all we have, aside from the Codex. Logic has its statues, its artifacts, enough architecture – worldwide, I might add – to permanently stamp their face on Earth's surface. We do *not.* We must not put ourselves at unnecessary risk!"

Elara dug in. "The only ones at risk are the ones who follow this extremist fool and make themselves targets for *us*."

"Taking precautions is never a bad idea." Oren chimed.

"Oren – shut up." Elara never took her eyes off of Marin. "We can't sit idly by and wait for destruction. We're already past the point where we can *hope* that everything turns out alright."

"Kali must live, not us." Marin sneered at her as though she were a demented, ignorant child. "'And She will outlast all of us through our words –'"

"'– As they strike on the drum of the cosmos'? Thank you for reminding me. Save the quotable lessons for initiates and lower circle adherents."

"Now, more than ever, we need to abide by our principles, Elara. We need solidarity, not doubt and divisiveness."

"We need *leadership*. Our cloister needs *us*. Our order needs *us!*"

"Our order needs Kali! We have to believe that our beliefs will sustain us!"

Inos' eyebrows twitched at Marin. So, he at least understood the danger in that type of thinking. How had Marin become so blind?

"Kali's Eyes! This is ridiculous." Elara planted a fist on the floor and pushed herself to her feet.

Marin lurched forward. "Elara! The Coven of Ascendants hasn't ended!"

"You mean the waste of time where we all sit around and agree with you? Where we listen to your contradictory ideas?"

Brae gave her a warning look. "Elara –"

"Brae … not now." She raised a palm towards him.

"Where are you going?" Marin demanded.

"To get answers."

"What? What does that mean? You owe us a better explanation than that!" Marin's voice was firm, but her little, weathered hands fidgeted with her robes.

At that moment, Elara saw the severe, dogmatic woman not as she'd first seen her in a Leviden years ago – darkly beautiful, a phantom of mystique, twisting the stem of a drink, eyeing Elara above the rim, thick lipstick matching the red of her dress – but as she looked now: reedy, slumped in her robes like a child wrapped in blankets, leathery face stretched into a mass of lines and creases. A faint, scorched wick. The bellows of her life had been blown to exhaustion. A charred wick could burn no fire. Chilled embers could ignite no more.

Marin was closed. Tired. Lost.

Elara couldn't let herself be swayed by sentiment or the ties of the past. Survival demanded brutality. Survival demanded absolute self-sufficiency. Survival meant becoming untouchable, invulnerable.

"I owe you nothing, Marin. All the debating in the world isn't going to save us."

Across the fire, the older woman glowered. Tiny embers sparked and spat at the air. When she spoke, it was a venomous hiss. "Neither are *you*, Ascendant Aeve."

The chamber fell silent. Only Inos' steel-gray eyes met Elara, stable and focused through spitting sparks and the singe of smoke.

Is one enough, Goddess? One ascendant worthy of Your mantle?

The rage in Elara's heart dimmed. In its place flooded an icy, dire resolve more lethal than an uncontrolled conflagration. It left her frozen, but hollow. Furious, but numb.

"Maybe the Great Mistress wouldn't save us, either, not if She saw how squabbling and divided we've become. Maybe *we* are the limbs that need to be cut from *Her* body. Maybe these ... *extremists* are exactly what we need to save us."

With that, she swept her robes aside and cut a path out of the Chamber of Sarcophagi, through the darkness of the cloister, without others, and therefore, without the dagger of betrayal.

CHAPTER 3
THE CODEX

Elara strode furiously down the corridors of Cloister Sangra, fuming, stamping down thoughts of the Coven of Ascendants. The *failed* coven. Adherents bowed and murmured greetings to her as she passed. She completely ignored them. Fragments of conversations from the coven, segments of looks, glances and scathing insults paraded in her mind as though stuck on a spinning wheel.

Damn Marin and her obtuseness! Her old advocate was a roadblock to reason. Oren was nearly as bad – obsessing over orderliness, plying for approval. Elara doubted her own worthiness, her own sanity, even, being raised by the Stabat to the company of such "ascendants."

No matter. She would act by herself, but she needed space and time to think. The solitude of the Codex – quiet and more conducive to focus than even her chambers, at times – was exactly what she needed.

Even if other Kali'ka, ascendants included, were willful and stupid at times, the order of the Kali was needed. No other refuge existed for those above. No other home existed for those who awoke from Logic. She had to do *something* about the crazed dissident in Advent Square, not simply debate in circles.

She passed through an intersection of familiar corridors that transitioned to an artificial sub-structure with hugging support arches under a semicircular ceiling. The pathway broke into a staircase wide enough for eight abreast that led down to a vast multi-floored interior chamber completely encased by a combination of plateglass shielding and the cloister's natural stone.

At the low-ceilinged, curtained entryway, a lone Kali'ka sat outside on the floor, legs crossed, one finger pressing on a spineback in her hands as she held it at a very precise distance from her long, thin nose.

"Kali sees you, Adherent Cassandra."

The lanky woman jumped as though bit. She starting to get up, but Elara held up a hand for her to stop.

Cassandra resettled herself and absently muttered. "As She see all. I didn't expect to see you again so soon, Ascendant Aeve. Looking up the usual information? Reverend Dogen of Sight? The philosophies of Musash the Twin-Bladed?"

Elara wrinkled her nose. "I, uh… I'm not exactly sure, Cassandra. I'll let you know if I need anything." Best not divulge the reason behind her visit. Easier to keep people out her way, too.

"Of course, ascendant." Cassandra's bony frame bowed from where she sat. She extended an arm to the curtained entrance. "The black blood of Kali beckons us all."

Elara nodded and grunted something interpretably committal before sweeping past the woman and into the Codex, where she was alone and able to breathe.

The air, though filtered and sterile, nonetheless carried the musty smell peculiar to decaying spinebacks. It was a comforting odor. The smell, combined with solitude, helped to balm her agitated heart and redirect her mind to what she did best: problem-solve in seclusion. Think alone, then act alone. Marin, the Gehana, the agitator in Advent Square – all of it started to fade into a neatly wrapped bundle in the back of her skull, visible, understandable, but non-intrusive.

As the only physical repository of Kali'ka knowledge in Cloister Sangra, the Codex was an oddly incongruous reminder of the technological advances eschewed by typical cloister life, yet commonplace in the world of New Corinth above. It resembled an antiquated Corinthian museum, filled with massive, mahogany shelves, standlamps, candelabras, hanging lamps, support columns, and cylindrical flowshields that suspended tomes revolving in strange waves of flickering particles, all consumed in the amber glow of dark wood paneling and brass.

The Codex served as an indicator of a lost segment of Kali'ka past. Knowledge was lost, history forgotten, no matter how well-preserved. Elara wondered at the past the stony stronghold of Sangra had witnessed. The scope and skill of the cloister's craftsmen, her forebears, was bewildering ... whoever they were.

Elara slipped between a set of display cases to a familiar array of shelves, letting her fingers run across cracked and faded spinebacks, crumbling slowly beyond recognition. Legal volumes, charters, treaties, fringe and mainstream philosophy passed her one after the other. Their authors now clattered only in meatless skulls, their passions and tireless labors embedded in only in these flimsy pages.

She felt like a listener to the great chain of the past, bearing its weight with each word read. Names of spinebacks rolled by as she slowed down and tilted her head to the side.

Debating Heuristics in a Burgeoning Pantisocracy.

Life as Noise: Sounding Dead.

Philological Comparisons: A Meta-Illative Approach.

Aegis Council.

At the last name, she felt her feet come to a stop. Following a strange, prickly sense, she reached up and plucked several volumes from the shelf and gently cradled them to her chest, turning towards a table in a nearby alcove. Their aged fibers creaked from the stress of being handled.

Short of storming off to other cloisters – a suggestion that Marin had mocked in their coven – Elara needed information. The past was the natural first place to look when asking how to approach the present. And among an order sworn to an unaltered constancy of belief, the past *was* the present ... at least ideally.

Off to the side, she noticed another Kali'ka meandering through a set of koans on hanging scrolls. He appeared engrossed in his search. His hands were empty, though. Strange ... she hadn't noticed him on the way in. She reminded herself to check with Cassandra on the way out to see if she knew him.

He drifted towards her as she neared her destination. His hood completely covered his face.

Why is it covered if he's looking for something...?

There was something strange in his gait: the vector of the feet; their placement on the ground; a twisting of the hips. His movements were too natural. Disturbing in their proficiency. There was no element of inconsistency.

As Elara reached her table, the man bridged the gap between them in an instant.

It was only because of the brighter light in the Codex that she saw his dagger, driving upwards towards her kidney.

She spun and launched her spinebacks at him in a desperate attempt to shield herself. He battered them across the room, laying into her with his blade, slashing, pressing forward, sliding his feet in flawless coordination, an uncoiled snake whipping out, striking with no wasted movement.

Wild, savage energy wrapped his limbs. There were no feints, no parleys, no terms. He struck only at vital areas: a bundle of blood vessels, a stalk of bulging tendons, patches of flesh covering pulsing organs. He was prodding her, steering her with his strikes, chaining them together three, five, seven in advance. He used his robe to cloak his movements, obscure his trajectory, and mislead her senses.

It was masterful. And inhuman. He couldn't be Kali'ka. He couldn't! His forms and stance were alien and focused solely on offense.

It was all Elara could do to keep up. Driven incessantly backwards, she dodged tables, chairs, standlamps, corners, while keeping her footing loose and her balance locked to the ground. Her body reacted instinctively, pre-decision. Muscle memory ruled. She ducked, slid, evaded, melding with his strikes, economizing energy and making motion brief. Survival depended on it. If she committed enough energy to block, he would've just re-routed and gutted her. Likewise if she attacked or diverted focus to cry out.

Aside from the swishing of their robes, the shushing of their feet, and the clipped panting of their breathing, they dueled in silent unison. In the shadowy cavern of the assassin's hood, ambient light revealed flashes of features, humps of nose and cheekbones, and the white of bared teeth.

Elara's sight began to fuzz and lose its crisp shell. Her attention began to slip. Darkness started to press in, and her surging heart sucked energy from her limbs. She would falter soon, if she didn't break their stalemate.

In that moment, when her mind and body coasted with the clouds, incinerating thought, boiling her consciousness, garbled bits of mantas and clips of texts flitted into her mind and fused into a single, solid concept.

…I feel pressed, so I am pressed. I feel pressured, so I am pressured…

Understanding's spark ignited, casting its light wide and bright, illuminating all it touched, filling the full volume of her being with staggering, instant awareness, as though she'd been given a key to an infinite, inner storehouse.

Her attacker challenged with speed, so she would not answer with speed. She stopped resisting. She stopped believing she was dodging, evading, under assault, or even threatened. She just moved with him, whatever he did. Soft met hard. Hard met soft. No threats, no fear, no harm. The shackles of her perception lifted like morning mist.

Frustration became evident in his movements. Strain took his limbs. He displayed carelessness. Fatigue caused overeager swipes. Huffs came from his hood.

You were trying too hard for too long … assassin. No conservation. Now I have you!

In a flicker of light, Elara saw his eyes focus on the hollow spot under her sternum, towards her fourth chakra and the yantra inscribed there in her flesh. Telegraphing his attack. Sloppy. He would leave his front side open.

She slid towards the outside of his thrusting arm as he began his strike. She pivoted to face the same direction as him and grabbed his wrist as his dagger slipped into the spot where she *was.*

Clutching his wrist to her ribcage, she rotated it inwards and up – leveraging his forward motion – dropped her body backwards, and pressed straight down towards the floor. His elbow clicked in a high-pitch.

A wail of pain tore from the man's throat. His dagger dropped from his trembling hand to clang on the floor. His legs kicked, and his other arm slapped around his wriggling body as she pinned him in place.

Elara gnashed at the air. "Who are you!?"

He didn't answer, but only continued to howl and writhe, sputtering unintelligible clusters of syllables.

"Silence! I said, who are you?! Who sent you?! How did you get in here?! Are you Kali'ka? Answer me!"

His lips sputtered a hoarse, contorted yell. "Whore of Kali! I'll kill you! I'll fucking kill you!"

Elara's mind ignited. Wrath took her. In one motion, she wrenched the assassin's arm forward and out, torqueing viciously. A thundering of small cracks and pops rattled the air as his shoulder stretched and snapped. His agonized howls redoubled.

"Ascendant!"

Sound? *Talking to me. Someone.*

"Ascendant Aeve!"

Family name. Formal form of address – family name instead of first name. Had she answered? A person. The location solidified in auditory memory. She turned her head towards it source.

Adherent Cassandra stood there clasping her mouth, staring in horror at the pinned assassin. She must've ran from her station at the entryway to the Codex when she heard him scream.

"Ascendant Aeve! Oh Kali... What happened?! Are you ok? Oh no, oh no...!"

Next to her, another figure stepped forward. Ascendant Oren.

"Ascendant Elara! Are you ok? What ... what happened? What's going on?"

"Oren, what are you doing here?!" Elara growled.

He took several seconds of lip flapping to produce an answer. "I – I – thought I could – I could find some information that might help, like you, I would imagine. I –"

"Never mind! Get over here and help me!"

Oren just stood there, fidgeting his feet and glancing at the assassin.

"Kali's Eyes! Cassandra, come here and grab his other arm!"

Cassandra stepped past Oren and dropped next to Elara on one knee. The assassin still struggled despite the tremendous pain that must have been wracking his shoulder and elbow.

"Focus, Cassandra. Third kana. *Sunken Hammer.* You can't be squeamish about this! Are you... Yes – eleventh circle. Ok. Listen. Palm to your – no! Wedge it in the corner of your shoulder! Good! Good. Hold firm and press down! Straight down! Bend at the waist. Focus, focus. Yes. Forehead to center to floor... Good!"

Once Cassandra had locked the assassin in place, Elara hoisted herself to her feet. The dusk of glowing combat stormed through her brain. Her muscles wobbled from strain. The musk of her sweat filled her nostrils.

She found herself drawn towards tangible, physical things, one to the next, in a compulsive stupor, pulling them together like threads. She lifted the seam of her robes. Countless tears, gaps, ragged holes, and missing flaps of material ran through its fabric. Her skin was visible through the holes, whole and smooth, completely, impossibly unharmed.

Scattered across the floor laid the spinebacks she'd hurled at her attacker. She stalked over to them and rifled through them, snatching them up and running her thumbs across their covers. She'd be damned if she left without retrieving the things that could've cost her her life.

On the ground a short distance away, the dagger glinted in the lamplight of the Codex, thin, double-edged, easily half the length of her forearm, hilt longer than the grip of a fist.

She strode over to it and let her hand hover above it – debating, assessing – before plucking it off the floor.

Her eyes tracked the gleam of its edge as she twisted it in the air. No etchings in the blade, no decorative designs or relieves along the hilt. No language anywhere. No adornments, nothing superlative. No sign of age or previous use.

It was an implement molded in the form of its wielder, streamlined and uncomplicated, having no other purpose other than being an agent of death. In the world of Logic, where abundance, Levitant-induced bliss, and a lack of physical conflict were absolute, who existed to make such a tool?

Having it so close to her face, so near to her lips and tongue, under her control, away from the man who wielded it... The dagger felt comforting, somehow. Having it close felt exultant, almost. Jubilant.

Familiar.

Nothing would be more intimate than piercing her … and killing her. No other connection would last as long.

"Oren, Cassandra…" Elara's voice hummed in a daze. "Take this … assassin … to Ascendant Brae. Inform him what happened. He'll know what to do."

She turned to face them – Cassandra restraining the assassin, and Oren clenching his hands together – only to see them staring lock-eyed at a patch of shadow between two shelves.

The shadow shifted and warped, pressing out like a black teardrop, growing and resolving into a shape of limbs and a torso draped in the gray of Kali'ka robes.

A Stabat, caretaker of Cloister Sangra.

It just stood there, wrapped in unnatural stillness, monitoring, observing, its third eye lodged in its forehead, surrounded by clay-like flesh and its two blind, clouded eyes. Its bald head jutted upwards out of its robes like the end of a maggoty protuberance.

Instead of jittering around like usual, its third eye pointed straight at Elara. At the sight, a tingle grew in her spine and shimmied upwards to implant itself in her brain, spawning worry, paranoia, and anger.

What could it possibly want? Did it not care what just happened? *Could* it care? It was a manifestation of Illusion, without ego, seeing all, knowing all, reflecting what it was shown. And like a mirror, the Stabat's walking, entombed flesh was ultimately empty. All the Stabat, all twelve of them – hollow constructs.

"Ascendant." Its voice rasped like paper dragged across stone. "You have crossed into Circle Nineteen."

Elara blinked. Surely she'd misheard. Behind her on the ground, between the assassin's pained grunts, she heard Cassandra gasp and Oren mutter something that sounded like disbelief.

"Circle Nineteen. What…?" Elara stumbled over her words. "What are you talking about? For saving my own life? I did what I had to. I had to protect myself! What else was I going to do?"

The Stabat said nothing. Its cyclopean eye stared at her, large and unblinking, dispassionate like the sheen of fog.

After a second more of numbly staring at the Stabat, Elara tossed the dagger towards Oren. It clattered dully on the floor. Oren reached for it pensively, lightly, as though its mere contact could destroy him.

"Bring that to Brae, too. Let the Master Inscriber do what he does best. Have him examine it … and this man on the floor. Tell Brae 'no restraint' – remember that. Those words exactly."

"Yes, Ascendant Elara," Cassandra managed.

"Ascendant Elara, we can't leave you alone." Oren babbled a bit before his mouth caught up to his thoughts. "Danger could be everywhere. We have to be careful! *You* have to be careful! Allow me to get you an escort. Protection. Something!"

"Ascendant." Cassandra spoke up, nearly in tears, half keeping a wary gaze on the Stabat. "You don't want someone to go with you?"

"No… No. I don't. I'm fine. I can't… I have to go. I have to go. That's all."

In a mind glaze, Elara turned to leave without looking back, clutching her spinebacks to her chest like armor. She left Cassandra, Oren and the Stabat as they were, amidst the parchments and shelves and standlamps of the Codex.

It didn't take one glance to know that the Stabat's third eye was still riveted on her, even as she wound her way up and into the corridors of Cloister Sangra.

Only a few Kali'ka speckled the corridors to see her. The necks of every single one turned with her as she passed, gaping at the little flaps of her slashed robes whipping around.

She barely noticed them. She felt not a smidgen of embarrassment at the looks she got, nor the slightest need to volunteer any explanations. Any attempts at communication were met with complete disregard or an upraised hand. They were mere upright images, their movements the depthless mechanics of caricatures shifting across a canvas of shadow. She felt empty.

Circle Nineteen. The Stabat are watching. One circle closer to High Ascendancy.

Being raised to the next Circle of Ascendancy, being attacked in the Codex, seeing the edge of the dagger glinting, flashing in front of her face

– all of it swam together in a jumbled mass in her mind, spiraling, tumbling, engulfing her, pressing down, down.

The tales of the crazed man in Advent Square, the rumors and their fears... It was all undeniably, undisputedly true, twisted by a crushing conclusion.

There was a schism in the Kali'ka, and she, Elara Aeve, had become the target of the other side.

CHAPTER 4
ADVENT SERMON

The Basilica Formata set nestled in the center of New Corinth like the overturned bow of an ancient, monolithic ship. A man-made construct large enough to rival a small mountain, its megalithic stone body, cream-striated marble and stucco-textured synthstone, dominated the skyline like an ever-burning, noonday sun. Its rounded, sweeping architecture minimized flat surfaces and maximized flow, while flying buttresses and interlaced support structures ran across its exterior like a meshed exoskeleton, connecting ancillary buildings, towers, domes and skyramps to courtyards, entryways, amphitheaters, ballrooms, and living quarters.

Depending on the wing, the Basilica was fortress for the Magistrate, boarding school for fledgling scions, tomb for the deceased, reliquary, cathedral, or home of the largest complex of offices under the canopy of Logical law and custom. It was the beating heart of billions of Logicians worldwide and the pulsing soul of the citizens of the city of New Corinth; the shining jewel of Logic, as unending as the Eternal Day, as undying as Lord Logos Himself.

It was as much an impregnable edifice as it was a monument to insoluble passion, and what can be created when hands put chisel to stone in the relentless pursuit of belief. From stone-and-mortar masons to grav-tram operators, the labor of mankind stacked in aggregate in the Basilica's history and body.

In the Sacristy of the Conclave Wing of the Basilica, the High

Devotee of Logic, Jacobs Osgood, sat amidst the teeming bustle of pre-Advent preparation with a host of attendants buzzing around him, dabbing makeup on his skin, blotting at his eyes, combing fragrant oils into his hair, cutting in and out like flies that landed and left before they could be swept away. Whenever his hands weren't busy signing sheafleaves proffered by racing seminarians, or tapping away at the cool, blue glow of compads – they restlessly picked at the golden thread trimming the plush velvet armrests of his cushioned, antiquated wooden stool.

"No, no! You see that birthmark under the eye? I want that a shade lighter. And make sure my forehead doesn't look too large." He'd have to do something about his receding hairline; it was inexcusable for the High Devotee to be seen aging.

"Lord Logos wants us to look our best at all times, remember. If we look our best, we *feel* our best. That matters most of all. Elation, pleasure, and the bounties of wealth are paramount. The Godhead must rise."

He cleared his throat at the end of his impromptu soliloquy and glanced at the rubricians being primped to either side of him. Only *his* Seat was honored enough to be raised above the height of an armchair. Members of the Reserved Cove of the Chosen or not, none were as elevated as the High Devotee.

Through the beveled mirror in front of him, he watched seminarians speed by lush, hanging wall tapestries, dart around vaulted columns, race past amber standlamps, and circumvent guided tours of dignitaries who'd paused to admire alabaster statues of Lord Logos, typically nude and barrel-chested with a reared phallus. Every seminarian had their fingers to their earlobes, depressing their comchits, chatting like an arrhythmic, clattering rainshower.

Jacobs barely noticed the weak-chinned man with an aloof brow and a bored sneer staring back at him from his mirror's platinum frame.

"…viewscreens in the Plaza of Perdition's Absence are lagging by 0.2 seconds. The million-plus Corinthians along that vector won't have access to the Spirit at the same time as…"

"…and when you're done, let's have a final count of pre-orders for the revised Epicurial Apologia. Make sure to include a copy of the recording of Advent Sermon for every order."

"...be *much* more apt to donate once they've received Penance, remember. Leave the credit scanners open until vespers."

"...our final light and sound check. Be absolutely sure the RGB frequencies of the holo-lenses in the pulpit are tuned to project His Holiness' transformation to the rear of the Mausoleum."

Groups of broad-smiling, clean-shaven, gorgeously bedecked scions, typically in the liturgical purple and white of Advent Season, strolled at a slower pace, gesturing as though intensely engaged in a debate regarding some subtle point of doctrine. They nodded and waved reflexively in the general direction of people who may or may not have noticed them.

Above their heads, clusters of tiny, floating glo-globes gleamed warmly, shifting owners, hovering in spaces before clinging momentarily to passersby, ensuring that pockets of dim light never persisted for more than mere seconds.

Jacobs recited the Epicurial Apologia to himself, whispering *'Shadows are cast from those unconcerned with the light'*. In the lighthouse of the world, he had learned, the integrity of the Eternal Day required incessant maintenance.

At that moment, a slight disorder in rhythm of feet and shuffling of clothing emerged in Jacobs' field of view, in his mirror's reflection. A small, slinking man emerged from the din, eyes locked on Jacobs, weaving his way through the crowd with unconscious mastery to stop and hover at a distance. Dressed in a single, white shift, he hunched like a shrunken, osteoporotic cadaver, too frail to even support his own meager weight. Lit by standlamps and flitting glo-globes, his mottled, jaundiced skin looked wrapped in filmy plastic.

Jacobs grit his teeth and quickly scanned to see if anyone was paying attention. At least comeyes weren't allowed back here. No need for them; magisters screened everyone who entered the Sacristy.

Jacobs lifted one finger towards his mirror and crooked it at the man, who slipped through the jutting elbows of Jacobs' attendants and leaned in with a low-pitched, slick drawl that melted syllables into each other as if he was speaking one long word.

"High Devotee, you honor me as always. If you might allow me the opportunity to address an item of potential interest, I'm certain that we may come to discuss, and hopefully conclude, on said item in a manner we both find interesting at the least, and doubtlessly beneficial at the greatest." His yellowed teeth glowed dully through a fixed crescent smile. The pungent odor of alcohol and bacteria wafted from behind his thick, purplish lips.

Jacobs cleared his throat and swallowed down bile. By Logos, the man was off-putting! No matter how many words Jacobs and he exchanged or traded, the man absurdly insisted on playing the role of a well-bred debutant.

"Mendicant Hegil, there's nothing surreptitious at all about making a show of appearing to be hidden. I thought the words I used last time were 'limited public contact'. You do understand what that means, don't you?"

"Certainly, Your Grace. Certainly." Hegil's rheumy bug eyes rolled right, left, probing non-stop for information.

Jacobs' eyes watered just by looking at him. "I would hope, Mendicant Hegil, that your affinity for ancient dialectics hasn't stuffed your head with an inability to understand common language. Not even the High Devotee of Logic can stay above weighted glances if I allow you unrestricted access."

"Oh no! I would never besmirch your station by exposing you to mendicant *filth*, High Devotee."

"Nihil Obstat! You know better by now. Watch your tongue."

"If only I could, You Grace, if only I could." Hegil nodded thoughtfully, pursing his purple lips. "But I'm afraid the object of rhetoric is far removed from its distant origins."

"As are you. When the buried surfaces, we are only forced to question how much dirt was unearthed."

"An allusion to the Epicurial Apologia, nested within an allusion to my usage of Nihil Obstat? Well done, Your Grace, well done. I believe the passage is, *'The buried cannot unearth themselves lest I provide the cord'*? Spoken by Lord Logos, himself. So true, so true. I'm thankful for the utterance of our most holy words, and I'm further blessed by these words of truth as expressed by your voice. The most recent revision, though, I hope. I heard that sales are going quite well so far."

"Thanks be to Logos, yes, despite your tiresome platitudes. Be assured though, mendicant, that there is never a moment when we are above reminders of His grace. Nor is there ever a moment when we can curtail the needs of the Logical masses of New Corinth." Jacobs smiled and nodded at a group of passersby.

"We can always take a stroll through the Epistemic Wing and regale the young scions in estuary about the rudiments of Logical theology, Your Grace, if you believe we should continue along this course."

Jacobs spoke through a clench-toothed smile. "What do you want, mendicant?"

Hegil's grin deepened. The man enjoyed banter far too much. "Lucrece Dagon is here to see you, High Devotee."

"Who?" A circular clock on a nearby wall displayed the time. "Now? Advent Sermon is in twenty minutes! Why are you bothering me with this? And here, in the Sacristy?!"

"She said it's about her daughter's Breaching on Advent Eve. In your parish."

Jacobs bobbed his head around his attendants' arms to get a head-on view into his mirror. He twitched the alb draped over his shoulders till it was equidistant length on either side. "Who, Hegil? Her? But I thought – what did you say her name was, again?"

"She's of the Aeve family, Your Grace. Dagon is her claimed name."

"Oh yes! Aeve. Aeve... One of her sisters lives overseas in the Esdrin Regime, does she not? The middle sister, yes?"

"So the Lady Lucrece has said," Hegil muttered, sidestepping a journalist with floating vocorders trailing behind like mechanical balloons, their oscillating grav-drives humming like the snore of a giant bee. The images they recorded were being projected to swiveling holo-displays that an entourage of chattering attendants edited in real-time. Jacobs' eyes trailed after the group. He made a mental note to check polls to see how well-received the upcoming sermon's edits were.

"The Esdrin Regime ... isn't their entourage here, Hegil? The High Minister and his family?"

You signed the release yourself, Your Grace. They've been given priority seating, of course, in quite a superlative location for a congregation of over 350,000, if I might say. In the Mausoleum, in the north, under the twin ivory status of Lord Logos, bless His name."

"Mm, yes – bless His name." A cluster of passing scions ducked bows in Jacobs' direction as they passed. They all made the sacred sign of Logos across their chests. Jacobs lifted his hand and absently twiddled the sacred sign in response, skimming his eyes over their vestments. As soon as they fell out of sight, he hissed.

"Did you see Rubrician Cecil's stole? *Synthetic!* Loose threads at the edges, even!"

Hegil gasped melodramatically enough for several of Jacobs' attendants to glance at him. "Your Grace, Rubrician Cecil's parish has had superb attendance since he was raised from scion late last year. There's no reason for such a lack of indulgence in his apparel. I could always arrange something. A loss in the intake of new relics, a dip in sales of his statues and holy visages, an embarrassing comment at dinner..."

Jacobs repressed an exasperated sigh. "Lucrece Aeve, yes? Dagon is her claimed name. The Aeve family lives in the Superluminal District in the Uppers. The mother and father are at Levidens so often, I'd have a hard time forgetting them."

"The Aeve family elates quite well, Your Grace. The Spirit of Logos flows through them, from His Holiness to you, oh High Devotee – them and their extension family, both. Especially this close to Advent, when there are so many pageants, the Aeve family and the rest of New Corinth has their hearts and eyes on those who lead, govern, and cleanse them. The whole world, in fact, is looking to our golden hill for guidance."

Hegil finished, standing docile, outwardly placid, with those damned tufts of hair limply hanging from his liverspotted skull.

"Two minutes, Hegil. Two."

"Certainly, High Devotee." Somehow, Hegil's grin deepened.

As soon as Hegil left, Jacobs occupied himself by scrutinizing the viewscreens stationed near the ceiling above him. Reporters commented over a brassy musical score as Corinthians filed in from the Elysian Plazas that acted as gateways to the Basilica, through the Atrium of Lack's Bane, up the grand, platinum-veined, crystal Steps to Glory – blindingly luminescent in the never-shifting light of the Eternal Day – into the whizzing, game-filled lobby-arcade, and finally into the Masoleum.

From such a distance, they all looked like a single blur of milling, pastel colors. If Jacobs descended to get close, would he see individuals? Would he see a strained look tugging at their eyes? Would he see preoccupied minds beneath their glossy surfaces? Would he see a crack in their veneer that not even the orgasmic bliss of the holy draught Levitant – thanks be to Lord Logos – could suppress?

The citizens of Logos' holy city had gotten a glimpse in Advent Square of the terror lurking beneath their feet, of the subversive, disgusting band of fringe lunatics who worshipped some dark deity, threatened the pristine, undiminished glory of the Eternal Day. Jacobs himself had had no idea, beyond records in Reliquary, of how ravening and mad the cultists of Kali actually were, until he'd watched the recordings of that horribly scarred man, lifting a dagger to his throat, and … and…

No! No, the Magistrate would keep them safe, electrolances in hand. His Holiness would guard them, even if it meant choking the cultists with his own beaming, glorious, white-lit hands.

Choking … how curious. Such a violent analogy. *Violent:* a Nihil Obstat word, never to cross the lips or minds of Corinthians.

Why would I think of that word now?

***

"High Devotee, the Lady Lucrece Dagon, eldest daughter of the House of Aeve." Hegil slid away after his introduction and stood off to the side. Jacobs sat in his seat and drew the sacred symbol of Logic in the air as Lucrece curtsied, her little daughter at her side.

Lady Lucrece's limbs floated with effortless, practiced grace, as though the metallic rods of some strange organic gearwork lie surgically lodged in her joints, delivering a needlepoint balance between muscle tone and softness. Every lift of the leg, every swivel of the head, every tilt of the arm: all flawless. Her skin was the typical creamy bronze of New Corinth, darkened from a lifetime of exposure to incessant heat and light.

"High Devotee, I'm delighted that you would take the time to see me and my daughter, especially in the midst of such a busy event as Advent

Sermon." Her silky, fluid alto tickled Jacobs' spine. "It's absolutely *beyond* expression that so wondrous of an event as my daughter's Breaching will be conducted by the High Devotee of Logic himself. Sophia's been waiting for this since birth, I assure you! I wanted to thank you personally for making her fit to be a Bride of Logos."

"Oh no no, not at all, claimant Dagon." He swished his hand around and strung some pre-fabricated phrases together. "Not even Advent and the Pageant of Miracles can deter me from my everlasting duty to indulge those in my parish, particular those of such a noted family in Logical spheres. You never slack on your lack of restraint! I know Logos himself must be beaming his excess down on you right now."

Lucrece made a some mindless quibble. Jacobs barely heard it. The two of them rifled the same staccato laugh. Seminarians continued buzzing around him; they were finally on the powder and stencil layer of his makeup. Someone passed by Jacobs' face with another sheafleaf to sign. Nearby, a duo of square-jawed, powerfully built scions nearby laughed in deep baritones.

Amidst it all, Lucrece kept talking, faced away from her daughter. The girl barely made it past Lucrece's waist. Short for her age? Jacobs could never tell.

"...and so my mother showed us all the vocoder footage from when she was Breached. We all sat around, hearts fluttering, nearly weeping with joy! It was all there on her face, when she was receiving the gift..."

Lucrece's fully dilated pupils left only the slimmest rim of olive green around them. She'd misted, what, forty minutes ago, perhaps? Depended on the brand, of course. She must be sopping by now. Ready to receive the gift of Logos.

Jacobs found himself compulsively studying her as she prated. She was voluptuous with old-world features rarely seen in modern times. Budded lips, deeply red and moist. Her face was framed by deviant curls of hair tumbling in large spirals of strawberry-honey across her exposed collarbones, atop a dress scooping in a wide arc from shoulder to shoulder. Her beauty was up-front and punctuated, like a slap in the face.

It was odd and confusing, though. Nothing about a woman's physicality typically roused Jacobs' attention at all. Why this one woman?

New Corinth was overflowing with gorgeous women and potential claimants, many for whom he'd conducted Penance. They were common in the way that the least rare gem was ordinary.

"...and so I said to him, no, no, of *course* not! Why would we settle for viewscreens when we can physically be there? To feel the waves of energy flow over us as Logos ascends in Advent Square! Oh, I'm sure it will be just glorious. None of the footage Sophia has seen from her study time using doctrinators will *ever* compare!"

A seminarian swooped in with a platinum tray of truffles. Jacobs made shooing motions with one hand. Lucrece made a scandalized – or perhaps mock-scandalized – blurt of sound before plucking a truffle off the tray and popping it in her mouth.

"Oh, but, High Devotee, the sensation is so wonderful! It feels so good. Isn't that why Logos bestows us with his bounty?" Jacobs watched her tongue slip around her truffle in a thick, wet churn.

"Mmm – My dear Lucrece, I can't have a bit of chocolate on my teeth or in the corners of my mouth when my face is going to projected into the homes of billions, now can I?"

She tittered in reply and laid a hand on his arm. The angle of her wrist said that she was demure yet confident.

Jacobs rotated towards Lucrece's daughter, standing pretty with dirty blonde hair, tinged with ruby as though stained by pomegranates, in a frilly dress that projected holo-flowers that spun as though their petals were caught in the wind. No expenses spared. Always a blessed sight.

"And how about you, little one?" Jacobs propped his smile up. "Are you happy to be brought into the fold of Lord Logos? To have His Spirit pour into you, and to begin the everlasting process of cleansing and rebirth? To have His bounty fill your life? To imbibe the holy draught Levitant for the first time? Misting, as your mother might have called it … in the vernacular, of course." Lucrece and he shared a politely coquettish chuckle.

Nothing. The little girl said nothing and did nothing. No bouncing about, no spastic glee, no flushed features. She just stared at the floor like a stump of hardened clay, dull-eyed and regressed into some inner world. Jacobs felt his smile slip as he stared at her. Was that a scar across her left eyebrow? No, no, no... Impossible. Access to plastein was quick and ubiquitous, especially for a household from the line of Aeve.

Seeing her daughter's flat affect, Lucrece trilled a nervously embellished laugh. "We've just had a long stroll around Market Canal, High Devotee. The weather is still perfectly lovely at this time of year, wouldn't you say? She must be a bit fatigued from the experience. But it was a joyous one, I must say!"

She settled her gaze on her daughter, and a strange expression ghosted across her face. It came and left so quickly, Jacobs only recognized what he saw a second later, as his mind raced to catch up to his now-slack face, staring in suppressed shock. Again and again, he tried to convince himself that he'd seen incorrectly.

Hatred. Malice, sucking away all of her softness and pouring cold, cruel imperiousness in its place. Quick and powerful, flashing then fleeing. It was so venomous, so intense, that it bordered on pure enmity. For a second afterwards, Jacobs fully believed that this woman was going to *hit* her daughter.

To the side, Hegil stood recessed into the environment and nearly invisible, with his hands up his sleeve, watching Lucrece adroitly, intently, tapping notes away on a compad strapped to his arm, most likely. He must have seen it! This time, Jacobs wouldn't begrudge his presence.

"Oh, um – well, certainly, Lady Lucrece." Jacobs lifted his chin for an attendant. "Physical activity has a way of invigorating as well draining. I'm sure once Sophia has been Breached, and has had access to Logos' holy draught, Levitant, she will certainly perk up and be receptive to Logos' bliss, much in the way you embody his elation every time I see you."

At that comment, all vestiges of anger drained out of Lucrece like poison sucked out of a snakebite. She was once again full of nothing less than the same vibrancy with which she approached him.

"Well, High Devotee. For the grace and courtesy you've shown us, especially during such a busy time, I will not forget. We both look forward to seeing you on Advent Eve, in your parish, and then again afterwards, at the Pageant of Miracles in Advent Square." With a masterfully practiced, flowing curtsy, she lowered herself to the floor. Jacobs found himself staring directly down her neckline.

Jacobs hustled to remember the traditional phrase. "Bookpraise to Logos, Lady Lucrece Dagon, eldest daughter of the House of Aeve."

Still, Lucrece's daughter didn't budge. Jacobs was unsure if he'd even seen her blink the entire time she'd been standing there.

"Praise His name, High Devotee of Logic, Jacobs Osgood. Come along, Sophia." With a whirl of her dress, Lucrece and her child left his side. In his mirror, Jacobs watched the strawberry-blonde woman float like a specter, gliding in and out of bustling seminarians, Hegil trailing along at her side.

The phantom of her near-outburst lingered like a silhouette imprinted on his heart. The anger. The scorn. The lack of control. It reminded him of the footage from Advent Square. The lunatic in a gray robe, prowling back and forth, howling and gnashing like an unchained daemon, ready to slash his own throat. Welling blood, piercing screams, and frantic terror.

"Lady Lucrece!" He called out before he'd realized what he was about to do.

Lucrece spun towards him with a bright, perky face. The sight roused a deep, unrecognizable burn within Jacobs that he didn't understand.

"You can come straight to my Penance booth after Advent Sermon, Lady Lucrece. Just cut through the lines. Your husband will be quite pleased that the High Devotee of the entirety of Logic poured the Spirit of Logos into such a ravishing claimant."

CHAPTER 5
INITIATION

Along the Fourth Avenue of Reclamation, one of six pedestrian-only spokes that ran from the sprawl of central New Corinth, a young woman weaved in and out of the flowing bodies that strolled and dallied and chatted along any and every divergent or tributary street. She reflexively dodged traffic veering in and out of storefronts, hearing her heels click tok, tok, tok, on the plasmold-coated emerald and garnet pavement. Everblooms swayed above her head, lining the streets' medians.

The iridescent bag in her arms stayed tightly clutched to her chest as she bobbed a cheery, "Excuse me!" or a self-effacing, "Oh, I'm sorry!" picking things up from squawking hawkers, putting them down, lingering momentarily at a diamond-inlaid headpiece, slowing at a a viewscreen rotating above the ground, bouncing from one spot to the other like a piece of wind-borne confetti.

Riding atop the nearly limitless clutter of Corinthians swaying together like the open sea, she was only one tiny bit of flotsam.

It was easier than she thought it would be: the Levitant-induced grin; the bodies slicked and toned like hard shells of resin and tissue numb from repeated use; skin flush from synaptic floodings (skillfully applied makeup in her case). The capriciously asymmetrical clothing was simplest of all – thin, clingy, cut to accentuate groins, chests, the inside of thighs, lower backs, anything that could be construed as sexual.

No one noticed her, implausible as it seemed. No one could see through her appearance. The voice of her kin resonated inside, warning and giving instructions. Logic hid everything in plain sight, they said, so don't hide and no attention would turn towards her. Behave *no differently* than usual, and Logical assumptions would take care of the rest. She was only just learning what "usual" meant.

But the eyes ... they were the hardest fraud to maintain. Corinthian eyes were waxen and limp, resuscitated through dose after dose of Levitant like flat props. Their eyelids flit shut like the twitching of hardened insect wings out of fleshy compartments.

How she wanted to blink. Just blink, in a pattern that came naturally. Had she really ever looked like that? Had she ever looked so empty? So full of nothing?

All around, the beaming effulgence of the Eternal Day pounded again and again, bearing down from crimp-walled superstructures that rose to absurd heights. They magnified, intensified even the smallest bit of light, fusing with the blazing sun above to consume everyone and everything in the haze of the Eternal Day.

All of them, drowning. Gurgling in their senses, beyond escape. Too much of too much vibrancy. Not underwater, but underlight. Everyone, small and gagging, drowning in the runoff of white. Every man, woman, and child, pastel blips and blobs on a milky canvas.

All kindling in Logos' perfect blaze.

Zinging flo-globes spun and darted overhead, blaring proclamations over brassily triumphant sacred music.

"...in honor of the birth of Sybarite the Carnal, tours are now reopened in the newly remodeled reception hall and vestibule of the Conclave Wing at the Basilica Formata..."

"...don't want to forget, during the weekend prior to Flint Crowning, Penance logs are mandatory for all Service attendees. In the interest of..."

"...is currently offering a discount to expectant parents scheduling their daughter's Breaching. Hurry! These days, to ensure an unhindered event, many are choosing the brief version..."

"...By the blessing of Logos, we are welcoming an increase in production of VacTin! Worldwide, this staple of home plastein is now receiving due attention by the..."

Other flo-globes broadcasted the Cardinal Premise in a volume tucked right between comfortably ignorable and persistently loud, like a never-ending mantra of the unconscious mind – a collective intent, emitted through an unfeeling, mechanical proxy.

"We submit to the Godhead. The Godhead will rise.
The Godhead will open. From its tip He will flow.
We join with the Godhead. We join with each other.
Logos speaks through rivers of white."

"Oh!" she chirped. A small boy nearly crashed into her. His open mouth dribbled something sticky and fizzing. His empty eyes looked at nothing. His parent was laughing absurdly at a street performer. One of those niche acts, tangled in a jumble of spinning, whirling, flickering plates. The parent joined others herding their children into a nearby lines, to pose beaming-faced on the knees of scions for family imprints, girls in boothwear and boys in miniature vestments.

She quickly looked away. Had they seen her looking? Couldn't show too much unusual interest. Couldn't appear out of place.

Corinthians were looking more, *seeing* more. Under the gloss, here and there, she saw dents in the armor of Levitant and faith. Flattening of smiles, shifts of the eyebrows, restlessness of movement. Something was slipping in, taking shape, forming itself into the mold of its original wearer, but humming with lethal intent.

The face of New Corinth was changing forever, now that it had been placed face to face with its inner self. All it had taken was that one, unknown man in Advent Square, and now all the old instincts – to fight, to flee – were rising to the surface.

She wouldn't be the one responsible for compromising their way of life. Extra caution was needed. Caution had kept her brethren unknown for generations, a full and self-sufficient society embedded within another.

Passing through the center of the plaza at Iesu's Navel, the young woman circumvented the illustrious Fountain of Angel's Tears, where Levitant-laced wine spouted from twined fish rising from its center.

Scions stood nearby, dunking crystal goblets and passing them out to passersby, while others delivered impromptu Catechist services.

The scions themselves had clearly imbibed the holy draught Levitant, judging by their sweat-logged vestments, flush skin, bulging eyes and protruding phalluses. Groups of Corinthians, mostly in threes or fours, had taken to conducting Penance right there in the street.

Their orgasmic gasps were enflamed by the encouragement of the scions. "The power compels you! The power compels you!"

"Compel me! Compel me!" claimants screamed. The claimants' men could manage nothing more than incoherent slathers. The wine must contain a higher than average dose.

She passed by them and squeezed through a final few people, making her way to a rack of necklaces. Hovering a finger over them, she made a show of settling on one and hoisting it up. Some combination of crystal bejeweled with sapphires. It would do.

The enormous grin of the vendor grew wider. He prattled some nonsense. She had no idea what her responses were. They were practiced enough to satisfy him, it seemed, and that was all that mattered. Growing up in New Corinth produced some advantages, it seemed.

Clamping her bag in one arm, she held the necklace up to the omnipresent light of the Eternal Day and rotated it this way, that way, looking for the perfect sliver of refraction to… there! The useless trinket snared the Eternal Day and flashed like a winking star that puffed itself up in a trumpeted display.

In the necklace's polished planes, a warped, stretched version of her face stared back: high, prominent cheekbones, olive skin, and jet black hair pinned together with crystal sticks splayed upwards. Within the crystals' depths, kaleidoscopic colors coursed and smashed into his each other in little, zooming eddies.

Several seconds later, someone smashed into her shoulder.

"Logos preserve me!" She ducked her head and instinctively gripped her bag tighter.

A man swiveled around – the one responsible – to garishly proclaim some apology in mid-step, his coiffed hair fuming fragrance. He waved a piece of skewered street meat around like a scepter, its charred, pinkish wobble dripping juices.

Him? So convincing. So authentically Corinthian. Dazed, she led the necklace back to its rack and smiled something about inconvenienced bliss to the now overly sympathetic vendor.

She'd seen the direction, though. The meat skewer had been pointing firmly at the lane that circumvented Advent Square and marched on towards the Path of Gold. His timing had been perfect. She knew her final destination from there.

From one point to the next, she moved with soldierly diligence, counting in her mind: a flickering neon sign – the old non-holo style; a stall selling wafer-shaped sweets inscribed with the sacred symbol of Logic; the objet d'art shop with the white platinum sign. Two, three, four intersections, over bridges and past parks. Onward towards the Path of Gold with the rushing, sparkling Tame River in the distance.

Passing over a network of skyramps, she turned without pause down a narrow passage that crooked between buildings. The door was straight ahead. With a quick twist, the old-fashioned knob clicked and she was inside.

She pressed her back against the door and leaned. The room echoed in silence, while her blood rushed in her ears. Slowly, coolly, she scanned the interior of the building, a never-finished business bought to use specifically for purposes like hers. The Eternal Day refracted through evercracks in the ceiling and permeated the interior. No windows.

Quickly, she tugged out her hair clasps, tousled her hair and doffed her clothing, shucking layers, discarding arm tassels, stilettos, ankle and leg chains, earrings, bracelets, garters, undergarments, underbuckles, and of course, her scarlet dress: white sparkles with a lacey neckline – a favorite.

She stared at it a moment before burying her face in it and scrubbing her makeup off. A well-worn, well-conditioned part of her wailed like a colicky infant at the dress' defacement.

Her reaction was a trained reflex. Her newfound kin had taught her to isolate reactions from conscious choice. She accepted her response, but didn't act on it. She just observed the defacement of her dress, sensed her remorse, and let that be the end of it.

All she needed to do was *not* act, they'd said. Inaction existed before action. Silence existed before sound. Emptiness existed before fullness. Absence existed before presence.

Her advocate kept telling her that all people were born in full possession of everything they would ever need. The crushing tides of time and hardships broke on the shoals of inborn dignity. Dignity must be jealously guarded, her advocate warned, like a sacred secret. Graceless acts yielded graceless minds, and eroded even the staunchest person, Kali'ka or not.

Her mother, father, friends... If they didn't aid her, they were a de facto hindrance. If they would shun her for her choices, for who she was, then they were less than family, less than human, less than nothing. They were empty non-entities, existent only to be discarded and snuffed from memory, just like a scarlet dress.

What was hers would remain hers, she'd determined, and hers alone. It was *her*, her coven said – the place that hummed within; the untouchable flame. The flame came from her. It *was* her. The flame was Kali Herself, dwelling within in the realm of Illusion.

The heat below. Kali is the heat below, she heard herself repeating.

No longer would she be a cheap commodity chewed up in the gullet of Logical doctrine. No longer would she debase herself for the pleasures of scions. No longer would she believe she was worthy of Penance.

She stuffed her dress into the bottom of her bag, and squeezed the bag to assure herself that the small shape of her other item was still inside. Both were needed. Both ties to the past were critical for what was to come.

Possessions in hand, clutched to her chest, she turned down a hallway towards a back room, by choice forever lost to the Eternal Day.

***

...Darkness engulfed her, watery and soporific, textured with shudders of vibrations. Self evaporated. Space and memory disintegrated. The forever-realm pressed outward into nothing, containing nothing, contained by nothing. She existed in a skinless vast without boundaries or divisions,. She was continuance. She was essence itself, gliding in frictionless shunts,

self-propelling, unraveling, comingling with her own echoing ego, imprinting herself aimlessly, expanding eternally…

The young woman's lungs snapped open as her feet touched down on hard stone. She sucked in rattles of air and stood curled around herself, nude, coughing a hoarse, wet bark, shedding the speckled dreaminess that stuck to her senses.

The *pore* behind her – pitch black and nautical – clung to her body, roiling along her legs, wrapping tendrils around her arms, before reluctantly receding in an fluid retreat. Like a slab of unmoving ink carved into the wall, it stayed where it was. Passing through a pore was supposed to become easier over time, she'd been told.

In front of her, darkness spread into a rocky, underground chamber. Firepots smattered the floor, bouncing light from far corners. It was as though a scoop of stone had been sucked out of the under-earth, leaving a pockmarked shell in its place. She could see no visible exits. Straight ahead, several stone steps led up to a flat dais.

Murmurings arose from the darkness, regular and rhythmic. Adherents in dark gray robes stood facing her in a semicircle, hoods forward, arms in their sleeves. The light glazed them, barely, as though nervous.

She slunk forward. Their murmurings abruptly stopped. Silence submerged her ears. The chill of the air pressed against her skin and started to numb her bare feet. Frigid air sliced through her chest and plumes of ice blew from her shuddering lungs.

On the dais in front of her, three figures stepped forward and lifted their arms. A thunderous cry hammered the air. Everyone spoke as one voice, while the young woman cringed and tried to shrink.

"Hail, Kali! Hail, Great Mistress! Hail, Goddess of Time! Hail, Shadow Slayer!"

The three figures on the dais raised their voices. "All hail, You who are dark and powerful! You, who guard the transition of ages! You, who wait on the surface of water!"

The man in the center of the dais rumbled. "Who dares seek the face of the Great Mistress?"

Trembling from fear, shivering from cold, the young woman grasped for her rehearsed line. "One – One who seeks to return to her original mind!"

The figure on the right replied. A woman. "Who comes to us seeking to be stripped bare of falsities!"

"One willing to embrace the innermost reasons for her actions!"

The figure on the left spoke. "Who seeks to return to the womb of the Goddess?"

Was that … Ascendant Cyrus? Her advocate? Was he there like he said he'd be? She shook herself and focused on her response. "One, who comes from nothing, and will return to nothing!"

The three leaders spoke in unison. "Fire, blood, and shadow. Three facets of the Goddess. Three paths by which we approach and know Her."

Like a chorus, the entire room resounded. "Fire destroys the old life. Blood is the path to new life. Shadow is where She dwells. To shadow you must go. To shadow you must go. To shadow you must go."

The man in the center held his hand out to two concentric circles etched into the stone floor that made a single ring shape. "What do you bring?"

Cautiously, huddling her bag in her arm, the young woman slid forward and lowered herself into the center of the ring. The cold floor bit into her knees. The ring circumscribed ornate inscriptions resembling those the young woman had come to see inked into the bodies of some in her coven.

She placed her bag and its possessions at the edge of the circle. "My favorite outfit, and…" She hesitated, suddenly embarrassed. "…my doll." In her own ears, she sounded ridiculous. Frail, like thin porcelain.

"Who gave you this doll?"

"My … my mother. When I was young."

After a few seconds of silence, the man in the center spoke. "That mother is a facsimile. She is a suture for your ego, like these objects. These objects are you. They are what you seek from your life. They represent the mists that cloud your vision and snuff your inner flame, where Kali seeks to blaze."

An adherent stepped out of semicircle of gray robes surrounding her and held out a rod – short, black, encircled by chains of minute, indecipherable inscriptions. Hesitant, she reached out and took it. It felt like metal, but soft to the touch and strangely warm.

The man in the center of the dais gestured towards her doll and robes. "A light untested is a light unburning."

After a moment, she understood what he meant her to do. She leaned forward to extend the rod toward her possessions.

A ball of white fire erupted around her doll and clothes. The air squealed with the change of pressure and motes whizzed around. Her arms jerked up to protect her face and the rod fell from her hand.

The flames flared for a moment and were gone, leaving only bright streaks swirling in her sight. She blinked again and again, and when her vision returned, she saw only a meager pile of milky ash where her possessions once were. It was fine enough to be blown away by the most careless breath.

"No!" The ash accused her, glowering, irreversible and absolute.

The speaker on the right continued. "A light unburdened is a light unknowing."

Figures swept in and snatched the young man's wrists. She screamed, twisting and kicking, but they were brutally efficient. Before she could cry out, they pulled out long, silver rods and drove them into the soft, exposed skin of her wrists, sliding them up her forearms like new, metal veins.

Jets of fire and pain cascaded through her arms. She could do nothing but choke on her own swallowed screams. Blackness, woozy and spinning, gripped her sight. They slipped the rods out, leaving terrible, fleshy holes that emptied red mist in petulant fits.

Someone had placed bowls to either side of her. They filled with her pulsing, dribbling blood. Overshot sprays of red spattered the floor as much as the bowls. Her arms began to tremble to the point of convulsion. The men no longer gripped her arms, but she was paralyzed by the pain. It blanketed every sensation.

The man on the left spoke. "Live like the sun, and fade in time. For even the sun will die. Where will we be then, if not for the light inside?"

She recognized the voice – her advocate? *Cyrus!* It *was* him! He *did* come! Did he know this would happen? Did he?!

Delirious, she could do nothing. Darkness rose through her body, throttling her thoughts. Dimness crept into the corners of her open eyes, melting with the blackness of the room, throbbing in time with her strained heart. She was falling behind her loss of life, further, further.

Someone was talking, but she couldn't tell who. "You must admit before you can accept, and accept before you can embrace. By opening yourself to the Goddess, be assured, She will show you what you need to see. Your comfort, your assumptions, your constructs, your artifices, your mind, your senses, and your body must be razed. They must be made as nothing!"

There was some jostling she could barely make out. A sound like the scrunch of wood on wood, again and again.

"You cannot approach the Great Mistress as you are," the voice resumed. "Her power would consume you. You must be concealed from Her third eye, for a time. You must be masked in the vestiges of your old life, and empowered by the new life within. Death to life, life to death, end to fore, and from it forging a singular circle of power."

There was pressure on her face – rough, sliding over her skin, back, stomach, and legs. It left a residue behind, smeared but precise, in lines that interwove. She felt places touched that only claimants and scions had touched. She felt her own nudity, but felt nothing about it.

Her head drooped, and in a moment of clear vision she caught sight of her arm. Gloppy stickiness ran along it in a dirty red streak, curving to connect to another streak, then another, all the way to her elbow and beyond. The streaks tracked along her entire body, creating one giant emblem that used her joints like fulcrums in its pattern.

Her blood. Her blood and the ash from her possessions, comingled to make a new substance.

"Division is the fundamental flaw." Again, the voice spoke. "Contradiction is the bane of time. The Goddess seeks to reconcile you with yourself. Illusion exists, waiting inside."

With those words, every flame in the cavern disappeared at once. Her remaining sight was plunged into a thick nimbus of darkness.

"Wait! I can't see! I can't see anything!" Her words sounded bizarre. Had she even said them? Her consciousness faded further no matter how much she resisted.

"Then you have no choice but to look within! Relent, and know Her! This is the sight you always wanted! This is the sight you've denied yourself since birth! This is the sight all of New Corinth refuses to see! Remember that! The Goddess will show you, swiftly and decisively, who you really are, and you must embrace what you see, or be lost forever! Sight beyond sight is yours, and will be, again!"

Her heat seeped out of her frame like fleeing vapor, sliding like her blood into hidden crevasses of air. It and she, bleeding out into a weightless realm of dark and cold. Inner heaviness sunk her down, down, and in its place an icy torrent rushed in.

Something shuddered inside of her, revolving in the vacuum of her mind, more and more like ripples on a pond. It grew and expanded to a fulminate bulge, an undiscovered momentum swaying round and round in a pendulous rotation. From eternal blackness, nothing yielded something. Through contrast, movement was born. *Presence* came to be.

A singular speck of white light radiated in her inner volume. It grew larger and larger, looming, expanding into a blazing sphere rotating on a single point, spreading heat vast and immense, glorious and golden. Unbroken fire wreathed the point of light as it grew into a burning core of magma, oscillating within gossamer crests rising and falling in shades of cream, snow and ivory.

The light resolved from outline to core. It snapped into place. Sight shifted from blurry to distinct, into shapes both familiar and divine.

It was a woman. The core was a woman. Ashen-skinned, sitting cross-legged, hefting a wicked, curved sword in one of Her four hands, and a human head in another. An avalanche of long, thick, black hair spilled down Her back. Her two great, onyx eyes glared widely, while a third in the center of Her forehead gazed at nothing. Fire roiled in Her mouth, behind protruding fangs.

Kali! The Great Mistress... Within me!

There, at the smallest point inside, the Great Mistress lived, unchained, uncompromised by perception, revolving in an inner infinity.

In Illusion She dwelled, forming the seed of consciousness, abiding, exploding, radiating, permeating to fill to bursting the limitless potential of physical Creation.

She was the single, unseen vent breathing life into every action and fire into every thought. She was the spark that churned the cosmic mulch of matter and energy into an ocean and spun the great wheel forward, forward, onward forever.

The third eye in the center of Kali's head rolled directly at the tiny, other presence that had made its way to Her and now observed Her.

I SEE YOU.

The young woman's identity – her sense of self – disintegrated in the maelstrom of Kali's fire. In a single instant, the young woman saw and knew the full spectrum of her life.

"...Daddy, look!" She knelt on the floor, proudly displaying a crayon-drawn picture. His flat, disinterested face glanced at her before turning back to smile at household guests...

...Each slight, each unkind word, each hedged feeling, each inkling of her true, unadorned self coursed deeper, deeper like trenches of a blade hacking into the same gutted flesh again, again, and again...

"...Come on, get off of me!" Her claimant's face – the first since her Breaching – twisted from affection to irritation. He pushed her off of him and onto the grass. He stood above her, yanking dredges off of his already rubbery penis, slinging them next to her. She lie there on her back, feeling him ooze out of her and onto the grass they'd shared, watching him stalk away out of sight...

...Desperate need, cruelest anger, deepest wrath, profoundest sadness, all returned to her at once in a series of living words and images, as vivid as they once were...

"...The power compels you! The power compels you!" Clap, clap, the scion's groin rebounded from her as he grunted his lines. Her mind

wandered and her body felt nothing. Penance was an accepted institution of Logic. Levitant was the gateway. Bliss was the means. There was no other way. Not since childhood. So she told herself, again and again, while inside an inferno slowly bourgeoned in her heart, expanding from a once cold, lifeless ember...

...One after the other, every choice compounded her pain. She swelled under the weight of every action and non-action like a boil straining to pop. Pressure and grief needled her core. Somewhere within, she was certain that her body was a lacerated, bloody mess, so keen and tangible was the pain and agony. Soon, she'd explode in a shrapnel-storm of bone chips and flesh scraps.

"I see Her! Oh Goddess, I see Her!" The full power of her feelings loosed itself like an unshackled beast. "The darkness! I admit it! I embrace it! I hate them! *I hate them!!*"

Instantly, the vision of Kali vanished. The young woman slammed back into her body, gasping and coughing, kneeling and bleeding on the cold ground of a dank, moist cavern. Flames sprang to life all around. The entourage of gray-robes still filled the room.

The middle figure on the dais spoke, calmly and gently. "In darkness, young one, we see clearly. From one generation to the next, it is our duty to remember the sight that can never be unseen, which those above refuse to see. Never let it leave you. Harness it, embrace it, and let Her be your compass."

The hiss of plastein lit the air. A cooling bubble rose from the young woman's wrists. It was like a soft tickle that also itched. Slowly, the agony in her pierced arms lifted. She glanced down to see ash and dried blood running across her skin in a coat of emblems and runic symbols.

The man in the middle continued. "She has cracked open your third eye. You now come to us in knowledge of yourself and ready to learn. Only the gray may enter from here."

A group of adherents stepped to either side of her. Around her shoulders they swung a gray fabric that settled heavy and firm. A tad too coarse to touch, a hair metallic in scent.

"The Great Mistress has seen your face. You belong to Her, now."

Through a blur of tears the young woman saw past the speakers on the dais into the back of the room. There, torchlight caught the inside of a hood just so, illuminating the horribly mangled face of a man standing off by himself, grinning intensely. One of his eyes was scarred shut.

In the corner opposite him stood a pasty, upright man-creature with a single eye in the middle of its forehead. The eye jangled like a bead in a pocket. A Stabat.

"Welcome, Initiate Oyame Nagai. Welcome to Cloister Mors, third of the cloisters of the Kali'ka."

She could barely comprehend the two insane figures – one a disfigured man, the other not a man at all – opposite each other in the back of the room. She could barely hear anything through her sobs and mutters.

The man on the dais' left raised his voice, swallowing back tears. "Now, you are Kali'ka."

Cyrus, her advocate. It *was* him. She'd been right. He'd been there the whole time. He'd witnessed the entire initiation.

It didn't matter, though. Not Cyrus, not the Stabat nor the scarred man in the back of the room. She could barely feel anything beyond the thick, radiant cord that trailed from her core outwards into infinity, connecting her forever to the Goddess of Time, Kali.

For what seemed like hours. Oyame wept in the darkness, dazed, screaming at times, unable to shake the vision roiling within.

Blessings and thanks to Kali poured from her incoherent lips the entire time.

CHAPTER 6
MUTED FLAMES

In her small, personal chamber, behind a cracked door of worn wood that led to the warrens of Cloister Sangra, Elara Aeve shifted her hips, slid her feet, slammed her fists and smashed her elbows into the empty, dark air.

She was a bundle of driving kinetics one moment, a tassel of rippling waves the next, transitioning flawlessly from one kana to the other like a viper in water, encircling itself again and again. Consumed by the elements of stone and night, she swept around and around the firepot in the middle of her floor, shifting in and out of its crackling orange convulsions, her loose hair a whip of fire, her fair skin coated in an armor of sweat.

Around her room, her few possessions watched in silence: a set of ink brushes and their kamiboard; a cracked ceramic sink with a warped mirror above it; a tattered cot; a polished blonde wood shinsen propped against the wall, its six tuners glinting like the winks of a collusive eye.

Did she make a misstep somewhere? Was she not good enough…? Was she not able to protect herself after all these years, despite all the training, all the self-deconstruction, all the hardening? The assassin had gotten so close, so near, even though his blade never once skimmed her skin.

Her chambers provided no respite, no place of solace, no matter how hard she practiced, no matter how deeply she meditated, no matter how high her consciousness rose on the waves of kinetics and controlled wrath. When left alone, she was once again consumed by the visions that rose from a font of nightmares to flood her mind.

...Puckered canyons like earthen wounds spewed gouts of magma across a ruddy horizon of barren mountains and scarlet dunes, sending their fiery rain to engulf the charred and split bodies saturating those desolate plains, a tinder of flesh for an oceanic, cascading inferno...

There was no space, no room, no time to reconcile herself to the attempt on her life, let alone address the threat creeping to surround their order with weapons raised.

There was no respite from the waking world, even in sleep. No escape from sleep, even when waking. The Great Mistress couldn't help – thoughts of Her soothed nothing, salved nothing. The nightmarish visions taunted her from within, in a place she could never escape, forever out of reach but forever flickering like a phantom dancing along the her mind's outline.

A bolt of pain smashed into Elara's foot. She stumbled and caught herself. The room's light shrunk. She stood there, frowning at the source of her misstep, resettling into her body, coming back from her trance.

Her iron firepot lay on its side, its round rim tottering back and forth. From its open mouth spilled an upturned mess of ash and pulsing embers, strewn like a gritty, flaming puddle on the stone floor.

"Fuck," she huffed, propping her fists on her hips. She flexed her toes, cringing at the pain.

She never made that kind of mistake. She never lost awareness, not of her surroundings, her body, her being, her relationship to her environment, *nothing*. She was distracted – that was it. Second guessing herself.

Was the firepot in a different spot than usual? Had someone moved it...? A quick reassessment of the room – its dimensions and the distance between objects – told her no.

She would've noticed. Nothing passed her by. She'd made herself indestructible, as much as was humanly possible. No one – *no one!* – would hurt her, not again, not since escaping New Corinth and refusing to submit to its will of shame. No one would come close. Certainly not an armed coward who attacked an unprepared opponent.

The upended coals of the firepot said otherwise, spreading towards the evidence they needed to assert their point. Like a finger, their trail pointed to the spinebacks Elara had taken from the Codex, arrayed on the floor. *Debating Heuristics, Philological Comparisons,* and *Aegis Council.*

The spinebacks chided. They mocked. She should be dead, they said, skewered and bloodied like any other water-soft creature. A superior foe, the disadvantage of being taken by surprise, the shock at being exposed to a violating force within bounds and sanctuary of Cloister Sangra. Her, reduced to bare survival, pitted against a man whose sole obsession was to pierce her with an instrument of death.

Somehow, it all constituted being raised to the next Circle of Ascendancy. In Elara's mind, she still saw the Stabat's third eye staring at her in the Codex, tracking her as she sped away.

Meanwhile, the spinebacks just lay there, pages full of vague philosophizing and mundane bylaws from unknown centuries. Useless. They told her nothing.

She could almost see hear Marin chastising her through a thin-lipped frown, denouncing her like a meddling pet. How long had her former advocate been an ascendant, now? Over fifteen years? Growing evermore rigid, watching her pupil below her rise to her equal? Elara could almost understand the stubborn woman's frustration.

Fists clenched, Elara exhaled slowly. It would be useless to resume kanas again. Her throbbing foot pattered on the stone floor as she stepped gingerly across the room.

Next to her cot, the shinsen leaned, pristine and exquisitely crafted, alluringly surreal yet tactile. She dragged her fingers across its smooth surface, letting her fingertips linger on the edge of its neck.

She'd never learned to play it. She could appreciate its music, to be sure, but more so she appreciated the player, the one who gave it to her and dazzled its frets, knowing that it was the one tether that Elara couldn't refuse, to the one person in her former life that she'd unwillingly foregone. It had traveled with Elara when she'd left New Corinth and the Aeve family loft in the Uppers to dwell in secret catacombs under the city.

A sudden, powerful rapping shook Elara's door. Knuckles on wood, clipped and unhesitating.

Elara glanced from the door to the firepot to the spinebacs to her cot. On her cot laid two robes: a tattered mess of slashed fabric and a new, whole robe retrieved from storage – one given when she became an initiate and one claimed after the Codex. Two halves, one old and one new. Two garbs, one woman.

After a moment, she snatched the new robe and slipped it on. Its coarse, unused fabric settled uncomfortably on her shoulders, hips, and bust. It protested her and filled her nose with dry musk.

She kicked the spinebacks under her cot as she adjusted the robe. Best to leave certain things unspoken of … for now.

She purged lingering thoughts and construed scenario after scenario for how to defend herself within the confined space of her room. She wouldn't be taken unaware again. Not only could she not trust those whom she saw, but also those whom she couldn't see.

When she pulled her door inward, she blinked in surprise at the unlikelihood of the sight in her doorway.

It was Ascendant Inos.

CHAPTER 7
A LIFE GIVEN

Against the shadow-laden hallway, Inos was a gray statue swathed against deeper black. The folds of his robes hung from his stately frame like melted stone captured in mid-drip, while the top of his closely-shaven head knifed upward. His hands were clasped in front of his waist.

His level eyes stared at her. The little white scars dotting his face and ears caught the light from her room strangely.

Even before Elara finished opening the door, Inos' eyes scanned her, twitching from her to her room, back to her face in an instant. He'd masked the scan within his natural blink cycle. Only a shift in the white encircling his gray irises gave him away.

Impressive. It would be a shameful loss to them all, if he'd come to harm her.

She glanced past him into the shadow-engulfed hallway. No cluster of Kali'ka gathered around, pointing at her, pleading for attention, whispering to their fellows. No kneeling initiates, begging to have questions answered. It was beautifully empty.

"I shooed them away." Inos pointed his thumb behind him. "But I can't say I blame them. Hiding in your chambers is the best way to draw curiosity. I wanted to give you some space after the Coven of Ascendants, but I think the time for waiting is over."

She stared at him, saying nothing, growing impatient.

"By the yantra on your temple, you've been to see Ascendant Brae?

Circle Nineteen. Can you feel the pattern actuating your crown chakra? For me, it took a week or so to have any real effect. Clarity of mind, heightened intuitive sense."

She lifted a hand to her right temple. Like him, she now had a yantra on each temple. The inscription was still tender, slightly inflamed, but yes, should could feel it re-synching and aligning with her meridians. It felt like a bubble pressing outwards from her skin to fill the air around her head.

"Ascendant...." Her hoarse throat stuck in place. She cleared it before continuing. "Ascendant Noscent. Now's not a good time."

She took a step back and swung the door shut. It rebounded as though it hit a tree trunk. His upraised arm barred her door from shutting.

"Elara, this is important. No one knows I'm here. It's just me."

Elara. No title or formal greeting. Her name flowed so naturally from his lips that she was more surprised at its normalcy than offended at his forwardness.

Had they even *spoken* before? Had they ever held a conversation? She'd intentionally addressed him by his last name.

"What do you want?" She eyed him warily.

He became distant, like his body was a separate entity through which he observed her. In a far place he hovered, high above, gleaming like the light of a night-borne star.

"I know what happened in the Codex. The assassin. I wanted to see you right away, but I left you alone to meditate, to commune, to sort through what happened. But, we can't ignore the danger to our order anymore. Not when it comes into our very home."

For several seconds, Elara stood there, weighing, considering, assessing, trying to figure out what he was driving at.

Inos took the chance to say more. "We need to work together. You wanted to take action – so do I. You wanted to talk to other cloisters, but *this* cloister is right here. *I'm* right here. I'm willing to help."

Elara felt her fingers twiddle with the edges of her sleeves. His words made sense. On that basis alone, she was willing to hear him out. Sense was in too short of a supply to turn it away, no matter the source, no matter her discomfort.

Nonetheless, she mentally homed in on his joints, pinpointing key locations, walking through the steps required to cripple him in two, three strikes at most – given his height, weight, length of his limbs, and depth of his gait. Only then did she step back and pull her door with her.

"Come in."

In a few long strides he was in the center of the room. His board-straight back extended his tall height even higher. He swept his head left, right. Every motion seemed calculated and measured, ironclad and firm. Elara recognized the technique of no-sight, soaking in every detail as one holistic image rather than getting caught on minutiae.

"An assassin isn't about to jump out of the shadows, you know. This room, at least, is safe." She crossed her arms and rotated with him, keeping her back towards the nearest wall.

"I have to make sure." His face drove forward as he scanned. The obsessive subtext of his comment wasn't lost on her.

His presence fished at submerged memories. Images of the Gehana rose to spread over Elara's sight like a darkened, heat-warped film: her standing over him, chest heaving; the disconnected feeling of being a marionette of herself, simultaneously controlling and being controlled.

And now ... he was concerned about *her* coming to harm?

His eyes lingered on the tattered robe on her cot, then the spilled firepot on the floor. "Are you ok?" His face held an odd blend of skepticism and sympathy.

She quickly set about to grabbing matches and candles, using it to cover up her observation of him. The dwindling bloom of her spilled fire provided a good pretense.

"I hope you didn't come here to critique my cleanliness."

"Why don't you have guards outside?"

"I didn't have guards in the Codex." She struck a match, pointedly not making eye contact, and lit a few candles along the wall.

"If you won't take steps to protect yourself, then the rest of us have to." His voice was hard, yes, but coated in soft touches.

"When have I ever given you the impression that I need help?" She pulled her arms into her robe and gripped the handles of her firepot to tilt it upright, struggling a bit but managing.

"We *all* need help, Elara. You didn't find your way down here by yourself."

"Oh yeah – Marin, my estranged advocate. Thanks for reminding me."

He just sighed and ran a hand across his head.

"Inos, you want to know why there aren't any guards outside?" She stabbed a finger towards the shredded robe on her cot. "That's why. They'd look like that robe! I won't be held responsible for endangering anyone else."

Standing, she gathered her hair behind her head before crossing to her cot and swiveling onto it to sit hunched over her knees. "And, I won't have them slowing me down."

Inos just watched her with those penetrating eyes. Instead of pursuing the point, he said nothing. It was only then that she realized she'd used his first name. It irked her.

"Elara, I don't think the assassin was sent here just to kill you."

Elara frowned at him as though he was a lunatic. "What?! Why, then? What else did he want? Grab a spineback from the Codex and sit down for some tea? Have a nice chat and then slice my kidney out? Ridiculous."

He ignored her facetiousness. "No it's not. This –" he pointed to the tattered robe next to her, "– is too deliberate. Too direct. Just to *kill*? No. Think of what we've heard about Advent Square. Their leader wants a reaction. He wants to see a transformation. He's a *performer*. You yourself said that there are deeper layers at play."

At the sound of her own words quoted back to her, Elara felt her frustration loosen and her thoughts start to straighten. "Why would they train one man only to sacrifice him? The assassin."

"I think it's pretty clear that their leadership has little regard for their own followers. And besides, whoever trained him is still alive. And, we don't know if they *only* trained one man."

The words were startling at least, horrifying at worst. A scene unfolded in Elara's mind – an entire army of interlocutors and guerilla savages lurking in the periphery of Cloister Sangra, wielding gleaming daggers. Elara could only conclude that the image was probably what

Corinthians thought *all* Kali'ka were like.

"So ... what, Inos?" Elara glared at his tightly bound, reserved, annoyingly controlled face. "What do they want, then? Hm? Provoking violence will only destroy them. *We're* not their enemy, not really." She lowered her voice to a murmur. "Certainly not me."

Inos leaned against a wall and shrugged. "To see how we respond. Force our hand. Provoke us, like they're doing to the Corinthians."

"You think he was sent here to test our defenses? To what end?"

"Check our limits. Our resolve. Send a message."

"To show us ... what?" she asked.

"That they can get to us whenever they want. Wherever. And..." Inos sighed. There was that sympathetic look again. "...At whoever."

Elara blew on her hands for warmth. The sweat on her skin was drying and clinging, and the ever-present cold of the cloister was creeping in. Staring into the blackened, unlit corners of her room, her eyes sharpened like the edge of the dagger that could've ended her life.

"Leave us alone," she whispered, "or you become our enemy, too. That's the message. You and the Corinthians, both: enemies."

Inos said nothing. He was frowning as though mulling over something.

"Inos, maybe we *should* leave the dissidents alone. Let them rampage across the surface of New Corinth. Logic is a hateful blight and a foolish disgrace. Let the scions rot. Their entire culture of stupidity and usury should be obliterated." Elara scrubbed her scalp and, with more force than necessary, shook out some snarls in her hair.

"And then what?" Inos crossed his arms and stepped towards Elara's firepot. The squat, round cistern of coals and embers glowed dimly, its upturned contents starting to smoke and cool.

He scattered some ash with his foot. "We become used kindling. Muted flames. A mockery of a once proud order, unable to intervene, unable to guide lost Corinthians. All it would take is one misstep, like this fire here. Do you really think the extremists will stop with New Corinth? There'll be nothing left, eventually. Nothing left of them *or* us. We split once – the Kali'ka – and we split forever."

Elara sunk her head into her hands. His words cut into more deeply than the assassin's dagger ever could. He brought reality to bear under a single, austere focus, like a hammering blade and a cleaving sword fused into one tool, building, breaking interchangeably.

She found herself whispering the Chant of Ages, staring off into the dark corners of her room, feeling her mind tumble and lock and link together fragments of thought rising from buried conclusions.

"In darkness, your eyes shine, oh Kali. Tilt the wheel to carry us onward, over the ocean of birth and death."

In her inner eye, she saw the assassin lunging at her, striking like a snake, wielding his dagger like an extension of his body. She saw the blade's edge plunged in a golden haze of light, flashing and swiping in front of her face.

To the eyes, he looked frantic and rabid. That assessment, however, ignored what lay beneath the surface, hidden within esoteric rationale.

He embodied what Elara told adherents again and again while practicing kanas: capture your enemy's attention and you've won. Redirect their eyes and they're yours. Musash the Twin-Bladed was long quoted as saying that all conflict was distraction; all combat was diversion and inveiglement.

To win such a fight, she would have to respond in an unexpected way. An unpredictable way.

"The assassin. I have to see him." She pushed off her knees and turned to leave. "Brae won't like it, but … whatever."

Inos took a step between her and the door. "I want to go with you."

In the middle of her room, Elara stood facing him, scrutinizing him as intently as his gray eyes examined her, both of them measuring, considering, searching.

Mistrust. It came so naturally for her. It was her place of safety. Was it really so hard to believe that someone like Inos simply wanted to help? Would she corrupt the clarity of her own mind by blocking a source of reason?

Inos didn't resist her, not directly. He didn't confuse her. He didn't complicate things. She saw her own image reflect out from him, undistorted and immaculate, shaprer than how she looked otherwise. His perspective was a lens attenuated her comprehension into a solid, crystalline form.

He didn't really have to *do* anything except be who he was, and she felt ... *clearer.*

She tracked her gaze along the inscriptions on his temples, scrawled in jet-black lines and interwoven crescents, like hand-drawn segments of thorny vines, or fragments of a broken crown. Left, right, and one at the base of the skull. They proclaimed his ascendancy to Circle Twenty, a mere single circle away from the Stabat declaring him High Ascendant, when he would shave his hair to the scalp and have his final yantra etched at the articulation point at the crown of his skull, symbolic of the connection that beamed forth from the ground and up through his essence to stream into the cosmos.

In Sangra, only Marin had been raised as high as Inos, and it had taken her decades rather than a handful of years. Marin, though, refused to grow, and so reverted.

High Ascendant was the end, though. No one moved beyond it. No one Transcended. *Transcendence.* Even the word was shrouded in near myth. There were no rites and no strictures beyond ascendancy. There was no objective means of gauging progress at that point. There was no one to *ascertain* Transcendence, nor even develop an objective definition of it. Not the Stabat, nor any force or entity.

A part of Elara wanted to muster whatever poor apology she could manage for nearly ending Inos' life. A part of her wanted to confide in him about the crackling *presence* that raged within her and sought to devour her conscious identity.

Instead, with ruthless efficiency, she cut down the desire. She beheaded the need to have someone to disclose to. To have a peer, an ally, an equal. To not be trapped within herself, always silent.

As she hacked her true emotions at their root, she felt her heart shrink to a lump of darkness as muted and chilled as the spilled fire on her floor.

"Inos..." She spoke, carried along on a compass of intuition. "...Why are you really here?"

He never broke eye contact, but his demeanor cracked for the first time since he entered. It shrunk into apprehension and vulnerability. An effusive energy radiated from a source deep within his gray eyes, like a storm crackling behind the canopy of an overcast sky.

Yes, she thought. She'd asked the right question.

"At the Gehana…," he whispered. "…You let me live."

CHAPTER 8
HEIRS OF EARTH

At the end of a dead-end hallway in Cloister Sangra, Elara swept a divided curtain aside and stepped into the Scrbe's Sanctum. Inos following closely behind.

Across the ovular, cornerless room, Ascendant Brae leaned towards a wall mural from the top of a tall, rolling ladder, tapping away with a fan brush like a plump finch pecking at its nest. Elara could make out a distinctive 6:4 ratio in the proportions of the leafy pattern he was painting – the Golden Ratio – from the entryway. Ever tinkering, Brae was, never content to not experiment.

At the sight of Elara and Inos, his face assumed a devilish glow. With an agility that belied his girth, he pattered down the ladder and sauntered towards them, wiping his ink-laden hands over the stained, white apron stretched around his mid-section. His arms stuck out of his scribe's vest like elephant trunks.

He passed through slim shadows cast from free standing columns that sent emblematic patterns stretching across the floor. Wheel-mounted standlamps and an adjustable mirrors allowed him to create and view whatever pattern he needed to examine.

Before he reached Elara and Inos, he cavalierly tossed his brush into a wooden box of jumbled writing implements on the floor, paused to adjust an easel and canvas depicting a stenciled heron, and re-assessed the tilt of one of the sanctum's mirrors.

"Elara, there you are! I was wondering where you'd disappeared to.

Back so soon? Gotten to Circle Twenty already? The Stabat probably have to take shifts just to keep up with you."

His guffaw shook the massive beard wringing his face. He settled into a toothy grin that displayed perfectly aligned incisors. "And Ascendant Inos! I'm either in serious trouble or seriously needed. Although, it take it by your demeanor that it's more likely the latter, hm? Maybe."

Elara tucked an errant lock of hair behind her ear and chuckled to herself. The man was an uncontrollable force. "You enjoy pricking me with needles, that's all. You're a sadist."

"Well, no one does it better, do they? So … I take it by the lack of an entourage that you snuck down here."

She could only sigh. "I'm fine. I'm safer by myself than anyone is with me."

"Oh, I know, I know. I don't doubt it. It's a bad decision. That is, it's a bad decision to *sneak*. Encourages rumors." He gestured towards the entrance. "Our adherents need to *see* you to believe you're ok."

"Some of them did as we were walking here. They'll spread the word, believe me. I'm not responsible for their peace of mind."

"No, but you can't deny your influence. You should –"

"Later, Brae. I'll deal with them later. Not now."

He stood there with for a moment, silently observing her with a dubious eye. "Just realize that even though they're all in awe of you, they don't all *trust* you. That's a dangerous combination. Especially now."

Behind her, Elara could see Inos standing with his arms tucked into his sleeves, observing. His eyes said that he was worried, Strange… Was she already getting better at reading him, or was he willingly letting his thoughts show?

"Elara." Brae lowered his voice and leaned towards her. "Some of them blame you for the assassin, you know. Some say you let him in yourself, that the whole fight was staged. The Codex is completely isolated, and no one actually *saw* you two fight. Cassandra and Oren only saw the aftermath. Some even say that you're the mastermind behind the whole dissident movement. Some, in fact say –"

"Listen, Brae…" She probed for tact, but immediately gave up. His words didn't upset her. They were just … *in the way.*

"I need to talk to him." She pointed towards the lone wooden door at the far side of the room.

Brae straightened to his full height, barely eye-level with her, and crossed his massive arms over his chest. The yantra on his left and right temples – eighteen and nineteen, respectively – caught the sanctum's light, matte and flat. It was odd to think they were the same circle, now. Had he inscribed the yantra himself, she wondered?

"Absolutely not," he stated.

"I'll just go in, anyway."

He barked a laugh. "No you won't. You're in enough danger without endangering *yourself*."

"There's no danger from him at this point, in the crypt back there."

"No danger? Do you want to break his solitude? Give him leverage? Strengthen his connection to you? You should know better than to even ask. He's a *prisoner*, understand?"

"It's my right."

"You'll botch the process. You're not involved. Period. This is my territory." He turned to a bench and began fidgeting with his tools – ruler, some compass-and-needle contraption, charcoal nubs – picking them up and examining them one at a time.

"I need my own answers, Brae. He has them."

"That's why I'm here," he muttered, not looking at her.

She stepped next to him, peering into his face, stressing each word. "*I need to see him.*"

He turned on her. "*I'm* the Master Inscriber of this cloister, Elara! I've read the shape of his meridians, the nuances of his articulation nodes, the character of his blood. That's what I do. You doubt my talents?" He winked at her and a large scalpel materialized from nowhere into his meaty hands. Its cold, hairline edge twirled round and round in his surprisingly nimble fingers.

She lifted an eyebrow at him. "I know you haven't been able to get him to talk. That's why you're out here and not in there. Letting him simmer a bit longer."

"Well." Brae's impish grin faded. He flipped his scalpel towards a nearby table. "I wanted to wait until I was finished, but I'm sure about one thing, at least." He took a deep breath. "He has no yantra. No inscriptions ... whatsoever."

Elara glanced at Inos, who frowned and gestured 'I don't know.' She asked the obvious. "So he's not one of us?"

"No, no. That's not what I mean. He is. I found evidence of scar tissue around articulation points related to the root and sacral chakras, and the first of the *hara* triad."

"Scar tissue. How?"

"Cut. Patches of skin ... *cut off*. And not delicately. Afterwards, they healed by themselves. No plastein."

"Kali's Eyes," Inos breathed.

Elara tried to make sense of what she was hearing. "Seven scars? That means..."

"Circle Seven, yes." Brae started inspecting various hanging scrolls. "This man was of the seventh circle. And I'll say 'was' because whatever he was, he's no Kali'ka now. He's...." Brae drifted off and just shook his head.

"The seventh circle...." Inos spoke as though half to himself. "Denying external influences. Learning to co-exist with base impulses."

Elara recalled the rest. "Beginning to learn how to not pass judgment on violent, angry thoughts and desires. Instead, learning to integrate them into your natural flow of thoughts and feelings."

Brae walked here and there, running fingers along the edges of easels. "Which is related to the larger issue of unfettering preconceptions that we would *assume* an inflammatory, extremist group would have problems with. He hasn't progressed past that point, Circle Seven. Whatever articulation his yantra once provided to his meridians was stolen, in a moment. He lost his mind. His energy sunk to his sacrum, where it stays."

"Our foe is using the susceptible." Inos made no show of hiding his disgust. "Those too young in Kali to know better."

Elara rushed up to Brae and riveted her jade eyes on him. "Brae, listen to me. I won't deprive myself of the right to face him. I want to hear *why* from his own mouth. I want to see the reasons in his eyes!

"We all have unique perspectives as facets of the same Goddess, correct? I might be able to draw out answers that you haven't been able to. Do you want to risk missing a chance to find out what's going on in Cloister Mors? Cloister Ignis? Aboveground in New Corinth? Because of pride? Because being our scribe is your *art*?

His face soured. He was well aware of the hubris he held towards his own work.

"The scions didn't commission you this time, Brae. Not like in the old days. You're not up there anymore. None of us are!"

He scratched his beard and grunted. "Elara, I'm not sure I like it when you make sense."

She folded her arms and stared at him.

He lifted a single finger. "You won't use any of my tools. I don't want you ruining my reputation."

"Fine."

"And, I'm staying."

"I want you to."

He threw his head back and bellowed a deep laugh. Slowly, his chuckling torso quieted. "I wouldn't do this for anyone else, you know. Remember that."

"I know." Elara gripped his arm and stepped passed him toward the crypt in the back of the sanctum, in and out of shadowy lines cast from the room's free standing columns. Here and there, fragrant streamers from incense lashed around her as she strode through them.

Brae turned towards Inos. The two men stared at each other through indecipherable, opaque gazes. After a moment, Brae bowed with fingertips to forehead. Inos returned the gesture and moved to follow Elara.

"Elara," Brae called.

She stopped with her hand on the rear door's rickety handle, keeping an ear towards him. Frigid air seeped in from the room beyond, through cracks in the doorframe.

"I hope you find what you need." His gruff features assumed an uncharacteristically aged, severe pose.

All she could think of was the raging, fire-streak sky in her visions. All she smelled was the acrid stench of sulfur and old blood carried on flinty, unbreathable air, rolling over fields of corpses.

All she could think of was losing the order that had rescued her, the place she now called home. All she could see was the face of the Great Mistress howling in Illusion.

"Something already found me, Brae."

Without waiting for a response, she twisted the handle and stepped into the Yantric Crypt.

***

As soon as Elara entered the Yantric Crypt, she gagged and lifted a hand to her mouth. The stench of gore lay thick in the chill air of the low-ceilinged, barren room. A single oil lamp of archaic design lit its unadorned, stony features.

A splintered wooden table stood next to the door, arrayed with crudely worked blades, rust-stained barbs, hooked tongs, and inexplicable, hinged metal mechanisms. Dark, glistening slashes marred the tabletop, here and there indistinguishable from the stains coating the gruesome instruments on its surface.

In the middle of the room, like a macabre centerpiece, lashed in place on a solid slab of deep, iridescent obsidian rested the naked, unconscious body of the assassin, contorted into a bloody spectacle.

It was exactly what Elara expected – and wanted – to see.

Fine, scalpel-thin incisions ran down the length of his sides, along the contours of his muscles. His scalp was rolled back. A chunk of flesh was hollowed out of his midsection; somehow, he didn't bleed. Raw bands of flesh encircled his wrists and ankles where he'd clearly raged against his restraints. One shoulder was a gnarled clump of odd protrusions saturated in deep purple.

Brae hadn't set the joint she'd snapped. Good.

Off to the side, on the floor, atop smears of caked blood, lay the dagger that the assassin had brought with him. Bathed in the crypt's single lamp, its tapered blade was a dully gleaming grin whispering wicked promises.

The door clicked shut behind Elara. Inos stepped past her and to the side. She'd never seen his face more emotionless. The gentle pressure of

Brae's large, warm palm came to rest on her shoulder.

She recognized his bearded face as he leaned in to whisper. "His will is focused no matter how misguided his mind is. Don't let him manipulate you."

She nodded and stepped forward to circle the man. Her slippers softly crunched on the gravely stone floor in a deliberate, steady pace.

This was the person who could've ended her life. A human tool of a rogue sect wielding a metal tool made by human hands. She saw herself as she might have been: impaled, blood pouring out onto the cold floor of the Codex, while he quietly slipped away into whatever dark crevice had spawned him.

Elara felt words flow from within the rhythm of her steps, seething from a primitive locus of cruel motives. They coiled up from the deepest, harshest places of her mind to mold the shape of her lips and the pitch of her voice.

"Kali sees you," she hissed.

The assassin's eyelids fluttered open and his rolling eyeballs struggled to right themselves. Spittle dribbled from his parched, bloody lips.

The instant his eyes latched onto her, he howled in rage and his body lunged against his restraints. "You!! You'll die! You'll fucking die! I'll kill you! I'll kill you!!"

Elara kept her breathing even, refusing to react, refusing to push back against this man, even though an inner need begged her to destroy him.

He would not control her. She would meet him, as she had in the Codex: fast for slow, hard for soft, left for right. Information, she reminded herself. That's all she needed. That was why she was there.

"Tell me, initiate…" With the reins of her voice pulled tight, she kept her tone on the cusp between disinterest and disdain. "Why did your master send someone as inadequate as you?"

"You stupid whore! If I'm so inadequate, then tell me why I almost killed you. I still can! I can carve any of these fools into a bloody pulp! Tell me why, you stupid, Breached whore!"

Out from the shadows Brae stepped in a motion that radiated powerful and clear menace. Elara lifted an arm to stop him, but never took her eyes from the assassin.

Inos didn't even appear to be breathing. She was grateful that he understood her well enough to let her do what she needed.

"You didn't 'almost kill me', initiate. You didn't even nick me."

"Let me try again, then, whore of Kali."

"This time maybe not by yourself, nor in a well-lit area?"

"Shut up! I'm not as easily manipulated as these other pathetic excuses for Kali'ka!"

"Clearly not."

"Shut up!" He railed against the stone, snared by restraints, consumed in an insane frenzy. "You can't trick me! You can't trick me! You can't! No! No!!"

Elara waited for him to quiet down. "There are no tricks, initiate. The Goddess can be a trickster, but She doesn't lie."

"*The Goddess*," he scoffed. "What right do you have to invoke Her name?"

"I have as much right as any of Her children. Which begs the question: what right do *you* have? I'm your ascendant, no matter which cloister I come from."

"My ascendant? You're not my ascendant, nor anyone else's! I know what you are!"

"*What* I am?" She stumbled over his odd choice of words.

"Yes! You are the false face. The threat! You are the one who will break us, if allowed to live! If you are not struck down, the entire edifice will fall!"

To the side, Brae looked dumbfounded. Inos' eyes probed the man for unspoken answers.

The assassin's words had the ethereal, almost visionary quality of rhetoric, similar to Logical maxims and euphemisms. Scions always made impassioned pleas for irrational action wrapped around mock reason. Their "rationale" was always justified through a self-made calculus of checks and balances, irrespective of physical truths, contradictory interpretations, or external observation.

Worship, they called it. The assassin's words had a similar ring.

Elara resumed her interrogation. "And tell me, initiate, who told you to recite those very clever lines if you were caught?"

"One who is far more dangerous than even you!"

"I doubt that."

"He is! He is the true Transcendent!"

Her eyebrow twitched. Transcendent? *He.* A man. Were the rumors correct, then? Could one person alone really be controlling an entire cadre of Kali'ka? A singular seat of charismatic power?

"There *is* no Transcendence, initiate."

"I'm no initiate! Stop calling me that!"

"You don't like that title."

"We are not initiates. Not adherents. We are all *ascendants!*"

A genuine laugh burst from Elara. "Except for your master, of course, who has Transcended."

"Yes!"

"Right. You're not even Kali'ka, you blind fool."

"I am a *true* Kali'ka!! "

"A true Kali'ka doesn't take a life not asked for."

"A true Kali'ka does as he wills!"

"No, initiate, he doesn't!" She brought her open palm down on the obsidian table. "By attempting to take my life, you're *asking* for yours to be taken. And the Goddess will happily claim it!"

"Then do it! Kill me right now! Kill me!! But you can't, can you? Because you're afraid! You're afraid of me! All three of you! Three *ascendants* –" He spat. "And you can't stand the sight of a truly free Kali'ka, without shackles and inhibitions. I am the power of the Goddess! We're all Her representatives, aren't we?! Do as She would, then! My life is Hers! Destroy me!"

A voice inside Elara warned her against confronting this man head on, but she shoved it aside and obeyed her impulses, stepping right up to him and screaming in his face. A part of her wanted to fragment him into a spray of fleshy soup and bone slivers.

"Kali strips away falsities of the *mind*, initiate! She destroys illusions! She dismantles the constructs of our *ego!* She leaves us broken and able to change! *Then* we become her representatives. The Goddess is not a *tool* for you to use! She doesn't exist to justify whatever you say and do!"

"*Lies!!* You just accept whatever you're told! You don't even realize it, do you?! Those lies have covered up our true purpose for centuries! Used to milkfeed the weak who demand that we all hide like frightened children, while those pathetic Corinthian creatures deride us! Mock us!! They and their dead god! We will not be controlled any longer! We are the most worthy! We are the heirs of Earth! Through us, Logic will come to know the true face of Kali!"

Heirs of Earth. What a curious phrase. Elara stored it away in memory.

"Is that our 'true purpose', then? Being … heirs of Earth?"

The man clammed up. Nervousness crept into his face. He was catching on to her tactics. Her door of access was shutting fast. Brae started twiddling with a long, thin silver rod that had someway made its way into his hands.

"How did you get into this cloister?" she demanded.

The assassin stared at her, tight-lipped. The thin-lined, red cuts along his skin started to seep, here and there.

"Where did you come from?"

Nothing. His resolve and composure solidified.

"Is there anybody else here with you? One of your cohorts?"

The second the question left her mouth, the door into the room crashed open.

Elara spun around, dropping her center and readying her mind for combat. Next to her, Brae and Inos did the same.

In through the doorway stepped the frazzled face of Ascendant Oren.

"Oren!" Brae bellowed, waving his silver rod around. "What do you think you're doing? Get out! This is – You're not allowed in here! This is an effrontery! A violation! This is the Scribe's sanctum! This is *my* sanctum!"

Almost directly on top of him, Elara joined in. "Oren, what are you doing?! Get out! Get out of here!"

Oren shifted his weight back and forth, one leg to the other. His eyes had riveted themselves to the assassin, and he appeared unable to pull them away. "I, uh … I understand that I shouldn't have allowed myself in, but I had to find you right away, Ascendant Aeve. This supersedes any improprieties or norms. It's – It's important."

"You're sure it couldn't wait? Kali's Eyes!" Elara stalked towards him, intending to snatch his arm and haul him from the room.

Oren lifted his hands in defense and took a step back. He managed to pull his gaze from the assassin and make eye contact with her. "It's your sister, Ascendant Aeve. She's here. Your sister is here. In the cloister."

Your sister ... here. The words rang hollow and telescopically distant. The world stopped. Sound cut out. In the span of a moment, the same impossible sentence stretched and repeated, repeated. *Your sister ... here. Here. Here.*

"What ... she's here? Right now??"

"Yes, ascendant."

"But, where? Where is she?"

"Where? Uh ... here. In the cloister What do you mean –"

"*Where* here, Oren?!"

"Oh! Oh, um ... In your room."

"My room."

"Yes. In your room."

A second later, he cleared his throat and continued in his best attempt at a conversational tone. His eyes kept glancing at the assassin.

"Ascendant – I'm, uh, a little confused about this. Not about having a sister, of course – we all have relatives aboveground, I assume. Families we've come from. Well, that's beside the point, I guess. What I mean is, uh – I don't see how it's possible she could've known how to get in. I mean, she had to have been *instructed*. The pores would've killed her, otherwise."

Outrage stormed through Elara's chest. She punctuated each word. "Oren, shut – your – fucking – mouth. Don't say a *word* about my sister! This isn't a problem to deconstruct, understand? There are no figures to tally, no lists to compile. Can't you see what's happening here?" She pointed at the assassin. "And you're standing there talking about my *family?!*"

From behind her, the assassin jeered in the darkness. "A sister? And she came *here*? You really *are* the stupidest whore I know. You led her here!"

Elara burst towards him, ablaze with violence. "What do you know?!

Tell me!"

A vicious grin split the assassin's face. He said nothing.

"Tell me, damn you!"

"We know you'll never make concessions. You're Unchanged. Weak and petty. You'll never ask for quarter, and you'll never have it. Your obstinacy has already defined your end." Sickening, indulgent malice dripped from the his voice.

"I'll find her when I get out, you know. That sweet little meat you care so dearly for. You know I will! You know I can! And I'll kill her! I'll fucking kill her!"

I'll find her... I'll kill her... They were the only words Elara could hear. In the span of a moment, the same impossible sentence stretched and repeated, repeated. *I'll find her... I'll kill her...*

"I'll gut her open, your lovely little sister. And as her life bleeds out, I'll fuck her dry! But first, I'll come back here and have her watch me do the same to you!"

Oh Kali, no... She's here, near this man. It's all my fault. My fault. Nothing else mattered. Nothing.

"This is what happens when you undermine our order, *ascendant!*" His mockery of Elara's title was clear. "First your elite circle, then the rest of the fools in Cloister Sangra, then your family! One by one, until no one is left! Your blood will pour like a river into the gullet of the Goddess!"

A white torrent of wrath annihilated Elara's mind. All she saw was the delicate face of her sister, side by side with the bloodied and mangled *monster* laying in front of her.

Before she knew what she was doing, she pulled her arm back and smashed her fist into his ruined shoulder like an iron hammer.

"AAAaaa!!" His body cringed and twisted as much as his restraints would allow.

Again, she smashed her fist into his shoulder. It crumpled in a cascade of tiny pops. His yells of pain twisted into sputters of blood that shot through his lips.

"Y – You're not ... as strong as you think, Ascendant Aeve. You're not invulnerable. Indefensible. All of you ... nothing left."

Again, Elara struck his shoulder. Where bone met bone, her knuckles cried out in pain. She barely noticed.

"You … can't stop us! Your sister, all of you … dead. We are the true face … the true … Kali …."

Elara snatched his jaw in a vice and pressed her wild, furious eyes to his. Rage burned in her belly like a pit of coals, fuming up from her nostrils and sliding through the cracks in her bared teeth.

"No, initiate … *this* is."

Sudden and explosive, she smashed his head against the obsidian slab. A deep, nearly inaudible thud came from the impact.

She cradled his forehead in her palm, squeezed his sodden hair between her fingers, and waited.

The second he tensed his neck, she smashed his head against the stone again. His eyes rolled. He resisted, slightly.

Again, Elara smashed his head into the stone. Harder. Blood spat from his head. His muscles started to give.

Again. His eyelids stopped moving, and his neck gave way.

Again. Blood erupted onto the stone. No reaction came from him. Nothing.

Again. Elara didn't stop until his crushed skull lathered the obsidian slab in a thick coat of smeared red. Only then did she pry her fingers from his hair.

The assassin's head dropped like an unmanned puppet. Discolored splotches ran across his forward from where her palm had pressed into it.

At his sight, Elara felt nothing. Terror, hope, rage, empathy … all of it evacuated like steam. Nothing was left but a cold, solitary void and the numbness of blank fury. Nothingness. Emptiness.

It felt exactly like bliss.

"You can't harm my sister now, can you … *initiate?*" Her words sounded strange in her ears. Hollow and mechanical. "May you drift aimlessly on the ocean of life and death … wretch of Kali."

Brae started to lift a trembling hand towards her. Fear curdled his face. Oren was flush against the wall, drained of all color. Recessed in shadow, Inos didn't take his eyes off of her. Not even when she was a second from slicing him open at the Gehana did he appear so perturbed.

It didn't matter, though. Nothing mattered beyond her own fault. Oren was right – it was her fault that her sister knew how to enter the cloisters. It was her fault that her sister was neck deep in a dark conclave of danger. It was her fault – her, Elara Aeve – that her sister was within arm's reach of murder and conspiracy, so close to this man on the slab of obsidian.

No place was safe anymore. Not for her, not for those she loved. Never again. Never.

I led her here. Oh Kali ... no. No. Please, no.

Without another glance at the any of them, she stalked out of the room, leaving Brae, Inos, Oren, the assassin – his crippled arm, his butchered body, his crushed skull, and the bloodied altar he lie on – exactly as they were.

On the floor lay a puddle of blood with a streak through the middle, from where Elara had deftly pilfered the assassin's dagger. No one noticed at all.

CHAPTER 9
SISTERS OF AEVE

Elara lightly placed her trembling hand on the wooden handle of her chamber's door, allowing the grain and embossment to slide across the underside of her fingers. With her free hand, she combed out her hair and straightened her robe. Possibilities rolled and spun within – how words would play out, what tact she should take, how glances and the unspoken would be mimed and digested in turn.

As deftly as years of training could be applied, she stuffed the memory of the Scribe's Sanctum into a tiny locked corner in her mind for whenever she could deal with it. Not here, not now – not when the wrong word could damage what must be kept safe. At least the walk back to her room had given her a little time to re-center.

Kali's Eyes, the assassin had deserved it. He was a threat. He couldn't be allowed to live. He couldn't.

Again and again, she repeated these words to herself. In expert fashion, she stuffed down all emotions. She couldn't let her anger or anxiety show. Her sister would smell it. Elara wouldn't risk getting her involved, even if it meant concealing how she felt.

Tucked into her sleeve, the assassin's dagger lay cold against her skin. No one had seen her take it, she knew. She wasn't even sure why she did. She just left it there, aware of its presence, mindful of keeping it in place.

Taking one deep breath, shaking away flecks of shock and confusion, she entered her room.

In the nearly empty, shadow-cloaked chamber, her younger sister sat on her cot, staring down, aloft within smoke that curled and lingered from the dwindling fire in her upturned firepot.

Her younger sister looked like a living silhouette lifted off an austere stone background to form a new, elemental creation. Her silent shape seemed the vague shading of an impassioned artist who shunned precision, preferring broad emotive strokes, leaving a young woman so quiet and gentle, her mere presence demanded a repose resembling reverence.

Elara stood in the doorway, staring at her from across the empty space of her room. "Charlotte."

Charlotte looked up, wide-eyed, and bolted across the room to clutch Elara's middle and graft herself into place. Elara kissed her on the head, lightly like the faintest brush of wingtips, and they embraced. A familiar, floral scent clung to Charlotte's skin and wafted from her hair; she smelled like *home* – a real home. She was velvet – so soft. Completely at odds with the harsh, explosive violence Elara still trembled from, inside.

Separating, Elara held Charlotte at arm's length, and was shocked to realize that she was standing nearly eye to eye with her. Those eyes, round and darkly emerald, regarded her with open expectancy, large and glowing, almost sparkling. Her shoulder-length hair shone lustrous even in the feeble light of the room, amber with fine strands of reddish and golden fire.

"You look good," Elara glowed, feeling light surge through her, mending, caulking broken bits, carrying away refuse.

A warm, unrestrained smile split Charlotte's face. "You look like hell." Laugher percolated from her lips. "You're exhausted. Your skin's all red. Have you been practicing those ... what-do-you-call-thems?"

"Kanas. And no. I ... I just got here as fast as I could." Elara hoped her small smile covered her half-truth.

She noticed the torn skin over her knuckles as they gripped Charlotte's shoulders. Layers of red and pink. They ached. They'd just killed a man.

Even up to the end, he'd had proved unable to harm her. Only *she* had harmed her, herself.

Charlotte's intensive, detail-hunting eyes tracked the trajectory of

Elara's gaze. "El, what under Logos happened to your hands?!"

"Don't say that name in here. You know better."

"Don't avoid the question! You know it's just a phrase."

"It still matters. What you confess with your mouth…"

Charlotte rolled her eyes. "Becomes reality. You've told me. Many times, in fact. So what happened?"

"Char … there are only so many things I can explain unless you've done them. And at that point, I wouldn't need to explain."

Charlotte just squinted in response. It was her version of sticking her tongue out. Always the riddles, Charlotte thought. Always the riddles with her sister.

"Listen, Char. This is very important: were you followed here?"

Fear welled up in Charlotte's face.

"Were you followed here? Think. Carefully."

Charlotte didn't answer.

Elara tightened her grip. "Were you followed here?!"

"No."

"Are you sure?"

"I – I, I mean, I don't think I was."

"You don't *think* so? So that means you're not –"

"No! I'm sure. I mean, I don't see how it's possible; I only used the routes you showed me, like usual."

"Azure Lane, off of Brickfelt Avenue?"

"Southwest from Advent Square. The fourth alleyway. It leads out to a bakery on the left, the one with the round, purple sign."

"And?"

She looked off to the side, counting with her fingers. "Oh! Browse for three minutes, buy a knot roll. Pay with six gold, not credit. He gives four gold back and suggests I browse inside."

Elara arched an eyebrow at her. "And then?"

"I go inside, give the gold to the clerk, who lets me through the curtain when no one's around. Down the hall, second door on the left."

"Good. And once you're inside?"

"Down the stairs, don't close the door behind me. Clear my mind. Everything becomes dark. Focus on the point of light in the distance.

Imagine I'm there. Then, I step through into the cloister. It'll feel like stepping through a cold waterfall."

"And you're sure no one followed you."

"Yes."

"Charlotte...." Elara paused, considering and rejecting approach after approach. "This is a dangerous time for you to come here. What are you doing here, anyway? You're not supposed to be here for another few weeks." She released Charlotte's arms and took a step back.

Charlotte looked away and wrung her hands a bit – somehow making it a graceful movement – before turning to glide into place on Elara's cot and fidget with the coverlet.

"I ... just missed you, is all. I wanted to see you."

Elara exhaled deeply and mopped her face. "You scared me to death. What did Oren say to you? Tell me. Everything."

Charlotte frowned. "You mean the man who found me? Nothing. He was pretty jittery. He seemed surprised to see anyone." She was plucking at Elara's tattered robe on the cot. "What is this gross thing here?"

"Nothing. But really, Oren had to have said something. He didn't touch you, did he?"

"No. He just made me follow him here. And then he ran off really quickly. He seemed more distracted than anything else."

Elara started pacing, squeezing her fists into tight balls. "What was he doing? I specifically chose that route because no one uses it. No one has caught you before. Not even close."

"Did I ... get you in trouble?" Charlotte whispered timidly.

Elara started at the spilled mulch and coal on the floor. They looked vomited out.

She'd explained to a non-Kali'ka how to enter Cloister Sangra. She'd exposed their world to an outsider. By extension, she'd thrown the gate wide to anyone who happened to be clever enough to get the information from Charlotte. There was, simply, no more heinous of a crime to the wellness and sanctity of their order.

But there was no other choice; there never had been. She would never leave the safety of her sister to chance, even if that safety included the risk of necessary danger.

In truth, Charlotte was, for the present, perhaps more safe aboveground in New Corinth.

"What's done is done, Char. The responsibility is mine. If anyone has anything to say to me, they can say it."

Charlotte just shrugged. "I know. You're going to do what you want, anyway."

The comment struck Elara as a compliment. "Kali shows Herself in ways we don't necessarily want. Uncomfortable ways." Her eyes flit to the location under her cot where the spinebacks from the Codex laid. The assassin was dead now, because of them. Because she went to the Codex. Because of the failed Coven of Ascendants. Because of... Kali's Eyes – the extremist leader was tearing them apart without even being there.

"El...." Charlotte exhaled a light sigh. "You know how I feel about all that. When you talk about ... Kali." The name of the Goddess sounded odd on her lips. "I hear the words. I understand the concepts. But, I don't even really know what any of it means. I think things are simpler, or can be. You know that."

"Simple isn't real. It's ignorant."

"Come on! Let's just forget about all that stuff, for now."

"It's what I *am*, Charlotte! I can't leave it out of *anything*. Should I be a breeder squeezing out babies that grow up to contribute to Logical coffers? Is that a simple enough life?"

"Forget it, forget it. Alright?" Charlotte crossed her arms and stared at the floor "I should know better than to say anything."

Elara knew she should just drop it. It was absurd, the amount of times they'd traversed this same topic. The treads of this argument had been worn deep enough to skim bedrock. Their mother was present in every indirect accusation. Their father was present in every passive, silent nod.

Lucrece, the eldest sister of Aeve, was present in every snide insinuation. Elara killed that line of thought before it went any further.

"Char, Logic exists to rob you of your greatest gift. Mom and dad are going to start pressuring you soon – hard. Fourteen years old is *scandalously late*, after all." Elara injected as much resentment and sarcasm as she could.

"They already do." Charlotte was wearing her pouty face.

"What have they said?"

"I think most of their energy was used up on you, El. They've already convinced themselves that they have a second screw-up daughter. They provide excuses for me at galas, Levidens, private mistings."

She flipped a hand and started swinging her legs. "Just like they did for you. Their lies about you have grown to include an elaborate narrative, a background story and everything. Something about the Esdrin Regime."

"The nation in the Enclave?"

"Yeah. I keep dodging them, though, don't worry. Lucrece, too. She's easier to avoid, actually. She stops by now and then, but just to complain about how her husband doesn't pour the Spirit of Logos into her enough. And of course, mom and dad still tout her as their perfect daughter. Logos' own Bride."

Elara stared at the wall, blinking through the light of flames that spat and died around her room, from candles that burned at different, haphazard angles.

"I don't care about her, Char. She made her choice. They all did. Is there any particular reason Lucrece would give a shit about anything but her make-believe life with that trophy asshole and her showpiece daughter?"

"I ... wouldn't call her 'showpiece'. She's – well, I feel bad for her."

"Lucrece treats Sophia like a piece of jewelry. She always has."

"All parents do. In New Corinth, at least."

"That's the problem, Charlotte! Is there any reason why our parents should take an interest in their children except for when it makes them look good? Except for when it gets them another invitation to some highbrow Leviden?"

"El ... relax. If I cared what they thought, I would've never come here."

Elara exhaled deeply, feeling her bitterness eek away.

She sat down on her cot next to Charlotte. "I know. Me too. They didn't see you leave, right?"

"Of course not! Mom and dad weren't even back home yet from

whatever they were doing. It was about 5:30, I think. In the morning, of course. They're getting ready for Advent. Trying to recapture their youth or something. I mean, mom never meant to have me, anyway. She was so old! And you were thirteen. They've already forgotten I'm there." An impish chuckle rose from her throat. "Youngest daughter, after all. But honestly, I'm glad, because I can come and go as I please. The other day, they left to go to…"

Elara sat transfixed by her sister's agile features and animated gestures, half-hearing Charlotte's small voice fade to a mute murmur. Elara was snared in a time-locked frame that could have easily been ten years prior. Her the watcher, the keeper, the protector. Charlotte, the sister, the daughter, the beloved.

Elara saw Charlotte squirming on the floor as a toddler, squealing in delight at floating holo-com cubes that shifted from blue to green to yellow in a Logic-recommended, cognitive-pacification color pattern.

She saw Charlotte as a child, doodling on their loft's lawn with shimmer-pens whose markings popped up from the grass and play-fought with each other in the glowing light of the Eternal Day.

She saw Charlotte in their shared room, pleading with her not to leave, and instead bequeathing her cherished instrument as a tangible reminder of her presence.

She saw that same instrument propped up against the cold, dark stone of her chambers. Hidden and protected. Safe from harm, just like Charlotte should be. To have Charlotte nearby was too normal. Too real, and therefore unreal.

Elara could have lost her life in the Codex. If she'd died, her entire room would have remained nearly exactly as it now was. The only difference would have been that Charlotte would've been greeted by her sister's corpse.

"Char. You … deserve better, little one."

Charlotte abruptly stop talking and blinked in surprise. Her emerald eyes peered outward at Elara, shimmering with intelligence, crackling with vibrancy, glowing with an inner incandescence like glassy marbles. In darkness they grew brightest, occluding and drinking light in shifting effusion.

She's just like me, Elara thought. We are the same.

No, she retorted to herself. Not "just like". She doesn't have the hate. She hasn't been pressed, yet. She doesn't know Kali. Charlotte was at peace without pain, somehow, bafflingly.

Elara couldn't remember if she'd ever been that way. If so, never again. That epoch was gone. The era of feigned civility was lost. Now, strife was all. Duress was her chief lover. Conflict was her essence.

At that line of thinking, she felt her heart unbuckle and drop into a chasm that swept in from some deep, remote place. She fell into a long-forgotten abyss, vigilantly banned and blocked by the rote of conscious suppression.

Elara was forced to cast her inner eye upon a memory that shook her with its consuming vision.

...The small shadowed room. Stuffy with a wood-deep stench. Hands bracing on something encrusted. The scion. That man. His teeth invaded his speech. The ritual words. His loud voice was muffled by fat ringing his throat. His hair was matted with sweat against his brow. He was too fat everywhere. In and out, heaving obtrusively, at uncomfortable angles. Sloppy. His purple cloak brushed against her hips on either side. He never lowered his pants past his thighs...

It had been quick, her Breaching, unlike most girls. The Brief Version. Her parents couldn't afford to elate more in those days. He'd had a time-table, the scion. It had hurt and left her bloody. He had a towel. It was white. Parents had celebrated. Relatives had attended. She had spoken the lines, acted her role. But now, the merest image of the scion's face, the memory of his stench, made her retch and clutch her belly. She felt her legs unconsciously draw together. She wished she could tear her brain from its bony vault if only to rid herself of the memory.

I must have been mad.

Some women considered themselves lucky to chance across an attractive scion, or to be gregarious enough to garner the attention of a full-fledged rubrician. They spoke of it while doing chores. They spoke of it while buying things at Market Canal or the Path of Gold. They spoke of it while eating dinner. They spoke of it while tending children. They spoke and spoke and spoke, but did nothing. They were content to be mere icons. Insensate objects utilized and discarded just like bloody towels handed to little girls after their Breachings.

And why? What could be done when an entire race was bent like iron around remaining insane and consuming the lies of Logic?

Each person could only take care of herself, that's what could be done. Each left to her own end, though it bring them suffering and damnation. Each woman and man, harnessing the full hemisphere of hurtful, painful truths to shatter self-fashioned illusion.

So Elara had lived, and come to the same conclusion as others of the same mind, all congregated under the banner of the Great Mistress. The Kali'ka were *needed*, in the world of Logic, underneath the streets of New Corinth.

As the vision of her Breaching passed, the relative softness of Elara's cot pressed upwards into her legs, like her bed in her family's loft when she'd cried. They pressed in like the light of the cloisters, like the solitude of her chambers. They veiled her like the little white dress she'd worn at her Breaching. All pressing, surrounding, enclosing.

Elara numbly observed her little sister, intimately following the lines of her gangly, thin limbs. They seemed more sculpted. Harder. Even in the short time since they'd seen each other last, she'd gotten tougher, more sophisticated. Older. Her baby fat was shrinking.

Charlotte was trading the old path for the new. She was transfiguring into a woman of bursting angel, a creation of mist and light, a powerful being that seethed compassion and dignity. One who was capable of choosing her own partner and her own path.

Yet, she was still only fourteen.

Hardship and trials, and the right to experience them, could activate Charlotte's potential. So much potential, so much. But what of the right to live without loss?

"Char, you can't let them have you. You can't."

"I won't, El. I never have. I never will. Because of you."

Because of you. Charlotte's words, rather than comforting Elara, fazed nothing and changed nothing. And nothing – *only* nothing – was guaranteed in the world of Creation.

Elara felt an inner chain tug at her, reminding her of recent days, resurrecting the memory of her visions and the terrible sense of power lurking inside. That chain hardened and cooled. Its length tightened and bundled.

"Char – there are … listen, there's another group of Kali'ka out there. They're dangerous. Violent. You have to be careful."

"I know," Charlotte whispered, eyes fearful. "I heard about him. About *them*. The man in Advent Square. All of us have. Everyone's afraid. The whole city. They don't even know what they're feeling, though." She hesitated. "El, I don't know if… Do you…?"

"No, Charlotte. No. Is that why you came here?"

Charlotte nodded her head silently.

"No, little one. No." Elara leaned in and kissed her sister on the head. "We have nothing to do with them, believe me. I don't know anything about them. None of us do – not here in Sangra. They're holed up somewhere, they have to be. Cloister Mors, maybe. Cloister Ignis. I just know…" Elara felt her words come to a halt as the realization of what she was about to say struck her. "…I just know they have to be stopped. Somehow."

Charlotte repositioned herself. She could feel Elara leading her somewhere.

Elara didn't want her involved, but necessity brooked no compromises. "Char. if you know anything… If you've heard anything…"

Charlotte retreated into a quiet shell. "He… His face. People say it's terribly scarred. He only has one eye."

Elara licked her lips and probed for the right way to continue. "Ok. And… a name? Have you heard a name?"

After a second, Charlotte softly piped, "Fallow."

Fallow.

Charlotte laid a delicate hand on Elara's arm. "Please, El, tell me you aren't going to do anything reckless! I knew I shouldn't have told you. What are you planning? What's going on? Tell me!"

Fallow. Elara hammered it onto the anvil of her smoking intent, and vowed death to the man-daemon it echoed. Him, his extremists, his schism, his assassin: all of them.

Elara placed a hand on Charlotte's head, feeling her sister's softness. "You have to leave, Char. I've put you in danger. Don't go back to mother and father's. Don't go anywhere someone would recognize you. Don't even go anywhere you think someone would be able to predict you'd go. And take your shinsen." Elara pointed to it, leaning against the wall. "I don't need it anymore. You should have it. It's yours. The cloister isn't the place for beautiful things."

"El, why are you talking like … like…" Charlotte's face scrunched as tears welled in the cracks of her eyes. "You can come, too, you know. Why not? Please. Just leave. Get out of here. Come with me. Please?"

Full-throated weeps seized Elara's chest, but she mercilessly hacked down. The sight of Charlotte crying threatened to punch through years' worth of precisely laid defenses. She was shocked at how steady her voice sounded. "I can't leave, Char. I have to do my part. Down here. For now."

"Can't I do something to help?"

"It's not fair of you to be further endangered because of me."

"It's *you* I'm worried about! It's not safe here in the cloister, I can tell. Aren't you afraid for yourself?" Charlotte's cheeks were growing puffy and her eyes were growing red.

The question clamped Elara's mind in stocks. She felt a lock of her hair shift. Her palms felt clammy and tickled. When put to the question, she was unable to not examine the fringe perceptions, suppressed impulses, and layered phantasms of motivations that defined her inner state.

Sitting there next to Charlotte, something twisted into shape inside Elara. Being there in her chambers, so near to someone so often far away, Elara suddenly felt as though her body was a fabrication; her form was an untruth told to her since birth. Her muscles, the strength of her conditioning, the physical prowess she so greatly prized – all of it felt no more substantial than a wink of light or a flash of heat.

In that moment, her body became discardable. A husk. It became something other than *her*. It became a shell to be shed, a vacant hull. Something of null value. A thing of emptiness.

She felt no more fear for her life. She felt no more fear of physical harm. Thoughts of the assassin, his swiping dagger and his snarling threats, thoughts of a cadre of crazed, violent Kali'ka – none of it carried any threat.

Charlotte and those like her – if there *were* any more like her –were the ones who deserved to live. They were the ones who would carry the future forward, regardless of the nightmares of the present. So long as they lived, Elara could safely die.

"No … No, little one. I'm not afraid for myself. Not now. Not anymore."

Elara locked eyes with her sister, the only real thing in her life – sister in arms, sister in intention – as she stuffed down tears that would've weakened her, would've softened her, would've … *distracted* her.

Charlotte just sat there, shaking her head and crying, her hands clutched to her chest, staring at Elara's cot through the widest gap that had ever divided them.

To their side, the fire from the overturned firepot had dwindled to nearly nothing. The candles along the wall would soon follow.

Elara wanted to say more. She knew there *was* more to say, locked inside, but she kept abandoning sentence after sentence. No words could suffice. Nothing suited the moment.

You're better off far, far away from me, little one. She won't let me die yet. How can I explain? You don't belong to Her. Me, though… The Great Mistress won't let me go. Not yet… Not yet.

CHAPTER 10
THE BETRAYER

Fallow opened his one eye to absolute darkness in his chambers in Cloister Mors and immediately hissed in frustration. He knelt on the floor, his eye flicking back and forth, searching, grasping for the already-fading sputter of strange colors and odd-shaped objects swirling in his mind's eye. He could still feel the remnant of his scarred, dead eyelid attempt to twitch.

It was right there, the otherworld. He was getting closer, yes, to Illusion. So close! Why couldn't he see it?! It intermingled with the realm of the living, superimposed, co-existing but out of reach.

Fire... so much fire. Streaming across the sky and exploding from volcanic rifts in the earth. Red earth, red sky, and the titans of old waging eternal war. A primal time captured in the untapped memory of living men and women, persistent in the present, couched in the sediment of the unconscious, when the Goddess Herself lived and walked and talked on Earth....

He pointed directly towards where his prized possession, as silent as a gravestone, stood in the corner, trapped by a few etchings in the dirt and a few syllables muttered in the ancient Kali'ka tongue.

"You think you can remain without sides, do you? An uninvolved participant?! You're responsible for *all* of this! Your meddling. Your lies. And for how long? How long?! You have no power over us, old one!"

Pathetic. It had been so easy. So ridiculous. Its eye, he was sure, flitted around like a paranoid insect trying to escape the simplest of prisons – a body.

A shift in shadows brought Fallow's attention to the bar of light under his door. The torchlight in the hall had flickered. Someone was approaching. An intruder. An unscheduled visit by anyone made them just that – an intruder.

Fallow heard his door creak open. Light spilled in through the doorway, and the shadow of a man fell into Fallow's room.

"Transcen –"

Before the word was finished, Fallow's dagger was out and at the throat of the intruder. A moment later, the man jumped and become rigidly still, mouth caught in mid-word. Crouched low like an unsprung serpent, Fallow could see his dagger's edge prying up the two-day stubble around the man's Adam's apple.

"Do you know, *Ascendant* Oren." Fallow whispered slow and languid, letting the moment prolong itself, sliding syllables off his tongue-heavy lips. "About the first man? The one before Kirsh, Iesu, long before Logos? The one made of dust and breath. You hum his eulogy every time you speak. This little ball in your throat vibrates, and from it you sculpt words. Like the *Aum*, casting itself outwards into the blind void. Words really do create reality, just like the Epicurial Apologia tells all those fatuous, hateful skinbags breathing, walking, purchasing, smiling, fucking overhead in a Logical stupor."

He grit his teeth and hissed. "Of course you don't know! Because you're just as stupid as all of them. Only *I* perceive the full stretch of time! Only *I* adopt the principles of the past and learn from the blights of dead empires! And that preparedness tells me that you – have – *failed!*"

"No, Transcendent! No! Not me! I haven't! I won't!" Little sweat beads dotted Oren's panic-stretched features. His eyes were looking away and not at Fallow's face. Good. At least he was behaving like he'd been taught. "I had to come. Something has happened. There's –"

"I told you that personal messages are no longer necessary. The journey is too risky for you." Fallow whispered breathily, distracted by how tensile Oren's throat skin was. When pressed with the flat of a dagger, it bounced back every time.

"Our footholds are in place, Oren. The Veneer can do nothing to contain us; our bastion there is being built. I have hand-crafted the weapons that our enemies lack. Mors is all but ours, except for that wretch Cyrus and his holdout loyalists. Advent approaches. You should be focused on the forthcoming era, conducting your business in Sangra, not frittering around – frilly, tongue-flapping, defective in reason.

"Our cohorts are out right now, taking care of their part, while you waste time prancing your way down here. It leaves you unfocused. You become a burr in the clothes of our labor, rather than a thorn in the side of our enemy. And, more importantly ..." he growled in rage, "you disrupt my solitude!" A line of red grew from Oren's throat as Fallow twisted his blade. "I require time alone with our would-be overseer in the corner over there."

"T-T-Transcendent ..." Oren glanced around, licking his lips. "He's failed. The one so trained has failed. He's been captured. They've interrogated him. There's no telling how much he told them. I only got there at the end, when it was too late. She killed him. There ... There was nothing I could do to help, not without revealing myself. And ... she's completely unharmed."

Fallow crouched unmoved, blinking. A moment later, he laughed in throaty bursts. Spittle flew onto Oren's terrified face.

"You think because she has no bruises or cuts that she's 'unharmed'? You think this won't galvanize your efforts over there? You think the weak-willed Kali'ka in that cloister will remain unaffected? Your lack of insight remains just as amusingly pervasive as it was when we first met at Selenist, those four short years ago. The Unchanged are as pathetic as you."

"But, Transcendent, the assassin ..."

"His failure was his fault, my little broodling," Fallow cut him short. "She survived the attack, and so she is worthy of acclaim. A god can be martyred, true. A god martyred is a god worth emulating, but moreso is the killer. A killer is only a killer, but a god-killer is a god."

Fallow ran his tongue across his teeth and grinned. The raw gristle of his scarred face squeaked. "So why not wait?" He released the blade's pressure on Oren's throat and stepped back, sliding into shadow and out of sight.

The most trusted of Fallow's brood glanced around in maddened confusion, trying to locate his master in the darkness, "Is that the goal, now, Transcendent? To let her live?"

"If necessity dictates it. We have precautions in place." Fallow slipped around, spinning his dagger in the fingers of his right hand, lacing it between, around and through. It flowed like liquid glass molding to his skin's surface. He sensed an odd imbalance. The coordination of his left side had always been a tad more adept than his right. Irksome, that.

"Why train him for months, then, Transcendent? He died, serving no purpose."

"It was not without purpose, Oren. He isn't the only one who's been brought to the true path. You've seen them. In rows and columns, grunting and slicing their blades in the echoes of our shared underground. The entirety of our brood is one harmonious, synchronous. It's my system, don't forget. I drew if from the recesses of my mind and snapped it into place like a whole picture drawn at once."

"So ... we seek her awareness," Oren ventured.

"We seek her *crisis*. Pain is the most apt facilitator by which life validates life. Or simply, *life to death*. The statements have never been untrue, but the *method* has been. Like a bloated, red giant star, our order wobbles purposelessly in a vacuum! It feebly declares its once-radiant power through puffy-throated maxims, unwilling to admit its impending death, and unable to compensate for its former glory!

"But Oren, even the most heatless stars collapse into a cosmic inferno of lucent brilliance. The ideology of the Unchanged – our misguided kin – has never actually been embraced except in word. And what is word next to action? Who else better to test ourselves against besides those of our own lineage?"

"Isn't there danger, though, in letting her remain free? She is a rallying point for the Unchanged. A spark of inspiration. I see it every day. They fear her, yes, but she is the parapet behind which they huddle. She is... exceptional. You've said so yourself."

Fallow snickered at the man's obtuseness. "That's exactly the point, Oren! Can you not even grasp this simple idea? Direct the head, and the body follows. Direct the eyes and you control the head. So *we* – we control the eyes! You've learned this in your time as Kali'ka. Acknowledgment makes a thought real, like a fetus in-womb. And birth, my broodling, is the greatest distress of life."

Along a perfect, mid-brain tickling pitch, Fallow modulated his voice. "Clinging to rhetoric, finding sanctuary in camaraderie, suckling on rituals, worshipping ego and personality... All surrogate actions for the bawling wail of a helpless infant still cringing in fear at a loud, bright, cold world.

"She is the ultimate idol, our auteur in Cloister Sangra, who by her own nature unintentionally encourages frailty. This is what it means to inspire worship, Oren. Gods are built martyrs, reliant on their creations, and creations always mirror their gods. She will lead them, and we must let her. Remember – the sound of screams echo on the wind."

Oren perked up at the key words to their recitation. "And lodge in the mind."

"Restlessness reveals fear."

"Fear reveals weakness."

"And there is the point to strike. Exactly! The greatest of our enemies will make herself our ally, and she won't even realize it. And as for the assassin, well ... I doubt he told them anything they'd understand. Trust me."

There was no way he would've succeeded, no matter how quickly he'd grown adept at Fallow's new method of armed combat. Fallow trusted in the skill of his chief enemy more than anything else, because her skill was how she became predictable. She would always follow who she was, like a self-guided pawn. Her, the one so trained, Oren and all the rest: all pawns with value derived solely from an inability to be unboxed.

"Fear is a lie of false expectations." Fallow brandished his dagger like a scepter. "You're apprehension, Oren, reveals your belief in *her*. But once you accept the reality of what you expect, beyond your own delusions, fear vanishes. We will succeed. Our demonstration in Advent Square has already had in irrevocable effect on the psyche of New Corinth. So you see, this doubt you have... There's no place for it here."

"Of course, Transcendent." Oren drew himself up as much as possible in an obvious attempt at recouping composure and pride. An absent glaze filmed his face like a lackluster finish.

Fallow snickered at him. Oren. The perfect crony. No true comprehension. No imagination, no sense of humor. Absolutely unengaging in every respect. Able to be ignored in a crowd of two. Mid-height, mid-weight, generic nose, roundish jaw, brown eyes, brown hair. Without comparatives, it was impossible to place any precise definitions on the features. The perfect diecast figurine for his throwaway role in their Kali'ka drama. The perfect infiltrator, a man no one paid attention to. The perfect provocateur: the average man.

What was an average, though, but the net result formed by extremes? What was variety but the conflux of averages? He himself – Fallow – was the outlier. It was his talent that gave meaning to his horde.

"Transcendent, there's something else." Oren's mouth worked for several seconds before he managed to speak. "Her – her sister was there."

"That blight-brained bitch living in oblivion, lapping up Levitant in that luxurious loft of hers?" Fallow snorted. "Unlikely."

"No, Transcendent. Another one. A child."

Fallow stopped meandering around the room. A child. The possibilities poured from his mind in torrents, rushing to tumble over each other, crossing flows, crashing in crests and troughs. As images unfolded in his mind's eye, he felt an animal heat stir below the waist. It reminded him of times now past, in these tiny, cramped quarters in Mors, when he indulged in secret, small pleasures. It also reminded him of the foundation of their dominion being built in the Veneer.

Time to visit soon. He required the … *diversion.*

"Are you sure? How old?"

Oren fumbled over his words, "Um – uh, I don't – maybe twelve, thirteen …"

"Never mind! How well-composed was she?"

"Fairly well-composed, Transcendent. Not what you'd care for."

He hissed. "Fine. Now tell me. Did you watch them interact?"

"No, Transcendent. But when she was told about her sister, she was consumed with fear. She… That was when she killed the assassin."

Fallow tapped his fingers on his lips and started peeling strips of skin off them. "Remarkable, that she kept her younger sister secret this entire time. It tells us all we need to know about the child's importance. Track her, but don't intervene unless she becomes a nuisance. Be ready to strike in an instant. Even then, only capture her. Do *not* harm her." He spit little flecks of skin from his mouth. "I estimate it's past the point where we could leverage her for usefulness, but we can never be sure."

"Yes, Transcendent. As you say."

"Did you think of the child?" Nearly giddy with glee, Fallow inched his way closer, biting his lips till blood oozed from them. He found his hands compulsively gripping and releasing the hilt of his dagger in tight pumps. "Imagine what it would be like?"

"No, Transcendent. I thought only of how she might be useful to us, and how she might compromise our plans. She –"

Fallow lunged at him and viciously reamed the back of his hand across the man's cheekbone, dropping him to the floor. Fallow felt no anger or irritation. He felt, in fact, absolutely nothing.

"Of course you imagined it! All action is to seek or avoid pleasure or pain. You were thinking of it now, even. Don't lie to me. I can tell."

Oren pushed himself up from the floor, one hand cupping his cheekbone, eyes dazed. His skin appeared to have been spread wide, the little epidermis pushed back like kneaded dough.

The analogy made Fallow laugh.

"Oren, this is the path of Transcendence! Remember how you feel now, and clutch it firm. Use it to invigorate your languid bones at the lowest of hours. The mountain pass to the gods' summit requires hands torn on thorn and rock. But there we will take our due seats with Kali Herself, when we finish constructing our aboveground-Babel.

"All will become darkness, and people will yearn for it because they will no longer be burdened by the expectations of light. And in that afflicted, mortified state, they will bear witness to their own true nature, denied for centuries by a tiny enclave of privileged, hateful, stupid beasts!"

"Of course, Transcendent. I am yours. No horror left untouched." Fallow's protégé stared at him, hinged along rapture and terror. Blood was starting to leak through the cracks between the fingers cradling his ruined cheek. There was too much blood in any one body, to be sure. So much better uses for it.

Fallow grinned and gripped the back of Oren's neck with nimbly placed fingertips. Leaning in towards his ear, the most delicate puffs of breath hissed from his tattered lips, as his hand slid up Oren's neck like the slow creep of an adder poised to strike.

"Precisely…."

ACT II

CONFLAGRATION

CHAPTER 11
HOUSE OF DAGON

L ounging on a divan in the Dagon family loft, Lucrece swayed in light-headed pleasure while cradling a goblet of robust, spicy wine, watching the family viewscreen amidst a lush sitting room of marble busts on pedestals, purple tapestries and abstract-patterned paintings.

She stretched and let out a long, squealing exhalation as her entire body shuddering. "The Pageant of Miracles is going to be absolutely amazing this year! I knew it was the right decision to indulge on reservations to go there in-person. We might even see His Holiness! Playing the role of Lord Logos, that is."

On the viewscreen in front of her, vocoder footage flickered and glowed from the week prior at Advent Sermon. Lucrece watched His Holiness dissipate into a filmy vapor, vanishing from the pulpit of the Basilica like feathers of clouds swept away in a final blink of streaking light droplets. Trumpeting music rose in the air, and scions began their post-Sermon ceremony and exeunt.

Lucrece's full, moist lips – painted blood-red – curved around the rim of her goblet as she grinned at the silver-framed, black and white lithograph of the High Devotee on the mantle of her fireplace. Signed, of course. A personal gift, before they started going on sale in Market Canal a couple days ago.

At the sight of the High Devotee, she drew a long, deep mouthful of wine and lapped its heavy richness before swallowing. It tasted delightful.

And what felt good *was* good, and right and true. The High Devotee himself would have said as much.

Along the upper edges of the walls, evercracks emitted light from the Eternal Day, bathing the sumptuous, modern residence in a bright, effusive white that never altered, never diminished. Datapanels, holo-projectors, doctrinators, and translucent furniture around the loft reflected a unified, mutual glare. From their elevated height, the Dagon loft's plateglassed view in the parlor spanned across the entirety of the Superluminary District. Outside the window, the spires of the Uppers, from high to low districts, pierced the sky like golden grass across a hilly field.

Lucrece reached to a nearby datapanel to set the Sermon on continuous playback. Glo-globes flocked above her head, to hover and dance, filling an imperceptible dip in the local light level. She barely noticed them. As soon as she leaned back, they flit away.

"Adam, our copy of the revised Epicurial Apologia should be coming soon! We can recite some of our favorite quotes, right along with His Holiness. Oh, and the High Devotee, of course." She drew a deep breath, attempting to control her dizziness, and took another long drink from her goblet.

She heard some general sound of agreement from the direction of the kitchenette. It was halfhearted enough to make her giggle. The expression on Adam's face when she'd snatched his hand and dragged him off to her Penance with the High Devotee had been absolutely, wonderfully, worth the entire trip to Advent Sermon.

"Mommy, the scions were saying the same as last year. Did you hear it? Do you remember?"

The tiny voice came from the corner, where Lucrece's daughter Sophia sat playing with toys – little synthetic things that lit and whirled and made foolish sounds. Sophia sat among them with a dull, morose expression.

"What does it matter, Sophia? Does that take away from its truth? Its beauty? Why can't you just accept it?! Logos *moves* through his scions. Imagine receiving Penance from the High Devotee, like I did. Mmm... You're quite the lucky girl, you know. Soon, you'll be bonded to Logic for all eternity. You're even going to be Breached before your auntie Charlotte. Imagine that!" A shrill giggle slipped from her smiling lips.

Sophia said nothing. In the viewscreen, scions draped in full liturgical ensemble commented on Advent Sermon. The square-jawed, powerfully built men laughed in deep baritones as they gestured powerfully around a roundish table.

Lucrece felt an acidic, derisive burn in her heart as she observed her daughter. "Why can't you just accept your own joy, Sophia? Bliss is the natural state we all aspire towards. This is why Logos bequeathed us His holy words through the Epicurial Apologia, and bestowed on us His holy draught, Levitant. This is why we celebrate during this time of year, child. Logos' ascendance on Advent is the pinnacle of rejoicing. The Pageant of Miracles is when we can behold the ascendance with our own eyes! At least, the reenactment in Advent Square."

Again, nothing. Sophia just stared at the floor and clacked some toys together.

Damn you, child... You're not going to take my life away from me! Lucrece resettled on the divan and placed her attention back on wonderful, lovely, bright things.

Advent Sermon – yes, now *that* was astonishing! Even as she watched the vocoder footage again and again, she knew that nothing could possibly replace the memory of being there a week prior, within the in-person glory of the Basilica, one with the elation of thousands of bodies wrapped in the same light, who thought, breathed, laughed, and cried in ecstasy as one.

In her mind's eye, she saw it all play out in a single memory.

...In the pulpit of the Mausoleum, vaporous beings of mist solidified into naked couples in sexual throes, their Levitant-flushed bodies gripping, thrusting, squirming in spasms of body and voice that sent undulating cries of orgasmic bliss throughout the Mausoleum. Comets zipped around, facing attached to their fronts, laughing, sprinkling the air with slowly descending confetti sparkles like the pinpricked outpourings of pastel stars. Scions leapt from rafters, striking mid-air poses, hovering weightlessly before landing gently with a flourish in row upon symmetric row.

At the core of it: the being of vibrant light, floating on an unfelt breeze, flowing down to the podium, morphing, shifting like clouds. Arms outstretched, soaked in white, so much white, suffocating, thick enough to inhale and swallow in the gasping throats of all. A scene from dreams, of milky blocks of shadowless cells. Breath given the form of flesh by a fathomless miracle, blown from dust to walk and reason and communicate through properties of a conscious mind.

From it, the apex of man sprang and deigned to elucidate the holy truth of Logos, made incarnate in His Hand and Will, the Miracle of Ages, the Bosom and Beloved of Light, the Son of the Father, Husband to the Widow, Father to the Orphan, Majesty in Us, the High Pontiff, the Lion of Logos, His Holiness Johann Ambrose Descartes IX...

It was glory overflowing! Palpable rapture, spilling out of Logos' own brimming body, to engorge the faithful in gushing, white-hot waves. The magnificence of boundless pleasure and the magnanimousness of uncorrupted, pure feelings. To receive, receive, and have everything always so perfectly right.

So vivid, even a week later. So well-defined. The sharp lines and effusive colors and tones dwelled in Lucrece's mind like an everlasting commandment. She never wanted to lose that saliency – the reality she felt during Advent Sermon.

There was one way. One way only for those in the realm of carnality to recapture the epiphany of the spouting Godhead.

She felt her hands drift around the front of her loose blouse, across her stomach and abdomen, sliding further down.

She swung her head left, right. "Adam! Where's my mister?"

"I think I saw it in the bedroom," Sophia piped.

"I wasn't asking you. Get out of here!" Lucrece gulped the last of her wine and tossed her goblet on the carpet.

"But my holos are all set up here, mommy, and I think –"

"Fine, then – stay!" Lucrece hoisted herself up and shuffled through scattered jewelry on a nearby end table, while one of her hands probed her crotch. She could feel the heat below. Her fingers glided over her sheer undergarment, uneven from ruffled pubic hair.

"I think it's in the bedroom. I'll get it, Lucrece," Adam muttered, shoulders slouched, head tilted, stepping in from the kitchenette and out through another doorway. Munching on those damned dehydrated fruits again.

Ready for his forthcoming duty, though, Lucrece noted. He knew her habits. He was useful in at least *one* way.

She continued to rifle through clothes tossed over armchairs and footrests. "Hurry, I can't wait! You heard what His Holiness said! Now is the time to cleanse ourselves and our household. We must allow the Holy White of Logos to flow!"

Adam's muffled yell echoed from the other room. "I'm looking! Where did you put it?"

"I don't know!"

"Got it!"

"Then bring it here!"

His feet came thumping down the hallway. Lucrece sneered in his direction. "You *did* remember to grab your dose, too, did you not?"

"Yes, Lucrece. It's right here."

Before he could fully extend his arm to her, she rushed him and snatched her mister from his hands.

Lucrece flipped the device over, scrutinizing its aesthetics as her manic fingers fumbled with its clasps and clamps. It was so glossy and plastic-seeming. It looked like nothing more than one of her daughter's fake playthings. An imitation of an actual something.

She tsked to herself for not having purchased this month's design. Some of the newer models promised enhanced aeration, she'd heard.

"Soon, little one, soon, you'll be ready for Penance!" She beamed at her daughter, who stared back through hollow eyes. "Once you've been Breached, you can receive the Spirit whenever you want! That's our role as claimants. From Logos to His Holiness, to our husbands, to us! That's the natural order. Oh! And the High Devotee! Mmm!" Memories of their rabid, frantic Penance pranced inside. Just in conversation alone, at Levidens or balls, Jacobs Osgood had elevated her high enough that no one would forget.

"Mommy, is it alright if I go –"

"Shut up! I'm busy." It was important not to lose focus on details while securing her mister. Every infinitesimal particle must be absorbed.

No slack, nothing too loose. Her head was growing lightweight from excitement. Adam was off to the side prepping his.

There, done! Placing the actuator over her face, she depressed the pump on its side, inhaling and keeping her eyes wide open. She felt a fine spray moisten the soft tissue of her lips and nose. Its telltale decompression was like the prolonged pant of claimants in the throes of Penance. On the viewscreen, she vaguely saw scions conducting interviews with enraptured attendees of Advent Sermon via mobile vocoders.

"Mommy, I have a question for you, if it's …"

Everything started to look blurry, and the mister fell from Lucrece's hands as a biochemical firestorm devoured her.

Yes, Spirit, come to me!

She felt her interior walls thicken with the rush of blood. Sensory acuity surged upward like a waterfall erupting towards the sky. Bright became hyper-bright, loud became hyper-loud, hot became hyper-hot. Touch ascended cognition or comprehension. Vaginal fluid seeped through her undergarments and ran onto her inner thighs. The merest pleasure was nearly painful. All it would take was one touch to her labia to send her into a frenzied orgasm.

She squealed and began sucking on her own fingers simply for the sensation.

A quick glance at Adam showed him swooning on his feet, eyes wide and glassy, pupils distended, laughing hysterically while an animal bulge grew in his pants. His mister was on the floor at his feet.

The lights in the room grew to white incandescence. Logos! He was here! She couldn't see it before! He bathed them in His haloed glory!

"Adam, now!" Her saliva-coated fingers glistened as they reached towards the light of the Eternal Day, penetrating through the evercracks along the ceiling. So bright, so bright!

Adam ripped his pants down to his knees. His colossal phallus reared like a papery-sheathed spike primed to burst from blood-bloat. Stone-hard erectile grafts – implanted in Corinthian boys as early as five years old – supported the unnatural weight with built-in spongiform elasticity.

"May the power compel you!" he roared.

"Compel me! Compel me!" she shrieked.

Only a few more ritual words escaped their mouths before sensation wrested all cogent language from them. Within minutes, they descended into distorted bursts of syllables. Seismic thuds shook the walls and ceiling as often as their muffled, blathering cries.

"Compel me! Compel me!"

Bestial, savage, Lucrece and her husband howled and screamed, submerged in a depthless ocean of chemicals. Their self-awareness slid towards oblivion, wherein resided the plateau of emptiness and oneness sought by the highest realms of Logical theosophy, the place reverent sages and saintly mediums had labored for centuries to find.

"Compel me! Compel me!"

Oneness was now discoverable through the beneficence of Logic and a stroll to the local parish. The one final resting place of non-change and penultimate joy: conveniently administered in one, two, or three-hour doses.

"Compel me! Compel me!"

Enlightenment was at hand, at any time of the day, thanks be to the grace of Logos, through His most holy scions. The Holy White would flow. His Spirit would spill over the brim.

Somewhere in a small, fortified location in Lucrece's mind, her thoughts resonated in complete clarity, as they often momentarily did during Penance. Among exquisite luxury, undeviating pleasure, and the promise of faultlessness, her thoughts strayed to the same person as always, the one whose familiar mane of auburn hair swayed like the free wind, whose untamed eyes pierced like lances of jade fire.

She was out there, oh yes! Out there, with *them*. She was with the man from Advent Square – their leader, it seemed. Who really knew what they were about, anyway? They were sick. Deviants. She was out there, yes, picking apart Logic's idyllic, golden-spun city one strand at a time.

Elara, the prodigal sister of the House of Aeve.

If you could see me now, young one. You have no idea the type of life you gave up! You thoughtless, selfish, depraved harlot! Making a mockery of our family. Leaving me – just me! – to carry the name of Aeve! Me, our disgraceful baby sister, and my embarrassment of a daughter!

The moment these thoughts coalesced, they were consumed like a whisper in the hurricane of Levitant. They vanished like the sweat evaporating from her creamy, bronze skin.

In the corner of the room on the floor, Sophia watched her mother and father. She frowned through a slightly creased scar that split her left eyebrow.

Beneath her frown, her round, sea green eyes betrayed no thoughts. Her posture revealed nothing. Her hands refused to move. Her tiny frame remained motionless. Little holo-cubes scattered on the floor flashed a dead, neon light across her face. The dim chatter of the viewscreen murmured in the background. In the recording, she could recognize the preening, nasal voice of the High Devotee.

Sophia watched as her mother's luxuriant, strawberry-honeyed hair was yanked by a man who bore the name of "father," a man who now barely resembled the hunched mute who shuffled around the house aimlessly at whenever his non-work hours were. She watched as her mother laughed at what obviously hurt, and ground herself into the thrusting meat shape slathering behind her.

Their snarling, twisted faces, the jumbled mess of puffy organs, the squishy sounds, the wetness and clawing – every tiny detail passed directly through Sophia's never-wavering gaze to imprint itself on the elastic gray matter of her mind, unforgotten and eternal.

As the effects of Levitant wore off over a matter of hours, and Sophia's parents roused themselves to a slow, gummy sentience, they uncoupled from each other. Their flat faces, reddened with Afterglow, stared vacant and unblinking.

Her mother lifted her hair from her neck, gathering sweaty strands and wandering wisps, waving herself cool in huge, voluminous sweeps while making loud "phew!" or "woo!" sounds. Her father mechanically set about wringing clothes, spraying antiseptics, scrubbing out semen and the occasional blood stain. Not once did they glance at each other.

"A-daaaaam," Lucrece crooned, examining her figure in a mirror, "Make sure the loft is ready for the Dresdons. They do enjoy prattling, so I expect we won't get out to the Catechist gala at Juniper Springs any earlier than compline, at the least. The wine we purchased from that

lovely rubrician along the Path of Gold last spring – what was his name…
Cecil? Yes, Rubrician Cecil – will suffice for the evening. Such a
handsome scion, that one."

Without waiting for an answer, Lucrece started walking towards the
bathroom. She glanced at Sophia, stopped and cocked her head, "tsked,"
rearranged several strands of Sophia's dirty blonde, ruby-tinged hair,
paused to assess, and rearranged one of the strands again.

Satisfied, she smiled proudly and resumed walking towards the
bathroom, working though her typical post-Penance muscle ache,
humming in a singsong lilt. Off to draw a bath, no doubt. Sophia watched
her naked form vanish around the corner.

"Sophia! Get ready, darling! The roadshine along the Path of Gold
should be particular lovely right about now. As soon as I'm cleaned up,
we're going to go shopping! You need to look your best for the High
Devotee!"

CHAPTER 12
THE GODHEAD

Elevated high above the Epistemic Wing of the Basilica Formata, accessible via a series of vine-wrapped, trellised ramps inlaid with ivory appliqués, the High Devotee of Logic, Jacobs Osgood, knelt in front of a wide, semicircular altar. Here in his personal chambers – his Laetus Domicilius – nucleus of everyday Logical operations, he communed with his god's surrogate.

He barely saw the opulence behind him, where alabaster statues of couples joined in union, decorative columns rose high, rare paintings hung on walls – reaching back to Salome's *Lily of Nine Thorns* – and milky, marble friezes spanned the spaces between.

Like so many countless times before, he could do nothing but kneel in a ball at his altar, compressed and crushed into subservience. Glo-globes flit above him as he gestured and spoke, racing in and out of pockets of too-dim light.

"Ah, yes, Holiness. The delegates from Amaranth and Ri Lank are scheduled to arrive Advent Eve. They've been designated quarters in the Epistemic Wing."

In front of him, on a throne composed of interlocking, pure crystal, sat a man projected via holos into the form of a being of pure, white light. The ethereal, luminescent entity thundered in the same forceful cadence as always – incisive, articulate, proud, dogmatic. Jacobs could unerringly anticipate each pause and pre-hear each inflection.

"Inform them that a visit to the Northern Outlook to view the bounty of the Tame River would be magnanimous. Ensure that the foliage visible from that vista does not obstruct the worthiness of Logos' holy city. Place Rubrician Seymour in charge. It's said that Princess Leandra has received Penance by him."

From an untouchable summit, His Holiness dominated the world, enshrined like a living icon in the Tabernacle on the other side of the Basilica, where he sat on the Crystal Throne, twin to the throne Jacobs knelt in front of. Sequestered for the entirety of his earthly life, attended to by a legion of seminarians, the Lion of Logos had no direct contact to anyone besides Jacobs, the High Devotee. Out of the entire world, no one else had access to the Crystal Throne. No one saw His Holiness, not ever.

Except for Advent, the one day each year when he emerged from the Tabernacle wrapped in holo-projected light. On the grandest of holy days, he donned the mantle of Logos in the reenactment of the Ascension, at the Pageant of Miracles in Advent Square.

Stolen glances at the throne – expertly practiced over years – showed shimmers of color shifting like stained-glass across the surface of His Holiness's projection. Jacobs swore that if he peered closely enough, he could pierce the veil of light and get a glimpse – just a glimpse – of the sumptuous, gorgeous chambers His Holiness occupied. To see with his own eyes the glorious, famed One-Hundred Diamond Lights of His Holiness' Keep, sparkling in a single oceanic gleam from chandeliers dangling at the ends of silver chains overhead ... magnificent!

"Of course, Holiness. And the edits to the official transcript from Advent Sermon?"

"By the Hand of Logos, He spoke much to me that day, and I remain humbled by all He continues to impart. All shall, in due time, be related to everyone in a comprehensible, beatific manner."

"We await patiently and ardently for anything Lord Logos has to say to us."

"Also, High Devotee, remember to send word to the scions in Melati that a translated copy of the revised Epicurial Apologia will be sent to them, once I declare the work recto-verso. I want a penitent-native ratio update every three months. Graph it along with a cost-revenue assessment of our resources there."

"As you speak, so it shall be done. I'm sure the natives will be quite pleased when their first shipment of Levitant arrives. And the wording for the Injunction for Freedom from Moral or Doctrinal Error?"

As His Holiness started to respond, Jacobs silently cursed the antiquated hiccups in law that necessitated assessments such as these. It was awe-inspiring to be in the presence of His Holiness, certainly, but in the present day, when all internal communiqués were catalogued moment to moment... Why the need for such tedious bookkeeping and wordplay? It was terribly annoying.

"...in granting the texts recto-verso, no implication is contained therein that these texts are not disallowed interpretive leeway, within theosophical guidelines pre-established by Logical treatises – strike that – Logical precedent. I agree with the content, and any extrapolations bear no resemblance to statements expressed by any scion or anyone else related to or in the direct service of Logic, nor do any such statements indicate any fault on the part of..."

Jacobs' mind drifted to the seminarians stationed next to the door, swinging their censers like the slow swoop of a ticking pendulum. Sinuous streamers rose from the censers in billowing plumes to gather near the dome overhead, painted in imitation of a clear sky-blue.

They ceaselessly chanted the Cardinal Premise – all day, every day, in shifts – lifting their voices in unison like an eternally rising blessing to the ever-rearing Godhead.

"*We submit to the Godhead. The Godhead will rise.*
The Godhead will open. From its tip He will flow.
We join with the Godhead. We join with each other.
Logos speaks through rivers of white."

"...pending my approval, you may begin the proper processing. Our work in this manner should already be complete, and speaks of our lack of diligence, rather than resistance on the behalf of those whom we are attempting to help. There can be no excuses. The Shriving must proceed undaunted. Our theocracy must substantiate its everlasting dominance, through..."

"We submit to the Godhead. The Godhead will rise.
The Godhead will open. From its tip He will flow.
We join with the Godhead. We join with each other.
Logos speaks through rivers of white."

"...find it quite difficult to believe, High Devotee, that there even remains such dark, untouched corners of the earth. Enclave nations are the last blight remaining on our unbesmirched world. This close to Advent, I'd rather our attention is turned on the Pageant of Miracles."

Jacobs' breath stopped. In auditory memory he heard the implication again and again. No, no. His Holiness couldn't see his preoccupations, couldn't peer past his clothes and his face to the core within. It wasn't possible.

"Uh…" Jacobs cleared his throat, gently. "Construction is underway, Holiness. Grand Magister Hammar himself is overseeing the site, as aided by Magister Julian and a newly raised Magister Philip. Nothing less than flawless execution, Holiness."

"As expected. I anticipate little interference on the part of circumstances, let alone direct hindrances, for that matter."

Jacobs stared at the floor, his eyes skittering around as he tried to wrangle his thoughts. Another implication? Two times in a row. His Holiness would never insinuate except to address a potential problem directly. Was he trying to bait him? There was no choice but to follow suit.

"I … would imagine, Holiness, for Advent we would require an expansion of the Magistrate's presence. Especially as we cycle through the rest of the week. There's still Catechist, tonight, then Flint Crowning, and then Vigil for three days prior to the Pageant."

"Has Grand Magister Hammar mapped out the Magistrate's disposition for Advent Sermon?"

The tangential question threw Jacobs off-balance. It came off pre-planned. "Well, uh … of course, Your Grace. Grand Magister Hammar continues to serve with admirable diligence."

"And, have the magisters' patrol routes been designated throughout

New Corinth? 1.3 times density along major commercial thoroughfares? Not a single magister more, in keeping with custom?"

"Well, yes, Your Grace. That's always the case. Comeyes comb the remainder, and transmit all data to the Oculus. Nothing has changed in that regard."

"So it seems that the Grand Magister has determined a proper course of action. Did he, who is an expert at what he does, suggest increasing the disposition of the Magistrate at any point?"

Jacobs dabbed at his forehead with his wrist. He'd have to tune the environmental controls. A slick forehead was so unseemly! By Logos, what was His Holiness getting at?!

"No, Holiness. Grand Magister Hammar has not suggested any such increase in the disposition of the Magistrate. There is, however, the issue of..."

The second Jacobs started his sentence, he knew where His Holiness had been leading him. He had no choice but follow through. Yes, the Lion of Logos *could* see his heart and mind.

"...the issue of the Kali worshippers. As you may be aware, Holiness, they seem to have altered their attitude towards us. They don't seem content with staying out of sight, anymore. They've disrupted our way of life. Their ... *demonstration* in Advent Square was an abomination and a mockery of our way of life. It teemed with Nihil Obstat imagery and words, Your Grace. It stands to reason that –"

His Holiness bellowed before Jacobs could finish. His voice shook the air. The floor under Jacobs' knees quaked.

"High Devotee, they are a trite, trivial group of misguided, fringe deviants! They have never had the will to do anything other than subsist, whispering in the cold dark under the streets. Have we not spoken of this already?"

"They have demonstrated a willingness to employ violent means, Holiness. Mustn't we match them? Increase the disposition of the Magistrate? At least by several hundred? Perhaps swap the electrode tips of their lances for bio-nihilate attachments?"

"Those haven't been used for centuries, and under much more severe circumstances. The citizens of New Corinth will have all but completely forgotten about the Kali'ka after Advent."

"But, Your Grace, that's my point precisely. His Holiness Gregor Juniper Friedrich VI – all grace to him under Logos – waited until it was almost too late. The Hale Riots, as we call them, were just a disorganized band of Veneerians who dragged up the courage to try and cross the Bridges to Paradise into New Corinth proper. They weren't organized, and their numbers were far less. If comeyes hadn't –"

"The cultists have no reason to go to Advent, High Devotee. Logos is not their god! Their saber rattling is no more than the impotent cry of a toddler unable to affect his world in any meaningful way."

"Holiness, at least reconsider the tradition of personally attending Advent! There's no reason for you to play the role of Logos in the Pageant of Miracles. Any player could perform the role admirably!"

"Jacobs, when we adopt a defensive stance, we admit our weakness! Do you not shield your most vulnerable parts when expecting to be struck? And why? Fear! Fear is Nihil Obstat. Fear is anathema to the environment we seek to engender. Fear is what we would create with a display of force. But the invincible, the untouchable: they do not fear. And we, Jacobs, are beyond untouchable – we are immortal! As immortal as Logos Himself! In Logos, there is no fear. There is only bliss and pleasure. We have everything we would ever need. Or do you doubt the injunctions of millennia? The visible efficacy of the ages? *We* are all that remains of the treads and trends of time!"

"Holiness, if I may, the Epicurial Apologia itself says – Second Partite, Book of Mammon, Cadence 5, Dram… 34, I believe, '*Let your tongue confess what your eyes have seen.*'"

"I do not require the work of Logos' own lips to be recited back to me, High Devotee!"

"Furthermore, Your Grace, if we say nothing, or make *no* kind of pronouncement, then we've given the Kali'ka leeway to influence whatever, whomever they want!"

"Enough, Jacobs! Your preoccupations are a disgrace to your station. Your compulsive attentiveness to irrelevancies mars your visage. The cultists are beneath our attention! I think there is no Corinthian who is as focused on them as *you*."

Every sneering syllable, every fiery word, lashed Jacobs like a barbed whip. His Holiness' voice pounded.

"This is your fatal flaw, High Devotee: imagination. Imagination coupled with predictability. Your own self-doubt twists their paltry numbers into a great beast beneath our feet, but I assure you that they are no greater than a speck of dirt on the heel!"

Jacobs licked his lips and kept his eyes riveted on the sacred symbol of Logic in the ground in front of His Holiness' throne. Some great force he didn't understand was pushing him, compelling him to press and not let the point go.

"Holiness, I... I understand these reasons. I just think a more proactive posture is necessary in this situation. Surely as a precaution –"

"High Devotee! Your job is to be the hands of the body of Logic, while I am its *mind*. All you need do is dwell on what is good, what is beautiful, what is pleasurable, and all will be well. We need a concerted focus on issues of state, especially this close to Advent. This behavior is not fitting of the least elevated of us!"

"But, Holiness –"

"This assessment is over! By Logos, within the Palm of His Hand, we carry forward."

The official closing words were like giant book covers slamming shut. His Holiness moved on undaunted, if a bit hurried to Jacobs' ears.

"Your continued diligence is appreciated, High Devotee, as well as your continued compliance. Logos exalts in the handiwork of your labor, and all of Logic is blessed in turn. As for the cultists, there will *be* no response. I am the Lion of Logos! His Will in flesh. He speaks, I hear; that is all. I will call on you when needed. In the meantime, attend to everything we spoke of, in turn, with your usual dutiful ... attentiveness. Blessed be you."

The silhouette of light shifted its weight, and a creak of leather managed to slip through the Crystal Throne's audio filters. Leather worn by a person. A man.

The holo-projectors blinked off, their servos whined down, and the boom of light and sound faded to near silence. Jacobs was left alone, kneeling in the same spot, blinking through white splotches blotting his vision. Subsumed by the same crystal and ivory brilliance of his residence, with his body on the same hard, tiled floor, hearing the same unaltered chant of seminarians at his back.

"And also you," he whispered.

In front of him, the empty throne stared like a silent tongue. Accusing in that familiar, demonstrable tone. Deriding him for his uselessness. Insinuating his incompetence. Same as it did at all hours, in use or not in use. Infringing on his space, pressing in, invading, never leaving, reminding him incessantly of year after year of hollow, fruitless tête-à-têtes where his mouth mirrored the words of His Holiness like a mechanical echo. Year after year of wielding terms like "joy," "elation," and "purity" in the same breath as "schedule," "manage" and "produce."

How could His Holiness not understand about the Kali'ka? Wasn't he supposed to be an infallible font of wisdom? A flawless executor of ecumenical and philological convergence? The embodiment of the Godhead itself, from which the Spirit of Logos flowed?

Confused, fixated on the acerbic bundle of emotions in his chest, Jacobs rose and stepped towards his desk like a leaden, numb machine. His hands moved of their own accord, manipulating the ceremonial steps of ablution, sanctifying himself after contact with the Lion of Logos. He watched himself lift icons to his forehead, uncork vials of consecrated water, upend small flasks, fold towels over his forearm, and make gestures in the empty, light-full air.

At the final step, Jacobs hefted a small, tin-thin ceramic pitcher and stopped to examine it. Such a dainty thing, tiny beyond pragmatic use, ornate with dense scrolling and holy symbolism. Such a fragile, fine example of exquisite craftsmanship. So much effort, so much care, just to pour its water over his hands and watch it spatter into a basin in jittery spits.

His weak, soft muscles quivered and his grip on it tightened.

"Seminarians! Leave me."

In swift, economic fashion, the two men at Jacobs' door stopped chanting the Cardinal Premise, put away their censers, bowed and backing out of the room.

The second the door shut behind them, Jacobs released a gut-deep shout, spun and hurled the tiny ceramic pitcher he cradled in his hands. It struck a far wall and ruptured in a misty explosion of pottery and water.

He ground his fists into the plateglass surface of his desk and shoved his jumbled stack of compads and sheafleaves to the floor. Heaving, trembling, soaked in sweat, consumed by unrecognizable and terrible sensations, he peered into the dull smear of his own face stretched across the desk's reflective surface. Darkened, inverted. Vague and unrecognizable.

All he could think about was the gray-robed man in Advent Square, his one eye and his virulent hatred, Roving, snarling, shouting, slashing the white marble with his blood, on the exact ground where the most important of Logical holy days took place. That, and how His Holiness disregarded him. Shoved him, the High Devotee, aside as though his life and his efforts were nothing.

The two feelings fused into one behemoth of terrible, ruthless intent.

A sharp beep snapped Jacobs' reverie short. Repetitive and whining, from the companel inset into his desk. He mumbled a quick fragment of thanks to Logos that he and the other scions didn't have to get those horrible comchits implanted in their earlobes, like seminarians did. Their bodies were inviolate vessels for Logos' Spirit, after all.

As soon as Jacobs depressed the receiver on his desk, the gruff, stony face of Grand Magister Hammar stared directly at him. Jacobs started in surprise at seeing the face of the man he'd just been talking about with His Holiness.

Hammar was consumed by a grave and focused expression. Clearly, Jacobs was about to hear something unpleasant.

"Grand Magister Hammar, why are you contacting me directly? This isn't exactly what I'd call an opportune time."

Hammer clasped his fist to his heart and bowed. The man could never avoid ceremony, even when it got in the way. The tip of his electrolance wavered in and out of view.

"Blessed be you, High Devotee. I wouldn't disturb you at a time as busy as the week prior to Advent, but an urgent matter requires your attention. Are you … alone?" He glanced around the border of the viewscreen as though he could peer around it.

The ominous sense in Jacobs' heart expanded. For Hammar to show any sign of hesitation or trepidation spoke of danger more than anything else.

"Get on with it, Grand Magister. No ears exist but mine."

Hammar visibly braced himself, as if unsure how to proceed. His full but neatly trimmed beard wriggled as he scratched a cheek. Jacobs had no doubt that the powerful man, when in doubt about how to proceed, would resort to blunt directness. It would be either a blessing or a curse, depending on the news.

"Your Grace ... a scion has been murdered."

Jacobs just blinked at the man for several seconds. He didn't his jaw fall. "What?! H-How? How is that possible?"

"I don't know, High Devotee. He appears to have been, well, castrated before he was murdered."

"Castrated?! You mean –" Jacobs made a snipping motion with his fingers.

Hammar cleared his throat. "Yes, Your Grace. It's still in there with him. Judging by the blood, he was engaged in Penance."

"Penance... Then this was in his booth??"

"Yes, High Devotee. It appears so. On the Cusp of the Veneer. There's no blood outside, so he must have been killed in his booth, not dragged inside."

"What do you mean 'here'? You mean you're still *there*? At his booth? Out in the open?"

"Yes, Your Grace. We're rerouting foot traffic through adjacent streets, and getting the scene in order."

"By Logos..." Jacobs ran his hands through his thinning hair and began pacing. "Who? Who was it?"

"Scion Driscol, Your Grace."

Driscol, Driscol... Ah, yes! Jacobs conjured up his face. Nobody of note. Nobody of any kind of distinction. A middling scion no different from hundreds of others, in a small district in the southeast of the city. Not overly elevated.

He noticed that Hammar's straightforward, unwavering bass had continued to jog on.

"...but his booth was otherwise in pristine order. No struggle, nothing knocked over, no claw marks. It makes me believe that the act was sudden. It believe it was planned, because no cutting implements exist in Penance booths. Perhaps a kitchen knife? However, because those are deliberately manufactured to be too dull to –"

Jacobs dashed to the viewscreen and snatched the edges of his desk. "You haven't told anyone, have you? No one else knows, right?"

Hammar's eyebrows twitched in confusion. "Ah – Well, I had to contact you before anyone else, Your Grace. Such is the holy hierarchy. I might be the only one who actually knows this bylaw, but nonetheless, I –"

"Good! Good. Tell no one! Do you understand? Block off the area from public view. Completely, you hear me? No one gets in or out. Supplicants will have to use other batteries of Penance booths."

"We've cordoned off paths that lead to this spot along the Cusp of the Veneer, but –"

"Not enough! I want the whole vicinity on lockdown. Send a relay to the Oculus to turn off all comeyes along the Cusp off until future notice. The whole grid if need be. Confiscate footage for the past twelve hours. Has anyone started looking at it yet?"

"They're starting to work on it now. I haven't heard any –"

"Stop them! Let no one see it! No eyes are to cast themselves on its vile, sordid influence!"

"But, Your Grace – if we're to conduct an investigation, we'll need access to –"

Jacobs hunched over his viewscreen, drilling his manic gaze into its glow. "No! There will be no investigation. The footage will stay out of sight! It was clearly the cultists, was it not? It was obviously the Kali'ka. How could it be a Corinthian? Right? Right?! What further evidence do you need? Murder?! No. Not yet. You and your men saw the cultists in Advent Square! You know better than most. The terror! The threat!"

Hammar's face paled further and further as Jacobs continued throwing out one forbidden concept after another. "High Devotee, I of course trust your decisions, but under the grace of Logos, I highly recommend that we at least review the comeye footage from the time period in question."

"No! Just do what I say, Hammar! In times of crisis, we don't need questions. We need obedience! We need solidarity! And believe me, this is a crisis. Now more than ever, we need the aspect of invincibility. We need to react nimbly and as one body. Do you understand? Dissenters weaken the foundation. We must be unified in our intention. We must be focused on the true enemy! You must trust your Godhead!"

"Yes … of course, Your Grace. Of course."

Intermittent screams came through on Hammar's end. A general bustle of magisters accompanied the noise.

Jacobs perked up. "What is that? I hear screaming."

"The citizen who found Rubrician Driscol is with us." Hammar hooked a thumb towards the area behind him. "After her discovery, she found Magister Timothy on patrol nearby, and brought him back here."

"Keep her there! Quarantine her. And shut her up! If I can hear her, who else can?"

"You Grace, the Spirit's flow needs to be restored in this woman. Levitant will return her to her bliss. We should first take her to the Oculus and take a thorough account of what she's seen, and then –"

"Grand Magister." Jacobs clipped the words like a command.

Hammar stopped mid-sentence, and at the sound of his title, lifted his chin high. "Yes, Your Grace."

"Exactly how much of a subversive element do you think that woman would be if she was released back into the populace of New Corinth? Hm? How many daggers would her eyes shoot, how much venom would her lips pour? Do you think it would prove anything but disastrous to let her roam around?"

"I – well, High Devotee, I'm not sure. We've never dealt with this sort of situation."

"Do you think Levitant and Penance will make her *forget*?"

"Well … no, Your Grace. I suppose not."

"Then she must be *removed* from the body of Logos. And shut her up, I said! Now!"

"Well, yes – of course, High Devotee. You know best."

"Of course I do! And I..." Jacobs was instantly rapt with a sudden possibility. "I'm coming down there. I ... I want to see it."

Hammar's face fell to shock. "But, High Devotee – there's no need at all for you to expose yourself to this! The sanctity of your countenance demands that you be kept away from..." he struggled with the Nihil Obstat, "... m-malice! Away from darkness!"

Frantically, Jacobs blurt out. "No! No. I... I want to. I want to see it! Understand? No. No... Yes! I want to. I want to see it!"

Hammar had moved beyond baffled and into the realm of disturbed. He just stood there, while Jacobs' intense stare bore through him.

"I'll ... tell the Magistrate to expect you, Your Grace."

"Good." Before Hammar could reply, Jacobs closed the communiqué and plopped into his soft, cowhide chair. An idea was rolling and growing in his mind, gathering momentum and collecting snippets of thoughts and information from source after source. Like a vortex, his idea sucked him in, latched onto him and embedded itself in his mind, possessing him utterly.

Where under Logos did the Kali'ka come from, originally? Generations upon generations of unaltered stasis had left the common Corinthian knowing nothing of antagonistic forces. Lack, unhappiness, and pain were only vague inferences of unspoken ideas. Had the cultists just subsisted from age to age, back to pre-Logical times?

Maybe they were just a scrabbling bunch of maniacs, not content to accept what had been freely given: abundance, comfort, pleasure. Maybe they were throwbacks to an era of evolutionary dead ends, where societies dwelled on deep-rooted personal defects or unquenchable self-loathing. Maybe in the end, they really were just a band of disorganized, useless slogs. Slogs with a flavor for tacky, drab, cheaply manufactured clothing and a penchant for morbidity.

No matter. They would serve their purpose. They would serve *his* purpose. They would be the fulcrum – the method and means to solidify his role in the future of Logic forever, as the true representative of Logos on earth.

Jacobs' long-suppressed ambition flooded into him like a desperate tide, icy and burning. All heard in the back of his mind was the derogatory tone of His Holiness.

He tapped at his viewscreen to connect to seminarians in the Transport Hub of the Basilica. Sound only. A hiss of static and the voice on the other end came through clearly.

"High Devotee. My apologies, Your Grace. We weren't expecting an audio communication. An honor and a blessing to hear from you. How may we serve?"

"Prepare my flo-car. I'll be traveling along non-beautification routes."

"The old municipal tracks, High Devotee? Surely a more splendid view can be afforded you along your journey."

"The non-beautification routes, seminarian." With the last word, he tapped the line shut.

He sunk into his chair and picked at its armrest. What was that old frequency? Hopefully the man on the other end would pick up, and hopefully he wasn't busy at his duties, slopping Penance booths or recalibrating electrocoils or whatever *low* things he usually did. Jacobs had all but commanded him to stay completely away at Advent Sermon.

Inputting the frequency, hoping he'd correctly wrested it from memory, Jacobs sat and waited. After several seconds, a familiar face popped into his viewscreen.

"High Devotee!" Mendicant Hegil's watery, bug eyes stared at him. The scene behind him was obscured somehow; it was impossible to see where he was. "How unexpectedly pleasant of *you* to be contacting *me*. It is unfortunate, though, that recompense is not something that could actually exist in a land that lacks nothing, wouldn't you say?" His drawl oozed like honey and communicated something approaching giddiness.

"Mendicant Hegil. An opportunity has arisen that requires your talents. If I'm right, then this will be what finally cements us – *both* of us – into the positions that we've come to rightly deserve."

Hegil's yellow-toothed, crescent smile spread wider, "Bookpraise to Logos, Your Grace."

Jacobs grinned in return. "Bookpraise, indeed. Logos is Lord."

CHAPTER 13
ERRATI

A young man sat isolated in a dingy, narrow alleyway in the Veneer, back propped against the stained synthstone wall of a dilapidated building. His pale blue eyes, whitened like the shade of a blizzard's gale, cut through the fissures between eaves overhead, along a straight line towards the golden spires of the Uppers driving their way heavenward, gleaming in the Eternal Day.

Mere street corners away, out of direct sight, hundreds of thousands throbbed in an ever-present buzz. Unintelligible shouts and terror-filled screams pierced the ceaseless wave of human noise and bustle.

The sheer indigence crushed them all like a never-ending insult. The Veneer remained out of sight and out of mind of the rest of the city, separated by a massive synthstone wall that ran alongside the Tame River. It and its people remained ignored, cordoned off like cattle in one smallish sector of New Corinth proper. A damned district where people were born only to die. Living first in swollen wombs, then swelling on the streets as bloated corpses. Replicating by droves in filth-coated alleyways, starving what meager resources they shared. Death was the only escape to their interbred caste of hopeless, generational poverty.

How thin and fragile the glowing needles of the Uppers looked, bunched on their knoll, saturating the crisp, blue sky. A sky that never waned, never switched off, but blazed deep into the night. Veneerian nights, every night, which grew dimmer and darker for want of the ever-present light in the east.

The young man in the alleyway raised a large, heavy hand – oversized and broader than his lengthy teenage limbs would imply, like the paw of a juvenile dog that would one day grow into its own mass – and one by one, wrapped his fingers around the Uppers, seeing their glowing needles snap in his mind like blades of sun-burnt grass. With each flex of the finger, a rusted, metal hoop half-embedded into his forearm twitched, and his overly broad shoulders tightened like a mantle of stone resting around his neck.

Scions... he snarled, fixating on his fertile, simmering bitterness. *Nothing can prepare you. One day, we will reclaim what rightfully belongs to us.*

A small, shuffling sound jostled the air, delicate enough to be out of place. It rustled in the mouth of a nearby, narrow alley.

All the muscles in the young man's body coiled. He expected, demanded – hoped for, in fact – catharsis. Slight adjustments to the positions of his feet and balance enabled him to respond instantly. His breath became a latch waiting to spring. He didn't move, but he prepared to destroy.

Out of the alleyway stepped a gangly girl nearly as tall as him, her long legs craning over a pile of strewn trash. She alighted only a few meters away. Her amber hair, disheveled and sweaty, matched the disarray of her clothes. The instant the young man saw her, the tension in his chest vanished.

Before she could take a step, half a dozen figures dropped to the muddy pavement in splats and splashes, from rooftops and overhangs above. They circled around the girl, crouching, growling.

"Errati!" The young man smashed his fist into the ground, more for show than need. "You didn't see her coming, and now you drop in? Get out of here! She's under my protection. She can come and go as she pleases. You know that!"

Making a reluctant show if it, the Errati turned and vanished into grime-slick nooks, glassless windows, and half-barricaded doorways, glowering through faces punctured by rings, hoops, chains, and rods.

The girl just stood with her hands on her hips, waiting.

"Nyx, what are you doing here?" he asked.

"Nice to see you, too, Devin. You and your … friends." She shot the retreating Errati a glare.

Devin chuckled to himself. *Friends.* "The timing seems strange, is all. You were just here." His mind wavered and his eyes floated back towards the Uppers. He resettled against the wall behind him.

"Hey, I didn't come all the way here just so you could ignore me." She craned her neck over her shoulder and brushed bits of dirt of her clothing.

"Hm? I'm sorry."

"Don't say 'sorry.' I didn't teach you that word just so you can be apologetic." She turned her attention to fishing crumbles of refuse out of her tangled her.

Devin stared blankly for a moment, mouth churning as he considered several options. "Pardon?"

Nyx rolled her eyes. "Good enough. I know you never talk, and probably haven't talked to anyone in the past day or two – except to yell at them, or order them to steal some food or something – but we have to talk. Now."

"How did you know I would be here?"

"How would I *not* know?" She pointed to his clear view of the Uppers.

Devin saw through the layer of hardened glassiness Nyx was putting on. Her face, voice, and posture were … *concerned?* That was the word.

"Ok, I'm listening."

Nyx sighed in relief, confirming his suspicions of how she felt. "My sister is in trouble, Devin. I need your help."

"I thought you hated her."

"Not her. The other one." She blinked several times, as though hesitant to continue, and licked her lips. "And I don't hate her, the one you thought I meant. I never said that. I… I don't hate anyone."

"The Kali worshipper, then? She's the one in trouble?"

"She really hates that word."

"What word?" Devin asked.

"'Worshipper.' 'Worship.'"

"She hates it?"

"...Presumably," Nyx offered. "I can only assume she hates it."

"Why do you have to use doctrinator words?"

"Like 'presumably?'"

"Yeah."

"It's not a doctrinator word, Devin, believe me."

Devin, confused, broke eye contact with her and started fingering the metal hoop looped through his forearm. He knew it for an act of nervousness, though others seemed to find it troubling for some reason.

Out of the corner of his eye, Devin caught sight of the heaps of decaying refuse spread, piled, and clumped around him. Conspicuously colored liquids pooled around them in between shattered glass, dented metal scraps, scattered needles, disposable misters, and dismantled bits of technological baubles from New Corinth proper.

Sticky musk always enveloped this place until the depths of winter. At that time, moisture adopted a clammy stickiness rather than a slick flush. The stench was relieved during those months, but still caused fits of gagging even to lifelong residents when it rolled along the streets in aggregate waves. It was arguably worse near the Cusp, where the warmth of the Eternal Day competed with the stifling heat of the enclosed crush of buildings.

Devin glanced up at Nyx. Somehow, someway, it seemed to never bother her.

"They've been showing up everywhere, Nyx. The grays. More than usual. It's different, like something is about to happen. Patterns have changed, routes have changed. There's ... haste?" He looked for her approval at using the correct word. She nodded softly and crossed her arms. "Haste to their movements. They're hurrying. There's even one of them that has himself holed up in the streets and buildings near the outer wall. Has guards. He thinks we don't see him and don't watch him. Something happened the other night. Someone tried to get in there, I think. But these..." He rolled his wrist as though trying to conjure the word.

"Kali'ka."

"Kali'ka. This isn't their home. Some of them might be *from* here, but this is *our* place."

"Any idea what they're up to?"

"No. But some of us have gone missing. Veneerians. Not the usual kind of missing, either. This is different. We think they grays are … *responsible*?" Nyx nodded again. "Responsible," Devin confirmed.

Nyx clasped her hands behind her back and started pacing. When she carried herself that way, she looked older, somehow. Sturdier. "It's just like what Elara suspected. They're held up in Mors. The cloister under the Veneer."

"The what? Under us?"

"I can't go back. To her cloister. To Sangra. She'd kill me." Nyx half-spoke to herself.

"Kill you? I thought you're trying to help her."

"Not *literally* kill me."

"Literally…" He mouthed the shape of the word, inferring its meaning. He picked at one the metal spines perforating his ear and repeated the word several more times to himself. Across his chest, neck, and torso, slivers and hooks of metal pierced his still-young flesh.

"Going back there wouldn't help," Nyx continued. "I can't do anything except tell her what she already knows. But I have to help somehow. The Kali'ka here in the Veneer – the ones you've seen – they dangerous. They want to harm her. Elara. My sister. I know it. They're trying to…" She snapped her fingers, looking for an explanation. "…*change* the Kali'ka. Make them aggressive. Violent. But that's not what they're about."

"Violence is necessary. In the Veneer, you fight or you die."

"I know that, but the Kali'ka focus on *themselves*. Knowing themselves. Changing themselves. Not harming others. Not changing others."

"Sounds like the ones who are trying to harm your sister are trying to take what isn't theirs."

"More or less."

"If somebody tries to take what belongs to the Errati, they get hurt. If they try again, they get killed." Devin flexed his fist and mused about what it felt like to grab someone's skull in his palm.

"Well … hopefully it won't come to that." Nyx waved a hand as though shooing away the idea. "There's one of them – he only has one eye, and a scarred face. I did a little listening on the way. Took my time getting here. People are talking about him, even out here in the Veneer. Ever heard of a guy like that?"

"Hm? Yeah. Fallow. He's the one I mentioned. The one holed up near the outer wall of the city."

Nyx's pacing halted. "What else do you know?"

Devin eyed her curiously, wondering where she was leading their conversation. "Not much, except that when his name is spoken, people shut up."

Nyx nodded. "Fallow's at the center of this. He started something."

"The center ... of *this*," Devin repeated.

"Of whatever's going on. The Kali'ka. Why I came. And I doubt it stops with just him and Elara." Nyx's eyes pierced the air as though it contained the answers she sought.

Devin planted his knuckles into the ground and shifted his weight. "The Errati can find out. This is our home. People listen to us. Fear us."

She nodded absently, staring at the ground.

Nyx... Devin knew that wasn't her real name. They all took their own names, in the Veneer, just like he took his. Her name didn't matter, though, ultimately. None of their names mattered. That was the point. One name or the other wouldn't change anything. People were born, and they died. What came between was incidental.

Devin took a deep breath before venturing a comment. "You never talk about her."

Nyx glanced at him and said nothing.

"Why not?" he asked.

"She's... It's difficult."

"What about it?"

"It's complicated. Too complicated to talk about, especially now. Family stuff. You know."

"Yeah, I know." Devin glanced at the dried blood along the half-molded entrance where his metal loop pierced his forearm. It had bled earlier today, like it sometimes still did. No matter how much the loop bled, though, the scar tissue atop it never moved.

"Family," he growled.

His father had clamped the loop to a chain and used it to yank him around as a boy. The wrenching agony would ignite his entire nervous system and set his muscles ablaze, causing him to pass out for hours at a time.

That is, until he killed his father with that very chain several years ago.

He had been free ever since. A proud Errati, bred in the shade of New Corinth's bowels. Free to make his *own* family. He and the rest of the young people of the Veneer, clutching the tools of their torture proudly, lifting them in sectarian cries. They used their bonds to forge newer, rawer creatures of metal-imbued flesh, one post, one lance, one piercing at a time.

Still, the Veneer was a forever prison. Inflexible, relentless, merciless.

"What can I possibly do?" Devin stared at the loop driven through his arm.

"A lot. You're here." Nyx's hands encompassed their surroundings.

"Exactly. No matter what, Nyx, I'm going to die here like everyone else. New Corinth –" he gestured towards glowing Uppers "– will never know we existed. They never have. They don't remember."

Nyx frowned and tilted her heard to one side. "This doesn't sound like you. What's wrong?"

Devin scrubbed a hand on his head and ran his fingers over a rod driven through the top middle layer of skin on the back his neck, driven in by himself.

No matter how much he fidgeting, no matter how where his eyes landed or what his hands touched, he couldn't keep focus. Nyx's presence contorted his thoughts. Words became what they weren't intended to be.

"Devin … this is serious. Please, I – You're basically the only person I know I can trust." She stood straight, refusing to slouch. A minor quivering shook her body, as if she were a lone leaf on a wind-blown branch. Her eyes watered and sparkled in the failing day of the pre-dusk light starting to enshroud the Veneer. It was good that she'd made it there before dark.

Strange though, how she never seemed afraid of night. Even though she lived in the Uppers, in the middle of the Eternal Day, in a land that never saw sunfall, she never seemed frightened by the dark.

This girl was an impossible sight in Devin's eyes. An impossible beauty, especially in the Veneer. Even sweaty and haggard with deep, purplish circles ringing the underside of each eye, she was benevolence incarnate. Utterly incongruous with his home. A singular oddity – one totally at ease among muck and filth.

She was completely unlike other Corinthians. Completely unlike any Veneerians, too.

She risked much coming here, as she always did. Levitant gangs, forced prostitution, assault, the ever-present possibility of offhand murder. Her resourcefulness was astonishing. It was born inside her, derived *from* her. She came and went completely unscathed each time she visited, finding narrow slits of paths past danger. It was as though she had been ordained for safety and was untouchable to any malefic force.

On the contrary, Devin risked little by staying. He was in a fortified location; he was surrounded by a cadre of Errati; he was larger than his peers – stronger by the day as his muscles filled out his lengthy frame. He was destined to become a creature defined by near invincible strength. By the standards of the Veneer, where men and woman died as easily as flies were swatted, he was nearly untouchable.

He simply idled, waited, hoped, and watched for *something* he didn't understand. That something would soon rise, he felt, like the moon over the horizon in the west. Like twilight, swelling to offset the never-dying sun of New Corinth proper. In the meantime, he knew Nyx would return to him, every time.

In two strides, Nyx crossed the distance between them and placed a hand on his arm, squatting to meet him at eye level. She didn't flinch at the metal piercing his flesh. She didn't spare a glance for the blood, the dirt, and the scars.

He, however, *did* flinch.

Her touch was the lightest kiss of a spirit's indulgence – one of those old guardians that some superstitious Veneerians still swore hovered above their heads, unseen, protecting where they could. Her touch shocked what physical punishment couldn't. It penetrated when pain wouldn't. It was more real than metal, more solid than stone. His torso buzzed with an odd chill beyond cold. He hummed with heat beyond warmth.

Their eyes locked, hers to his. Green flame met white-blue dawn in a typhoon of emotion.

"Please, Devin."

He fought the urge to look away. He fought the urge to never look away. Their rising breath intermixed as they faced each other, joining, traveling, journeying.

"You knew I'd help, Nyx. That's why you came."

The smile that bloomed on her face evaporated his fear and apprehension.

She spoke swiftly, like the night soon to descend on the Veneer – only the Veneer – while the Eternal Day persisted, untouchable untarnished.

"Let's see if we can get into Fallow's little hideout."

CHAPTER 14
IN DARKNESS

Initiate Oyame Nagai kept her head down as she shuffled through the dank, dripping caverns of Cloister Mors. Her breath puffed in front of her wide eyes and slipped into the darkness. Like a heavy cloak, the endless night, the cold, and the earthen scent never left. They stalked, haunted, and constricted her at every moment. She gripped her own arms for a semblance of warmth, thankful that her robes were wool.

Ovular patches of torchlight bloomed at the edges of passageways, or far in the distance beyond spires of stone that speared up towards the vaulted ceiling above. Clusters of Kali'ka stood whispering, gesturing, casting askance glances at anything that encroached on their sphere of vision. Those moving from place to place, always in pairs or more, some scuttling along the peripheries of paths while others strutted with chins held high, snickering and tapping their compatriot's shoulders whenever anyone passed.

So it had been, every single day since she arrived: Whispers. Rumors. A nameless, faceless figure stalking in the dark. Secret meetings. The fervency of raised voices and charismatic phrases. People disappearing, leaving, coming back with profound changes in demeanor. Division and discord. Kali'ka in the cloister seemed to purposefully espouse a hard-lined, extremist version of their beliefs, prodding others into contrary perspectives.

It was madness. Wrong. Sour in a subversive way, like meat almost-bad meat. Daily life was an end-on-end pantomime of harsh, unyielding devotionals, coldness, and hunger. She barely ate. Her eyes were slow to adjust to the incessant dimness, after a life in New Corinth. She walked in figurative and literal blindness.

Were all cloisters like Mors? It was completely different from the mutual brotherhood she'd been exposed to in secret covens aboveground.

Images from her initiation danced within, and she clung to them like a sail in a windstorm. She gently placed one hand on the still-sore yantra directly above her navel. The brand in her flesh felt hot, especially in the robes she never took off except for kanas and for bathing. It didn't feel inflamed, though. Their master inscribe said the heat was from how it was actuating her root chakra.

Eventually, her inscriptions would climb all the way to her skull and mark her face in a way that forever disallowed returning to New Corinth. One day, she would be an ascendant of Cloister Mors.

This was the dream she would live, if she managed to live at all.

Thank you, Great Mistress... Thank you. No matter what, Oyame never ceased uttering these words to herself. Like a secret, she planted them and whispered to them to grow.

Along a path that curled down into an open, communal area, Oyame found her attention drawn to twin doorways bordered by massive iron censers that hung on either side. Activity was busier here, conversation less restricted, attitudes less shielded.

She slipped into Virgil's Navel, nexus of geometric power for Mors, keeping her eyes down as she past Kali'ka gliding in and out of the chamber. She found a spot within among row upon row of gray robes, all bowing in one pose, facing one direction. A host of blank people in hoods. Unknowns with unknown intent, lost to shadow.

They all hummed the Chant of Ages.

"In darkness, your eyes shine, oh Kali.
Tilt the wheel to carry us onward,
Over the ocean of birth and death."

Oyame knelt and lowered her forehead to the floor, keeping her hands in the shape of a triangle around the spot her skin kissed the stone. Her voice joined the chorus, indistinguishable.

Within the hum of their drone and the sizzle of firepots, Oyame allowed herself to drift into a blessed, beautiful, static emptiness, where words spilled freely.

"In darkness, your eyes shine, oh Kali.
Tilt the wheel to carry us onward,
Over the ocean of birth and death."

It was then that she felt the tap on her shoulder.

She rallied her attention, and careful not to interrupt her mantra for fear of being noticed, counted to one-hundred and twenty using the limited split-consciousness she'd learned in training, before getting up and quietly exiting. Several turns took her out of sight and into the agreed-on alcove. She stood in silence along the rim of a nearby torch's light, listening to the shuffle of feet echoing through nearby passageways.

A good minute passed before a tall figure stepped out from a patch of darkness along the wall and pulled its hood back. Soft shadows lay across the face underneath.

"Kali sees you, Ascendant Cyrus, my advocate." Oyame lifted her fingers to lips and then forehead, and knelt to one knee. He must have been waiting nearby, watching, ensuring their safety before emerging.

"As She sees all, Initiate Nagai. But," he reached down to grasp her arms and pull her up, "formalities aren't needed at a time like this. Nor should they overreach common respect."

"Yes, ascendant." She gripped the cuffs of her sleeves – an old, anxious habit – and struggled to pull her eyes from the ground. "Why have you asked me here?"

His breath caught. "To ask you to leave."

Oyame blinked in confusion. "But – what? No!" Cyrus gestured for her to lower her voice. "No," she repeated, softer. "I'm not leaving. I just got here."

"You don't have to be cloistered, Initiate Nagai. Only ascendants do."

"It was my choice! Why are you telling me this now? My initiation was, I don't know – five, six…"

"Nine."

"*Nine* days ago! Why – am I – what am I doing wrong?"

"Don't think that this has anything do to with you."

"Nothing to do with me?! How can it have nothing to do with me and still *affect* me?!"

"Sometimes you can do nothing wrong and still have wrong things affect you, Oyame."

As Cyrus spoke, Oyame got a clear view of his face. His eyes moved quicker than normal. Small, tiny changes in his mannerisms – pinched eyebrows, tight lips, an overly calm voice, immobile hands – added up to a telling portrait.

He was … diminished, somehow. Distressed, distracted, smaller. Changed, just like the cloister. Like her.

"Then why? You're the one who brought me here! Saw me on the Path of Gold. Met with me for months even before inviting me to my first coven. Showed me the true nature of the Goddess! And then, at my initiation, you…" Oyame's throat caught. She swallowed back tears that she didn't realize were there.

Cyrus sighed. Some of his former self relit. "I'm sorry, Oyame. We all go through it. You can't be prepared. That's the point."

Oyame stilled herself. "Where is Adherent Silvia? I haven't seen her since I arrived."

"You know that we can't talk about coven members – "

"To the void with that rule! I consider her a friend. You haven't even talked to me since I got here, and now you want to start dictating to me? I'm worried. Have you seen her? I need to know. There's something… Something's not right down here."

"Oyame, I –" Cyrus stopped and lifted a hand in a silencing gesture. He tilted his head as some noise bounced through the cloister.

The vague, jumbled cacophony grew in volume, resolving into a mess of scrabbling and blabbering. Oyame heard a single, spastic voice masked by occasional shouts, interspersed with gravely sliding.

Oyame and Ascendant Cyrus pulled up their hoods and pressed themselves against the walls. Into vision passed an insane sight: A gnarled, withered man, howling, hooting, and scratching at the floor as he was dragged by a small cadre of Kali'ka that Oyame didn't recognize. They pranced around him as they dragged him and jeered.

One of them smashed a fist into his face. *"Shut up!* Pawns of Logic have no voice down here! You're the one who came into the Veneer! You came looking for us. This is your doing!"

Another delivered several quick, vicious kicks to his head. "Shut – the – fuck – up! Nothing you do will save you! It's too late. We can't be stopped. Nothing you do will stop us! Nothing you do will stop *him!*"

The man whined and bawled through a shattered face. The group just kept laughing as they dragged him out of sight. Eventually, the sounds of their commotion vanished.

"Kali's Eyes." For the first time since Oyame had met him, Cyrus seemed legitimately stunned.

"Cyrus … what's going on?" Fear clenched Oyame's throat. "That was a mendicant of Logic. I'm sure of it. You saw his vestments. What's a mendicant doing down here?"

Cyrus lifted a hand to his forehead and spoke in a daze. "Child, I… I'm so sorry. To join us now, of all times. I would have never believed that the skills you learned aboveground could help you down here. Listen: you have to stay out of sight. It's not safe. We can't meet for awhile. This threat is different from the danger we accept when we embrace our inner darkness. This is something none of us could have foreseen. This is a perversion."

Oyame was snared between trembling terror and anxious anger. "Advocate, this is supposed to be a haven. The one place we can commune. The Great Mistress is supposed to reign here, not –"

"You're not alone." Cyrus reached out to grip her wrist. "Even if you're the last person standing, you're never alone. Remember what you saw during your initiation. Around Kali make your vigil. She is your shield, not the Kali'ka. Certainly not me. That's the most important distinction you can make. We're just representatives of something far more real and far more powerful."

Oyame found herself listening to Ascendant Cyrus' words as much as soaking in his features: a still-full hairline, graying above the ears; the inky yantra slashing across his right and left temples; the strong vertical line leading down to his jaw; the mournful eyes whose vague focus seemed lodged half between the realms of Creation and Illusion. His calmness and fortitude were a bastion that she'd come to rely on.

"Cyrus... Kali protects Her children, like She always has. We have a need. She will save us. She eradicates all fear. All apprehension. Why are we hiding?" Her mind rifled through the stories she'd learned, the precedents, the axioms, everything and anything to sturdy her strength.

Ascendant Cyrus observed her silently. The signs in his face shone clearly – regret, sympathy, pride – all bundled into one struggling snapshot that rapidly slipped through filters of emotion. Although Oyame didn't understand *why* he felt that way, she perceived *what*.

Cyrus became as blank as the dawn was silent. Without budging an inch, he receded further and further into an inner thought-scape. He spoke, and as he spoke, understanding seemed to come to him.

"Because, Oyame, even gods need the hands of people."

***

Above Cloister Mors in the Veneer, hidden in a spiderweb of sprawling, debris-packed alleyways and stained synthstone walls, Fallow dwelled among his brood in his own hand-made stronghold. His place of peace. His *Ashram*.

He glided untouched in the unveiled darkness of a Veneerian night, through a stygian courtyard lit by the flutters of scattered firepots. Rolling his dagger along his fingers, Fallow scrutinized his Kali'ka – his devoted followers – with his one living eye.

Around the courtyard, they were hunched over hewn, half-living bodies that leaked bloody rivulets and squirmed like maggots. With gore-slick daggers in hand, they set to work, slicing, skewering soft flesh, lifting bloodied sheets of skin and pinning them into place, crafting a great, sprawling emblem to the smallest, exact detail Fallow demanded.

For the emblem to work – for his plan to work – every last stitch of flesh, blood, and bone had to be perfect.

Against a far wall, Fallow's forge belched steam. The antiquated, hulking contraption of iron and hammers, chains and fire, and troughs for molten metal, radiated heat that crawled over the courtyard. From it, Fallow himself had constructed the framework for the future of the Kali'ka.

It was all there in the daggers. Invasive tools crafted by his own hands, down to the last cowhide binding and chip of metal scraped from the desolation of the Veneer. They, the creations, mirrored the will of their creator. He and them both: implements having one, singular, defined purpose: to invade, to force the hand of another. To slip in the space between the ribs of New Corinth and pierce the heart of Logic. To no longer be passive, no longer wait for the future, but to *make* it. To forge fate, like the daggers themselves.

"You!" Fallow pointed at one of his Kali'ka, who leaned over an emaciated, filthy Veneerian man on a rotten, viscera-slick set of planks with his dagger in hand. Fallow stepped into place over the Veneerian and proceeded to instruct as he set to work with his own blade, applying precise pressure, digging deftly.

"More like this! At an oblique angle."

The man on the table howled and whipping violently against his restraints. Fallow's broodling to the side frowned and fought through his reflexive, physiological repulsion.

The reaction made Fallow smirk. He didn't *need* them to perform this task, not precisely. He could have done it himself, the whole thing. More reliable that way, too. But through the act, they would learn what *he* had learned. They would discern how to cast their inner eye on the pain of another and observe what it produced in them: nothing.

"Never forget that you belong to the Goddess, ascendant." Fallow leveraged his elbow as he corkscrewed his dagger to get a better angle. "She watches at all times, and applauds our efforts. You and your fellow Morsmen are Her true heirs.

"There. Yes! You see that spurt? You see the deep red? That's the pulmonary vein. It will drain him effectively. Don't worry about mistakes. The Veneer has plenty more of these rabble. Do try to catch all you can, though. It'll make the symbol on these walls that much more potent."

Fallow tapped a bloodied bucket nearby with his foot and turned away, leaving his broodling to his task and tucking his dagger in his sleeve.

No one would miss the Veneerians. Random disappearances were as common as death in the Veneer. Cheap lives effortlessly snatched from doorways, lanes, lean-tos and alleys, discarded like single-use syringes. They needed only to live long enough for their purpose to be fulfilled: to complete *his* purpose.

This was the pathway to true enlightenment – to Transcendence – never embraced by the Unchanged Kali'ka except in word only. Pure necessity painted the scene of what was needed to surmount and live from one day to the next. A scene forgotten to Earth, lost to the annals of history. A plane of ruthlessness, where the unworthy existed to facilitate a future that the powerful envisioned. A realm of survival, where the brutality of the past, of Kali Herself, provided the foundation for the pre-ordained of Logic to live along solid gold streets and drink heady wine from crystal fountains.

They'd forgotten Kali, the citizens of New Corinth. Millennia ago, they'd taken paradise from Her lessons and wasted it on the unworthy. Paradise, without friction.

Fallow chuckled as he weaved through the gorgeous morass of his Ashram. Friction, coupling, coitus... Space and texture in contrary motion. Halves of one. The means of perpetuation. To spread and populate, consume and grow, absorb and convert. To re-write the stamp of life as a virus unchecked. To sprout from a meager seedling, unfold again and again. Dividing to multiply, separating to flourish, splitting to survive. Cells of tissue, groups of cells called animals, groups of animals called communities, groups of communities called society: all the same template.

A divided cell, now, were the children of Kali. Two from one, and so to persist ... forever. Because of *friction*. Because of *difference*. Because of *contradiction*.

History would remember him as the savior of the Kali'ka. This, he was sure.

Fallow's head jerked, startled by an emergent motion in the din, at odds with the rest of the movement. A small cluster of his Kali'ka ghosted past limbs and blades, dragging some lanky, misshapen creature behind them. They stopped meters away.

"Transcendent Fallow." All three of them bowed in unison. One of them grabbed the creature and shoved it forward into the blood-soaked dirt. It knelt there, slathering nonsense noises and wringing its hands. Its jaundiced skin was slack with pure terror as it glanced around and babbled through a bloodied, beaten mouth.

Through a saturated layer of oily grime, patches of sodden discoloration, and smeared feces, Fallow saw its clothing. Off white, rimmed in purple at the hem. Simple. One layer. Vestments. A cassock. One of the hated ones of Logos. *There*, in his Ashram.

"Please, please!!" It wailed grossly. "It's so dark! Can you please make it brighter? Please! I can't – I can't see anything. Oh. Oh! The Eternal Day! Over there, to the east! The Eternal Day lives! It is a gift to all of Logos' children! His excess pours in milky whiteness! We elate through His holy draught, Levitant! We abide in rivers of... of... We – We..." The words dissembled to unintelligible, weeping blubbers.

Fallow circled around the creature, his one eye steaming like a chasm of flame. "Why... is this *thing* here?!"

One of his three Kali'ka spoke up. "He asked to speak with you, Transcendent. By name. He'd made his way to one of the pores that leads down to Mors. Past our sentries. Some of the Veneerians had seen us tracking in and out of it and led him nearby. He didn't make it any further."

Hmm... Fallow scrutinized their captive. The scraggly, repugnant annoyance had accomplished what no one else could? Tracked through both the Veneer's own grotesque inhabitants and the surveillance of Fallow's own brood?

"So you brought it here? Directly to our heart? Why didn't you at least gouge his eyes out? It's still too well-composed!"

They grew hushed, like chastised animals that didn't comprehend their master's displeasure.

"*We* dictate the attention we want, ascendants! Otherwise, we remain unseen! And you've done the exact opposite! Fear must lie in the *mind*! In imagination! It must nest there first! You feed it, and then leave room for it to grow! This thing –" Fallow slashed a finger at the whimpering, huddled form in the dirt "– would've served a much better purpose out there, among its brothers! Able to spread its fear like the carrier of a pathogen!"

Off to the side, the tiny creature chirped. Out from its bloodied mouth came a thin, wobbly voice. "Um … Your Grace, if I might have a word?" Its bug eyes were darting around the courtyard, clearly not understanding what it saw.

Viciously, Fallow cracked the worthless creature on the side of the head. It dropped like a brick. Its eyes fluttering like insect wings.

"No, you may not, you feeble idiot! This is the first thing you have to learn: even the stupidest dog understands pain. And I have confidence that you are, in fact, at least as insightful as the stupidest dog!"

Fallow turned towards the three who'd intruded on him, hollow, frozen with empty contempt. "You've performed admirably in the Cusp of the Veneer, as you know. The Godhead has been severed. Disgraced. The scions of Logic know that we can reach them at any time."

Yes… They all needed reminders sometimes, of why *he* was Fallow. He gestured to a nearby set of hooks and cranks attached to a pulley and bolted into a makeshift table.

"Add your lifeblood to the tableau of the future. Your contribution will last far beyond the confines of the realm of Creation. Your deeds will echo into the illusory realm, where Kali and Her pantheon resides. I will find you there, my ascendants. This is the gift I grant you."

They bowed in unison, hands clasped to their chests, before shuffling away to their deaths. "As you will, Transcendent."

The cringing little creature on the ground watched the three Kali'ka leave, eyes boggling, jaw agape.

Fallow rounded on him, hands behind his back. "Surprised, are you? Loyalty without bribery. Impossible for one of the hated, Logical elite to understand."

The man-beast pulled its eyes up to Fallow with obvious difficulty. It said nothing.

"Now tell me, creature… What do they call you?"

"H-Hegil."

"Hegil," Fallow mused, hand perched on his chin. "How ironic, that you doubtlessly have no understanding of how our contrary perspectives typify your namesake's philosophy. If I may: 'We find in our actions evidence of an explicit existence, to which we refute with implicit knowledge, and so come to an absolute measure of ourselves.' Sound familiar, frail slave of Logos?"

Hegil just knelt there, eyes as wide as dual moons, mouth working as he tried to recall fragments of words.

Fallow sighed melodramatically. "Nevermind, wretch. Nevermind. Now, how is it that one of Logos' snow white lambs comes to dirty himself in the realm of the forgotten?"

At the opportunity to speak about something he comprehended, Hegil almost fell over himself in sycophantic glee. Almost, just almost, he seemed to forget his surroundings.

"Mmm, yes, you are indeed wise to ask such a question, Your Grace! If I may, I'd just like to say that if I were in your position, I would doubtlessly find this a bit unnerving, to have my place of solace encroached on. But rest assured, there is little in the way of trouble I could cause you, despite such an egregiously abrupt interruption of –"

Like the strike of a whip, Fallow pounced on him, squeezing his throat and grinding his face into the dirt.

Spit sprayed from Fallow's lips as he shouted. "From the instant I saw you, fool, I've denied myself the pleasure of watching your face scream as I butcher your body. You see these Veneerians around you? Just like them! Not because you're a mendicant, but because you're a toothless disgrace – even by Logical standards. Because your own decisions have led to a life of slopping filth from Penance booths. Don't look so surprised! Yes., I can tell. *Mendicant* Hegil. No stole around your shoulders, no cincture, no alb.

"What happened when you were in estuary, *mendicant*? All the upturned noses and backbiting didn't take to you? The derogatory sneers from your scion teachers must have left quite a scar on that fragile, sensitive mind of yours. All while pontificating on the indulgence of Levitant and the unblemished elation of Logos' heart, worship His name! Or maybe you didn't wrap yourself tightly enough around your scion's

... preferences."

The disgusting goblin mumbled something unintelligible as Fallow held him in place.

"Oh! Does that image disturb you, mendicant? Your cowering face says it does. Or is it the thought of me meandering through New Corinth's gilded streets of pastel smoothness?"

Drool and blood slung from Hegil's babbling mouth. "No! No, of course not, Your Grace. I understand the need to –"

Before he could utter another word, Fallow struck out and clasped the man's jaw with steel fingers. He snatched the nearest yellowed teeth he saw, all slick with blood and chewed out flesh, and twisted, turned, and yanked, again, again and again.

Maddened laughter burst from Fallow's throat, riding on the storm of the courtyard's torture and bedlam. The howls of the mendicant spiked towards a climax of frantic animalism.

One final tug, and Fallow hurled Hegil's front teeth across the courtyard. Their tiny clacks were lost to the all-consuming screams of Ashram. Hegil howled and rasped through a gap in his ragged gums. He spewed his own blood to avoid choking.

"You see, mendicant?! Now, you really *are* toothless! This is what happens when you don't wait to make *sure* I'm done talking! And the correct answer is, 'Yes, Transcendent.' That is the response I will accept. Try again!"

As soon as Hegil's whimpers quieted, and he'd spit up enough blood to clear his mouth for speaking, he managed a tiny, slurred pip. "Yes, Transcendent."

"Good. Now, speak!"

"Th-The High Devotee has a request." Hegil's words came out gummy and thick.

"The High Devotee himself?" Fallow started twiddling his fingers. "Well... I can't think of a better reason to listen to you. Gold and fame aren't sufficient enough for him, then? Or for Logos, either? Why doesn't your prurient god simply suck his people dry, like the whore that he is?"

Hegil moaned and shielded his face with shaking hands as he shivered on the ground.

"Your discomfort betrays your frailty, mendicant! Words effect you. All I have to do is open my mouth and you are controlled. Your beliefs are a shackle that dictate your actions, not a tool of liberation. This is why you deserve what happens to you. Now, answer me!"

Hegil hesitated before speaking. "The High Devotee. He – that is... He needs one of your robes."

Fallow scoffed. "A robe. Interesting. The wool of a lamb *should* be most comforting to a shepherd of men, wouldn't you say? He must be bored of his well-appointed vestments. I take it he wants his baby-soft skin to get chaffed, just like in estuary? What a sick man he is. He no doubt wants something in return, correct?"

"The terms, T-Transcendent..." He fumbled with the word. "...Are up to you."

"Well! I wouldn't want to abuse your master's trust by asking for too disproportionate a favor! He should already be beside himself with bliss, at having aided the heirs of Earth."

"Of – of course ... Transcendent." The 't' sound was especially difficult for lack of his front teeth. "What do you ask for in return, then?"

"I ask for *nothing*, wretch! I *take*. I do as I *will*! Did you actually think you could come here and strike a deal with the most resolute, all-powerful force in existence? There are no constraints for followers of the Goddess. Her power is absolute, and as an extension of Her, I am an absolute being!"

Hegil sat cupping his mouth, weeping salt onto his bloody face. Fallow snickered at the sight.

"It's time for your life to have purpose, mendicant. You can track so well in the Veneer, after all. *You* will be my liaison, slipping in and out, performing what tasks I need done. But I fear you will never see your precious High Devotee again. Others will bring his *request* back to him."

"What – but – who? But I have to! Who else can get in to see him??"

Fallow sneered. "You think we live here in the Veneer, only? Or under the ground, only?"

Hegil's fluttering lips slowly mustered the courage to speak. "W-Why... ?"

"What did you say, little man?"

"Why... Why do you hate us?" Cringing in anticipation of being struck, Hegil's knobby hands and their spider-like fingers lifted to limply protect his face.

"*Why??* Look at you! That's why!"

"W-We've always left you alone! Alone! For centuries! We keep to ourselves. We don't interfere with your goings on!"

"You think that expunges your deeds?! You think you're neutral and without blame because you don't *actively* contribute to the hunt?! You're passively complicit! All of you! Your entire Logical way of life!"

Confounded by Hegil's obtuseness, consumed in a jumble of consternation, Fallow strode here and there, running his hands through his thick, black hair. He swept by blades and hooked tools without a glance.

"The old Logical law of sanctification can't save you in this life, mendicant. There *is* no purification, only consequence! Defensive wars are never won. Only by extension, by motion into enemy space, do we dominate! The Kali'ka will wither to nothing if nothing is done! Your Logical world has demonstrated as much. The weak have everything, but have earned nothing, and know nothing, while *we* – the worthy – atrophy in shadow!"

"War?" Hegil seemed legitimately confused. "Corinthians don't even know that word! We're not at war with you. Logic is joy. Logic is abundance. We harm no one!"

"Logic is manipulation! Logic lies! That *is* war! You are at war with *us!* Your very existence *precipitates* war! Your entire philosophy is an insult! Corinthians know *nothing* of themselves! The face of the Goddess is lost on them! You distract and inveigle. You pass around bottled enlightenment to your masses and then claim their choices as evidence of your own goodness! They have no other way of life!" He lunged towards Hegil, snarling, "Except *us*. Except *this*. Except the Kali'ka. We are the result of *you*."

"No! You can't hurt us! His Holiness won't allow it! Only by the grace of Logos – bless his name – and through the auspices of His Holiness, have you subsisted. We know! Don't you think we're aware? The meetings, the rituals? You just don't matter enough for us to do anything!" Blood drooled from the cracks in his fingers. Every word sent him wincing. Curious. Maybe a bit of tooth was still embedded in his gum.

"Ha! Is that what you've been taught?! Only by the crushing weight of numbers and the passion of dogma, hm? You'll subsist on constancy alone? Then cling to your long-held rhetoric, mendicant, and use it as a shield against the dagger rising under your ribcage. Then, tell me how safe and immutable your empire is! Not even His Holiness will survive the coming bloodstorm!"

"You can't! You can't! The Magistrate will stop you! And if not them, what of the rest of the world? Logic is everywhere! The other nations won't let you just conquer us!"

Fallow's scarred face crinkled into an indiscernible pattern of stitchings, like a skin-mask of various patchwork pieces, sewed at contrary angles in the semblance of a man.

Conquer... Such a simplistic, short-sighted man.

"It's already decided. Mendicant Hegil! The beginning marks the end. *I* will guide us to an era where the Eternal Day of New Corinth has no meaning! The beating heart of ignorance will pop in agony, like a blood-filled balloon to gorge your golden streets red. And with the center cut out, the body will die! All will become darkness, and people will yearn for it because they will no longer be burdened by the expectations of light. And in that afflicted, mortified state, they will bear witness to their own true nature, denied for centuries by a tiny cadre of privileged, stupid beasts who worship a fabricated god!"

Hegil started scooting away on the ground and slipped into a nearby firepot. It fell over, spilling light on a laminate smear of soupy, frothy blood-mixture half-trailing off into the darkness of the night. Screams were erupting all around. Chains were violently rattling. The edges of daggers flashed in lights' edges, grinding or hacking. Hegil was staring at the blood-soaked earth, paralyzed by fear. Was his untoothed mouth babbling something?

Fallow slid towards him, giddy.

"Kali is change! Kali is time Herself, spinning the lifeblood of the cosmos in strands of death and fire. No recourse can be employed quickly enough to catch us, let alone supersede us, Her only begotten sons and daughters! We are the heirs of Earth!"

Weeping, begging, Hegil planted his forehead on the ground. The skin on the back of his neck, exposed and wrinkled, faced straight up.

Fallow lifted a foot to smash one of the frail little man's hands.

"And you, my mendicant toy, are going to help me erase Logic from Earth's memory."

CHAPTER 15
A HALO OF WHITE

Light flared through Ascendant Marin's closed eyelids, tinted red through her skin, as she took the final steps up from the basement of a Corinthian building that led out from one of Cloister Sangra's pores. Even with her eyes shut and shielded, the Eternal Day scorched her vision. The heat was damnably sweltering, even so close to the winter solstice – Advent, as Corinthians called it.

After so many years underground, Marin couldn't remember how she'd ever believed that perpetual light was *natural*, or how she'd even managed to sleep at "night." Corinthians trained themselves to relentlessly check the clock. Once it was compline, they knew it was time to sleep.

Marin huffed in frustration and smoothed the edges of her blood-hued dress … the same dress she wore when she first met Elara in that Levident, years ago. Only by focusing on the task at hand did the muddled mess of thoughts and feelings inside her come to resemble any semblance of clarity.

Elara, again… Of course it's you, again! Another fiasco. Almost murdered? In the cloister?

Cracking her eyes open, Marin found a mirror in the clutter of the building and double-checked the makeup covering her yantra before settling into the Corinthian demeanor she adopted whenever she left Sangra to cloth herself in the role of advocate: blank eyes; face vapid but vaguely contented; steps bouncy from unfiltered glee. What was her alias this time, for this coven? Oh yes – Orchid. Adherent Orchid.

She stepped out from the building into the Eternal Day and closed the door behind her. After several minutes – when she was able to not blink for at least twenty seconds – she slipped from alley to alley and out into the well-populated bustle of Market Canal, keeping an eye on the rooftops above for comeyes. Flo-globes flit everywhere in flocks, as usual, blaring announcements or sacred music.

She turned down road after lane after avenue, passing Corinthian after Corinthian who had no idea that she was any different from them, had no idea that she was *gray*. The place was as banal and senseless as ever. They would likely take her pale skin for one of those artificial whiteners that was en vogue during her generation; at least the presumption would fit. The cloisters slowly sucked the bronze tone out of the skin of anyone who lived there long enough.

Marin focused on the task at hand. Only by finishing the upcoming task could she shift to the undertaking after. As she walked, Marin's thoughts fell inward and she found herself dwelling on the same chain of conclusions that last possessed her.

Elara attacked, and what did she do? Run and hide just like she'd done before. Be the whitecap that overturned their already tenuous cloister-bound life, and then vanish to escape responsibility. Again.

It was all her fault, the damn girl! Her disrespect, her insolence, her invitation to forces beyond their control. Forces that they, as Kali'ka, willingly chose to associate with, beckon, respect, perhaps ally with, but never swing the door wide to allow in.

Elara was a blind tidal wave whose undertow captured those who somehow escaped her swell and crash. No amount of talent or insight would change that. Whatever happened to her, she brought it on herself!

Even as these thoughts took shape, a tiny voice within Marin chastised her. A younger voice. A less bitter voice. No, it said. No one deserved to be shamelessly murdered. Especially without warning or a chance to defend yourself.

It was petty to lose sight of the overarching implications of what had happened. An armed assassin had somehow managed to infiltrate Sangra, enter the Codex itself, with the sole intent to murder one of their cloister's most renowned members, in an act where the circumstances surrounding the attack were overflowing with striking unknowns.

How they even knew the relevance of Elara to their cloister was a mystery. Four years prior at Selenist, the last ceremony where all the Kali'ka met, Elara was just another mid-level adherent, albeit one with the potential she'd come to show. And, Elara hadn't advocated for anyone yet – she hadn't been an ascendant long enough to – so she should have been completely hidden to anyone outside of Sangra.

That was just it – Marin couldn't begin to think beyond her own dumbfounded incredulity, which was doubly consternating. Even now, several days after the attack, she couldn't select which piece to focus on, because they were all equally baffling: the man in Advent Square; the assassin and the weapon he wielded… And the antecedent to it all – the horror of whatever happened when Elara donned the mask of their Goddess at the Gehana.

The gears needed to fit, to be constructed into a cogent machine of reason. But it was too much, too much, especially when compounded with the potential disaster facing their order. The rift. The divide. The *schism*. Even though the words were real and their truth was apparent, the eternally staunch skeptic inside Marin refused to accept them as fact.

But this was her strength. Her specific talent and the root of her fortitude: *disbelief.*

Above it all, like a revolving cipher of sanity, Marin heard her own fears spoken to her in Elara's iron voice, drifting in and out of consciousness, locking and splitting, fracturing before reassembling again.

An inner layer. Deeper workings. Inner and outer. Rise to the surface. Like heat and water. Layers. A deeper purpose. Specific and misleading. To manipulate. Corrupt. Dissemble.

Marin knew that it was all related to the man in Advent Square and his brazen agitation of Logic and its citizens. *We respond, they respond. Then we respond, and they respond.* Soon, it would be unclear who struck first.

Something was already sprouting in the populace, just like in the cloisters. Something was different. Skewed. Tiny tugs along the edges of the eyes. Too-quick glances when exchanging goods and talking in small circles along the side of the street. Nervousness. Hairline cracks were spreading along the shell of New Corinth's collective mind.

Should she stop by her chalet along the outskirts of the Uppers? Check on the residence, make sure all was in order with those correspondences who only knew her by her Corinthian aliases? No, no – she wouldn't succumb to the same paranoia. She'd only carry it with her and pass it along like a contagious whisper fuming through Cloister Sangra.

If there really was another group of Kali'ka out there, then their strategy was clear. They were forcing an attitude of fear. Fostering a reactionary position. On both sides. *All* sides. They, the other, what – Group? Faction? Sect? – were seeking some specific reprisal. Watching and waiting even while deceiving. Not a small, tiny band of rogues, either, but a well-organized movement with focused leadership.

Marin and those in Cloister Sangra were too far behind. They lagged behind their adversaries. Behind *them* – the others. How could this have happened to their order? Maybe Elara's assassin hadn't infiltrated from anywhere. Maybe the assassin had been waiting in the shadows of Sangra for Kali knows how long, primed and coiled, relying on some unseen cue, some cloaked code transmitted in secret to advance a grand, divisive plot.

That was why Marin must find an answer for herself. She had to confront Elara one-on-one, in private – *consult,* perhaps, would be the word she used – straightaway after finishing aboveground. Elara wouldn't like it, but then again, the girl rarely liked being challenged.

Girl... Girl... The word repeated itself in Marin's mind, as she ran headlong into her memory of the first time she met Elara.

...The Leviden. The thrum of bone-throbbing music. The flickering, multihued strobes. The rows of fleshports. The stench of sex masked by profuse fragrant oils. The effervescent tang of Levitant drifting from sloppily inhaled misters. The light glimmering through the curtains of lush, private compartments.

Separate from everyone, leaning against a wall, sulking, staring out into the slithering mass of bodies slipping and squirming on the floor, a young woman stood with a gorgeous mane of earthen auburn hair wrapped around her like a lush vine. Making no attempt to mask the depths of her disdain. Boldly displaying her dissident emotions for anyone with eyes.

She stared straight into the face of what she hated – the shade of her own inner darkness – implacable and unflinching...

From that moment, Marin knew Elara was already Kali'ka in her heart. Marin understood, in that single frame of time, the core of the young woman who'd she taken into their order. She knew, even then, that one day Elara would peel away layer upon layer of ascendancy with ease, and outstrip her. Outstrip *all of them.*

In all of their covens, all of their training, all of her tutelage, it was as though Marin had done nothing more than remind Elara of what she already knew. Elara had likely inspired Marin more than Marin had aided Elara.

But that kind of burden ... the burden of awareness, the burden of exception, marked Elara indelibly. It left her overly bitter, overly severe, overly soon.

Great Mistress ... have I steered myself wrongly? I'm the one responsible for bringing her into our fold. The choice was mine, as advocate... Her actions are also my weight. My burden.

Marin had been there at the Gehana when the Earth trembled, in the back corner, along with the rest of them. She'd been present on the day when Kai'ka wailed and lurched on the floor in agony, and their Goddess breathed in human form in front of their eyes.

All the evidence Marin needed had been right there in Elara's face when she yanked the mask of the Goddess from her face and flung it to the floor.

...The eyes of striated jade, blazing bright enough to dim the paltry flames of the room. The fury. The intelligence. The restrained power. The proof of ten thousand generations and their cumulative strength to survive, stringing back to the beginning of their shared human lineage...

Elara was the evidence of will. The fortitude to wrench free of the shackles of dumb thought. To howl in defiance at the controlling forces of pain, pleasure, and death. To heave them aside and reach to the realms of the gods. To smash the stars themselves and rupture their fiery matter in a conflagration of kinetics that matched the nucleic fire of a single woman's heart.

Girl? No... She was no girl. Woman. *Goddess.* A maelstrom to be always respected, often feared ... and likely avoided.

And Marin had turned on her.

Marin had antagonized her, and she had to make good on it. To reconcile with their most powerful ally, and bring her to the Kali'ka as the leader they needed. Maybe ... maybe that was her true purpose, finally. Maybe Elara was *exactly* what they needed.

After the coven, though. First things first, then the rest. Obligations must be fulfilled.

Marin turned right at an intersection and followed several more landmarks to arrive at the back door to a fabric shop, a custom tailor who specialized in poly-vicose undergarments. At least, that was who locals knew him as.

As Marin entered the shop and closed the door behind her, she felt her feet involuntarily slow to a stop. Empty. No one was there. Evercracks near the ceiling emitted the Eternal Day in their typical, even shine.

Where was her coven? Where was Adherent Forsythia? Where were the rest of them?

Marin's instincts rose to a series of pitched screams, but she cut each exhortation down. She denied the urge to ... run? Why would she need to run? There was no danger. She saw nothing!

And then, against an armoire – a glitch in the room's unbroken light. A patch of shadow, completely still.

Marin's eyes blossomed wide. She took a step back, preparing for something of which she had no proof.

The shadow shifted and exploded from the wall to sprint directly at her, two hands like claws reaching towards her throat.

A person, clothed in the gray of the Kali'ka.

Marin dropped her center, planting herself, while trying to hasten her mind and reconcile disbelief with action. *Now? Here? What's going on?*

Cradle the Sun. The kana snapped into place without thought. Marin lifted her arms to block her attacker's hands while pivoting her body to face behind her. She dropped her weight, projected her arms forward, and cut down. The figure flipped over, flew through the air and crashed against the wall.

It was only then that Marin saw the second assailant.

By the time she realized what was happening, it was too late. She rammed an elbow towards the second assailant's face, but he had already circumvented it. A tremendous force gripped her head. Panic consumed all of her attempts to react. She knew what to do, how to save herself, but her body failed her. Age won.

Her skull smashed against the crimped, synthstone wall. A dull thud and a deep crack boomed. Sound winked away. Sight receded and bloomed like the flash of a spinning lighthouse. Her cheek and temple twisted at the behest of an iron fist that ground her head into a surface that didn't yield. Flesh tore, pain cried. Fingernails stabbed the skin of her cheek, gripping and pressing deeper, harder. Somewhere inside, a singular mote of awareness cried out, horrified at the mortal distress being done to her body.

Marin's conscious mind roiled on a windblown thundercloud like scattered leaves.

No! Kali take these bastards! Curse me! Too slow. Fatigued. Dulled. Distracted. Not paying attention. Alone. Sight obscured. Guard was down!

And underneath, a layer of word-thoughts floated like driftwood, clear and lucid as the light of a waking dream.

…Strike at the spot 'cause no one's there. Slip under the skin. Tear and wrap. Replace my face with the face of my enemy. Make me strike at the face of myself…

Inos had been right, she realized. It was too dangerous to go to the surface. They'd been compromised from the inside out. Why hadn't she listened? Oh why?!

They found my contact! Followed her back here! My coven – my fault. On the heels of the assassin… the perfect time! A diversion for a diversion for a… oh Kali! I have to help them! I can't leave yet! More time! Someone –

– Elara! Elara, help –

In the middle of the never-ending white of the Eternal Day, everything fell to darkness.

CHAPTER 16
COMMUNE

Elara gasped as her lungs snapped open and her eyes popped wide. A slightly fungal, mineral odor slipped in and out of her nostrils as she drank in the frigid, dank air of the Chamber of Sarcophagi. The twelve upright forms of the sarcophagi rose in the darkness like a field of pillars – null spaces in the air that reflected no light. Only the twitching, overlapping shadows from the Undying Firepyres, roaring and crackling, allowed them to be seen in contrast with the floor. That, and the meager torch she brought with her.

The Sixth Arteriole, one of twelve entryways to the Chamber of Sarcophagi, seemed like the best choice to enter by. Less foot traffic. Less witnesses. Fewer complications. The chamber should be empty for some time.

The Kachina stewarding the sixth entrance said nothing and did nothing. He simply continued stoking and tending his firepyre. His ovular, white mask stared at her blindly through tiny holes for eyes. His breath rattled shallowly through the mask's thin slit.

At least the Kachina would never, *could* never, reveal what happened in the chamber. They were living beings without a voice. Able to listen, but unable to communicate. Unfazed by the pain of thrashing cinders. Stifled by the heat of a mask. Bodies sore and burning from relentless movement. Restricted. Shackled. All for the will of the Goddess.

In their slow, endless churn, their mad tedium and their willful enslavement, Elara saw herself – chained to a wheel of smoldering purpose that spun inexorably, inevitably to this exact moment, in this exact place. She could only affect what could hear her voice, what could see her face, and what her hands could touch. She was blind to the greater confluence of circumstances. Beyond the ability to intercede. Too many points needed her. Too many places required her presence.

A dark hemisphere of whispers and grim intentions encircled their order and encroached on their way of life. *Fallow.* That was his name, Charlotte had said. The one who trained lunatics and then handed them weapons to slay strangers like pigs. Author of their divide. Arbiter of the threat that pursued them relentlessly.

He coiled through the very stone of Sangra, through the soil between cloisters, and grasped them all – grasped *her*, specifically – tearing away their haven. No good choices could be made. No place was safe.

This is what happened when masters of secrets turned on each other: *nothing* was transparent, and everything was suspect. What was skillfully buried stayed adequately covered, but resoundingly alive.

Elara was left with no other choice but the most extreme. Her body was a tool. She was a shield to use against the enemy. Nothing more, nothing less. None of them could afford anything otherwise.

Charlotte deserved more. Her bright, expressive eyes were due purer things. Her pale, unblemished skin – soft like a whisper, airy like her flower-scented hair – was owed something greater than the darkness of a broken Corinthian family and cursory visits to an underground nightmare.

Soon, little one – I'll make this world safe for you... For all of us. I swear it.

Elara stepped through the field of sarcophagi, passing by the spot where she'd sat with Inos, Brae, Marin and Oren in the Coven of Ascendants. At the direct center of the chamber, where leylines converged, from pores to Undying Firepyres, to sarcophagi, through the five points of ascendancy, she stopped and waited, gazing through the crags and cracks of the black stone underfoot. Darkness lay thick like the mist of a pre-dawn morning. She laid her torch on the floor and waited.

Below her feet dwelled manifest, crackling energy. A conflux where Kali and Her celestial pantheon had more space to flex and breathe. It called to her, that realm below, where sights dwelled unseen. It charmed with vapors of violence that rose to slither their way through her chest and sight, leaving the imprint of a black, lovely, horrible seduction.

The mask and blade of Kali were down there, entombed under the stone floor. Expectant. Waiting for her – only her, it felt – same as when she wielded them at the Gehana.

Softly, Elara ran her finger across the object hidden in her left sleeve, like her tongue across sweet skin. Its flat, thin surface stayed cool in the dark. Metallic. Unfeeling. She flexed her hand, feeling the painful ache through her bones, the torn skin spread over her knuckles. Darker bruises were giving way to layers of purplish yellow.

It was in her blood to fight. It was her nature to harden. She and the Great Mistress were one, in this way. Or at least, she'd fought for so long, so hard, that she'd convinced herself that there'd never been another choice. Fight and suffer, or capitulate and suffer.

Such a choice was no choice at all.

She looked out towards the Kachina, sensing a strange kinship with their mute figures. From where they were standing, light-blinded by plumes of flame, they would see Elara only as a vague impression. As unidentifiable as themselves. Equally unknown. Equally anonymous.

These were the ones she was left with. The only ones she could keep close – the faceless. They were the only ones she would trust herself around. They were the only state she could aspire towards

"Kachina," she intoned. "Leave me."

Stutters in movement betrayed their shock at the breach of silence. They knew full well the severity of what could happen if they left their duties and the light of the firepyres cooled to mere cinders.

"Leave me, I said. Now." Elara reached to pull her hood back, loosing her signature mahogany hair. Her eyes glinted in the firelight. If they didn't recognize her before, there was no mistaking who she was now.

After a moment, one of the Kachina lowered her rod. One by one, the others followed, reluctantly and jerkily as though their puppeteers' arms grew tired. They turned to their respective pores, took several moments to empty their minds, and vanished.

Alone in the center of the chamber, Elara began her kanas, just like any other time of practice. One by one, she entered and exited the full 72 hand positions, transitioning fluid and unbroken like slowly unwinding yarn. Hands to hips to feet, she slid and stepped across leylines invisible to the eye, punctuating her forms at key indices, facing into the chamber's darkness at each cardinal direction – north, south, east, west – then at each point of a nonagon, sliding along adjacent lines to the next set of loci, then at each point of a pentagon, onward through various shapes, inward and outward, across and through.

Each form had to be impeccable, each curve artfully shaped, each angle nimbly cut, or else she'd finish and nothing would happen. This is how the Stabat knew if she was indeed ready to don the mask and blade.

She kept her breathing even and her stance wide, empty of mind, full of body. At the end of the last kana, *Crown's Light,* she drew her feet together, exhaled, and closed her hands in front of her navel in a single, conjoined fist.

Instantly, the ground shook. A massive upheaval shuddered through the chamber. The stone floor cracked, and a black line severed the stone underfoot, in the center of the chamber. In layers, the megalithic blocks of the floor slid down, descending in an ear-splitting grind.

The tremors stopped, revealing rudely hewn steps leading down into a devouring darkness. Neither the light of the Undying Firepyres nor the torch in her hand could penetrate the pure sanctity of shadow.

The Well of Kali awaited. Elara stood at its edge, feeling its stony maw drawing her in. It sucked her down and collapsed her senses into one, compulsive, intractable *need.*

The gaping chasm was one more piece of evidence of the knowledge of the cloisters' progenitors. Their understanding of the currents of life and death, Illusion and Creation, energy and matter ... time and again proved unparalleled.

The Stabat, the only ones who might know more – if they indeed were conscious of such things – would never reveal their secrets, no more than they would their own origins.

The restless, dire presence inside of Elara quieted. It felt soothed, so close to the Well. The relics of Kali reverberated from their shrine below. They beckoned, cunningly. It was as though they were the end goal desired by her otherworldly, fire-streaked visions. She felt as though she'd never taken the mask off, but kept it grafted, in spirit, onto her flesh, sealing her to a terrible, unbreakable pact. The sword, she felt, was an extension of her – a tangible afterimage that shifted in purpose along with her own inner changes. *She* was the true sword.

Inos couldn't help. Brae couldn't help. Marin, most of all – floundering and lost in murk – couldn't help. No one and nothing else could be relied on except Kali. They never had.

Elara would commune with her true mother, human to god, woman to woman. She would re-attach herself to her original purpose: to rend the poisoned manacles of Logic; to sunder the bondages of self-slavery; to carve them out, pluck them from her chest, and stamp them to an obliterated nothing; to pour into their place enough cruel fire to determine for herself who she would be and what she would do.

Dire forces lived within, hungrily awaiting invocation. Sight beyond sight was hers and would be, again.

Only as long as the firepyres burned, she reminded herself. That was the cut-off. If anything went wrong, no one else would have to suffer for it. No one would be able to enter or exit the Chamber of Sarcophagi again. The chamber would become just another tomb for one who'd flared like the sun, but left nothing behind.

One foot in front of the other, she descended into the pit, slowly, holding her torch aloft, sensing the long, thin object in her sleeve. She had no idea what would happen. She only knew that waiting accomplished nothing.

Soon, her body was engulfed by shadow, and her thoughts and intentions were committed to an impenetrable, suffocating shadow.

***

"Fire destroys the old life."

Kneeling in the Well of Kali, Elara and thrust both arms in the air, wrists up, letting her sleeves fall to her shoulders.

The dagger in her hands gleamed frigid in the meager light of her torch, crackling on the floor. In front of her, the fanged, howling mask of Kali and the Her curved, single-edge blade hung along chains of silver bolted across the thirteenth and final sarcophagus, focal point for the Great Mistress as she moved between realms.

In her mind, Elara rehearsed the dagger's motions, the sweeps and contours, the looseness of the wrist, the firmness of the fingers, the words to be recited.

The shape of the inscription mattered, yes. The location mattered, as well. But, the substance mattered most. Brae always said so. And in the cloister of blood – Cloister Sangra – she herself would be the substance, imbued into the rite as a living, breathing participant. An emergent rite, a new rite birthed in her mind, cobbled together by scattered teachings, fragments of parables, the curves of yantras, and the flow of kanas.

"Blood is the path to new life."

Elara turned the dagger downward and pressed its fine point to the sensitive, vulnerable skin of her inner forearm, directly aligned with the yantra on her palm – all the while, staring across the pool of water towards the mask and blade of Kali.

A stream of words flowed through her mind like the rustling of a deep undercurrent that barely churned the surface.

...The moon is the shape of the mirror. The image of a god, forever forward and forever behind. Image and source, reflecting themselves without origin. Close the gap, and you will see through the back of the mirror to what lies behind...

The darkness around her bristled and crackled with buoyant energy. It knew what she wanted more than she did. It tickled behind the ear, coaxing things, demanding things.

"Shadow is where She dwells." Elara's voice quavered.

A push, a pinch of pain – to which her refused to react – and the tip of the dagger slipped through the sheer, smooth skin of her inner forearm. A small bead of blood bloomed at the tip of the dagger. Perspiration welled on her forehead and slid down her temples and cheeks.

...I project, and see myself resting on the surface of the water. Pale and quivering, waiting to wane...

The rise and fall of Elara's chest, the expansion and contraction of her lungs, each breath, one by one, dispersed layers of thought and sensation, stripping her to the skin of her unconscious. She milled with the brew of elements, body reflecting stone, stone mirroring body.

"To shadow I must go. To shadow I must go. To shadow I must go!"

In one motion, she bore down and jerked the dagger towards her. Her flesh gave way like plowed soil. The shock of pain swallowed her scream. Her wounded arm and its white-knuckled fist quivered uncontrollably.

"Come to me ... You who are dark and powerful!"

Without lifting the blade, she carved a second curve. A shuddering gasp rattled her chest.

"Strike my ego dead!"

Another slash and arc. A searing burn rose in her flesh. She could barely breathe.

"Let my fire join with Yours…"

She raked the dagger right, then hooked it left. Spidery fractures of red-rimmed flesh glared up at her.

"Let My face become Your own!"

Once, twice, two swift rips tore. Blood welled up. Agony swelled to numb her arm. Saltiness leaked from her eyes.

"Hail Kali, the Shadow Slayer! Show me! Show me!!"

One final tear through the same trench as the first, except away from her, and the dagger fell from her hand to clang on the stone floor. She lurched, swayed, and huddled over herself on the floor of the Well, blood drizzling from the trenches in her arm to drip into a splotchy puddle.

Somewhere in memory, she remembered the exact combination of feelings at her initiation, years ago.

Anguish swam through her in a flowing headiness. Her focus collapsed, her vision blurred, faded and swooped. Shadows crept around the periphery of her sight. The storming, electric pain in her arm arced through her shoulder, torso, from skin to core.

"In darkness, your eyes shine, oh Kali…" Her jaw and tongue moved by themselves, drawing words from an unknown, empty source. Further and further, her senses dulled and shrunk to a far-flung fleck. The room dimmed. Light washed away to a shriveled, gray pallor.

"…Tilt the wheel to carry us onward…"

Darkness swelled to engulf the air. The air negated into the surrounding darkness, imploding to become nothing.

"...Over the ocean of birth and death."

The darkness bubbled and pressed, melting and solidifying into shapes both horrifying and familiar...

The Stabat. All of them. The entire host from all three cloisters, standing in a semicircular ring with her at the keystone. Enclosing her, there in the dead dark.

But ... no, not all of them. There was a gap. Only eleven. One... one was missing.

They stepped towards her, hoods forward, hands in sleeves. They surrounded her and the small pool of water. From a remote, paralyzed orbit, Elara eyed their anemic, clammy flesh. All the leaden white, waxen and translucent in the moonlight. Splotching the darkness with pallid blurs.

Great Mistress.

As one, their voices rasped inside Elara's mind. She heard their coarse, grating words, though their lips never opened.

"Old ones, you still answer My call." Her body moved independently, like during the Gehana. Her voice echoed deeply, at a pitch not her own. She watched herself, alone and cold, like a prisoner wedged in a distant fragment of self.

"Speak plainly. The other place beckons, and My Vessel has much left to do."

Great Mistress, the true image clings to life after death. The Stabat hissed like one great snake. As always, they spoke in conceptual, cryptic language and semi-formed ideas, like an open tunnel to the unconscious.

This time, though, she heard through the syntax to the essence below. Their words were simple, cogent ... almost like a child's.

Elara's lips parted of their own volition. "This is as expected. Her will reflects My intention. The divide between realms is but a pane, membranous and flexible. Whoever rejects her, rejects Me."

The transition of ages looms. Realms collide.

"The end remains the same, regardless of the path. I will be there in the final hour. What news is this?"

The great wheel passes a single point, infinitely.

"This is why I was birthed. This is My purpose. The form that the daemons take doesn't matter. Their death is pre-supposed."

Presence cannot be filled by what is pre-existent. Another rushes to fill the gap.

"I will know it when I see it, this new enemy of Mine, just as the Bloodseed knew Me. The time of the sword is upon us. My face will be known to all, again."

Nothing cannot come from something. Two points are required to portray contradictions.

"My successor will carry us forward to that point. She will soon reside here, in the realm of Creation. We will let their Her risk what She chooses. Her coming burden brings all points together."

Yes, Great Mistress.

"Leave me now! My Vessel will arrive soon, and I must return to see her."

Yes, Great Mistress.

With that, the Stabat bowed in unison and took a single step backwards. A chant rose from their motionless lips to scrape across the interior of Elara's skull, where she screamed and struggled vainly.

In darkness, your eyes shine, oh Kali...

A bleary, swaying dizziness raveled Elara's body. Her consciousness expanded, clamped in place but accelerating outward.

Tilt the wheel to carry us onward...

Beyond body, beyond room, beyond sky and stars, outward she coursed while inward she fell, down, down into nothing.

Over the ocean of birth and death...

Mind evaporated, consciousness dissolved.

You are the heat below.

CHAPTER 17
THE FIRE WITHIN

*U*nder a thickly red, storm-torn sky, ragged with clouds that raced in streaks of burnt orange and blonde-tinged rust, Elara pressed against the gale-force of wind, grit and heat. Fiery meteoroids like bloody drops barraged the scarlet dunes around her, leaving magma-charred pockmarks rimmed by molten spillage.

Clutching her gray robe, shielding her face for protection in a wind-whipped hood, she drove forward one foot at a time. Pockets of crimson earth gave way with each step and burdened her burning muscles more and more. Each breath was an inhalation of soot-laden pain.

The dead spread across the dusty dunes like unmoving waves of ruptured flesh, torn faces, and split bones. The blood from their desiccated, empty shells had long since soaked into the dust, painting the horizon red, marring the sky with the vapors of its stench.

Only she stood. Only her.

How long had she been here? How long before her body quit? She had no memory of arriving, and could foresee no end to her staying. There was only constancy, persistent as a wheel. A perfect circle of endless, boundless time. Only the goal. Only the top. She must get there. She must!

There, in the distance, it grew steadily in size – the rise that started small and climbed upwards beyond sight. The jagged peak that breached the unbroken sky like a cracked bone from the tissue of land.

In dreams, she'd seen it countless times. Since the night of the Gehana and perhaps before … streaming back beyond time and memory. It beckoned. It tethered her insides like barbed rope that coiled around itself and tugged her deeper, further. There, she would find it. The source, the font. Her focal spark. Kin to bedlam within and mayhem without.

Reaching the mountain's toothy face, she gripped and hoisted, hand over hand, higher and higher, robes flapping wildly within enflamed, turbulent swirls of copper and orange fibers of light and dust. The plains and their gouts of fire and their heaped dead spread wider and further below.

One final pull, and she mounted the cliff edge. The apex of the mountain flattered into a small plateau.

Flush against the utmost edge of a far cliff, framed against the crimson-slashed sky, the solitary figure of a woman knelt staring off into the distance.

Etched into her ashen skin was a tapestry of dirt-caked gashes, raw abrasions, and bloody bruises. Her white fur belt was torn and matted with crusty gore. Her right hand leisurely hefted a single-edged saber, dented and dully gleaming through a mask of scratches and stains.

In a single movement of grace and control, she rose to stand. Like a pillar of alabaster, she stood completely motionless except for the slightest swivel of a head surveying the wasteland spread below. Wrapped within the wind-blasted summit, her mane of wavy, jet black hair whipped wildly behind her bare back like a war banner.

She opened her mouth to speak and the air boomed as though struck by a hammer. The ground throbbed like a gong. Her voice thrummed within, deep and dense as stone, yet mellifluous and light as air.

"I did it... There is no one left."

Elara steadied her feet, uncovered her ears, and shouted, "Who isn't left? What is this place?! I – I've been here before!" Her voice was consumed in the storm, inaudible even to herself.

The wistful thundering of the alabaster woman continued, "Those who I have not killed have fled. Those who have fled will not live long. But this... this is what I wanted. This is what they asked for."

"What did they ask for? What are you talking about?! I'm standing right here! Answer me!"

"... Now there are no lovers, no rivals, no enmity, and no hope.

Nothing can hide, so all is revealed. In my absence, they sleep, those fraudulent seers. Soon, though ... soon I can join them. Soon, I can die again, and kill anew."

"What are you talking about? Please, tell me why I'm here!"

"The other place beckons. By need I am summoned. And in turn, so are you. Time, though limitless, draws nearer."

"What are you talking about? Answer me! What's going on!?"

"You... You are a living record. You are a monument to our boundless power, and a testament to our limitless ego. You are the memory of what remains of this place ... Vessel."

At the utterance of that final word, Elara's heart plunged into an icy pool of irrational terror. Encased in blackness below, frozen within the word's depths, steeped within the confines of its consonants, tones, and stresses, brimmed the answers she sought. Unseen, unknown, quelled, yet howling for light.

"But now you must leave. Leave and show them. And if I gaze at you, do not gaze back. Even for one such as you, this place is dangerous now. It is not yet time."

"I can't! Not yet. I need to know –"

"Leave!"

"No! I can't leave yet! Not until –"

"Leave!!"

The ivory body spun to face her.

Elara gasped as she took a step backwards and stumbled to one knee. Solid black eyes of burnished obsidian bore down on her, from sockets dry as sandpaper, cracked and bleeding. Those glinting nuggets were a dead, chiseled mockery of the blazing, animal fury rending their owner's face.

And that face; oh Goddess... Low hairline... Rosebud lips... Bobbed nose... Heavily knit brow... High, firm cheekbones...

It was the face of a fox. A face barely recognizable, though intimately known.

Her face. Her – Elara Aeve.

"Leave, Vessel! NOW!!"

In the middle of her shriek, the alabaster woman's torn lips twisted and spread wide. From the depths of her maw, a brilliant volume of light *rushed to engulf the hilltop and blast it with radiant power.*

The blinding, searing torrent consumed Elara in white-hot agony, skin to bone. Her screams were lost before they were heard.

Phosphorous fire engulfed the illusory world.

***

In front of the cavernous, rocky entrance to the Well of Kali in the Chamber of Sarcophagi, Ascendant Inos prowled back and forth, faced off against a mob of at least twenty Kali'ka. All of them were speaking over each other, some yelling towards him with stabbing fingers, some gesturing aggressively towards those nearest them.

In the middle of them, Ascendant Oren stood hunched, palms out, simpering – corralling and herding like a ringleader, crooning to some, whispering to others, placating with upraised eyebrows *and an expression of likely, but vague acquiescence.*

Kali's Eyes…! What is he doing? This is exactly what we don't need right now. This is exactly what our enemy wants.

"Where is she?" One of the adherents yelled at Inos.

"We know she's here!" Another shouted.

"We have no right to intrude on the business of ascendants!" This from a woman in an opposing cluster. "She's earned our trust by now!"

"She's violated the chamber! She has to be down there! We know it!"

"If she's even alive! Ascendant Inos won't let us down there!"

"We can't go down there! We can't risk it! The Stabat are watching! They're always watching!"

Inos observed them all through a detached, shocked disbelief. It was all wrong – all of it. Impossible, surreal, forced and artificial. There was no reason – no reason! – why it had to come to this. Simply by a confluence of circumstances, leading to misinterpretation upon miscommunication upon misevaluation, growing, billowing like the firepyres ringing the chamber. Set to distend and explode and wash them all dead.

He couldn't afford to succumb to the indignation that flared within, sharp and scorching. Not here, not now – not when they needed him to be controlled and contained, more than ever. He could only watch, wait, and protect – those were his functions.

Still, the tiny scars across his face trembled from restrained anger.

"It's the relics! The mask and blade. She's after them!"

"It's just like the Gehana. She'll kill us if we let her loose! She has to be stopped!"

"She's always sneaking around! She's hiding something!"

"Right when Ascendant Marin goes missing, she shows up here? We all know they didn't get along!"

"She *has* to be up to something, down there in the Well! It's too unlikely of a coincidence!"

"You can't know that. We don't have enough evidence to know the reasons for her actions!"

"Ascendant Marin could have left to work with the dissidents! Ascendant Elara could be trying to stop her!"

"If she really is responsible for Marin's disappearance, we should be running in the other direction! What is this mob going to accomplish?"

"It's clear that she's a danger to us! Look at the Gehana. Then the assassin. Then *this?* Ascendant Inos, we need to do something before things get worse!"

The Kachina around the chamber didn't budge or deviate from their tending of the firepyres. Inos almost regretted bringing them back, countermanding whatever Elara's orders were and potentially undermining her purpose for being there. When his conclusions had led him to the Chamber of Sarcophagi in pursuit of her, he'd been horrified to see the Kachina standing outside, and the firepyres mere minutes from winking out.

That was two days ago.

In the intervening time, the reverent curious among their order had metastasized into the vocally belligerent. Even among the Kali'ka, the synergistic swell of paranoia had seeded itself firmly. The children of Kali, reduced to mania. The offspring of the most high Goddess, crumbled into bickering toddlers. Anxiety about the dissident faction, fear about intruders within the cloister… It was all simply too much for them to handle.

No, Inos thought … not even they were immune to such things.

The Kali'ka continued arguing amongst themselves, Oren chief among them.

"We are *owed* an explanation! That's not too unreasonable!"

"Forget about explanations. She should just leave. Get out of here!"

"Ascendant Elara is the only thing protecting us from the other group! We need her!"

"How do we know she's not working *with* the other group?"

"That's crazy! She's never been anything but loyal to us!"

"She's a menace! Trouble follows her wherever she goes!"

"I agree. We can't have the situation outside of the cloister *and* this going on at the same time!"

"Ascendant Elara has earned the right to do as she pleases!"

"Ascendant Elara is a power-grabbing whore!"

At the last comment, Inos' restraint winked out. Outrage tore through him like a hurricane.

"Kali'ka!" His powerful, resonant baritone shook the chamber for seconds on end. His hood was thrown back, huddled around his neck like a lion's mane. "This is your sanctuary! You're so incensed about violating the Chamber of Sarcophagi, but look at what you're doing! You want a *reasonable* amount of conflict, is that it? You want benefits without risk? Danger is everywhere, most of all *within* – that's where you should be focused! Don't blame your own disappointment at what you find inside on one of your ascendants. Face *yourselves!* Save *yourselves! That* is why you're Kali'ka!"

At the sound of his voice, some of the more vocal adherents calmed down. Others shied away. Inos didn't allow himself to display his innermost emotions often, but when he did, everyone was caught in the volcanic fallout.

Their chagrin, though, didn't last long.

"Ascendant Inos is right. This type of persecution is exactly why we abandoned New Corinth. We can't turn on ourselves."

"We've already turned on ourselves! That man in Advent Square left us no choice. And now, we've become targeted by Logic." This from a woman towards the back, almost in tears.

"We're in greater danger down here, with Ascendant Elara!"

"Ascendant Inos, why are you protecting her? No matter how well-intentioned she is, we've seen what happens around her."

"Ascendant Aeve –" Inos raised his voice enough to suppress their outcries. "– is close to the heart of Kali. If you stand against her, I stand against you. Remember that." Icily, he lowered his voice. "And if you're foolish enough to provoke her, then may Kali claim you."

The rear of the crowd rustled and shifted as Oren squeezed his way to the front. The others spread to flex around him like a concave embattlement of robes.

"But – but…" Oren's face looked offended. "Ascendant Inos, such an unyielding position leaves us with few choices. We have to respond, in turn!"

"Oren, why…?" Inos whispered. "You understand what you're saying, don't you?"

"We have to be united!" Oren half-turned to the crowd, drawing sustenance from its encirclement, his boldness growing. "This kind of division – the kind caused by Ascendant Elara – only weakens us."

"You're telling me that we have to be united, but you see where you're standing, don't you?" Inos addressed Oren directly.

"We have to take action, Inos! We can't stop running!" Oren didn't turn to face him, but instead spoke to the other Kali'ka.

Inos noticed that the others had quieted to listen to his and Oren's exchange. Some of them started shuffling towards different directions, forming discrete, partitioned groups.

"Oren, we're already beset by a faction whose full intent is unknown, and you want us to turn on ourselves? There's no better way for us to fall!"

"We can't hide anymore! This is the first step! We've become lethargic, impotent, and ineffective. Ascendant Elara can't save us! She can only bring disaster on our heads!" Sporadic yells of support came from crowd.

"Oren, you are one of these Kali'ka's ascendants! They trust you, and they're listening to this bile you're selling!"

Oren's face contorted in anger. "What – so you think our Kali'ka incapable of understanding what I'm saying?"

"What – Don't you *dare* twist my words! You imply that I'm manipulating these people, but *you're* the one who's trying to coerce them into what to think!"

"Don't try to confuse the issue with clever speech, Inos! You've stayed silent while we've been slowly destroyed, and now you deign to tell us how to act?"

"Attacking me doesn't make your position any more correct!"

"But it *is* correct!"

"And saying the opposite of what I'm saying doesn't make your words true!"

"But they *are* true!"

"You can't hide behind rhetoric, Oren! That's all I hear. Words. And words can only protect you for a short time. You can only run from the truth for so long!"

Oren leapt on Inos' statement, making large, grand gestures. "Yes! That's exactly what I'm saying! We can't run anymore! Logic is a ridiculous farce! We must take our rightful places as heirs of Earth!"

Inos stopped pacing, instantly. His mind froze, his cold anger fled, and his muscles lost their tautness. Something in Oren's words – a twist of verbiage, a turn of phrasing – plucked at Inos' memory.

...Heirs of Earth...

Right there, Oren's outer surface shed to reveal the unnatural stillness of profound self-control. Affectation, manipulation, collusive motives: all of it brew beneath the surface. To Inos' eyes, Oren slipped out of his old skin and into a new sheath, where the possibilities, the connections, and the implications were more damning than Inos wanted to admit.

But Inos couldn't show his position, not now. He couldn't make his suspicions known, not yet. He would let Oren play his part. The man's own actions would reveal his true face, even more than they already had.

"Oren, you would only run because you haven't reconciled yourself to your own choices. You ... *have* made the right choices, haven't you?"

Oren stared back at him, detached, cruel, utterly transformed from a nervous, systematic thinker into a vicious, subtly confident presence. "I've made the choices that will ensure that we not only survive, but *flourish."*

The moment his words faded, hell erupted in the Chamber of Sarcophagi.

Screams like serrated knives burst from the Well of Kali to tear through the chamber. They echoed through the stony, frozen cloister like the wail of a thousand layered voices howling in agony. They swept around the chamber, audible to the ear but gouging at the mind like raking claws. The ground lurched and heaved in violent retches. Huge ripping sounds tore through the jagged, hematite walls. Tiny rocks fell from the shadow-cloaked ceiling overhead, bouncing and clacking on the floor.

The Kali'ka, Oren included, stared in shock, dumbfounded, unable to act. Some screamed, some dropped to the floor, huddling and covering their heads.

Inos braced himself, stabilizing his balance – balance of mind, balance of body – and turned his attention to the entrance to the Well, the source of the horrific, maniacal screams, and the seismic upheaval around them.

Below, Elara was alone with the mask and blade, communing in the dark with her mistress.

It's like the Gehana again! Great Mistress, no!

Inos dashed towards the entrance.

Oren slung a hand towards him, face screwed up in a perverse twist of terror and malice, "Inos! No! You can't go down there! You mustn't!"

Inos stopped with his foot on the steps leading down, glaring at the slithering man, no longer seeing him as fellow ascendant, but as a creature filling an empty spot of blood and loss. Writhing in their bellies, poisoning them all. An untouched and unaccountable presence.

Even as Inos' ears were split by unearthly screams, as rocks fell from the ceiling and the floor quaked, he stood firmly. The old viciousness brewed inside him – from the time he'd so deliberately submerged in Kali'ka training – the brutality that had laid dormant for nearly a decade.

"If any of you follow this coward, do us a favor and get out of Sangra. The rest of you, help me!"

With that, he leapt into the throb of darkness under the Chamber of

Sarcophagi, silently begging Kali for protection.

***

Elara's eyelids opened. Her hands were limp. Legs were limp. There was a hideous smell all around. Sour, mingled with a sizzling sound. She became vaguely aware of movement. Sound, light, heat. Everything was red. Why so red? Fire? Fire. Little flames licked around her peripheral vision. What looked like feet were stamping ... a charred bit of robes? *Her* robes?

Hands started hitting her. Why?

She lifted her own hands to fight them off and was paralyzed by staggering agony. She could do nothing but stare at a charred object reminiscent of the shape of a hand. Black with layers of red underneath, white in between.

No ... they weren't hitting her. They were snuffing her out. Extinguishing her, all the little hands.

It's my fire! Mine! Don't put me out!

"Ascendant!"

"Kali's Eyes, no!"

"What happened?!"

"Somebody run ahead!"

"Get the plastein! Now!"

"Ascendant, can you hear us?"

"Help me lift her! Help!"

All the voices sounded so distressed. What was there to worry about?

"Elara...!"

"Elara...!"

Charlotte? Was that Charlotte? *Oh, it's so nice to hear you. I wanted to talk. I've missed you... I've kept your shinsen nice and clean, like you always did.*

"Ascendant Aeve."

A different voice. Its whisper sliced through the frantic noise and clatter like a blade through still air. Elara focused on where she remembered her eyes to be, and moved them to the point of the sound.

The too-pale face of a Stabat was standing over her, it's one eye quivering as though trying to yank itself away from her.

"Ascendant, you have crossed into Circle Twenty."

Memory somehow connected with the moment. The full weight and force of the words blasted her with shock – numbing, fragmenting her mind. Flabbergasted, she remembered the premise of the twentieth circle of the Kali'ka.

...Nothing from something must go somewhere...

The hands stopped beating her. They were shouting other things now, doing other things. Some great throb coated her entire face and scalp, arms, legs, torso, all the places between.

Didn't anyone else see the damned Stabat standing over her? The mummified corpse lurching in their midst? Something was there, on its near-human face and its putty-like skin. She strained further to draw it into sight, with whatever power of motion and focus was hers.

There on its forehead, surrounding its one eye like a fan. Creases. Wrinkled skin. It looked ... worried?

Another face pushed into view. It was bellowing at the Stabat, cursing and raging. No inhibition. Good! Someone with courage. Someone who wouldn't back down. A long, fatless face with a falconesque brow gazed down at her.

Inos.

His steel gray eyes with those little blue flecks were so concerned! So stricken with fear, welling with tears of panic. Focused on her, only her. She wanted to cry, too, but the tears wouldn't come. Maybe, though, she thought, maybe he could cry for both of them.

Her eyes twitched down to Inos' arms, and in a moment of clarity, she nearly choked.

The wool of his robes was blackened and melted to his skin. His hands and arms were bloodied and red, scorched, trembling furiously. He huddled over his wounds, sheltering them, beads of sweat coming from his face.

"Elara," he managed. "We're going to help. Don't try and move."

Oh no... Why?! Why did you do it? Why didn't you leave me? Why?!

Flaming spikes drove into Elara's arms, legs, back, obliterating her thoughts. No, not spikes: hands. Grabbing. Where the hands touched, brutal pain wracked her in spreading cascades. The agony beat on her nerves and pounded down to her marrow. The hands were razors that hammered, serrated hammers that tore. Her consciousness threatened to flicker away with each shudder and tiny motion. She wasn't sure if she was awake, asleep, alive or dead.

Elara wanted to bat all the hands away like bold mites taken with gall, believing they had the right to intrude on her space. But the hands came regardless, and she remained still. In truth, she was beginning to feel nothing, and nothing felt good.

Marin, did you see my hand positions? I got all the way through the sixteenth kana. Climb the Mountain. *I made sure to focus on my posture. You think I'll be ready for Circle Seven, soon, don't you?*

Bore aloft by those Kali'ka present, Elara was risen high above their heads in a weird fetal, crooked position. Their stabbing digits dug into whatever pliable tissue was left on her. She was unsure where her robes ended and her flesh began.

"Ok!" someone yelled. The voice reached her through the bustle.

Lucrece!? You're here, too? How did you get here? I told you, you see... Don't you remember? You could've left at any time. Logic doesn't own you. You owe our parents nothing!

Jostles from the hands sent renewed torture through her being. Sight blacked out, then back in. By Kali, she just wanted to close her eyes! She could close her eyes, couldn't she?

Through will alone, she followed an impulse and turned her head to the right.

Shapes discernible as other adherents gathered from all around, reaching upwards, too far away to help those directly underneath her. All of their hands bobbed up and down, as did she, upon fingertips and palms. In a slow underwater dream, the spread hands were rising crests of fins, whole schools of fish stacked and overlapped, coasting through broad waves in aggregate formation.

There was general movement in the direction of her feet, and they all moved together, she and the hands, a graceless entity on many feet. Were they saying something? Repeating something?

It was then that she remembered what she was looking for,

superimposed in her mind amidst the probing finger-fins. The central sarcophagus, the thirteenth sarcophagus down in the Well. A doorway of absence into nothing, pushing out from nothing. Standing silent as vacant space, a thing not real created from things equally unreal, molded solely from zealous wishes secreted away from the lips of fevered, kneeling believers. She saw it directly in front of her eyes, on the other side of her mind.

With her head turned, the thirteenth sarcophagi appeared to be lying down exactly as she was. Lying down, it became carried out as she moved. She became carried out in it, on a bier of painful finger-fins, she and it held aloft in a ceremony heralding the life of one lost.

Thus she saw her future, in the blank darkness of a solitary coffin. Risen above the ground but buried below it, forever lying flat, mixed with dirt and lost memories.

In rank and file, the procession continued out of the chamber up through the corridors of Clositer Sangra, gathering Kali'ka, spreading larger the higher it grew, like a tree stretching for the buds on its own limbs, reaching out for its Goddess as She passed itself by.

A low chant continued all the while.

"Elara…"

"Elara…"

"Elara…"

"Elara…"

CHAPTER 18
PANTHEON

Rubrician Cecil peered down at the impossibly thick tome cracked open on the podium in front of him. "A reading from The Epicurial Apologia, Second Partite, Book of Manichest, Cadence 3, Dram 57. Bookpraise to Logos."

"Bookpraise to Logos." The refrain resounded through the amphitheater of Pantheon, from crystal dome to porcelain floor, five-thousand voices strong.

"Worship His name." Cecil replied, chin high.

Jacobs sat nestled in his seat of honor in the south of Pantheon, squeezing his armrests, wrinkling his nose as he eyed Cecil's annoyingly blonde hair and marginally crisp vestments. Where did the man get such a shoddily embroidered rochet? It didn't even look like actual lace!

"Worship His name."

Cecil lifted his voice to commence the Recitation, clear as glass and soothingly even. Jacobs' gaze skimmed over row upon row of scions, of all ranks from seminarian to rubrician, predictably sitting at attention from their tiered seats above.

"There came a time when Logos was sitting under a tree meditating on the nature of suffering. Recalling the teachings of his time, he wondered at the trueness of the inevitability of suffering.

'Is it truly the nature of all beings to avoid pain and suffering?' Logos pondered. 'Are pain and suffering simply unpleasant sensations, absolute

and tangible, or do we undergo pain and suffering because we struggle against the inevitable? Is it outside the self, or is it created by the self?'

In this manner, Logos sat meditating and fasting, unremoved from that very spot for 14 days and 14 nights."

The tree story again? Jacobs glowered, sunk into his seat, scrunching and releasing his toes inside his purple boots, again and again. How droll! How many years was it, now? How many times must they engage in the same useless debates about obligatory doctrinal misgivings? Curse this ritual recitation and the delay it caused!

He resorted to humming a little folk tune – *Twin Rivers Twain*, maybe? – as he daydreamed about what His Holiness' Keep looked like, within the One Hundred Diamond-Lights in the Tabernacle.

"Passersby began to spread the word of Logos' meditations, and followers began to sit with their master, to aid in his contemplation. The monarch of a nearby nation heard of these deliberations, and was distressed, as he himself saw no solution to the quandary. This monarch was himself a learned and renowned man, scholarly and skilled at the tactics of warfare."

Hadn't they already decided *not* to include this story as canon in the Epicurial Apologia? It clearly contained illicit referencing to Nihil Obstat imagery, terminology, objects and actions. Corinthians were not to be exposed to it!

Jacobs leaned forward and aggressively repositioned the gold-tasseled pillow behind his back. Once power was in his hands, he would eliminate useless exercises like this one. He would find a way to make obnoxious scions like Rubrician Cecil disappear. Or better – make them *mendicants*.

Thinking of mendicants reminded Jacobs of the only crease in the perfectly ironed fabric of his plans. He hadn't been surprised, not really, when the group of Kali'ka women – in flowery Corinthian dresses, no less! – showed up at his parish instead of Hegil with the item he'd requested. The morbid fanatics were everywhere, it seemed, robes or not.

Damn Hegil and his incompetence! He shouldn't have allowed

himself to be placed in such a position where he'd be unable to escape the Veneer. Surely, there should be ways for him to slink out after making their bargain!

Jacobs snickered to himself. Hegil *was* a mendicant, after all. Maybe he'd found his true home. Years of scraping crusty semen off the interiors of Penance booths must have left him with some perverse yearning for close contact with grime.

The cultists' request was mad, though… The *trees*?? What did it matter where the exact positions of trees throughout the city were? What was their lunatic leader thinking…? Did his mangled, mono-eyed face leave the brain behind it unable to comprehend half of what he saw?

"The monarch thought to himself, 'But in the attainment of the goal, do we not belie the struggle? Pain is the method of correcting wrongs. Is it possible to maintain that upper standard of being, of life and joy, without a contrast? We would, surely, digress into a state of helplessness and stupidity, without struggle. The answer must exist for the question to be asked. How would the question be defined, otherwise?'

The monarch decided to challenge Logos. He thought to himself, 'If this One truly is blessed with insight beyond even my ken, then I will not be allowed to kill him if I approach him with my sword. He sees all. We will know then if he is worthy to answer me.'

And so the monarch traveled with his retinue with the intention of killing Logos."

Resting his eyes on the carved marble statues ringing the inset dividing mezzanine and upper levels, Jacobs smiled and counted them one by one: Attis the Magnanimous, Mithras of Eyes Withheld, Horus of the Sun, Kirsh the Ninth Body, Iesu of One Rebirth, and of course, Logos the Word. Dozens upon dozens of incarnations of the one, true, physical Godhead.

Jacobs saw himself mingling in their ranks of fame, cast forever in changeless stone, a beautiful, marble creation streaked with lustrous white and creamy tans…

"*On the morning of the 15th day from when Logos began his meditations, as the monarch and his aides approached the tree where Logos and his followers were sitting, Logos suddenly opened His eyes, staring at the sky, proclaiming loudly,*

'*I understand! The purpose is not to avoid pain and suffering. I have asked the wrong question, and so I received the wrong answer.*

'*True joy and abundance of spirit do not require an antecedent or the memory of violence. In joy, a person will be content unto himself, as an extended state, forever. I did not even need to ask any questions. In so doing, I created the struggle. I created the split in myself for my own finite humanity to fill.*

'*This is how we initiate pain and suffering: by doubting the innate rightness of our original creation.*'"

Oh, the admiration! The accolades pouring on him like confetti! The praises sung in his name! High above New Corinth, even, Jacobs knew there was a place of light to rise to. A place amongst the heat and glare of the stars, piercing the void of space, washing everything in the same, eternal shade of perfect white.

"*At these words, the monarch fell to his knees, dropped his sword, and moaned in grief. The truth of Logos' words had cleaved his heart twain, and the guilt of his own actions consumed his being. His retinue observed in shock as he wept openly.*

'*Logos, I confess that I came here to slaughter you, so benign was your countenance and repute. I could not bear to gaze on it, for I saw myself reflected so poorly. Now I understand that I too, have asked the wrong questions and sought the wrong answers.*'"

Jacobs perked up, recognizing the parable's end. The two magisters at the massive, pneumatically powered pearl gates and the two at the rear entryway stood at the ready, while Hammar waited at his side, supremely composed as always. One after the other, Jacobs recounted the sequence of events they'd practiced.

"'If it is your will, Logos, please take my life in return. A king who cannot act as the highest of his own people does not deserve his own kingship.'

Logos smiled and spoke in sympathy.

'My Lord, the only reason you became resentful is that you allowed yourself to slip from the arms of your own bliss. You harm yourself beyond even the death of my hand or any other if you do so. Your penitent act is enough recompense, unto yourself. Go, and do all within your power to be content and happy.'"

Thump. Thud. Rubrician Cecil closed the Epicurial Apologia and lifted his voice. "On this day in the year of our Lord Logos, 1754 AE, let this year's Pantheon begin." He lifted an archaic gavel and smacked it on the wooden slab on his podium.

Jacobs opened his mouth and projected his voice outward in a pitch perfectly tuned to the point between obsequiousness and command. "I invoke the Intercessor's Missive for the right to address Pantheon!"

Hushed chatter rolled through the scions above. Rubrician Cecil eyed Jacobs before stepping back up to the podium and smacking his gavel again. "This year's Pantheon now passes to the High Devotee, Jacobs Osgood." Another gavel smack and he dismounted to take his seat.

Jacobs slipped his face into a mask of unassuming nobility, gripped his armrests and pushed himself to his feet. He lifted his chin proudly and made an ostensible show of surveying the slick mixture of metal and masonry of Pantheon, tumbling his lines through his head again and again.

It was time! This was *his* place! *His* dwelling! The realm of wordplay, dialectics, rhetoric, and the cadence of verbal rhythm. By stepping onto the floor of Pantheon, into a sphere where he commanded attention, for as long as he needed, in the exact method he deemed, guiding and directing perception from moment to moment, leading by the nose, he was entering a place where he assumed total dominance.

This was his resting space, under the watery calmness of the crystal dome overhead, within a tiny spot of serenity inside, surrounded by a horde of indistinct faces, like dots of skin-paint dabbed on the afterthoughts of heads. White with purple freckles and specks of gold twinkles splashed across a tableau of seats.

"Brothers, scions, Logicians. Heed the words of your High Devotee!"

Creaks and shuffles flit through the seats as scions repositioned themselves.

"We grow ever-nearer to Advent and the Pageant of Miracles, in a year undifferentiated from those that have come before. From day to day, our own personal richness, elation, and pleasure persist. Our wellspring, Lord Logos, continues to bless the faithful with limitless abundance. Like a master to a journeyman, we take the hands of the nations of Earth and guide them to the glory we know to be true. None of that has changed, nor will it ever change.

"Nonetheless, my brethren, we find ourselves in a situation that is unique from our counterparts of ages past."

Smatterings of whispers flew through the amphitheater.

Then came the keystone statement that Jacobs had taken longest to craft.

...frame an understated, negative statement within an earlier clause that precedes a positively-skewed succeeding assertion, that itself leads to a rebuttal of the original...

"A short while ago, during this most auspicious, most blessed Advent Season, we – the community of Logos' own scions – underwent a setback in our expansion of elation. When our dear Scion Driscoll departed this earth to re-couple with his master and Godhead, it was at the hands of a small, yet determined band of misguided charlatans. Even though we reside at the apex of history, they scrabbled high enough up our peak to touch our hem of glory! And when this troupe of madmen – who willingly reject all we offer! – made contact with our perfect and sublime scion, they could not bear the sight, for how he reflected their own lack!"

Dappled mutterings of confusion swept across Pantheon. Had they heard correctly? Oh yes! Driscoll was *dead.*

"They have remained out of sight for centuries, subsisting simply because there was not a compelling enough reason for us to allow them to do otherwise. They've been given many euphemisms. Many names, all passed down from generation to generation, embedded in the memory of our society, blackening what is pure. The cultists. The grays. The third eye. Those who dwell under our feet. Those in the serpent's bosom. But amongst themselves, they are called ... the *Kali'ka*. They worship an unreal goddess – one who exists only in their minds – a sick, twisted portrait of humanity called Kali. A creature whose essence directly contradicts the bounty of Logos. An entity of death, pain, and selfishness!"

Rumbling murmurs ran through the sea of scions as they jostled. Blurts of voices interjected loudly.

Jacobs lifted his hands, palms out, and continued to saunter leisurely. "Now, now! Nihil Obstat is kept from Corinthians, but *we* may employ them in order to understand them and act on our supplicants' behalf! My fellow scions, may you maintain your visage, lest you be removed from the state of adulation that we, as representatives of Logos, ought to espouse at all moments! Especially so, when we are in each other's company, and when we are approaching our most celebratory time of the year!"

As one, the rumbling in Pantheon slowly quieted.

"I, scions, as your High Devotee, second only to His Holiness in the holy hierarchy, have taken it upon myself to resolve this circumstance with expedience and diligence. I have elected to shield you from grim thoughts, and with my own pure visage, remain unassailably whole in the eyes of Logos, even as I traipse through dirt and mud."

No one was moving. All eyes were trained on him. He *had* them! This was it!

"I, in conjunction with the Magistrate – the Sons of David, by the old, venerable name – have fished out the pebble from our shoe. We have plucked from our side the thorn that would have driven even deeper had we not acted! We have unearthed the one who, as a vector of a much larger illness, followed through on orders from a malign, wicked overlord: a high-ranking Kali'ka who has already made himself known to us – openly and directly! – in Advent Square some weeks ago!"

Jacobs stopped and turned towards Hammer, who stood to the side near Jacobs' throne. The man didn't budge, but just stared back at Jacobs with a stony glare.

What – What is he doing?! The timing on this part is crucial!

The two magisters at the rear entrance glanced back and forth between Jacobs and Hammar. What was going on?! He was the High Devotee! They had only to carry out their orders! Jacobs ran a hand through sweat that started to creep onto his forehead, while the full body of the scions of Logos stared from row upon row above.

After several seconds, Hammar turned his head towards the magisters at the rear door and nodded. They bowed in return and exited. Jacobs exhaled in relief.

They returned wheeling some large metal contraption draped in a soft, voluminous bedsheet. Tall rods and long poles poked through the sheet like rows of toothy tentpoles.

Scions buzzed loudly, turning to those nearest to them, pointing at the strange, ungainly monstrosity encroaching on the solemnity of Pantheon. Jacobs couldn't take his eyes off the outline of what laid concealed under the sheet. He listened to the slow creak of wheels turn over themselves as the contraption slowed to a halt in the middle of the Pantheon floor.

Anxiety, powerful and fluid like a river, poured into him and seized his body; he knew the sensation by now – intimately, by name. His jaw clenched and his legs shook. He watched the tip of his trembling finger point towards the device as he strode towards it.

"Ah – and – and *here!* Here is the one responsible! The canker in our bellies! The one upon which we heap our sorrows! The one – The one – The…" He gripped the sheet and ran his thumbs across its sheer, delicately spun fabric. His voice collapsed to a whisper. "…The one we blame."

In one yank, the sheet was off and fluttering to the shimmering, tiled floor.

The scions above him erupted in a commotion of sound and fury. Shouts, clamors, and upraised fists filled their seats.

"A Kali'ka!" Jacobs shouted through the uproar.

There in the middle of the floor of Pantheon, in the hub around which the amphitheatre revolved, lay a single woman strapped to an inclined, metal rack. Hinges and brackets and spires spread across its surface. Her wrists and ankles were torn ragged from fighting her restraints. She silently sobbed as her panicked eyes rolled everywhere.

A coarse, wool robe shrouded her. Gray, with a deep hood pulled back. The robe that Jacobs had unwittingly bargained Hegil's life for. Its dark tones blended almost shade for shade with the rack.

"Yes, my brothers! I have done this! Me! I – I am the one responsible! I have brought one of them here, into Pantheon!"

Jacobs strode the amphitheater's floor, hand to his heart. "I've done this to show you that they have no power over us! They are bodies, only. They are men and women. They are flesh, like us! You see? You see these restraints? The Kali'ka bleed like anyone else! You see how they cower? They are no match for Logos! They don't have the power to undermine our society! They don't even have the power to resist! They can only lay there and cry!"

The woman sipped in quick gasps of air and stuttered through sobs. "Please, High Devotee. I'm not one of them. You know this. I – I didn't harm Scion Driscol. I received Penance daily by him! I found him, but I'm not the one responsible. I'm a pure Bride of Logos. Please. Please! I have a family, a son in estuary. He will be a scion himself when he's older!"

The sound of the woman's voice pulled Jacobs down into memory.

…*Stepping out of his flocar into the gleam of the Eternal Day, waving magisters away. Turning the corner to the front of Driscol's booth. Her, the witness, kneeling on the gem-variegated, cobblestone street. Weeping, in shambles, babbling pleas to surrounding magisters who just stood there uncomfortably, unknowing of what to do or say. She repeated the same thing over and over again, about how she'd just arrived for Penance, the same as every day before…*

And now, she lay there in front of Jacobs in Pantheon.

Petrified, terrified at the dip in his resolve, Jacobs pushed back all the harder. "This! This is the garb of our enemy! This is how we recognize those who are different from us! They embrace a perverse, warped way of life! She lays here, on a rack that has rested in the Reliquary, a silent testament to times gleaned only through the dustiest records! And now, we embrace the past this tool has witnessed! They've attacked us! They've undermined the Godhead! They've agitated the citizens of our perfect city! They've killed one of our own! We have no choice but to confront them and eliminate them! I, as your High Devotee, am willing to take this step! I will be our champion! I will be the one resolute enough to carry us forward! We must remake paradise in our own image!"

He thrust his open hand toward Grand Magister Hammar, who like a pillar of stone stayed still, with his lance driven into the floor.

"Hammar..." Jacobs breathed, "if you don't follow through on this, I swear you'll be licking shit off the streets of the Veneer within a week."

Hammar's gruff, perfectly manicured beard quivered as he ground his teeth. A moment later, he extended his electrolance forward. Jacobs snatched it out of his hands and backed away from him.

Switching his grip on the lance, Jacobs hefted it into position. The snapping, blue arcs of electricity at its tip were aimed straight at the woman's heart. She wept louder and louder, crying and blathering, and Jacobs shouted louder and louder in turn.

"Now we take our retribution, scions! We do not pardon, we do not request restitution! We take up the mantle of our forebears, and claim the heritage that has built our world! We must address this threat! We've heard the whispers! We feel the tension in our parishes, see it in the faces of our supplicants! We can ignore it no longer!"

"High Devotee! Please! I've done nothing! Nothing!!"

"We must stare it in the face..."

The woman's wide, terrified eyes locked onto the tip of the lance, and her lips begged for mercy.

"...And watch it stare back!"

Like a spear, Jacobs drove the lance at her chest.

The instant it made contact, her body convulsed and froze in rigid shock. Electric arcs danced across the metal rack, leaping from spike to spike like pylons, piercing her body, rolling across it, as her eyes rolled into the back of her head and random body parts lurched.

Jacobs twisted the lance and ground it into her like a screw.

"We must eliminate the spot within! The dark wound – it drills into our spirit! All our words... All our hatred! It festers!"

White froth billowed up from the woman's throat to pour out of her lips. Her eyelids fluttered like butterfly wings. Amongst the crackling of the lance and her stiffened body, snaps of bones peppered the air. A faint, singed odor wafted.

"High Devotee!" A booming, powerful voice rose from behind him.

"You're out there! Polluting! Corrupting! Seeking our destruction! For what?! You won't have us! No more of us! Logos! Oh Logos! Save us! Save your holy city!!"

"High Devotee! Stop! Stop!!"

The electric storm crackled and leapt. Was someone laughing? Was *he* laughing?!

"Enough! High Devotee! Enough!!"

Inexplicably, Jacobs felt his hands release their grip on the electrolance. It fell, clacked, rebounded, and clacked again on the floor before rolling away from his feet. He stood with arms outstretched, panting wildly, drenched in sweat, jaw agape.

The Corinthian woman – witness to Driscoll's bloodied booth and slumped, mutilated body – lay there on the metal rack, one elbow and one knee protruding opposite their normal direction. Neck twisted up behind, a strange bulge jutting out of its side. Eyes popped out of their sockets, clouded and bleeding. Smoke rose from the gray robe and patches of her skin. She was already starting to look like some lifeless, wax prop.

Jacobs senses' dimmed to a numb bubble that cloaked his head like a shroud. He heard, but didn't hear, the cacophonous outcries on all sides. He saw, but didn't see, the frenzied faces contorting and shouting, clambering, shoving in a desperate desire to flee Pantheon. Everything, everywhere, erupting in pandemonium.

It was the vision in Advent Square come to horrifying, true, undeniable life. Tongues, limbs, lunacy. Horrible, misshapen havoc. Jacobs' quiet place, where he and he alone was ruler, lay smoldering.

Massive, thick arms engulfed his body and pulled him away from his victim.

"No! No! I am the High Devotee! I do this for Logic! For the perfection of our empire! For solidarity! For order! For – " Jacobs howled and kicked and futilely resisted, while the dead, clouded eyes of the

Corinthian woman receded in front of him, around the corner, out of sight as he was dragged down the hall. His bucking feet squeaked and skid on the perfectly polished floor of the Conclave Wing of the Basilica Formata, to an unknown destination. He thought he heard the jingle-clomp of Grand Magister Hammar's boot buckles leading the procession.

"Hammar! Release me! Release me!! I have to go! I have to go!!"

No one answered him.

Some minutes later, when his weak, childlike limbs grew too tired to fight, and he was in a series of passageways rarely tread, the High Devotee of Logic began to weep uncontrollably, and he had no idea why.

CHAPTER 19
BOUNDLESS

Inos pointed toward the kamisheet on the wooden table in front of him, where a nearby torch cast its shuddering light. He addressed a patiently waiting adherent. "Move these Kali'ka to the alcove west of the Inner Court. Easy access to the rest of the cloister. Multiple escape routes."

"Yes, Ascendant Inos." The adherent touched fingertips to forehead and slipped away.

Inos watched him pass out of sight, in and out of pools of torchlight, before releasing a deeply held sigh. It was getting harder to maintain appearances for the rest of cloister. Brae, across the table from him, started tapping the wooden surface with his meaty fingers. A fidgety habit. Kali's Eyes, the man couldn't keep still.

"Closer together, they make easier targets." Brae's face was dour, his massive beard shrouding his features in obscurity. He kept taking little steps. Tiny muscles twitched across his arms and chest, visible through the folds of his scribe's apron and vest.

Something in what he said tickled the back of Inos' skull, but he couldn't pull it to the forefront. Fatigue and worry were killing his ability to think, no matter how trained, no matter how self-possessed.

"We have no choice," Inos breathed. It sounded trite, but true. It also grated. "There's only a little over half of us left, anyway, Brae. The cloister's almost empty."

Brae sighed. He started poking at the cracked kamisheet on the table, one of many in a jumbled stack held flat by ink bottles and rocks. "Might be better they left us, Inos, than corrupt us. Might be."

"Except that now there's more of *them*, with the dissidents, less of *us*." Inos was running a finger down the list of food in the cloister. "There's still a lot to do. What about Shaka's Rebirth? It should be tomorrow."

"Prograde? I don't know." Brae's focus was cursory.

"Perform it retrograde, because of the conjunction between Saturn and Mars. Hoods up when the death biers pass, in remembrance of those who recently passed. Their energy … passes to us."

Three Kali'ka had been killed in the coup following Elara's infiltration of the Well. Their remains would be scorched to ash during the ceremony. Moisture-less, earthen. Consumed by fire.

Oh Kali… The flames… the smell…

"It figures that Oren likes to take care of organizing this mundane shit. Supplies, schedules. Suits him." Brae's vexation was palpable, his levity feigned.

"*Liked*, Brae. Liked. Past tense."

"He might have had a valid argument for defecting, if he had to do this all day."

Inos snickered mirthlessly. In memory, he saw Oren as the man last was, pressing into the crowd of Kali'ka as Inos emerged from the Well with Elara's cindered, enflamed body in his arms. Some Kali'ka darted in to help, while others fled. Oren receded into the darkness, into the furthest corner, like a viper retracting into a nest. Hours later, they'd discovered how many he'd taken with him.

Half. He'd convinced over half. Or, half had already decided that they feared Elara too much to stay. Or more accurately, they *feared*, as a general condition, and didn't know what to do about it.

Oren had locked eyes with Inos the moment before he vanished in the crowd, his face twisted by wicked flashes of deep-seeded malice, surging and receding, swimming through his features.

Inos swore he'd never forget that look for the rest of his life.

"Inos?"

"Hmm? I'm sorry – what was it?"

"I said: we have to find out where they went. How the hell do you just vanish like that?"

"The same way the assassin got in. Pores that we're unaware of. Has to be. These cloisters are ancient. In reality, we know very little about them."

Brae grumbled, his fists growing visibly tighter. "Too bad we can't ask the damn Stabat – they're useless. Or other cloisters. Not at this point."

Inos refused to make eye contact with Brae, knowing what the man was thinking: *Mors. Or Ignis.* They'd fled to one of the other cloisters. Either Cloister Mors, situated under the Veneer, or Cloister Ignis, situated under the Leeward Quarter. Or both. An entire cloister, or cloisters, subverted and commandeered as a command center. Inos suspected the thought was true; true enough to not need to say it.

"Inos ... we saved her life. You fished her out of there, and I... Well, I did my thing."

Inos beat down the images that welled into his inner eye.

"And your hands. We saved them. Good thing we had some plastein left over."

"There's no *good thing* about it, Brae. You forced me. Otherwise..."

Inos trailed off, possessed by some strange need. He held a hand up to nearby torchlight. So strong-looking, so firm. Long fingers, wide palm. Able to pulverize flesh as easily as cradle it. Matched in deftness only by how that deftness belied its grim power.

In totality, all fingers combined could wrench a living body in two. All fingers combined could create a society. The intricacies of history, ascribed to an artful stump peculiar to their simian species. The ability to investigate, interact, manipulate, alter, rend.

...Blood and toil rests in these two sweaty hands... All those who walked before, who gripped and grappled tool and foe for the present we have...

But against some foes ... well, they were completely useless.

He'd failed. He'd failed them all. He'd failed *her*, the one who'd spared him.

"Her face, Brae... I could've done something. Gotten there sooner."

"There's no way to know that. There's no way to say what could or might have been."

"Brae, that's just it..." Inos squeezed the edge of the tabletop. "I'm not sure she *wanted* to be saved."

"Inos, listen. Elara's too stubborn to let herself die, even if she wanted to."

Inos chuckled. A valid point.

"What about –" Brae cut himself off, clearly hesitant. He settled on one word, only. "Marin?"

"No." Inos shook his head. "There's no way she sided with Oren and the others. I refuse to believe it. Elara and her, they... No. The closest families argue. There's no way. She's been taken. I know it. She's with them, Brae, sure, but not in a way that makes them allies. I just hope... Kali's Eyes... I just hope she makes it out alive."

"Kali sees you, Ascendant Noscent."

The voice came from behind them. Before Inos turned, he identified the speaker as a non-threat, chastised himself for being caught unaware, and then cut down the instinctive face/body surprise-response that leapt to action.

Turning, he affixed a look of untouchable impassivity on his face. So practiced, for so many years. The face staring back, however, did surprise him. "Adherent Cassandra... As she sees us all."

Cassandra was looking directly at him, not towards the ground. A strange shape controlled her eyes: defiant, yet sheepish. Large and determined. "Ascendant Noscent, it's ... about Ascendant Aeve."

Inos's heart surged. Cassandra would never see it. "Yes, adherent. Go on."

"When Ascendant Aeve visited the Codex, when the assassin attacked, she took spinebacks with her. I don't know if they're relevant or not."

At mention of the assassin, Brae caught Inos' eye. The assassin's carved corpse was decaying as they spoke. The man hadn't yielded anything else, not after Elara had finished with him.

An examination of the Well had revealed that she had, in fact, taken the assassin's dagger. Inos could only conclude that she'd used it in whatever rite she underwent down there. The weapon of an enemy, finally able to draw the blood its wielder had craved. A wielder, now dead, unable to draw the blood he wanted.

"Thank you, adherent. Anything helps at this point." Inos forced himself to smile. It felt awkward. In a nervous, out-of-character action, he reached out and clasped Cassandra's shoulder.

She seemed satisfied with the gesture, returned the smile, bobbed a bow and swept away. Her robe whisked behind her. At least some of the Kali'ka in Sangra had remained stable and sane.

"We'll be here." Brae thumbed the air between him and the clutter-strewn table. He smirked, but Inos couldn't share his amusement.

"I'll be back shortly, Brae."

Inos stalked through Sangra, closely retracing a set of steps he used to arrive at Elara's chambers the last time. Whatever it took to help, no matter how tenuous the lead, he would do it.

While his mind quested and searched, those horrible moments from the Well rose like an iceberg that refused to be plunged, refused to sink.

...The sickening stench of burned flesh. People milling all around, watching with a panic approaching hysteria. The sizzle of plastein. So much plastein – almost all they had – applied through Brae's perfectly practiced hands like a balm. Again and again its bubbling, coruscating surface rolled over itself, solidifying, flaking off in rainbow shards. The skin below, whole, smooth, without yantra. Eerily blank. Pale like snow.

But her face... Oh Kali, her face. It was as though her face consciously rejected the plastein. Either that, or the fire must have been most intense there. What effect would it have on her already tenuous psyche?

He'd held her hand the entire time, when possible, though he doubted she'd ever know or remember. When it had become too much for his absolute composure to manage, when he'd begun to be unable to absorb his own fullness of feelings, he let her hand go and slipped out of the room without a word.

Now he walked alone. So long, alone. So shortly together. So shortly with someone to care for. The small taste was enough to leave him nearly crippled.

But he wasn't the one who'd had to wake up after a living

immolation. His feelings were a selfish indulgence. What Elara chose to do was her choice. It always had been.

Still, though ... he couldn't deny how he felt.

Elara ... where are you? We need you, now. Especially now.

***

...The same obsidian slab as the assassin. In the Yantric Crypt in the back of the Scribe's Sanctum. Unable to move because of the pain, yet the pain came regardless, tearing into her like jagged knives of heat. Scapulae pushed up awkwardly from the stone bed under her, compounding her agony.

Awareness grew, slowly. Sights solidified. Hands darted. Voices yelped. Frantic movement all around. No gore marred any surface. Strange, that. Brae must have cleaned it. No gleam of the dagger. That's right... She'd taken it.

Then the frozen waterfall. She could almost feel the coolness. So cold! The percolating, translucent bubble hissed like waves of boiling water. Itchy, itchy, tingly! Body encased. Fizzle and absorption. Coat upon coat upon coat, sucked up by the dryness of her skin, ravenously. Excess biological constituents morphed into sandy, rainbow dust that floated down in puffs...

Elara bolted awake. Mere feet ahead of her, two Kali'ka passed. Gesturing, whispering unintelligibly. As soon as their movement rustled to nothing, she counted down from sixty before moving anything more than her eyes.

A creak in her left knee and a stabbing twinge in her back were her only punishment for curling into a ball in a stone nook and falling asleep. For two hours or twelve, she couldn't say. Bone-deep weariness sunk her like an armada of anchors. Rest was an inert activity.

Would they have recognized her now, anyway, if they'd seen her? Would they have seen through the exterior to the true form beneath? Her body was a shield, after all. A barrier against the enemy, empty but weaponized. She now bore witness to the result that such a belief had wrought:

She *was* the exterior. She *was* the husk. Joined, unified. Inside had flipped outside, just like the fire that had consumed her in the Well. Just like the vision of Kali she'd seen, on that distant cliff edge, somewhere in the realm of Illusion.

There was nothing hidden anymore. Whatever she was *was* the true form... She would learn to accept it.

Keeping low, she propped herself up to a kneeling stance and hitched her hood forward. She was getting closer to the toxin of lies and conspiracy that corrupted the home of Kali's children, and she had to try and catch up to its seep. Detection was a non-option. But if it came to conflict, she would have to rely heavily on muscle memory.

Her eyes would never show her as much as they once did.

...She jerked up from the slab, shoving Brae away. Or, trying to. He barely budged. Her muscles buckled and filled with angry heat, twisting in bizarre, knotted ways. Like a toddler fumbling vainly for gross motor control, her hands clumsily tracked over her skin, squeezing, clutching, brushing away the iridescent polycellular dust left behind by plastein.

Everything, all back in order. The precise tone and length of her fingernails, lightly pink with a millimeter crescent of flat-shaded white. The thin layer of blondish hairs frosting her abdomen. The roundish and not-quite-flattened birthmark on her ribcage. She looked down, uncomprehending, flitting between spotty recollections and foggy focus.

None of it felt like her. She was in a non-reality, full of inanimate non-things. Her, Brae's room, her memories. Everything. The body she looked at was the milk-hued shell of a plastic mannequin, grafted in place over her true, inner casing of bloody cinders.

Then she noticed the great black blot cloaking her left eye like the dab of a mighty brush.

"...Brae." Her voice quavered like water's surface. He just stood there, still, face masked by a standlamp behind him.

"Why can't I see out of my left eye?"

Before he could answer, her shaky hands told her why.

The screaming gasp that left her throat terrified her more than what her hands felt. The animalism. The acquiescence. The complete and irreversible condemnation.

The lesson, indelibly learned. An unavoidable truth, ceaselessly present.

"Thank you, Great Mistress." The whisper slipped from her throat like a ghost, as she lowered herself back onto the slab and stared blankly at the ceiling…

Close to the floor, Elara roved like a semi-bipedal beast. Squinting through the darkness, staying to shadows. Distance was warped. Her hands groped at the air, in front of things she swore were closer. How long would it take, if ever, to get used to such garbled depth perception?

Time was a jumble. Old events transposed themselves with recent events. Bits of memories swapped and stuffed themselves into each other. Reality bled into imagination. She was sure that she was, in fact, still in shock.

It had taken mere minutes to define an entire future. Success, dependent on an artificial healing method. The long trudge of life's remainder, mapping itself out in sequence, had faced headlong astride an endless runway. Tended to by others, unable to even wash or relieve herself without assistance.

Then, those preparations were yanked out from underneath.

But their mark of ruination would persist.

…Brae returned to the Yantric Crypt carrying a set of brushes and paint canisters on a tray. Balanced off-angle to the rest, his most-used tool: a long, thin silver rod with a fine tip that tapered to a needlepoint.

"Elara, it's your yantra… They're gone."

She looked down again, disbelieving. Her skin spread unbroken like a field of virgin snow. Had she noticed before? It had been ten years, at least, since her initiation.

Placing the tray down, Brae held his hands suspended above her body and began moving them along the natural gradients of her meridians, along her contours of energy. Occasionally, he stopped to make circular motions, drilling into a trouble spot, before resuming the general flow. She heard his hands almost as an audible hum, felt them almost as a physical drag.

"*You have to be re-inscribed... All of them. It's not supposed to be possible.*"

She found herself compulsively caught up in watching his hands.

"*I can discern your nodes. But normally, the design of the articulation points provides the framework for me to continue working within. All of it becomes synchronized. Yantra are like poles spearing your unique imprint into place. Now, you're like a blank template. There's no foundation. Nothing to contradict.*"

His face was stern as stone, buried in a big, puffy beard. This time there was no banter, no smiles. His vitality had been drained as though hollow fangs had sucked him dry. She said nothing. She might have even thought nothing.

"*What I mean is... There are no restrictions. No upper boundary. You are like an unlimited reservoir that can expand forever, and always be full.*"

The words were incomprehensible. Empty. Without concrete values or recognizable substance.

"*But, we have to do it.*" *He dipped a brush in paint. The tip was moist with ink and came to a needle-like point, while tapering gradations fanned one side. He wiped his brush around the edge of a bottle, curling up at the end to catch any lose droplets.* "*Regardless of the consequences, we have no choice. I'm sorry, Elara ... to have to deal with this now, so soon after...*"

They meant nothing, the words. They only circled round and round, feeding themselves like a ballooning sphere. Expanding forever, yet always full, he'd said? In a world of space filled with matter, it sounded impossible. The sequence of words, the imagery they evoked, tugged at fathomless concepts. Could something expand without an exterior? Could something contain everything, yet have no boundaries?

Finite space without boundaries... Infinity?

"*Your nerves could be hypersensitive for some time. Cause weird pangs of pain for no reason. Cold-hot sensations, wet-dry sensations, metabolic imbalances. Sense of pressure, sense of pain, the reconstitution of minor blood vessels, the acclimatization of galvanic skin responses, the entire connectivity of your sense of touch to your spinal column. All of it, for such*

a traumatic experience, could take a very long time to reconstitute.
But just remember ... there's no plastein for the mind."

This was one of the last areas left to search – a set of switchbacks under rarely used storerooms.

The others had done their part. Inos, Brae, the adherents who remained in Sangra. They'd given too much. They all had. They'd sacrificed while she brooded. She used her strength for her, and her alone, sucking others into her vortex as a result. Unintentionally or not, this was the case.

Kali'ka or not, self-reliant or not, self-preservation wasn't enough. She realized that, now. She was capable, more than most, and she had to turn her attention outward. That was all. The balance of events required her not to simply subsist, solving her own problems, but to act on others' behalves.

Now, because of her avoidance, because of her foolishness – because of *her* – Marin was gone and half the cloister had defected. She could have prevented it. She could have done something more. If she hadn't detached herself, and had instead worked *with* the others, she could've intervened earlier. They all could have.

Now, she had no choice but to act alone. It was quicker, more efficient. That paradigm, at least, hadn't changed.

Marin's absence, however terrible, provided Elara with exactly the impetus she needed. It laid out the exact trail she sought. It would lead to them, the daemons disguised as Kali'ka. The usurpers, the destroyers. No more waiting, no more debating, no more compromising.

And Oren... Not even the Goddess Herself would be able to protect him once she found him. Death would be the greatest quarter traitors were given. Betrayal brooked no mercy.

They'd taken her old advocate – she was sure of it – perhaps to goad her to leave Sangra, on the heels of the assassin's failure. She didn't regret standing her ground against Marin's staunch and dogmatic way of thinking. She *did* regret that it took Marin being put in danger to realize that a difference in opinion, amongst allies, didn't create enemies.

And it had taken her being incinerated alive to come to her senses.

Marin, you old fool… I know you still have your fire, somewhere inside! You'd better fight them. You'd better not give up. Wait for me, my old advocate… Wait for me…

…She lay completely motionless as the bristles of Brae's brush tickled belly, thighs, neck, nose, and chest alike. Each fiber impressed itself, fanning outward. Brae began chanting, his entire body swinging with the sway of his arms, more and more impassioned, pausing again and again for a quick dip-and-twist in ink before resuming. Having lived through twenty inscriptions, Elara knew the procedure.

She following the brush's texture along her skin, spinning in its movements. Stunned. Severed. Lightly yet firmly, Brae attempted the impossible. The skeleton of her consciousness took form through the brush. Her arms and legs became one singular emblem. Elbows, wrist, knees, head became one machine described through the cutting angles of geometric/linguistic insignias.

Once the frame of paint was laid, the inscriptions began. Dot upon dot upon dot. She, the canvas. The silver rod, the tool. Slip through the surface of the skin, wipe the blood. Like she'd done to herself with the dagger, in streaks and slices of a digging tip. Destruction of flesh, construction of form, one in the same. Creation at the expense of life.

Hours to come, one after the other. One to twenty, again. The familiar pain of Brae's needlepoint rod quickly became numb. The tap, tap, tap of her newly inscribed yantra became a familiar companion.

Brae's chanting persisted, through the old syllabic language of throat and minimal lips. He was as her thoughts were, which were one with kanas, which were as ripples of water, storms in the sky, celestial orbits, mitochondria swimming in cells.

Like gems from sediment came clarity from crisis, separated in the surface stir of hands, swipes of ink, and stabs of needles.

The end was the beginning. Inexorably, one from the other. Her path was set with the first step. Her end was determined by her first intention…

Elara's fingertips caught on some kind of traction. The natural adhesiveness of her skin dragged across an odd consistency on the floor.

Worn, with a host of fine lines. Without the nuances that her renewed flesh detected, she might have otherwise missed it.

She stopped and looked down, turning her neck to look through her right eye – her living eye – towards the edge of a pool of jumping torchlight.

Scuff marks. Streaks. Leading towards a wall.

...A milieu of bodies saturated the corridor. Kali'ka, as one, cried out from where they lined the walls leading into the Scribe's Sanctum. Some rose. Other tore their robes wide in shrieks of fervent gratitude. Obeisance. Weeping of ardor. Reverence.

As she passed, they fell. Palms to floor, forehead kissing stone. Entire strata of prostrate bodies. A chain of hushed, frothing praise to the Goddess. Hands were lifted to support her litter and elevate her beyond them all.

Elara saw it then, what they must have seen. What they chose to remember, and what had already undoubtedly been catalogued as fact in their oral history.

Spontaneous immolation, birthed from nothing. Wild flames that melted wool to skin and refused to be quenched. Hands lifting her high, declaring her name.

There within the inner sanctum of Sangra, among the sarcophagi, Kali had come to them, manifest in Her favored harbinger.

They'd seen not an accident. They'd seen purpose. Structured intent. Cosmic will.

A miracle...

Elara's hands slipped across nearby walls, pressing, pushing, probing for the slightest incongruence. She kept her ears open to passersby. Visibly, this path was indistinguishable from any other. Was this where the defectors vanished?

She closed her eyes and relented to what the elements told her. The darkness was Kali's blood, she reminded herself. Its blackness was Hers, and she flowed through it as easily as Her children slipped through the shadows of their home.

There. The barest aberration. A murmur in the valves of Sangra. A sliver of absence in the flow of energy.

Without a second consideration, Elara emptied her mind, stepped forward and was consumed by a realm of lightlessness.

CHAPTER 20
SACRIFICE

Fallow emerged from shadow into his stronghold in the Veneer, into the sound of hooting, cackling, fist-pumping applause. His Kali'ka zealots shoved each other side to get a better view, gnashing at the air, pounding the ground in honor of their master. They were *his*, these converted denizens of the world below. They encircled him, dressed in their grays, and he stood in their midst, arms outstretched, head craned towards the sky, searching, striving for that place beyond the sun-brightened clouds of a rose-girded Corinthian firmament, to pierce the infinite darkness beyond.

He saw their future in that ever-expanding void, beyond sight and sense, in the otherworld of Kali. He saw it all around him, on the soil of Earth, whereupon lingered remnants of Ashram's construction. Here and there scarlet streaks, tissue fragments, and hooked instruments lay among firepots of smoldering coals and stinging embers. Blood-stench thickened the air.

This was their underworld upturned. A sanctuary architected as an extension of the body of Mors, in the shape of its creators. From it, his followers would be the arms and legs, slashing, striking, stabbing, grasping, and piercing the sacred heart of Logos. Culling the weak from the bosom of Kali, and ensuring the survival of the heirs of Earth.

There on the far end of the courtyard stood all the evidence he and his brood needed. Evidence of their superiority, their purpose, and their self-carved fate. There, a mound of dirt supported three wooden poles with cross-beams for arms. Centerpiece of the drama. Seed to the unfurling tree of death.

On the right cross hung the creature that Fallow had captured months ago in preparation for this exact day. The liar. The remnant. One of twelve. It remained utterly still, as it always did, except for that damned third eye.

On the left cross hung the disbeliever to the appointed mistress of Sangra. Yanked from her home, rid of her robe – a requisition for the High Devotee, no less – and put up on display. Bait for their great nemesis.

In the middle, between the two prisoners, an empty cross waited. For *her,* the only one who could stop him.

The moment Fallow's eye latched onto the robeless woman on the left, she roused. Her groggy eyes opened and her scream split the air.

***

Ascendant Marin stared in mind-stricken horror through puffy, red-rimmed eyes. The mass of teeth-bared faces faced off against her like a solid wall, shouting and cursing wildly atop jabbing fingers and shaken fists. Like a raw assemblage of jumbled human parts, they bobbed and shifted in primitive rudiments of shades, sounds and heights. All in Kali'ka gray.

Impossible! Who were these animals?! Again and again, her mind smacked into disbelief. It refused to decipher meaning, refused to desire sense, but merely darted as her eyes did, from one impossible sight to another, and another, then another.

They were somewhat below her, the mob. She was at a higher height. Glancing directly down, she saw her aging, lined flesh, bare and in full view of their leering, jeering scrutiny.

Nude! Oh gods!

With difficulty, she twisted her head to see crude rope bindings digging into her arms and ankles, cutting off circulation. It took all of her strength, pressing straight down through her calves, onto the tiny pedestal supporting her feet, to keep her from sinking.

Around them, the surrounding buildings formed a single, contiguous surface of disjointed synthstone, wood, and metal, several stories high like a courtyard. The Veneer?! Above Mors, then? From the eaves of the surrounding buildings dangled red-stained meat hooks, swaying like loose guillotines.

The walls underneath displayed a mortuary gallery of bizarre and incomprehensible fleshscapes: dismembered corpse parts aligned next to bones arrayed in patterns that resembled yantra, aside skin spread apart like hides sitting within emblems of runny blood. The stench rolling from it collided with the gag-inducing wave of ubiquitous Veneerian filth.

Once the scene composed itself into recognizable sights and smells, Marin's stomach lurched and liquid vomit spurt from her empty gut to spill over her own body and leave her throat and nostrils seared. Scattered laughter punctuated the insane noise of the crowd.

Somewhere beneath her shock, memories strained to reach through, hobbled by a skull-deep throb that pained terribly on the side of her head.

...On her way to a coven. Towards the agreed-on location, through the Eternal Day. A blur of blackness in the house. Two figures. Hands grabbing. Pain and darkness...

Kidnapped! They took me! Oh Kali, no! No! Great Mistress, preserve me! Please!

The crowd turned its attention towards their rear. From the center of their uproar stepped a single, undisturbed spot, like the eye of a storm. In that spot stood a man, dressed in the same robes as the rest of them, with his hands upraised towards the sky. Hideously disfigured, face torn apart by scar upon poorly healed scar. No plastein had ever touched that face. Only one eye remained whole. The mad crowd shuddered away from his wake like ripples from where a pebble sunk into a pond.

"Brothers and sisters! Ascendants! Listen to me! I am Fallow!"

Marin's heart froze. Time stopped. Through the pain in her body, the shame of her nudity, and the incessant fury of their shouts, she understood.

This was him. She was here – right here – in the snake's den. In the realm of the *others*.

Whoever they actually were, whatever they actually believed, they encompassed her like a living, savage prison cell. Her eyes swept the perimeter for an escape route, impossible as it seemed. She didn't even have her own clothes for protection.

"The sound of screams echo on the wind!" The man who named himself Fallow ripped the air with an impassioned, furious yell.

"And lodges in the mind!" Like an avalanche, their collective voice pounded.

"Restlessness reveals fear!" Again, Fallow raised the cry.

"Fear reveals weakness!" The chorus resounded.

"And there is the point to strike!" Fallow finished alone.

They couldn't be Kai'ka! They couldn't! Dissidents? Extremists? Rogue faction? Those words couldn't apply to the lunatic nightmare in front of her. No amount of persuasion or oratory skill could bend all these Kali'ka to the will of one single person … could it? How could they be led so far off course?!

Fallow opened his mouth and out boomed a voice of arcane control and surreal inflection. "Soon, my liberated ones, it will be the time for our purpose to be grasped! For our claim on the stake of Corinthian land to be sown! We have no chains! No harnesses but that which they try to brand us with! But as they tug upon our bloodied bullring, we will run up the slack and use their great yanks as a launching point for our counter-strike! We will take their plows and beat them into spears to plunge directly into the beating heart of Logic!"

The horde around him raged in a slathering, animal frenzy. But still, Fallow's voice rang loudest.

"Their cord will be cut, starving those incapable of nourishing themselves without a conveniently hung, golden teat! The hated ones, the ones who forfeited their lives from birth, who offered as a sacrifice the potential of their own divinity, will suffer as their invented god stares in effigy from its melted bust, its face consumed in the same fire as those it watches. And it will happen in a way no one thinks possible! No horror left untouched! No sight left unseen!"

The uproarious response was of no specific shape. Just the leaping, beating, howling mania of the droves within the courtyard. As soon it started to die down, Fallow snared the reins again.

"Here, my fellow Morsmen, we have one of the Unchanged! From Sangra, no less! One of those who would doom our order to atrophy! One who would yolk us to a feeble life of endless debate and unrealized potential! An *ascendant*." The final word oozed from his frayed, mocking lips. Cackles and shouts rebounded across the courtyard. Many made vulgar gestures or even bared themselves towards Marin.

"And here! One of the old masters! A surveillance tool to keep us repressed! One who forfeited life for immortality! A Stabat!"

The horde sneered and cursed as Marin, a second later, understood the words and looked to her left.

There, on the other side of an empty cross, hung the soft, clay-like flesh of a Stabat. Lashed to its wooden crossbeams. Nude, like her. No one had ever seen a Stabat like this, without its robes. It had no genitals. Its body was thin and asexual. Smooth and flaccidly muscular. Its eye flit around like an agitated fly.

Marin could do nothing but stare at the Stabat, speechless. More deeply than the shock of the mob, more embarrassing than her nudity, the sight of the Stabat bore its way inside like apocryphal venom. It broke her. To see one of the caretakers – somehow brought here and restrained…? In its sad frailty, she saw herself, reduced to a wretched, undignified, base display. The sight seared her numb and shattered her heart to slivered bits.

"You see?" Fallow continued, merciless. "Not even the all-powerful Stabat can defend itself from us! They are helpless when exposed to the true face of Kali! She has no mercy for those who do Her or Her children wrong, especially those who would guide us wrongly! And, the Stabat have guided us far, far astray from what we are due! They've taken us down an errant path towards a hidden, self-serving agenda!"

It was then, like the snapback of grass tipped over from a slithering snake, the crowd shifted. A sinuous line unzipped from the back, towards Fallow.

Out from the wall of bodies stepped a face both familiar and unknown. Features so average that Marin had to stare for several seconds before she recognized them.

"Oren! What – What are you doing here! Get out! Don't you know –

don't you... " Her voice died as she stared at the slow stroll of Oren, uncaring, secure. His face grew closer, warped from its usual, self-abasing quiver into a headlong glare of deep antipathy. He stopped to stand directly at Fallow's right. Without moving, the two of them stood fused in energy, in essence, beyond ease.

"Oren... Oh no." No one heard her whisper. Absolute condemnation filled her like a concussive, pounding force.

In memory, she saw all their covens as ascendants. All the collaboration, all the doubt, all the plans, all the disagreement... all the innermost information. All of it, funneled directly here to the ear of Oren's true master.

No one had known. No one had suspected even in the slightest.

She should be angry. She wanted to be angry. So, so, bitterly angry. She wanted to howl in rage and unleash the full wrath of Kali onto this man standing safe and smug like a loyal, leashed dog. Betrayer to the Great Mistress. The worm in Her bosom, eating away at confidence and unity like a consumptive disease.

But the flame wouldn't spark. The tides of indignation wouldn't rise. Marin's wick was pinched before it could light, and all she could do was break down and weep in full realization at her own helplessness and despair. Her head throbbed with a horrible, deep, bleary pain.

"You see!" The man called Fallow turned with his hands held high. "This is how fragile our enemy is! She doesn't fight back! She doesn't pick up the banner of her fellows! When faced with the harsh, unyielding truth, all she can do is *cry!*" Jeers spread throughout the crowd. Laughter and angry shouts.

"And make no mistake. Those who you once called brothers and sisters are our enemies! They are an impediment to potential! An impediment to the progress of our order! They cannot be reasoned with. Their weaknesses cannot simply be caulked up like a hole-ridden dam. They are as corroded and corrupted as Logic itself, and must be purged so that we can rise new and whole!"

Tears streamed down Marin's face, falling from her chin and nose to slide down her exposed body. She watched through watery disbelief the insane scene in front of her. All the gray robes – a symbol of solidarity and dignity – draped around bitter, vile creatures who made absurd noises and tromped around senselessly.

It was like being told by a strange that her most beloved family member had just died. Then the stranger turned and left her alone, naked, cold, unable to ask questions, unable to understand, unable to rage even at her own helplessness.

"She'll find you," Marin breathed.

Fallow slowly turned towards her, his mangled face contorting into something like disgust. The crowd simmered to silence. Next to him, Oren's smile started to slip.

"She'll find you." Marin spoke again. She wasn't sure if they could hear her. She wasn't sure if they could understand a single word through her weeping. She wasn't even sure that she was speaking aloud.

"None of you will survive," she pressed. "Do you understand? Down to the last. Gone! You'll be slaughtered. You act like animals, and so you'll die like them. She won't yield. I've seen her. I know. She has the strength! The will. All of this – your speeches, your justifications, your duplicity – in the end, you're just rabble. Children, demanding what you can't have! You'll all be burnt to ash!

"And you – Oren! You traitor! You fucking snake! She won't forget you! For you, a special type of vengeance will be reserved!"

Fallow stood there, boiling with rage, unbalanced by her sudden defiance.

"That's why you're so upset, Fallow! You know it's true. Our order has existed for thousands of years, and you're just one small person in that timeline. You know how feeble your life is. You know how little you've actually contributed. How trivial your role is. You're not content to know yourself! You can't let anyone else *be*, because of your own sickness. Kali rejects you! You're a daemon and a stain on Her name!"

"So now you're a believer?!" Fallow rushed towards her, explosive, wrathful. Those nearest to him pulled away and pressed back into the crowd. "*You* are the traitor!! Your fellow ascendant here – " He held a palm open towards Oren. " – is honoring his inner self! Stepping boldly to grasp what he wants, not simply obeying the strictures of outmoded traditions or the whims of the Stabat! Something you have never done!"

"Oren has told me of how you antagonize her. And now, when you need help the most, you adopt her as your *personal Goddess*? Are you expecting your false idol to save you, then? Go ahead! Beg for her! Demand that she make herself known! Demand that she save you! Cry out and pull her body from Illusion! She's already enslaved to your weaknesses! But you – you! – you've already chosen a master! And now, you're beholden to your choice! I won't let you forget! I won't let you distract me!"

"I *do* believe, Adherent Fallow! I always have." Marin ground her teeth and bore down on the one-eyed fiend with every bit of strength she had left. "I believe in Kali! I believe in Her wisdom! I believe in those who honor Her! I believe in how we restore those lost to Logic. I may disagree with Elara's choices, but I believe in anyone who so completely embodies our Great Mistress! You can't control her! That's what you refuse to believe! That's the truth you can't bear to see!"

Fallow released a bestial roar and brandished his dagger, pointing it directly at her face. "Then believe in this, you old bitch! You and all those hiding in Sangra and Ignis will die! They will break under the burden of true action! They will snap as twigs under the boulder of us, the true heirs of Earth! They will splinter like babies dashed on the rocks of our prominence, cast in a bloody ocean of death! The Eternal Day of New Corinth will be snuffed under the palm of our hand, and Eternal Night will fall on Logos' prized city!

"You will be the final pivot towards Elara's demise, feeble one. The final nail in her wrist! You, her greatest skeptic and doubter, will prove what I've said all along. And when you need her most, your false god will fail you! She will fail *all of you*! And I will sling her body on that empty cross there on the mound! I swear it!"

In three steps, he was next to her, lowering his voice for her ears only. His snarl rent his scarred face into a collage of pulverized meat parts. "And for making such a show here, today, you'll be alive to witness the end … in whatever state I deem appropriate."

His robes swished, and Marin gasped at a convulsion of electric pain. A tiny pinch twanged in her spine, and an inaudible snap rang in the most precious, most delicately balanced of chambers in her body's temple.

Her spinal cord had been severed.

Instantly, her legs collapsed and her lungs were crushed. She could barely suck in breath, and her shoulders twisted up behind her, crackling in small cartilaginous pops. She hung there, panicked beyond reason, sipping in whatever air she could through the full, unsupported weight of her diaphragm.

"You think yourself a martyr, Ascendant Marin. But no one is a martyr if they're not remembered. No one is a martyr if no one else cares." Though he stood directly in front of her, Fallow's cruel face grinned from a far away, pitiless distance.

He spun towards his masses. They were watching, listening, expectant, waiting and attentive until commanded, fused to their leader, master, teacher, savior, madman and butcher.

He opened his mouth and uttered a single sentence.

"Make ready the invasion."

***

Lying on the edge of an eave that looked down into the courtyard below, Charlotte cried silently, hands clamped over her mouth. All she wanted to do was look away. But still, she watched, letting her eyes fill with tears, for a moment yielding some small, blurry respite from the nightmare below.

Around her, the staggered rooftops of the Veneer – synthstone, plastics, even old-world wood and wattle – spread jagged and off-set like a random arrangement of decayed, rusted utensils. She caught at least ten Errati scattered within eyeshot on the rooftops around them, skulking, slinking, surveying, guarding.

"No... No..." It was all she could muster.

These people below were the ones who wanted to kill Elara? They were the ones who were out there in Advent Square? That was him? Fallow? So much hatred... He hated everything! It was like they had no minds. No hearts! What had ever been done to them? Why would they do that to that poor woman?! Didn't they see how hurt she was? Why didn't someone – just one of them – step in and help her?? If these people were out to do harm, then Logic, the Kali'ka – none of them were safe!

On her right, Devin's face repeated all of her thoughts back to her, wordlessly. His tight features tried desperately to maintain composure. He was unconsciously fingering the metal ring that hooped through his forearm. Little muscles in his limbs and torso were catching, releasing, wiggling the rods and brackets stapled across his body.

The blood, the anger, the violence – they were as common to him as blinking, she knew. Spending a lifetime in the Veneer exposed anyone to far, far worse.

But the people down there were behaving like this by *choice.* They readily adopted, for some insane reason, what another caste of people, for lack of any other option, spent a lifetime struggling with.

As one, hundreds of voices exploded. The scene in the courtyard turned into a commotion of action and a frenzy of bodies. Gray robes scattered towards the periphery. Charlotte could pick out the catalyst in their midst – the man Fallow – standing in front of the slumped woman on the cross, with his fingers clasped to his chest and his head lowered.

Then, as Charlotte's eyes ran across the edges of the rooftops, between the darkened splotches of rotten building materials and crumbling synthstone, she caught the contrary motion of a new, rising set of shapes.

Kali'ka. Hoods pulled forward. One, two, five, a dozen, more, pulling themselves up over the edges of the surrounding rooftops like the slow ascendancy of hooded serpents. Within moments, a swarm engulfed them.

Devin's head spun towards her. "Nyx! Get out of here! Now!! Go! GO!!"

Without thinking, Charlotte catapulted off their rooftop onto a nearby landing, stumbling and catching herself. She jumped over a pile of refuse and leapt again, keeping her legs moving while death dilated at her back.

Devin kept up with her on a nearby set of rooftops, grasping, clutching, hurling himself forward like a long-limbed projectile.

Out of the corner of her eyes, Charlotte saw their protective perimeter of Errati collapse as Kali'ka pressed on. Flashing daggers clipped on Errati skin embedded with metal spikes, or plunged directly into the soft spots between. The Errati were falling quickly, too quickly. Their focus was split between protection and navigating the rooftops to somehow fight their attackers on less lethal terrain.

"Get down to the ground! We can lose them there!" Devin howled and vaulted over a balustrade, his weight slamming onto a cracked landing.

He was right. They were at eye level with their assailants. They needed to break the Kali'ka's line of sight.

Down, down, Charlotte dropped, searching for any available path. Coming to an abrupt end a story up from the ground, she spied a wet, muddy area below. Softer than other spots. No broken glass or metal shards.

There was no choice: break a bone and maybe die, or stand her ground and definitely die.

She jumped.

Landing with a thud and a shower of mud, she sprawled forward, half-rolling over her shoulder, half-smashing onto her back. She found herself staring directly up towards the sky, seeing craggy overhangs drip moisture down towards her face.

Off to the side came a scuffling sound. Charlotte rolled onto her hands and knees and faced towards it.

In the narrow alleyway, crouching in the sopping filth underfoot, maybe three body-lengths away, one of the Kali'ka hunched with dagger in hand, growling from inside her hood. To either side, the alleyway spanned without end. No nearby crooks. No doors or recesses.

The Kali'ka raised her dagger to strike, and inside her hood Charlotte caught the shine of teeth bared from within a bestial face.

Before the blade could land, a hurricane roar shook the surrounding walls and surged down the alleyway. It barreled into Charlotte's attacker, blasting her off her feet and sending her smashing into the closest wall.

It was Devin.

Like a titan unchained, he hurtled himself at the Kali'ka assailant before she could recover, and with both hands, snared her robe and launched her to the ground. He dropped to the ground, pinning her between his knees, locking her into place.

In swift, explosive strikes, Devin brought his fists down again and again onto the small, wriggling, wailing creature locked under him. Blood flew and sprayed in sheets like a hemorrhaging fountain. Fracturing rifts of bone snapped and crunched within the face and body of Charlotte's assailant. Devin bellowed the entire time like a mind-lost beast. Merciless, savage.

Slowly, slowly, little by little, his blows came to a gradual halt and he knelt there, gasping for air, eyes wild and staring.

Under him, mashed red pulp gushed blood in retching fits, tangled within swirls of gray fabric. The dagger and various fragments of bone lay strewn in the muck. Slathered gore slicked Devin's taut, adolescent musculature. His chest rose and fell in deep thrums, and his sweat-drenched hair matted his forehead. His overly broad shoulders slouched from fatigue.

After several moments, he glanced around and stumbled upright. Dazed, barely blinking, he took two lurching steps over towards Charlotte, who knelt curled into a ball against the nearby wall.

Gingerly, he extended a trembling hand towards her. His hands were lathered in blood, his knuckles shredded and eaten away in jigsaw patches. He didn't seem to notice, or if he did, hardly care. He just stood there, wordlessly pleading for her to take his outstretched hand, cohesive thought slowly filling his face.

Once shock started to fade from Charlotte's mind, and she realized what he wanted, she reached out and gripped his bloody hand. She held it tightly, pulling him back to the world they both knew. She didn't recoil. She didn't hesitate. She never considered another choice.

Devin's breathing settled and calmness enveloped him. Like the quick tug of a string, he popped her up to her feet.

"She..." Devin started. "The Kali'ka was going to..." Unable to finish, he just stared at the ground.

"Devin..." Charlotte whispered, glancing at the heap of indiscernible viscera and fluid behind him. "Thank you."

His eyes, locked on the ground, welled with moisture. "Don't they realize what they've done? Coming into our territory... Attacking us!

Butchering Veneerians. This is our place! Our home! They should've left us alone. But now…"

She just laid a hand on his arm and gripped it. It was all she could think to do.

"We'll gather the Errati, Nyx. All of them. They'll know what happened here. We'll find all those gray-robed fucks. We'll kill them. Every single one of them. We'll tear that hideout apart and take revenge for what they've done. Fallow will feel the pain of every single Veneerian he's killed. I swear it!"

A gust of frost passed across Devin's pale, winter-blue eyes as he lifted them to meet Charlotte's. His voice seethed dire retribution.

"And if your sister is as tough as you say she is, she'll get her own personal army."

CHAPTER 21
EYE OF THE VOID

Amidst the clash of metal on stone and the clatter of trampling feet, Oyame swept through the catacombs of Cloister Mors at a dead run. In and out of pools of torchlight, breathless, heedless of the rocky, damp floor, she peered into the darkness, searching, scrutinizing for any sign of movement. Anytime she caught sight of someone, she veered in a different direction, never backtracking. Behind her trailed the hounding of snarling, angry voices. Howls of agony and terror lanced the air, echoing throughout the corridors of Mors.

She was certain the gang behind her had taken a different turn. Was there another group, maybe? No time to think. Too many had already fallen.

One by one, like a chain reaction, Kali'ka in Cloister Mors had spontaneously turned on those nearest them, like birds in flight obeying an unseen conductor. Where it had started, she had no idea. She only knew that it had spread through the cloister like a viral plume. They'd stormed like one body, stabbing, maiming, slaughtering with utter impunity. Clusters of resistance flocked together, but were slowly being pushed into the deepest, most isolated recesses of Mors.

Oyame had no idea where she was. All she'd done was run. She was whipped into a hindbrain survival-frenzy that refused to let her stay still.

But somehow in the middle of it, her unconscious mind started synthesizing an underlying pattern. Little bits of information, clipped apart and puzzled together from whatever natural talents she had, amplified by her short time training in Mors. In her mind's eye, the pieces replayed in time with the fritter of her sprinting feet.

...Nimble bands of Kali'ka trailed behind the murderous raiders. The frontline injured and murdered, and the rear guard skirted the victims off into whatever secret holes led back to their true den. They disabled then co-opted, crippled then claimed...

It was the perfectly executed strategy of a master – *no one* was able to be rescued. No one lay in the sides of passageways to be carried off to recovery or defense. Plastein was useless. Each who fell left a permanent dent in their numbers.

Oyame dug in her foot and banked into a sharp turn at an intersection filled with darkness. Her hand – reaching for balance – brushed on what she recognized as a splintered torch bracket, dangling from the wall. The fires of the cloister were dwindling.

Ahead of her down the hall, in the center of a sphere of quivering torchlight, stood a figure tall and proud like a monument.

Ascendant Cyrus. Cuts and bruises smattered his face.

The second Oyame saw him, her feet stopped dead and she slid to a halt at the edge of his pool of light. His head turned towards her, and in an instant of recognition, he somehow rallied enough composure to wave a hand low and convey a gesture of pointed desperation.

Stop! Get out of here!

Obeying, Oyame sunk back into the pure shadow behind her, flush against the wall.

Then she heard it: a mob of jumbled shouts and directionless pathos, surging from the other side of Ascendant Cyrus.

Cyrus turned his back towards her and stamped his feet in place like columns of stone. The peppered gray hair on his head faced her like the hackles of a lone packleader, above thick, sloping shoulders.

Moments later, even as Oyame shrunk against the wall, a crush of bodies rushed into sight like a crazed tide. In their fists waved daggers, rocks, spears of fractured wood, the men and women who wielded them howling murderously. They came straight down the hallway she would have run headlong into were it not for Cyrus.

As one beast, they converged on him.

They struck from all sides, leaping, swinging, hurling their bodies through the air, flailing their weapons with vicious, focused power. Cyrus moved within them like water split by river rocks. Two of their number went down, one more, then another, as Oyame's once-advocate unleashed the full suite of skill he kept hidden inside. Kana after kana struck and spun and snapped his attackers' joints. Controlled, economic, and direct, from the hips and out, his explosive knees, crushing heels and pounding elbows staved them off.

So like him, she thought … this display of lightfooted violence. Even in the most deathly of times, refusing to relent poise. So modest, so humble. So solemn and so severe.

She swore he'd always be there. Like the sunrise. Like water. Like the ground under her feet.

But there were just too many. Too many for him to focus on. For each one that fell, two more sprinted into the brawl. He couldn't keep up. Not for lack of skill, not for anything less than the limit of determination, but as a physical impossibility.

He couldn't face them all at one time. He was rooted in place. Surrounded. Unable to gain ground or shift his feet.

One kick caved in the side of his knee. Another took out his shoulder. He fell, striking with one arm at whatever met his fist. A blow struck his temple. He slammed someone in the groin and cracked his knuckles on another's kneecap. A dagger slipped into his back. Another. His wail of pain transformed into a snarl of rage. He lunged at nearby calf, biting, digging his fingers into the Achilles tendon like talons. A foot bashed his forehead, another from a different direction. His eyes hazed and his strength trembled.

Another blow, then another, and his body collapsed to the ground.

Once he fell, they swarmed on him like ants. In a rampage of fists, feet, blades, they pounded, stomped, slashed, and tore into his body. Within seconds, he was an unrecognizable heap on the floor in the dark.

All Oyame could do was stifle the scream that tore her soul apart. She knelt in a ball, shaking, eyes glazed.

One of their number stopped moving. From the foreshortened silhouette of his hood, she could tell he was turned towards her. He knew someone was there.

With her eyes welded to the mass of blood and robes on the floor, Oyame somehow roused herself to action. A solar wind of energy buoyed her body and propelled her legs. She thought of Cyrus as he was – calm, graceful – grasping at every image of him she could resurrect. She thought of her first coven, when her fears started to dissolve – fears she'd never realized she had. She thought of her initiation and the flame of Kali that beat within. The Goddess was her ally and fortress, darkness her arena, and choice her shield.

What began as a haphazard scrabble transformed into a solid, planted dash. With her pursuers raging behind her, Oyame dashed away into the darkness, having no idea what to do, where to go, or how to get there, knowing only the chase and the need to never, never stop.

***

Keeping low, Elara stalked through the dank caverns of Cloister Mors, unseen and unheard to the roving bands of dagger-wielding killers who prowled its depths. Sounds of violence rebounded overhead and pervaded every hall. Panting breath, scuffling slippers, or whisking robes flit in and out of earshot. She counted every turn and took note of every side passage, determined to backtrack her way out. Avoidance was key; dodging was always preferable to blocking, if the situation allowed.

She stayed hidden as groups of terrified Kali'ka raced down the hallway with violent marauders at their backs. Mors was divided, it seemed. Those who hadn't betrayed the Great Mistress, and those who'd allied with Fallow.

It was exactly as she'd feared – an entire society of interlopers skulking in their periphery. A twisted offshoot of the order of the most high Goddess. An entire cloister, one of only three in existence, fallen to apostates of the Great Mistress.

These dissenters lacked the skill of their assassin prodigy, though. Their raging force, their numbers, and the darkness of the cloister instilled them with lethality that they otherwise lacked. She saw straight through their unbalanced posture, undisciplined footwork, and uncontrolled eye movement. They were rabble in essence, but soldiers in execution.

The entire attack had the tenor of a coup, diving in hard, fast, when the enemy least expected, from within their ranks. But it was, in reality, an *invasion* – she had no doubt. A feint and riposte. Distract, then cut to the soft spot in one maneuver. Intrude into one place, spawn a base, then use that ground to drive forward.

It was clear to her what their next target would be. She had to get back and warn Cloister Sangra as soon as possible. Not until she was finished, though. Not until her search was exhausted. She had to stay focused on her goal. Now was not the time for revealing herself. Now was not the time for confrontation. She would meet them on her own terms. She would meet their strong strikes with the softness of unmoving air and the silence of shadows, as a being of whispers and breathy death. Open conflict would reveal her presence, delay her at a crucial time, and risk compromising Sangra.

And time, not physical harm, was her true enemy.

Then, though … she would find Fallow and crush his malignant heart inside of his very chest, with her own hardened hands, as the instrument of Kali Herself. The Great Mistress would enfold Her true children into Her embrace, either now or in rebirth, but those who defiled Her sons and daughters would be coldly abandoned in the ocean of life and death, their threads cut, doomed to drown forever, seeing Her ferry slowly drift on the surface above, always out of reach.

Elara swore this promise on herself rather than not see it met.

Ahead, a Kali'ka stepped through the threshold of a half-open door in a cautious creep, brandishing his dagger. Was he searching for something? Checking on a prisoner? Taking part in a secondary, supportive agenda? This area of the cloister was more remote than others.

A rush of dread poured into Elara like the bursting of an icy dam. She felt her great chain of purpose clamp down and heave forward. Torn by an inescapable gravity of intuition, an almost unbearable need, she left the security of the walls and their shadowy hidings towards the lone Kali'ka.

His back grew in sight as she glided silently towards him. In a single flicker of hallway torches, like a quick trick of the senses, she saw his target in the room beyond.

At that moment, Elara made her choice.

***

Alone in the cold, pitch black of her chamber, Oyame huddled with her arms around her legs, shivering, hearing nothing but her own huffs for air. Tears streaked her sweat-filmed face.

Her eyes stayed bolted on the thin, uneven slit of light peeking through the bottom of her wooden door. There was no way they'd find her in here... right? No way they'd hear her! She'd lost them several turns back. Hadn't she?

All the while, in the back of her panicked mind, in a vault of festering, stinging grief, smoldered the images of Ascendant Cyrus. Brutalizing his attackers, bold and direct, then crumpled on the ground and heaped upon. No matter how much strength, no matter how much skill, he couldn't survive.

She felt just as violated as when she realized what the scions had been doing to her her whole life.

Cyrus had faced his nightmare with eyes wide open, even as it had claimed his life. Never once did his fear master him. Never once did he try to avoid the inevitable. Never once did he fabricate excuses or construct a shelter of lies to parse his perceptions and present him with a burnished reality he'd wished was true.

He was a true Kali'ka ... unlike herself. All she could do was run.

Shushed crunches came from the hall. A pillar of shadow eclipsed the light under her door. Oyame's breath ceased. Her door handle creaked softly, clicked, and weightlessly whispered inwards.

In through her threshold, slow and sinuous, stepped a silhouette of purest black. Hooded and stalking, framed by an outline of firelight. One arm ended in a thin, straight blade. The shadow made no noise beyond the deafening silence that clung to its every movement.

Its turned towards her.

Oyame froze, paralyzed by terror. She couldn't escape; there was no room. She couldn't defeat him. Resistance would only compound the pain.

Her future had ended, right there in an underground, stone casket. The realms clamored for her entrance, and where the illusion of life would be shed, the reality of death would claim her. Death itself eased towards her, dagger in hand, soon to strike her record from the chronicles of time.

"Life to death. Death to life. Thank you, Great Mistress." The whispered exhalation that left her lips was all the preparation she needed.

But before she could close her eyes forever, her hunter stopped walking. Behind him, a second silhouette whipped into view.

Oyame's assailant spun and lashed his dagger at the second shadow. He swished through empty air and blended directly into another attack, then another. Quick, driving blows struck him in return, and the two shadows overlaid into one. Through their dark entanglement, Oyame heard grunts of effort, the commotion of shifting feet and flapping robes, and the thump of bone on flesh.

Within moments came a clipped grunt, the cessation of motion, and one shadow sliding to the floor like wax amidst a fan of hissing blood.

In its place stood a statue of darkness standing still in the doorway, body stretched low, framed at the end of a slashing pose. The malicious dagger stabbed out from the end of its arm, stretched towards the wall.

When it moved to stand upright, Oyame scrabbled away in panic, pushing into the immovable wall behind her.

"No! NO! Get away! Get –"

Her tongue caught in her mouth as the figure lowered its hood. Light from the hallway shone on the face within, and Oyame knelt shackled by awe.

Oyame stared through time at a vision of primal womanhood. Proud, straight-backed, defiant, fearless. She burned like the sun itself, infused with the spark of a star's spin. An alloy wrought of earth, fire, and metal. Deposited on Earth for purposes known only to the schemes of astral potentates. The will to survive and the grace to make it artful, married in an incarnate host. *Woman*, as an essence.

At the same time, she was stained by a grievous blasphemy.

Marring the left half of her face was a horrible disfigurement – an uneven and minced scar like a coating of ragged plaster, ghostly white. Lightly, it pattered down her neck like weeping water. It cut across one eye – her left eye. That eye stared out like a socket into the void – a solid, empty, black orb – peering at nothing, absorbing everything. The growth of her lustrous, auburn mane looked stunted on the scarred side of her face.

"Have you seen an ascendant called Marin?" The woman's voice rang in a gripping, authoritative alto. "Older, thin, not from Mors. Or, have you seen a newly arrived group of adherents? A lot of them." Even in the dark, her whole, untarnished eye fumed with a blaze of energy and intelligence, like coal-hot jade.

She projected intensity so powerful in presence, yet so incidental in intention, Oyame's mind felt wiped and wiped again like an ever-blank parchment. All she could do was shake her head.

In response, the woman sighed and hefted her hands on hips. She took a glance out into the hallway and slightly closed the door.

At the smallest sign of disappointment from her rescuer, Oyame felt mortified. She wanted to beg for forgiveness. She wanted to drop to her knees and clutch this woman like a baby would a mother, knowing that so long as she was near, safety followed. It made no sense at all – they'd just met, whoever she was, no matter that she saved her life – but the need to listen, to respect, and to obey was as overwhelming as standing in the direct path of a hurricane. The need felt ingrained in Oyame's bones, innate like an instinct.

A second later, Oyame found herself staring at the dagger in the woman's hands. She held it so easily, so naturally, like she was born an expert.

"Our enemies provide us with the weapons we need." The woman's living eye glanced up from where Oyame had been looking. The other eye – the eye of solid black – might've moved; it was unclear. Never had Oyame seen such reticence – and enchantment – painted on someone's face at the sight of a tool of death.

Oyame found herself drawn in and captivated by the woman's features. Rounded yet vulpine, soft yet severe. The more Oyame looked, the more the scar looked like a thin gauze ironed onto the true face underneath. Her disfigurement, rather than detract from her strength and weaken her bearing, seemed to only accentuate her nobility and inner beauty.

This woman had been consumed by fire, and rather than be destroyed, had emerged radiant.

A twitch of her hand, and the hilt of the dagger was facing Oyame. "Useful, no matter how they've been misused. Go ahead. I'll get another one."

As soon as Oyame mustered the courage to grip the hilt, the woman shoved the corpse of Oyame's would-be killer out of the way with one foot and gestured for Oyame to follow.

"Wait. I'm Initiate Oyame Nagai, *Ascendant*...?" The leading tone was obvious.

With the scarred half of her face shrouded in shadow, the woman paused, eyes lost as though considering the answer to a completely different question.

"Keep low and close, but stay out of my way. The Great Mistress Herself roams these halls tonight, and ... I don't want Her to mistake you for one of Her victims."

The second the woman turned to leave, she stopped. Oyame saw past her shoulder into the hall. Her heart nearly quit at the sight of a motionless object in the outline of a gray robe, as unmoving as an exhumed corpse. The face atop the robes didn't scrunch its features, didn't blink, didn't flinch at the screams echoing down the hallway. Its third eye stopped jittering and locked onto Oyame's rescuer.

The woman held an arm out for Oyame's protection. She settled into a combat stance, perched on the balls of her feet, and growled her words. "Stabat... I swear to you. Be quick, or you'll be next."

The Stabat's hoarse rasp slit the air like the scrape of a blade on stone. "You have crossed into Circle Twenty-one. You are High Ascendant."

***

In the Veneer, Fallow knelt on both knees in front of the three crosses in Ashram. That old hag Marin was out of his sight for now, until later, dragged down in the darkness of Cloister Mors by Oren. She wheezed and fought feebly – with only her arms, of course.

The memory was enough to make Fallow chuckle.

He glanced up at the buildings comprising the courtyard. So the smallest daughter of Aeve had been watching the whole time, hm? A resourceful little whore, like her sister. He didn't even have to find her, yet she came to *him*. She'd proven meddlesome, her and those Veneerian children. The pack of Kali'ka that had crawled up and onto the rooftops to pursue them would surely be enough to retrieve her, in whatever half-tattered condition she came back in. Less well-composed that way. More suited to his tastes.

Fallow filled himself with emptiness; Kali'ka meditative techniques were useful for some things. He needed to reconnect, bring end to fore, and align himself with events in the present. He needed to cast his inner eye on his impetus and spark. So close to the end, he needed to remind himself of his raison d'etre.

He probed the unlit sectors of his awareness, drifting, sliding towards the plane that cut sleep and wakefulness like clear glass, finding the nick inside that itched like a soft cut.

His thoughts trailed to nothing, and he allowed himself to sink into a wormhole of memory.

...Selenist. Years past. How he'd wasted his time, then, idling, conforming to pre-fabricated molds. They'd convened, all the cloisters – the only time they did, every four years – conducting ceremonies as their hemisphere flowed along the slow drag to a blind winter.

As they all sat and watched, cross-legged, Fallow knew she would never remember him, there in the flame-lit darkness, though he would never forget her.

All of her movements swam like translucent rods of ivory fire. They filled the background and foreground of his consciousness like the curve of the moon's arc through the sky. The rocking of her hips, the light step of her toe, the curl of her shoulders and the tilt of her neck. The circular grace of her kanas, the command of her gestures and the clearness of her voice. In a demonstration of all 72 hand positions, each one was precise, focused, cutting, and clear.

And those piercing jade eyes... They passed right over him, while he peered back. Right over him! Not a word, not an acknowledgement! He beheld her with both of his eyes then, without the big crescent eclipsing half his sight like a black blot.

What vanity! What arrogance! To ignore him, one of so much potential! Her slightest utterance, her merest glance twisted into a secret insult directed solely and spitefully towards only him...

Elara was the linchpin. Elara... Yes, that was her name. He would admit it. He spoke it internally, for the first time in the four years since he'd seen her. The core. The origin. The kindling for his insight and the compass for his path. Cosmically gifted, supremely powerful, and preternaturally disciplined. Since then, he'd heard the whispers – she'd only gotten better.

Soon though, she'd be crucified along with the rest of Sangra. Her body would be strung up on the empty cross in front of him in a howl of triumph. The triumph of rectitude over the ideology of the undeserved, the Unchanged. Their champion would be his prize, dead or alive. In the world to come, no one would outstrip him.

"A god martyred is a god worth emulating," he whispered, repeating his own words back to himself, "but moreso is the killer. A killer is only a killer, but a god-killer is a god. I am an heir, the true face of Kali'ka unmasked."

Fallow rose to one knee and turned his attention towards the pallid man-shape of the Stabat in front of him, hanging stoically in place.

The bloodied bodies on the walls of Ashram would be the keystone for the second phase of his invasion. Based on Oren's description from the Chamber of Sarcophagi in Cloister Sangra, Fallow simply substituted etchings in stone for bone, blood, and once-living flesh. The shape of the inscription mattered, yes. The location mattered, as well. Substance, though, mattered *most*.

Fallow gazed on the form and flow of the gory shapes around him. The ancient Kali'ka language, embodied in yantra, composed of meaty streaks, glistened in the falling Veneerian night.

All it had taken to understand their exact meaning was to lure words out of the Stabat in its typical, elusive, slippery metaphors. He had only to listen keenly, decipher, and decouple the links of verbiage and syntax in order to spill the abstract innards of the ancient language.

The chain of yantra around the interior of the Chamber of Sarcophagi – and those around the interior of Ashram, therefore – depicted the necessity of death in the threads of mortal rebirth. They described the world of the living, Creation, as the true illusion, and the world of Illusion, where the dead resided – along with Kali – as reality.

And only gods, it seemed, were reborn again and again, stuck in a forever loop, never allowed to pass onward into oblivion.

If what he suspected was correct, the future of Cloister Sangra and all its fools would be cemented, right here in Ashram. The next slab of pavement on the path of his plans would be irrevocably laid. All of the pieces were in place. The true nature of the seemingly omniscient Stabat was just another tool for him to utilize, as it should be for a true heir of Earth.

Never once did the Stabat attempt escape. Never once did the wretched thing even acknowledge its own captivity. Nonetheless, Fallow wouldn't alter the etchings in the dirt under it, not in the slightest, or mutter the barest syllable that would risk its freedom. He'd had its bonds reinforced repeatedly. He'd checked their integrity himself on whims, rewrapping them around the pole behind it, looping the rope under each shoulder twice before tying it under the chest and around the neck, as it currently was.

It didn't breathe, the Stabat. It didn't sweat. It was neither hot nor cold, only constantly lukewarm. Its head never drooped, never sagged. Its unliving façade could be mistaken for some kind of perverse serenity. By some glitch of perception, some aspect of form, Fallow swore it appeared restive, almost penitent, like an innocent awaiting judgment.

Little things were so ... accurate. Fingernails. Teeth. The way its tongue curled around diphthongs and alveolar consonants. With one ear gone, a man could still be recognized as a man. With no lips, with a disfigured jaw, an amputated nose even, still a man. With no hair, strange coloration – much like the Stabat – still human.

But alter the bi-symmetry, place an additional eye in the lower part of the forehead ... and a man changed into a monster. Could such a thing die? Was such a thing even alive?

Fallow reached his hand into his sleeve. Time to find out.

The instant his fingers gripped the hilt, the Stabat's third eye rotated directly towards him. Unblinking. Unwavering. It opened its mouth and rasped dreamy, weary words, echoing faintly as though slipping from a collapsing gateway.

"Ego ... sum ... paratus."

Fallow's heart froze and he felt his face go slack. Never before had the Stabat spoken voluntarily. Never before had it revealed even the hint of a discrete ego. The sound and sight seized Fallow with a long-forgotten sensation.

Fear.

More, Fallow recognized the words, from the old language of New Corinth.

I am ready.

With the shuck of metal on metal, Fallow's dagger was unsheathed. He would not be waylaid. Not now! Not ever! Stars and destiny be damned! His path was his own! Sangra would fall, just as Mors had! The walls of blood and flesh around him would aid him and make it so!

In a single motion, Fallow pulled his arm back drove his dagger to the hilt into the chest of the Stabat.

In a crack, the air snapped shut and boomed without sound. The Stabat's mouth stretched into a freakish chasm, and from its throat blared a horrible, sustained wail like the siren call of interwoven, tortured voices. A tempest of heat, light, and air, rushed towards the wound in its chest. Fallow's robe flapped like a wild flag as dirt and debris tore past him, condensing to a single point in the Stabat's chest.

An instant of stillness, a wink of light, and a gale of force blasted Fallow away. He soared through the air across the courtyard and smashed on the ground.

He awoke in a pile of clutter with a sharp ring singing inside his head. His skull beat like a drum. Every joint, every crevice, even his skin, hurt. He pushed himself up, disheveled, dripping blood from his nose.

The courtyard was an upturned wreck. Tables, chains and hooks, the runic patterns of body parts on the walls – all upheaved. His forge – a massive, impossibly heavy object – had been blown on its side, its sluices, coals, and chains scattered. Even smears of blood on the ground, the dirt itself, was blown in concentric trenches. The crosses were lying on their side, spread like flattened wheat.

It had worked. The Stabat was gone.

Cloister Sangra would soon follow.

CHAPTER 22
AN OPEN WOUND

Inos sat nude in the darkness of his chambers, on the coal-warmed stone floor with a small, rawhide drum cradled on in his lap. His steel-tinted eyes stared unblinkingly into the fiery red coals pulsing in the firepan in front of him, through whitish puffs and charcoal plumes spiraling up to vanish in the shadows of the ceiling. Sweat mounted on his forehead like rain building in heavy thunderclouds.

Where is it...? The solution. The answer. I know it's there! In the patterns. In the mists...

He tapped his drum in a syncopated, arrhythmic pattern, dipping his free hand into tiny ceramic bowls of salt, water, and lilac petals, leaning in, out, in, out, tossing them into his firepan. The coals stared at him like moistened, bloodied eyeballs penetrating the darkness. They scorched a path through his mind's crust to the unrefined mantle of consciousness below.

Petals fluttered down and blackened into curled crisps. A dash of salt crackled like an agitated tail. Water hissed and spat in fluttery bursts. Grounded in the physical realities of energy and motion, the patterns portrayed a story. They were the output of the interstices of realms as they cut through conscious reality. Inos, through Reading, created a space where the prevailing energies of Earth could be heard, like the visual voice of Illusion. Then, he had but to arrive at a pinpoint of clarity, like washed glass, and let the impressions pass through and be heard.

Through Reading, he'd learned that Kali'ka tradition was based on observation, not speculation. Based on supple guidance, not unyielding control. Confirmed by efficacy, not the whims of fledgling imaginers. Kali'ka divination was the engineering of the metaphysical.

There was little choice left for him, really. He couldn't leave, in case Elara returned. She was the footing for his feelings and the motion for his thoughts. Only with her, could Cloister Sangra and the Kali'ka move forward. He knew that more anything.

He had to support her for that moment. He had to do his part, with the talents he had. He had to decipher events behind the scenes. The rote of Readings allowed space for this mind to move and extract the answer he knew was already there. Minute details forced him to focus. Methodology forced his hands to be precise and calm. Procedural formats forced him to be patient.

Some called it a talent what he did. He called it necessity.

Off to the side of the floor laid one of the spinebacks he'd fished out from under Elara's cot – *Aegis Council*. It gnawed at him, confused him. Is this what Elara had dealt with? Is this what she was doing before going to the Well of Kali? Before her immolation? Did she undergo the same frustration, the same consternation?

Out of what he'd managed to read in the old, cracked tome, only one passage stuck to his mind, and it spoke to him again and again like a spinning riddle.

...In peace, there is rumor. In peace, there is the festering noise of discontent. It points like a finger from neighbor to neighbor, disbelieving the open-handed palm, determined to find the concealed dagger. Foes must exist. Scapegoats abound. Societal identity flattens and purpose dries out. Without an horizon, we have no direction. Without new territory, we have no solid footing...

Contrast. That was it. Fallow wanted contrast. He wanted to be recognized, like how a mirror displays an opposite image. He wanted to be remembered.

But first, he had to be noticed. He had to step in front of the Logic in order to reflect it. He had to distinguish himself from the rest of the Kali'ka. He had to gain attention, sharply and quickly. Like pain. Like a wound. Like the flick of an assassin's dagger. Like a gash that would last and not be forgotten.

What kind of wound could persist? What kind of wound would cut and then stay split? In a world of Logic and plastein and the lack of scars, any wound short of a mortal one could be restored.

Any wound short of a wound of spirit, that is. Anything short of tragedy.

Before Inos could Read further, a knock at his door jolted him like a cold slap. The everyday sound, hard and urgent, reminded him that he was sitting alone in the dark, nude in front of a fire, wrapped in a near-delirium of otherworldly preoccupations.

Inos placed his drum down, snatched his robe, slid it over his head, and crossed to the door. He felt no fear. A threat would not knock.

Clutching the handle firmly, he twisted his door inward as though yanking a sword from a fallen foe.

Steam poured out of his room into the corridors beyond, permeating the darkness as it was simultaneously smothered by it.

As soon as the steam dispersed and Inos recognized what he saw – the most unlikely of images – the rise and fall of his sweat-laden chest ceased.

In the torch-lit murk of the corridor, huffing, exhausted, with an unknown young woman at her side, stood Elara.

***

Inos couldn't tear his eyes from Elara's face.

He was locked in a bear trap of emotion, indecisive, unable to speak, and unable to accept the indelible, insidious wound that haunted her face like the memory of abuse.

A puzzle piece scar, white with gristle, covered the left side of her face. Her left eye, sable like the night of a new moon, chiseled like onyx with a glassy finish, stared blindly out of its socket. It drank light and heat, was colder and deeper than the vastness of space. In the vacant emptiness of that eye, Inos saw nothing but those awful, early moments in the Yantric Crypt, where she lied unmoving like the smoking tinder of a dying blaze.

It was as if his entire being had been held in suspension since then, as though he was a well-practice mime that walked, sat, spoke and thought in imitation of himself.

Inos forced himself quiet, saying nothing, clamping his mind shut. His muscle of self-awareness, honed and firm, braced itself, finding foundation in the habits of years. It was all within his control – all he thought, all he felt. Personal questions could wait; no need to hinder Elara with his own shortcomings.

He glanced up and down the hall, and extended an arm out to enfold them and usher them inside his chamber.

Elara didn't budge. She took deep breaths between strained words. "There's no time, Inos! We have to leave – they're coming. Invaders, from Mors. I went there. I found out how they do it – travel between cloisters. But I couldn't find her – she's – I couldn't find Marin. Goddess, I don't know where she is. The Kali'ka there, in Mors… Oh Goddess, no…" For a brief instant, she collapsed into sorrow.

The young woman at Elara's side stared at Inos, shivering like a cornered rabbit. One of her hands was slipped into Elara's and was clenching it so hard that both their hands trembled. If she wasn't holding on so tightly, Inos wasn't sure that she wouldn't bolt down the hall and never be seen again.

She still had the light-blinded, slick look of New Corinth about her. It clung to her like a moist veil. An initiate? What under Kali was she dong with Elara? Did she come from Mors…?

"Elara, I haven't seen you since… Listen, you have to come in. We'll only draw attention out here. Tell me what happened. Where you've been. You're – "

"No! It's too late. Kali's Eyes … weren't you listening? Mors has *fallen*. It was happening just as I got there. Those not on Fallow's side were being slaughtered. We have to let Sangra know. We're in danger. We're the next target – I know it. I came across Oyame in her room, seconds from being murdered. They…" She couldn't finish, but just quivered in place, seething frustration and buried grief. "And in the middle of it, a Stabat – it came out of nowhere, and … it raised me to Circle Twenty-one."

Inos glanced at the yantra on her temples, dumbstruck. "Then…"

"I haven't exactly had time to shave my head and have Brae inscribe the last one on my crown."

Her nonchalant attitude stunned him. "It doesn't matter. You're High Ascendant."

She nodded and stared at the ground. It wasn't the response he'd expected, although he didn't know what he would've expected, anyway.

Something about Elara was different, and not physically. Something had changed since the horrible incident in the Chamber of Sarcophagi, since the fire and the stench of her burning flesh, aside from the scar, apart from her physical body, regardless of High Ascendancy. An inner energy was blooming within her like the flash of a solar flare, beaming, lashing out at her surroundings, coiling, wrapping and pulling in.

It was as though all of the passion she'd pointed inward now projected outward, shining through her destroyed-then-renewed exterior to envelop her outer world. Like fused softness. Like an embrace. Like a mother. Like Kali Herself. The fire of the Great Mistress no longer hid within, but flipped out to face others.

Inos traced the curves and cuts of her yantra with his eyes, even the one slicing across her scar. New. Fresh. Brae re-inscribed *all of them.* A clean beginning on a fresh tapestry, attenuating all past experience through the lens of the present, rather than trailing backwards in a chain. Pointing from node to node, creating a single, living emblem of freeform power.

"By Kali..." Inos paused, rallying his thoughts, trying to coalesce them into a single, dense line of reasoning. "You – you're inscriptions. Your yantra. They're attenuating themselves all at once. It's as though *this* is your initiation, and all the Circles since happened at the same time. But ... the Goddess already knows you, so..."

Before he could finish his thought, a massive explosion rocked the cloister. It smashed the air like a sledgehammer. A pressurized shockwave rolled through them, filling their bodies and blasting them from their feet. The entire foundation lurched. Sections of floor shifted up and against each other like the tectonic plates. The ceiling creaked, cracked, and spit out shards of stone that scattered everywhere like a rainshower.

Seconds later, the tremors vanished, leaving a wrecked, lopsided corridor in its place.

Gripping his door handle to pull himself up, Inos looked around, not comprehending what he saw, blinking through puffs of dust that drifted towards the ground. Shouts and yells echoed through the corridors. Adherents started to rush by, some of them turning their heads towards Elara.

What – was that … a *bomb? In* the cloister?! Inos' ears recovered slowly, painfully, in a high pitched, muffled whistle.

You ok?? Had he spoken aloud? Had they heard him? Could he hear *himself?*

He aimed his voice at Elara and Oyame and tried one more time. "You ok??"

Oyame, on the floor, propped herself up with one arm. She gave a quick, shell-shocked nod. Elara was pushing herself to her knees, swaying. He extended a hand to her, half instinctively, but she just glared at it.

Inos glanced behind him into his room. Nausea gripped him. His guts wanted to empty themselves on the floor.

A massive cluster of boulders was sitting exactly where he'd been. His fire was smothered and gone. His implements, his bowls – obliterated. The hole in his ceiling gaped like a ragged-toothed mouth.

The spinebacks, gone. *Aegis Council,* buried with the rest. Their mysteries, lost.

With difficulty, he pulled himself away, though a part of him wanted to rush in and sift madly through the rubble for whatever was left.

"Come on," Elara said, waving them down the hall. Directly, simply. Inos thanked Kali for her decisiveness.

Together they loped down the hall, bedraggled, Elara in the lead, stalking low like a hunter. Inos kept his hand on Oyame's back as much for her support as for his. As they ran, Inos rallied his thoughts and collected his emotions as best he could.

There were no aftershocks, no collateral rumbles or lingering reverberations. Impossible for traditional detonators, even the sadistic ones he'd come across before – the ones with secondary, latent bitigniters.

It was extremely difficult to discern the direction of large explosions, especially underground. Instead, the three of them joined the tide of adherents starting to flow through the cloister, amassing one by one, group by group into a single, collective school that rushed like fish, twisting and turning through the catacombs of Sangra, climbing over rockslides, backtracking to bypass blocked routes, onward towards an unseen goal.

Before long, Inos was stepping out of a pore to emerge shoulder to shoulder with a crush of Kali'ka who rimmed the twelve entryways of the Chamber of Sarcophagi.

Each one had a mixture of shock and horror on their faces. Each one stood irresponsive as they stared at a single point.

There, under the vast emptiness above, lit by the plumes of the Undying Firepyres, stood the remnants of catastrophe.

Oh Kali, no!

One of the sarcophagi was missing. The twelfth one. In its place was a clutter of jagged rock blacker than night, strewn about the entire chamber. Fragments and splinters cracked as adherents shifted weight on their feet. Particles of stone dust glimmered in the floating repose of the firepyres.

A rope of outrage gripped Inos' chest and knotted tighter than tears or outcries would allow. Like his peers around him, he stared at the gash of an absence so large, no one had any idea how to respond.

The sense of violation was palpable like an open wound. Physically, truthfully. This place was all they had. All *he* had. The sacred had been senselessly blasted apart. *Something* had to be done! Some recourse must exist! A part of him wanted to call out orders, wanted to demand and plan.

A part of him recognized the need to apply rationale to tragedy, in terms of who, what, why and how. Another part of him craved nothing but vengeance.

He searched the hoods of all those present. It could've been any one of them. However the means, however the tools. What in the realms, though, could destroy a sarcophagus??

No! They couldn't – *mustn't!* – start down that path. Mistrust sowed by fear... What was he just reading about in *Aegis Council*?

When do we not seek truth, but only seek to blame?

Inos had lived in the same chamber in Cloister Sangra for twelve identical years, like a portrait unaltered, persisting with nothing more than the same small bag of personal items he had when he arrived.

His past linked to his present, and he viewed them in one transparent frame, a length of time that seemed short by comparison. He watched his body scar and harden, and felt that hardening soak inward to become the man he knew himself to be. The days and weeks alone, down to the lingering seconds between, extended out to months and years when he'd trained and honed and plunged himself in the crucible fire of Kali'ka tradition to temper himself a man anew.

All the death and despair he'd witnessed, he'd accepted as a part of himself. He'd collected himself in little bits, in the scarlet liquid of his own heart, clutching it firmly for fear of forgetting just how precious his life truly was.

He knew Kali. He knew far, far better than many. He saw Her face as a child, in every handmade shiv jutting out a corpse, in every desiccated infant in the road, in every woman raped and butchered at random by Levitant gangs.

Every Veneerian understood Her far better than most.

Life to death. Death to life.

The Kali'ka were all he had. Nothing else lasted. No one else stayed.

Inos stared out at the rubble in the Chamber of Sarcophagi, face wet by a salty feeling familiar as the passing of long years. A part of him felt suddenly selfish for thinking about himself. Someone slid fingers into his own and held his hand firmly, but he couldn't tell who. The hand was warm, the body that owned it solid. That was all he knew, and he wouldn't push it away.

Here and there, adherents moved to start clearing away debris, cradling bits of stone in their palms. They leaned over and stood up in offset, dazed patterns, like the slow sway of a field of wheat.

It was then, before Inos could even move to help, that row upon row of gray figures burst out from the shadow-engulfed perimeter of the chamber. They landed in combat-ready poses, snarling, shrieking, daggers flashing above their heads.

The Kachina fell before anyone could even react. One by one, their masked faces dropped silently to the floor, their endless tending of the firepyres cut short by the rake of blades across their wordless throats.

Before the Kachina hit the ground, their killers flowed directly into hacking, slicing, cutting through stupefied, unprepared Kali'ka who barely had a chance to turn around or look up. Screams of pain rose to collide with the cries of the invaders who set to razing the room with little to no resistance. Slowly, slowly, those closer to the center of the chamber realized what was happening and started crying out shouts of terror or warning.

Inos was crippled by confusion. Before he even realized that he wasn't intervening, he comprehended the damning, horrifying truth.

We're all here on one room... Oh Kali, no! We've been lured out. Baited to a single spot!

Only half their number was present to defend; the others had defected. The half that stayed was being torn down to nothing in the middle of fresh mourning.

The strategy was deliberate. It was as ancient as it was effective.

Attack us at our weakest! Demoralize, then strike!

CHAPTER 23
THE WAY OF KALI

Elara gasped as Sangrans – her sisters and brothers – fell like shorn crops. Swiftly, easily, they collapsed left and right, howling, clutching body parts. Blades flashed among them like specks of flashing light.

Fallow's killers crashed into them like breakers, sweeping them towards the center of the Chamber of Sarcophagi, caving in their circumference. One nick at a time, they crushed, pinned, and bloodlet the body of Sangra

Inos, just as fragmented as her, hadn't taken a single step. Oyame, paralyzed, was screaming.

They came right here?! No delay! Mors, then Sangra... then Ignis! All three cloisters leveled with one blow, in one night.

The Kachina... Kali's Eyes! – they didn't even get a chance to fight back! They didn't react, didn't shout out, but just fell straight to the ground in a pallid blur of white masks. Resigned, acceptant. Anonymous in life, unknown in death.

Without them, the Undying Firepyres would sizzle to nothing, sealing the pores, forever dividing the Chamber of Sarcophagi from the cloister outside. It was as though the cosmos, through a twisted, malicious grin, had given Elara exactly what she'd asked for when she was last here, demanding that the Kachina leave her alone. Insisting that everyone in the cloister simply vanish and leave her isolated.

Once the firepyres shrunk to embers, the pores would trap everyone in the chamber. How could any of them attain the clear mind needed to pass through a pore and exit?

They would die entombed in the dark. Unknown. Unremembered. Shadows in life, whispers in death. Every thread of aspiration, conviction, and sacred life snipped and reduced to inanimate, deteriorating husks. Fallow had brought Cloister Sangra together in one stroke – drawing them out, chaining as easily as if they'd willingly lent him their unshackled necks – from whatever safehouse he dwelled in.

He would move onto Cloister Ignis, unhindered. And once all three cloisters of Kali'ka were obliterated, Fallow and his followers could assault New Corinth with no one left to stop him.

No, no! Goddess – I won't let that happen! Not here, not now! Not to us!!

"We can't stay," Elara whispered.

Bolting like a spring, she dashed directly at the nearest attacking dagger. As its holder lunged at a slack-faced adherent, she snatched the striking hand and dropped it to the floor. The attacker flipped over his own hand, smashed on his back, and Elara twisted his wrist around in a sickened snap. Kana 23, just like practice. *Dip the Beak.*

She smashed her heel into the softness of his throat once, twice, again, until his pulverized windpipe could suck in no air. The man started gagging, thrashing and clawing at his throat, unable to even scream.

Elara lifted his dagger high above her and waved it like a banner. "Kali'ka! Sangrans! Here me! Rally! Rally!! Face your attackers! Face them!!"

Several heads turned towards her. As they pivoted, several more followed suit. She yanked her hood down. Let the enemy see her! Let them target her! Let her allies see her! She would hide no longer!

"Kali'ka!! Rally! Face them! Face your attacker!! Stare into their eyes! Destroy them! Destroy them utterly! Let nothing remain!!"

More and more, they turned to her. She knew them by who answered her call. "Destroy them! Rally! Place your backs together! Let them see the fire of Kali in your eyes! Let them know your contempt! Make them fear you!!"

Two figures shoved their way through the crush, daggers perched in their grips, tips pointed directly at her. She turned her head to keep them both in view of her right eye. Instinct and muscle memory took over, commanding her body, thrusting her into action.

She dropped low, hefting her own commandeered dagger. Before either attacker could strike, she sprinted directly at one of them and smashed into him with her shoulder, using her full weight to drive her weapon under his ribcage. The blade sunk to the hilt as the man was blasted off his feet.

Before he hit the ground, Elara pivoted and, bursting like a piston, smashed her foot forward and into the other attacker's gut. He doubled over, fell back and was trampled.

Snarling, rapt with glorious fury, Elara spun around, seeking, begging for another assailant. Around her, Kali'ka were locked in combat. Evading, punching in swift flurries, smashing with brutal elbows. Locking joints, rotating, cracking bones. Using the kanas she'd taught them, as their ascendant, employing the techniques she'd bestowed.

They'd heard. They'd listened. And for the moment, they held.

"Elara!" Inos' face pressed into view. One cheekbone was battered and sheered of its skin. Behind him, Oyame stayed close, trying to stay small and unnoticeable.

Elara howled through the din. "We have to find him!"

The twitch of a frown passed across his face. "Fallow?"

"Yes!"

"Now?"

"Yes, now!" She drove her fist squarely into the face of an onrusher, at the line between upper lip and nose. He dropped, clutching his face. The clash sent a lance of pain up her forearm, but she hissed and shook it off. Behind her, Inos lunged at a dagger, capturing it and rotating 180 degrees, hurling its wielder over his hip to smash on the stony floor.

"Yes! Now!" Elara's good eye scanned the whole chamber, employing the holistic focus of no-sight, cutting past the darkness that cloaked the left side of her sight. The scene zoomed in and out. Her lost eye contorted her balance, but didn't destroy it.

"Now, when they're not expecting it! We have to do exactly what they did to us! Follow on their heels! If we wait, they prepare! No more waiting, no more debating! We have to strike at their heart!"

Inos' gaze shot at a spot behind her. Immediately, Elara pivoted and hammered an assailant with the back of her fist. Inos slid past her, keeping back to back with her, driving his weight through his fist, plunging into another attacker at the soft spot under the sternum.

"Through Mors?" Inos rotated with her, auburn mane to shaven head, their eyes on the mayhem circumscribing them.

"No! It's too dangerous! We'll never find him!"

"I don't think he's in Mors, anyway! He considers himself separate! Superior!"

The words grasped for an elusive thought in Elara's mind. She broke formation, snagged Oyame's hood, and yanked her close.

"Oyame!" Elara screamed into the girl's hysterical, panting face. "Have you heard anything about a hideout in the Veneer?"

"W-What! I don't – I don't..." Oyame's attention came unhinged as Inos cleaved his elbow into someone's jaw.

"Focus, Initiate Nagai! Focus!! The Veneer! Are they there? The enemy! Have you heard anything?!"

Blinking through sweat, noise, and a thick glaze of terror, Oyame's words congealed. They came slowly, as though dragged out of her mouth. "Yes! Some of his people – they were dragging a mendicant through Mors. They mentioned something about the Veneer!"

"Then we exit aboveground!" Inos yelled towards them.

Elara drew a quick route through memory. "You know the edge of the Path of Gold along the Tame River? Near the Cusp of the Veneer?"

"I've seen it on a map." Inos blocked a forehanded dagger strike, grabbed the offending hand and rammed the dagger into the attacker's own throat.

I've seen it on a map? An odd comment. "Fine! We can exit there!"

"No!" Inos brought his fist down on an attacker's collarbone. The woman howled, staggered back and was caught in another brawl. "There are comeyes along the Cusp. We exit west of the Uppers! Straight towards the river, then track along the riverbed. At the fourth Bridge to Paradise, we cross into the Veneer! The wall around the Veneer has low spots there!"

In a time-slowed moment, Elara stared at him, uncomprehending. She was sure that she was talking to a different person.

His face slipped into a grin like the mask of a child planning mayhem. His eyebrow crinkled through a thin, white scar. "Trust me. I know the area."

She just nodded in response and set to searching for the next piece of her plan. The burn of intense muscle use crept into her limbs.

There. At one of the twelve entrances to the chamber, Brae sidestepped daggers like a nimble, featherweight boulder. The pore near him swirled in a twisted sea of dark glass. He plucked arms, legs, and necks out the chaos, snapping them like sticks. Some kind of slim object was in one of his hands, black fanned at one tip. A paintbrush? He probably didn't even realize he'd taken it with him from the Scribe's Sanctum.

Elara once again took up the cry as she inched towards Brae. "Sangrans! Here! Rally! Rally! To me! To me!! Clear your minds! Empty yourselves! Fill your bodies with power, and leave your minds empty!"

Slowly, ponderously, the entire body of Kail'ka shifted like a massive amoeba, flexing along its edges, following her and Inos as they fought their way towards Brae, who took notice of them and modified his stance to protect their approach.

"Brae!" Elara shouted. "Take our Kali'ka to Cloister Ignis! It's our last stronghold! Find a way in! Get there however you can! To the void with tradition! Defending yourselves with the Ignitians is the only way to survive! All of you, as one!"

Brae glanced between the two of them, wielding his brush like a sword. "What about you two?!"

"We're going after Fallow."

Brae paused for a moment. "If we exit north of the Leeward Quarter in the southeast, we should be fine! Scions only use that area for the Grand Guignol. Used to paint the ceiling there. Funny, huh?" His crazed grin split his heavy beard.

"Good. Go, then!"

"No! Elara! Don't go! No!" Oyame shrieked, scrabbling for Elara's arm as though she was drowning.

Elara wrested herself from Oyame's grip and grabbed the girl's shoulders in a hardened, iron squeeze. "Oyame! Listen! Oyame!! There's no time to argue! Events have led you here. Now, you must respond in turn. *This* is what it means to be Kali'ka! Now, *be who you are!!*"

The mass of Kali'ka were starting to constrict like a pinched balloon, funneling their way towards the pore nearest Brae, forming a natural barricade along with the walls of Sangra. Men, women, and the stone of their home, melded into one contiguous bulwark.

"Kali'ka!" Elara used her hands to amplify her volume. "Leave this chamber! Follow Brae! Follow your scribe!! Leave through the pores! Clear your mind! You must!! Empty your mind!! Empty your mind or *die!!*"

Brae stared at his brush for a moment before tossing it to the floor and yanking a Kachina's kindling rod out the nearby firepyre, hefting it like a crude spear. "This'll do!" He angled the tip directly at a link of attacks, and started swinging and stabbing. Oyame huddled behind him. "Elara, go!" He nodded towards the nearby pore.

Elara and Inos paused to clear their minds before stepping through the pore. As ascendants, they had the advantage of practice.

In seconds, they were dashing out and up out of the chamber, heading towards the surface, leaving Brae alone in the catacombs of Cloister Sangra to shepherd the rest to safety. She and Inos would do their part, within their grasp and capabilities … but the others must also do the same.

For their own survival, they had to be left behind, whether a fledgling initiate or a seasoned adherent. The way of Kali demanded that Her disciples claw and struggle. They must embrace their own darkness, at any cost. They must shatter themselves to know themselves. They must abandon their egos, their minds, and embrace whatever nucleus was left. If that core was too fragile to survive … then so be it. Passing through a pore was but a single symbol of the long, painful path of the Kali'ka.

The Goddess was the fulcrum of guidance, but they, Her children, were the levers of action and the hands of Her spirit. They were the manifestation of Her essence on Earth, in the realm of Creation. She was but the fire within, and it was within they must look – to Illusion. To potential. To the *possible*.

That night, the Kali'ka would rely on themselves and emerge more capable, durable, keen and hard than ever – those that lived, taken from those who stayed when others left. That night, they would step closer to seeing clearly and truthfully, that they'd always had the power to defy those who with willful diligence and perverse joy sought to debase, exploit, and annihilate.

That night, the Kali'ka would be distilled into their most potent form – the smallest, final fragment of greatest power.

CHAPTER 24
THE BREACHING

Isolated in the chevet of his parish – a small dressing chamber of cherry wood-paneled walls, lavish furniture and amber-glowing, decorative standlamps – Jacobs' trembling hands unfeelingly picked up, folded, and piece by piece donned the full Vestment of Pontification neatly laid out on the dresser in front of him. Gusting jitters of cold, detached anxiety cut through his shivering body and dazed mind. His voice quavered like a hanging branch caught in the wind.

"Oh Logos, honor this, Your servant, that I might be clothed in the Helmet of Your Benign Countenance."

The man in the unclouded mirror in front of him lifted the squarish fabric of his mauve amice and placed it on his head. Frazzled, unblinking eyes stared at him from gray, fleshy pouches. A sallow, rubbery scalp shone through thinning, receding hair. Middle-aged. Wasn't he in his late twenties? Early thirties? Early forties? The years and decades bled together and congealed like a solid block of motionless time. They left him a man he barely recognized, withered and broken like the victim of a consumptive disease.

"Let the Mantle of Divinity gird and sustain me."

He watched his hands slide across the fabric of his garments, making hushing sounds that mothers made towards infants. Along the deep purple scarf hanging from his shoulders, palms uncalloused by the march of time glided, soft as the fresh skin of newborn hands.

"Your Sash of Sanctity edifies this Temple of Your Will."

Moving with the practiced surety of long years, Jacobs fingered his vestments like most men would a lover's wrist. In his mirror, he watched his cuticles, pruned and supple, flatten the gold-fringed stole that wrapped him from shoulder to hip. He saw his nails, trimmed and buffed to a lustrous sheen, straighten the rope of white that cinched his waist.

At least his seminarians had been allowed entrance to prepare his garments one last time. And he had no doubt – it would indeed be the last.

"Let the Waistcoat of Solidarity shield me, and protect me."

Decades, and nothing to show for it. Nothing – nothing! – but the vision of a fractured woman's body stamped into his mind, striking clean everything prior and smothering everything to come.

No denial existed for him to clutch. No great vat of excuses existed to scoop from. No set of comforting verses existed for him to recite. No clever conjuring of words could banish the deed from his mind, or strike it from the record of history.

What he himself had wrought throttled him like a noose. They'd all seen it. Thousands of twin sets of scions' eyes. They'd heard it. Violence and pain and madness, for the first time, visible in a land that knew only ecstasy and abundance. Made manifest through a creature in the form of Jacobs' own mellifluous voice, his own crisp vestments, and own his soft hands, sliding up Hammar's electrolance like a slipknot, wringing, squeezing, its cold titanium chilling his flesh even as the shaft thundered in seismic vibrations.

His fingers still ached from holding on so tightly, from refusing to let go of the unquenchable need to see, finally, what he knew was true.

The Kali'ka weren't the enemy, no. He'd been wrong. They'd all been wrong. Horribly, horribly, wrong. The Kali'ka hadn't killed that woman in Pantheon. It wasn't their machine of torture she'd laid on, that he'd found in Reliquary. They weren't the blight. They weren't the abomination. The enemy was something far more elusive, far more nebulous.

He knew, clearly and cuttingly: the 'enemy' was a state of mind, and the mind was something all of New Corinth shared. It was an affliction that spread through silence, inference, and inaction. He – Jacobs Osgood

– was a symptom.

He had no idea what happened in Pantheon, what power he'd unleashed, or what profound and immediate force moved through him in the days since. Now, on the day before Advent, the holiest day of the Logical calendar – Advent Eve – he had never known or understood less.

But he knew that he'd been changed forever, the second he'd stared into that dead woman's face, into a face of his own creation. He saw that face within, every time he now looked in the mirror.

Now there was nowhere to go. Nowhere to run. Nothing to do except be an actor in the conclusion of his own life.

At least in his parish, he could conduct the basic rites, sacraments, and business left to each and every scion, highest to lowest. His Holiness had no Crystal Throne here. No all-piercing access, like in his residence. No comeyes or magisters – they'd given him the dignity of standing *outside* of his dressing room, not inside.

The tornado of whispers that must be going on outside, beyond the range of his hearing, citing his name, citing his deeds... By Logos, he couldn't cast his mind on it!

A knock, firm and regular like a timepiece, broke Jacobs' concentration. He stepped away from the mirror and opened his door. A magister – young, attractive, sturdy, in Magistrate red and white – stood in the hallway. In an odd blend of deference and embarrassment, the young man bowed, but wouldn't look Jacobs in the eye.

He knew. Of course he knew. They all did.

"Your Grace, we're ready to begin. Everyone is accounted for." The first chords of a great pipe organ's boom rattled the hallway beyond.

"Thank you, Magister ... uh ... what's your name, child?"

"Harold, High Devotee."

"Magister Harold, yes. Thank you for letting me know. I'll..." Exhaling deeply, Jacobs finished in a whisper. "I'll be right there." The young man bowed and turned away.

Out of habit, Jacobs returned to his mirror and stared at the fully assembled Vestment of Pontification cloaking his body. Bleached whites, steamed linens and creased lace all stood stiff and starchy, popping out like a bell, layered in combinations of shapes, colors and patterns.

He had always thought it looked so regal in the past, an icon of pride and wealth. So noble. The clothing itself *ennobled*, wrapping a person in a role as surely as skin wrapped the body. Others saw the dress, judged the dress, knew him by it and the role it signified.

In the Eternal Day, he beamed gloriously, but hazily indistinct and difficult to focus on. Light – never-ending, never-altering – streamed in through evercracks near his ceiling. The golden blur washed away details of his dress in lieu of a uniform glow. It soaked up nuances of color and texture and replaced them with vague impressions of cleanliness.

Lies. It was all lies. And he... He was the prime liar. *That* was the truth, and the truth was a trap because he'd made it so. He'd nurtured a method of deceit. He'd been complicit – he and Logic both – in creating and sustaining the same lie that he'd been told and had told himself since estuary: appearance was reality, and what Corinthians *did* was the same as who they *were*.

He might as well be swapped with one of the colorful clowns tumbling and jumping about Market Canal, lobbing balls while hooting through neon makeup at toddlers who stared blankly back.

Gripping the cool, smooth bronze of his doorknob, he twisted and pulled, and exited into his parish, the picture-perfect model of a scion, broken forever.

***

Right step, pause. Left step, pause. In marching time with grand, blaring organ music, Jacobs stepped up the port side of the apse of his parish, towards the pulpit and altar resting at the head of two columns of pews. Opposite him on the starboard side, the tiny silhouette of a small girl mirrored him, step for step. With each step, the bouquet of white lilies she clutched to her chest shivered as though they were caught in a capricious breeze.

The Cardinal Premise droned from seminarians to either side of the pews, through the rafters and vaulted ceiling high above, magnified and channeled through flo-globes that spun overhead like a flock of doves in the crisp, bloomy air.

"We submit to the Godhead. The Godhead will rise.
The Godhead will open. From its tip He will flow.
We join with the Godhead. We join with each other.
Logos speaks through rivers of white."

Amidst the clash of cymbals, the blare of trumpets, showers of confetti and sparkling light holos, the little girl's face – Sophia, was it? – conveyed all the emotion of a papier-mâché doll, plastered by flat, milky light. She locomoted, only, like a stiff mechanism compelled to action, irresponsive to stimuli, caught in the massive shaft of light beaming from the semi-circular dome above the altar. Reacting to nothing. Moved by nothing.

Just like Jacobs.

Why did she walk, then? Why do it? What compelled the precision of her steps beyond how much her mother, Lucrece, had coached her?

To the left, seminarians were walking up and down the aisles, passing out chalices of blood-red wine to a massive cavalcade of obscure relations, well-known Leviden-goers, and soon-to-be-impressed family acquaintances. The Levitant-laced wine would be held in hand until the precise moment that the Spirit of Logos flowed into His new Bride. Then, they would all fill their throats with deep swallows of Logos' holy draught and undergo Penance.

Twin magisters guarded the doors to the parish, mirroring the magisters along the walls to either side. Their poor attempts at appearing casual made their scrutiny of Jacobs' every movement all the more obvious.

Sitting at the head of the crowd, surrounded by an entourage of admirers, waiting expectantly with her hands clasped, face giddy, was Lucrece Aeve – or Lucrece Dagon, by her claimed named.

Her luscious drape of strawberry-honey ringlets flowed around the head and tumbled over a low-cut dress. Translucent bars of light slipped from the necklace draped around her exposed shoulders, a meshwork of silver and tiny stacks of fluted gold inset with violet and carbuncle gemstones. Non-holo jewelry was often used by Corinthians as indicative of long-standing wealth, especially through marriage.

She was closer than anyone to the pulpit and had a clear view of her daughter's ceremony. Her silky, languorous voice slid through the trumpets and fanfare like the slow flit a tongue.

"Quite handsome, don't you think, hm? Just like his picture. Yes, that's right, it's signed – *personally*. Right on the mantle of our fireplace." She giggled in collusive delight before leaning towards someone else and placing a hand lightly on her chest. "Oh, yes, quite right! This whole experience is so, I don't know – *sublime*. It's like poetry. It only comes one in a lifetime, you know! It must be perfect."

At the sight and sound of Lucrece, Jacobs' simmering anxiety erupted. It squeezed his chest until he almost blacked out. His sense of touch thinned, and his legs nearly collapsed. The need to flee swelled inside, stronger than any other conflicting, surging sensation. Overshadowing it all, guilt loomed like a glowering mountain.

Lucrece was the last person he'd cleansed through Penance, at Advent Sermon. Neither she nor any Corinthian knew one single thing about what happened in Pantheon. His memory of time since her Penance collapsed into a black quagmire of blind emotions.

Her daughter's ceremony was a sham. Another lie. Another distraction. An act, performed by a puppet whom he played.

Still, though... Lucrece and her hair and her skin and her smell – Oh Logos, the smell! A light floral waft twisted by cloying sweat – enchanted Jacobs' mind like a dark captor. She burrowed her way into his bowels, just like in the Sacristy when they'd met, tickling the underside of his flesh with squirming, orgiastic glee. The wrath he'd seen behind her eyes that day enthralled him as much as the blue crackles of an electrolance's tip.

Logos, Logos ... there must be a way out of this. There must be!

Several final steps, and Jacobs stood face to face with Sophia, directly in the center of the light that beamed down from above, through the ceiling. Little motes of dust wandered between them. Standing face to face, she reached his stomach. Her mute lips stayed closed. Her vacant eyes stared straight ahead.

His Bride. A concubine of Logos. A child fit for Breaching.

His left hand extended towards her, moving as though a separate, possessed entity, trembling in the light. After several moments, her tiny, child-soft hand slid into his own, so incredibly small it barely fit into his palm. He closed his fingers, locked hands with her, and both of them turned away from the audience, shoulder to shoulder, just like they'd been taught.

What choice was there but to follow through with the rite? What was left for him? What kind of life was left for her, for that matter? Penance, Levitant, bright and loud pageants? Existing solely as a token for a wealthy husband, eventually displaying her own daughter like she would a purse?

Jacobs screamed inside like a corked bottle.

I have to go! I have to get out of here! I have to flee!

The organ and accompaniment ceased. No sound broke the silence except for the occasional creak of a pew, a throat-clearing cough, and the flitting whiz of flo-globes overhead.

Comeyes joined them in the air, spinning and rotating in long swoops, figure eights, and high orbits, along pre-programmed tracks designed to record footage from the most dramatic compilation of angles possible. Jacobs had no doubt some of them were planted to keep an eye solely on him.

Backs to the audience, Jacobs and Sophia faced the altar and the alabaster statue of Logos, sitting atop a sapphire-veined predella. The trunk of Logos' phallus curved upwards between his wide-spread arms. On either side of the statue, dossals and banners depicted Him engaging in gratuitous sexual acts.

"Lord Logos! This one has come back to you, to be rejoined with Your flock. You, the Great Shepherd, recognize your own, for Your abundance and joy fashioned each of our faces and the innumerable hairs on our head. You know each one by name, these, Your Brides, even before they are brought back to You."

Releasing his hold on Sophia's hand, he lifted a maniple from amongst various implements on the altar, unfolded the little handkerchief once, re-creased it into a pinched triangle, once, then again, and placed it across his left forearm. It matched his stole shade for shade. Piece by piece, in this manner, he commenced with the Breaching, in delicate, whispery movements. The organ took up a quiet, genteel refrain. Tiny squeals of giddiness came from the crowd.

"Her unique oneness will be joined with the Body of Brides whom we present as our perfect offering, a libation sweet smelling and pleasing to your sight. The Godhead will rise."

Sophia placed her cupped hands above a bowl enchased with silver doves and entwined knots. Jacobs lifted a platinum ladle, careful to slide it between thumb and index finger from spoon to hook. Scooping gently in the bowl, he let three pours fall onto her hands before setting the ladle down.

"The flesh of two will become one. For this reason, a woman leaves her mother and returns to her true Father above, the Lord Logos. Thus her old life is traded for the new one, and a girl becomes a woman."

Jacobs turned to a tiny cabinet that housed a fluttery, white dress wrapped around a dummy. He opened the cabinet's miniature glass door and ran his hands along the delicate, sheer surface of the dress inside. Above it, on the dummy's faceless head, rested a dazzling, half-moon tiara.

Jacobs lifted the thin, bejeweled white gold and stared at it, transfixed. He found he could do nothing else, say nothing else, except stand there twiddling it in his fingers. His body stopped responding, stopped carrying out orders.

Behind him, the organ reached its transition to the next part and stuttered before playing around the ending cadence a bit. At a frantic gesture from a nearby seminarian, the organist looped around to the beginning of the last phrase. Strained, concerned hisses rose from those in attendance.

Jacobs looked towards Sophia, then back to the tiara. Back to her, back to the tiara.

How fragile they both looked … as if they would crumple in his hands. Bend, resist, then crack and snap in a flash.

Right now, he could do it, easy as a whisper. To break the head that would wear the crown, or crumple the crown that would break a head.

In memory, he stepped through the Breaching.

…Lifting her veil as she bends over, facing away from him. His

extended penis seeking its home, seeking enclosure in the firm grip of sanctuary. One veil lifting while another one is pierced, to re-enter and strive once more for the lost comfort of the womb...

Next to Jacobs, Sophia waited patiently and stared at nothing. Her dirty blonde hair, streaked with red like fruit paint – was pulled tightly across her scalp into two pigtails. Little wisps escaped here and there to float freely.

Brides usually weren't old enough to ovulate, true, but he didn't remember them looking so young before. So small. So frail. They just ... *were.*

The dead woman in Pantheon, whose life ended as she wept and begged for mercy... Did she start out like this little girl? The flower to Sophia's bud?

In that moment, the door of Jacobs' mind blast wide open and the light of comprehension, searing and penetrating, soaked into him.

He'd already made his decision. How long had he been seeking any excuse to make his choice real? Since long, long ago, perhaps. Since the first time he had been spoken to derisively by His Holiness. Since the first time when his sincerity had been mocked by the person he respected and emulated. Since the first time he stunted his true feelings – anger and embarrassment, along with all the other Nihil Obstat words – and channeled them into the head of sexual aggression. Since the first time he realized that Levitant only masked, but never created.

Penance wasn't to cleanse others. It was a failed attempt to cleanse *him.*

Had it all been necessary, to lead to this one moment of understanding?

If he made good on his train of thought, Sophia would be ostracized, true. Banished. Doomed to trek and wander, never to find shelter in a roof of a nation of Logos. Never to receive amnesty from any nation that bowed to the will of the Godhead. Never to infect another with Nihil Obstat thought and words. No Penance, no Levitant, no loft, no abundance. All of it, stripped away in one instant.

But, she'd be spared the abuse. She could choose with what little she had left.

And him... He would be spared the deed. The woman in Pantheon would be his last sacrifice.

One power was still afforded to him. The power imbued him by those in attendance. The power afforded by those who sat rapt, waiting for guidance. The power of the mystic. The power of belief.

Jacobs placed a shaking hand on Sophia's soft head. Faint heat warmed his palm. His unhardened palms rested comfortably, cushioned, sensing in the lightness of his touch the gentleness of shared breath that circulated between him and this little girl. In the constriction of a mutually enclosed space, they breathed. In, out. In, out. In, out.

Jacobs whispered the final ceremonial words of the Breaching, for her ears only. "Absolved, you may now walk reassured of your purity in the Eyes of Logos. He exalts in you, His perfect Bride."

Her eyes rose to meet his. They were green and twinkled like stardust. Not happy, not sad, just ... curious. Odd, Jacobs thought. It seemed that the strange little scar on her eyebrow was real after all.

"Excuse me, child. I'm going to raise my voice, but please don't be ... *frightened*. Do you know that word? No matter, no matter..."

He gripped his garments with both hands – the ones he'd so delicately applied to his body, the ones he'd worn year after year after year – and rushed the audience.

In one vicious yank, he tore the flimsy linen of his cassock in two.

"She is unfit for Breaching! Excision! Excision!"

The music stopped. Everyone gasped.

In the front row, Lucrece's chalice clattered to the floor, spraying wine in an arc of spattered plum. For a moment, its rolling rim was the only audible sound.

"Excision! Excision! Remove the girl from this Parish! Remove her! Immediately!" Jacobs stabbed his hands at the air. The words bounded off of the stone walls and floor. Every jaw was slack, blasted by shock. "Lord Logos rejects her! She is not fit to be His Bride! I command it! I, your High Devotee, command it!"

One by one, those in attendance turned to those nearest them, distressed, crying out to each other, crying out to the altar, unknowing of what to do.

The Magistrate left their positions, confused, taking half-steps, wondering if they should try and keep order. It was unlikely they even knew the procedure for such a moment.

Several seconds after they'd started to converge on the crowd, Jacobs acted. He leapt off of the pulpit, stumbling and smashing his knee on the floor, before scrambling to his feet and dashing straight through the center aisle in a tottering, shambling run.

He slipped through distracted and stunned attendees, confused magisters, and rammed the front doors of his parish open. He bolted through his courtyard, passed through the garden outside, and was through the gates and down the streets of New Corinth before anyone reacted.

One by one, he left a trail of discarded clothing behind him on the ground. The full Vestment of Pontification. Only his torn cassock remained on his body by the time he was several blocks away.

Strolling Corinthians turned their heads to stare, but he completely ignored them.

"Is that the High Devotee?"

"The High Devotee!"

"It *is* him! Oh High Devotee! Excuse me!"

"High Devotee! High Devotee!"

"High Devotee!"

Panting hysterically, pushing through the pain in his knee, Jacobs fixed his eyes on the first place he saw. Ahead of him, over the Tame River and towards the west, a dull gray pallor cloaked an otherwise untarnished horizon of gold.

The Veneer.

So be it! Hegil ... I'll join you soon. There's no place left for either of us!

Behind him in his parish, beyond the range of his hearing or sight, amidst screams and fleeing feet, and the gasps of a mortified Lucrece, the tiny half-moon tiara rolled aimlessly back and forth on the floor at the feet of an un-Breached, untouched little girl.

CHAPTER 25
TWIN HUNTERS

Through the hard-packed refuse of Veneerian warrens, Elara and Inos hunted. They bled from shadow to shadow, slipping through narrow, wall-compressed paths of decayed buildings and ducking under low, defilement-moistened rooftops.

They searched for any shift in the flow of skulking shapes that snarled as they passed, emaciated in scraps of clotted cloth, flesh coated in untended, sopping sores. They looked for any alteration in the rhythm of men and women who huddled against walls and rooted around in the vile, raw stew of filth and sticky fluids that saturated the ground like glassy pavement. They sought any marking of territory that might indicate an intrusive presence, while attempting to stay out of sight as much as possible of prowling, brazen Levitant gangs who pulverized random Veneerians into crippled piles of human tissue.

The Veneer was such a vile mishmash of rancid waste, animal musk, vomit and blood that it took all of Elara's fortitude to defy her instinctive, physiological repulsion, let alone focus on their task, ascendant of Kali or not. Everywhere, the dead or near-dead saturated pathways as often as the gibbering living. Every suck or sip of breath invaded hers lungs like a noxious contagion. She felt, simply by proximity, that some crawling desecration had sunk into her skin and invaded her veins.

Inos had assured her that it was unlikely the Veneerians would cause trouble unless the two of them broke any one of the host of the Veneer's expansive, implicit codes of conduct. If they did, they would be hounded till dead.

It was not a reassuring statement.

Overhead, the moon hung high, her pale aura surrounding her like an astral diadem. One curved sliver shy of perfect emptiness, of the night of the new moon, she was a narrow crescent bathing the decayed buildings and streets below in spectral bloom cleaved by black shadows.

Sunfall was swiftly descending. They were one day away from the new moon and the winter solstice. Advent Eve. One day from the Pageant of Miracles. One day from Advent.

In a skyscape that bled from bluish-black in the west to blinding white in the east, the moon took the aspect of a lone guardian standing off against an oppressive force of eastern light, mantling the sky and girding the heavens in a golden rim. The gleaming towers of the Uppers stood above the skyline like sentinels of gold, scorched in the relentless heat of the Eternal Day.

It was as though the Great Mistress Herself spoke through the celestial entity above, like a tether stringing itself heavenward from the center of Elara's body, leaving no space between. Like some make-believe childhood trip out of New Corinth, the moon had lived in her mind's eye only.

The Veneer was the one place in New Corinth where the moon could be seen and could shine her light down ... and the only thing she could illuminate was rot. All she could see was unfulfilled potential.

Tonight, Kali was in the moon, and Elara would reflect Her like a polished body of water, drawing her down, being the surface upon which She took shape below.

Elara glanced behind her, attempting to visualize the path they'd taken. The roads were an entangled, incomprehensible mess. First they'd been in the Cusp, staying out of sight along a series of dashes. Then, they'd been in the Veneer. The transition was immediate, as soon as they crossed the Tame River. From the Eternal Day to complete desecration, over the width of the river. Only the great synthstone wall, circumventing the Veneer like a moat, held back the bloated press of humanity from the indolent millions of New Corinth.

Inos knew exactly where its height allowed for passage. He knew every route and every nuance. He flowed like an untouchable ghost, a master at ease in his field of expertise. He was one with the environment because he accepted it. That acceptance, in turn, projected an aura of sovereignty so strong that the dark-socketed leers of starved or crazed denizens slid away whenever they caught sight of him. From deep within his hood, the winged yantra on his temples sharpened his roving eyes to a fine-filed edge.

"Stop looking like you're trying to appear inconspicuous. It'll make you a target."

Elara started, not realizing that she was doing anything of the sort. "I think we're a target, either way." Off to the side, a small cluster of Veneerians glared at her, hands limply pointing in her general direction. Some of their mouths dropped froth.

"We don't need to be wearing our robes for them to know we're outsiders." Inos whisked by an outstretched, trembling grasp. "It doesn't make a difference."

Elara pulled her arms further inside her sleeves. Rather than feel safer in her robes, she felt only felt more vulnerable. "I doubt Kali'ka gray helps, especially if Fallow's lot has been roaming around."

Inos only grunted.

Their robes were a uniform of honor in the cloisters, but an incensing stigma aboveground. This was the first time either one of them had been aboveground in years, and it was also the first time they'd ever been aboveground in full declaration of who they were and what they believed. Their identities were painted clearly for anyone and everyone who had eyes.

It produced a type of self-consciousness that Elara found detestable.

"It's odd..." Inos' voice broke Elara's reverie. "I don't see any of the Errati."

"The who?"

"The children of the Veneer. The young ones. They band together. Roam where they please, when they please, disregarding boundaries, defying their inevitable slide into the hopelessness of this place ... as long as possible. They never stop pushing back. They never stop fighting. They never yield. You'll recognize them by their piercings."

Elara's ear caught something in his tone. First-hand and personal, like a proud father. She remembered the multitude of tiny scars across his face and ears.

"You were Errati. You ... pulled out your piercings."

After a second, he nodded. "I was. And I did. I haven't been here in over twelve years. But, nothing has changed. The dirt and the bodies are in different spots, is all. They ... well – they didn't much like me leaving, the Errati. Chased me out. Otherwise I would've wound up in Mors, strangely enough. No one leaves the Errati, never – no matter where they'd end up if they stayed."

Elara looked over at him, seeing him through a new and compounded perspective, like an added facet of a gem. His behaviors, his mannerisms, his patterns of speech, his unique method of problem-solving, his slightly sunken cheeks, the deep creases along the sides of his mouth, his hyper-attentiveness to the environment. It produced a portrait that was obvious in retrospect.

It was quite easy to see him skulking exactly as he now was, except as a ragged boy. Pilfering for food, evading troupes of murderers. Slimmed down to necessity. Hardened through strife. Always fighting. Every moment of every day fighting simply to continue subsisting, or succumbing to die.

In her inner eye, Elara saw him escaping through the same channels they now walked. With his own two hands twisting, tugging, tearing metal rings and rods from his flesh in the cover of a night-cloaked alleyway, under a low-hanging eave. In a bloody, ragged sprint, fleeing the Errati who swore to kill him for wanting to leave.

And now ... he'd been forced to return.

More than ever, Elara understood at what point she and Inos connected. Their essences flowed together like conjoined waterfalls, strung like threads in the same tapestry. Him, the Veneer. Her, the offhand sexual abuse of Logic.

She wondered what she'd feel like if she ever had to retread the set of streets that led up to the Aeve family loft in the Uppers, let alone enter her old room and sleep in her old bed.

The flaw produced the strength, in both of them. The Veneer, on the surface, was one giant wound. But, it was only the very tip of the underside of an iceberg vast and deep. In its frozen belly was a blackened realm, a nest for every thought not admitted by Logic, every word unuttered by mothers, fathers, children, scions. It all funneled straight here to this place, the unseen consciousness of a Logical world.

The Veneer was their justification for denial. The Veneer was the realm that, by necessity, must exist for the play-world of Logic to persist in deluded, milky whiteness.

Elara had never known, not firsthand. She'd never understood how Kali Herself dwelled in these people, unrecognized and unknown to their conscious awareness. The Goddess was here, present yet untapped like an untainted vein of ore.

For now, the Veneerians kept their minds from searching. They saw, but didn't seek. They retreated inside, but never took the next step inwards.

But if they caught sight of the suppressed, whipped, brutalized dignity lurking deep within, and fully beheld their own potential... Elara was certain that there would be no barriers, no blockades, no power on Earth strong enough to stymie their bristling numbers from swarming out and devouring New Corinth in a maelstrom of wrath – deserved wrath; the wrath of the ignored. Certainly not the Bridges to Paradise, comeyes, or the Magistrate.

"You see our friend over there?" Inos' gaze roved through the environment, focus unlocked, employing no-sight. He didn't move his head, but she was able to follow his eyes to an aberration in the environment – a bobbing motion at the edge of sight. As soon as she saw it, it stood out as clearly as a figure of white on black parchment.

They were being shadowed by a scrawny shape sliding in and out of the general debris, slipping around people, ducking behind objects, adhering to corners. A syncopated, squirrelly, start-stop movement that lurched as often as tread.

The shade and shape of the clothes stood out more than anything.

"The vestments... A mendicant?" Elara murmured. "Oyame mentioned something about a mendicant being dragged through Cloister Mors."

"He's letting us see him. That works to our advantage. Let him play his part. His actions will reveal themselves."

Elara nodded in reply and kept her eyes forward, keeping some of her attention shifted towards the mendicant.

She and Inos reached the mouth of an alleyway and crouched down to observe the milling throng ahead. There was no way out except to push forward. The small little man-shape of the mendicant deliberately broke off and hobbled into an alleyway across the street.

At that moment, the crowd suddenly rippled as though a zipper pulled them apart. A figure bolted from nowhere down the road, slicing by people. Gray. A Kali'ka. Its robe flapped behind it.

The setup was clear – overly transparent. It didn't matter, though. She and Inos had no choice.

Elara teetered on the balls of her feet, ready to dash out. "I'll take the Kali'ka."

Inos slung an arm out in front of her. "No! They want to weaken us. Separate us!"

"Obviously! But we have to follow them. Both of them. We could waste a lifetime trudging around this place."

"What – How will we possibly find each other?"

She pointed up at the moon. "So long as we see her face, we have direction. We can find our way back."

"To where?" Inos bore down. "All the way across New Corinth to Ignis? Sangra is just as lost as Mors, now!"

"To the light-blinded Basilica – I don't know! Listen – there isn't a trap that could hold either one of us. I trust you to take care of yourself."

"Elara – I haven't done a good job of ensuring your safety so far, but – "

"Inos... I didn't come here expecting to leave."

He stared directly into her eyes, both of them – her black, empty eye, and her living, green eye – and was slowly seized by the realization of what she said.

"Inos ... Fallow took Mors. He took our home from us. He took Marin. I'm *not* risking him getting away. He's near, and there's no one else left to stop him from dividing the Kali'ka forever. That's why we came here!"

Inos' fingers ground into the dirt under their feet. "Fine. I'll take the mendicant. He'll be harder to track."

He made to go, but paused and turned directly towards her, holding his body in suspended motion.

Elara stared into his gray eyes, hard like refined metal, yet awash with the softness of the sky. The tempest of emotion that poured from them startled her.

The response it provoked in her startled her more. She suddenly realized that he was worried about her for a completely different reason.

She was even more terrified to find the same response inside of *herself*.

"I'll find you." He held his gaze for a moment, and then he was gone. All she saw was his robes dashing into the crowd, disappearing into the bustle.

Alone amidst thousands, Elara stared at the spot where he last knelt, unable to move. It was some time before she darted off in the direction of the Kali'ka robe.

She ran and ran, eyes locked ahead, dodging slow-trudging indigents, hurdling clumps of refuse, driven by a purpose as unyielding as a hammer-beaten anvil.

But within, her entire psyche remained mystified by the strange warmth that seeped into the cracks in her clay heart, smoothing and salving. Warmth, sparked by the static charge of equals.

Inos... I swear if we survive this, we'll find solitude and peace – somewhere, somehow ... innocent one.

CHAPTER 26
ASHRAM

Elara stalked from point to point, ears pricked to the wind, eyes wide to the earth. In this far-flung pocket of the city, the outer wall of New Corinth rose like an embattlement, tracing along the perimeter of the Veneer. Channels grew increasingly confined and isolated, with fewer and fewer connecting paths. Space between buildings grew tighter, leaving only a narrow band of starry darkness above.

The shade-blackened causeways of the Veneer were getting dimmer as the final moments of sunfall approached. Scattered, solitary people roamed the roads, keeping to walls and dashing across streets before slipping out of sight. Dogs barked in the chill sweep of a night wind that scooped down and flapped Elara's robes in fluid ripples.

Her quarry had ducked into the rubble and muck of a nearby alleyway, vanishing into its mouth, luring her, allowing her a clear line of light to see where he went. There were no guards, no patrols, nothing to indicate the entrenched, fortified presence she expected.

She glided into the alleyway, no different from countless others, and tracked forward, sliding in and out of shadows. The alley had no connecting passages. It fed directly into a wide-open courtyard circumscribed by a band of lopsided buildings, caved-in floors, and poorly constructed add-ons.

Elara stopped dead. Her feet stumbled and caught on the uneven dirt underfoot. Her hand leapt to her mouth. The stench assaulted her.

The walls were a solid, interlocking tapestry of hacked and hewn human remains, smeared with trails of blood. In the moonlight, the gore-slick mosaic glistened a colorless tone of black, matte and thick. Bones protruded from fibrous shafts of arms and trunks of legs that hung from hooks, swaying next to rib cages and blood-slick skin nailed into patches of viscera-soaked wood.

She could almost hear the screams, feel the knives sliding across their skin and prying it apart.

The entire scene was skewed, like its artist had tilted its portrait and shaken its parts. The ground itself appeared rent, lifted up and blown away from a mound of upraised earth across from the entrance, where laid three poles of decrepit wood, lashed with crossbeams, knocked onto their side. It was as if an explosion had rocked the courtyard's crafted palette. Off to one side, some kind of an ancient … forge?… lay toppled over, its coals and chains sprawled on the ground.

Among the gruesome wall remnants, she recognized spirals, curves, and slashes, pointing from spot to spot in an interconnected portrait. Lifted up and redrawn here, exactly to proportion, in the open air of the Veneer. Every emblem, every yantra, recreated in exact, meticulous, detail…

…The Spirals of Armistice…

…Julia's Recursion…

…Hearts of Light…

…The Belt of Pyramids…

It was the Chamber of Sarcophagi reconstructed as an abomination; a crude, perverse version fashioned from the ground, buildings and walls, refracted through a twisted, dark artifice into a sadistic, grotesque monument.

Amongst the fallen crosses, some oddness in the shadows drew her attention. They fused into a hard outline, like corporeal clouds.

A man. Still as the night. Clothed in Kali'ka gray. The one she'd been chasing? The abyssal opening of his hood was blacker than the starless night of the new moon of Advent, descended on a world far from the reach of the Eternal Day, where nightmares found life in a worldly vessel.

Fallow. It had to be him.

He lifted his hands to the edges of his hood and pulled back.

Pulverized human meat stared back at her, hardened and petrified into crusted, scabby scars that crisscrossed themselves and bulged like mountain ridges. Skin flapped from his tattered lips, freshly ripped and puffy. Most of his face, barring the section around his left eye, was a mass of dense disfigurement. His right eye was completely shut, heaped tissue having grown over it.

He dismounted from the dirt dais in fluid, serpentine steps. Elara faced him directly, refusing to react to his twisted appearance. She maintained distance step for step, senses keen and hyper-attuned to any deviation in his movements.

The two of them circled each other like satellites around an imaginary center. They bristled like ancient gladiators as their feet crunched through blood-soaked dust.

His one eye was a pit of welling scorn. Palpable, focused hate flowed from it in hammering waves. Elara felt – physically – the danger present in every left-right sway of his pelvis, every flex or twitch of his hands. The restrained violence, the craving for conflict, the explosive temper, the labile emotions.

Elara had infiltrated the den of shadows, and now she stood face to face with its emperor.

"Ascendant Aeve." His rich, oily voice carried a wealth of hidden intonation. "How generous of Kali's only begotten daughter to reside here in the flesh along with the rest of us. At least, with a little *less* flesh than I imagined." He grinned and tapped a finger on his scars.

Elara felt her hand jerk to the coarse, sense-numb skin tracking along the left side of her face and neck. The black blot in her vision – which she had started to become accustomed to – reared to the forefront to block her sight anew.

"For such a fiery creature, I'd expect you to be a bit more at home in flames, Ascendant Aeve. Unrepentantly willful and naturally avoidant is a dangerous combination. It invites suspicion. So often has fire, in our past, been used to scorch societies clean of such fringe or misunderstood people, especially those who look like you. Red hair, fair skin, gray robes. Interesting though, how ash describes nothing of what it used to compose. I'm left to wonder what *you* will leave behind, ascendant."

Memories of the Chamber of Sarcophagi, of light and heat and indescribable pain, flooded into Elara's mind. It burned her thoughts, distracting her, pulling her away from the moment.

A sneer twisted the pulverized flesh of Fallow's face. "My only regret is that I couldn't have been there to hold the flame to you and watch your skin crack, peel and blacken. You have only plastein to thank for your resurrection, nothing else. How does that strike you, hm? Not even the golden calves of our past would've made a better offering. They would've *melted*, at least, into something useful. Still, for a hand-made idol, perhaps you're a better substitute for our flaws. You live to be sacrificed again, just like these fools around us!"

He flung up a hand to the bloody tapestry strung across the walls. It scrolled as they circled each other. It was a struggle for Elara to not look away.

"What's wrong, *Ascendant Aeve*? Can you not even cast your third eye on these..." he flicked a hand dismissively, "...symbols of blood and flesh?! This is the true face of Kali! This is the true face of any of us. These rubbery sleeves we wear," he gripped the shredded skin of his cheeks and yanked viciously. Fresh blood oozed from caked crevasses, "...are meaningless!"

Elara swallowed back bile and kept her feet moving. His combination of feverish words and flippant attitude – disconnected but obsessive – disturbed her almost more than anything.

This was the leader of the unthinkable severance, she reminded herself. The spark of an unremitting brushfire. The font of division. The man who sent someone to take her own life, down in the Codex of Cloister Sangra. The man who barricaded himself in a hovel and used the ill and the indigent of the Veneer as a moat.

She had to press for information. He would not waylay her! He was the pathway to finding Marin, and that path would be closed if she showed her intent too clearly, too early.

As soon as she had what she needed, as soon she knew what he intended – what his plans and schemes were, regarding the Kali'ka and New Corinth – she would finish what she came to do.

"Is this how you did it...?" She lifted a hand to the bloody remains on the walls. "Is this how you destroyed the sarcophagus in Cloister Sangra? Using these body parts for some ritual? To mimic the inscriptions inside the Chamber of Sarcophagi? Is that what these people died for?"

"The torment of a few people, Ascendant Aeve – even entire generations – is irrelevant if it yields the end we need." His slow, liquid steps crunched in the dirt.

"It didn't even work, Fallow – your plan. I was there. We fought back. We *survived*. We stopped you from moving on to Ignis."

"Oh, I think it worked just fine, Ascendant Aeve. You're here, aren't you?" He lifted his hands in a mocking display. "I invited you into my home, indirectly, as both guest and gift. This is my Ashram, you see. My sanctum. The strife of the past built this place, just as the strife of the present builds our future. History is but a single monument of stacked stones!" The ring of his voice hummed, histrionic yet removed, effusive yet frozen.

"These were *people*, Fallow, not 'stacked stones'! Did they beg for the Great Mistress to claim them? Were they Her disciples? Were they innocents? Had they committed themselves to darkness? To the fire within?"

"Foolishness! These people were not the gods we are, Ascendant Aeve, have no worries. They hadn't embraced the trials we have. They fought it, every day, right here in the Veneer. Or, they avoided it completely and wasted away to nothing. But I… I found a use for their purposeless lives!"

Elara's anger spiked and poured from her lips. She continued to follow his movements, step for step. "You had no right! Just like you have no right to act as our representative! No right to divide our order! No right to unravel thousands of years of peace just to slake whatever defects live inside you! Don't you remember Reverend Dogen of Sight? '*A full mind is a mind of failure.*'"

"Reverend Dogen is *dead*, ascendant! These times are different! Kali'ka then were just as blind as Kali'ka now! We are the heirs of Earth! We are the Goddess made conscious!"

His body quivered from strident, white-knuckled intensity, and his fingers violently stabbed the air.

"We are Her hands, the appendages that grip the tools to forge a future of hammer and blade, are we not?! We see truly, to the untouched depths inside – to what we *really* think and feel. It's our right and our duty to be the elite amongst the chaff. We are the ones worthy!"

"We are the Goddess made conscious, yes, but…" She swept an arm towards the Uppers, towards the place of her birth and the home of her family. Images of her mother, father, Lucrece and Charlotte danced inside. "So are *they!* They just don't realize it, yet!

"That's why we're here, Fallow, to hold awareness within until they're ready! To take in those who've come in contact with the face of Kali *on their own*, and have no guide in a Logical society! They'll seek us out. You did! I did! We were both once Corinthian.

"We take them in. We instill them with the techniques and the fortitude to understand themselves! To know that they've been lied to since birth. We help them choose. To be in possession of their inner self. No one person is more worthy! There are only more worthy *actions*!

"We act on Kali's behalf, as –" she hesitated, her throat stuck with an unrecognizable emotion "– as their *mother*. Not their killer!"

Fallow sneered, his rent face stretching. "Don't you see? Logic is too immense! Their offenses are too egregious! You yourself have been *cleansed* by their scions, Ascendant Aeve! That's why you came to the Goddess. But you've been too long out of their world. Their pitiful lives have long since stopped earning them more time to *change*. You still don't understand what I want?! The Eternal Day must be destroyed!"

"What *you* want doesn't matter, Fallow! We're here, right now, only because you think what *you want* is what the rest of us *deserve!* I despise Logic as much as you, believe me. The manipulation, the deceit, the delusions. But a true Kali'ka acts as he wills without making demands on others! Without forcing anything on anyone! You to yours, and yours alone! Logic will maim itself, Fallow! That's what we teach!"

"Stop using my name!" He made an agitated, scattering motion. "You are not allowed to use it! You use it in vain, *Elara!*"

Her lips curled reflexively. To hear her first name on his tongue… He was subversively intelligent, using language like a virtuoso. His words had the shape of merit. He was also rabid and deranged. No matter the rightness of what he said, it was his illness – the great rift inside him – that drove him. No matter what internal validation he used, he remained led by the leash of frayed impulses, snared in a mind-trap, impossible to reason with or sooth. That, by itself, bespoke his danger, and revealed the false motivations that guided his rationale and actions.

"Fallow … any man can believe what he wants in his own mind, but it doesn't change what's around you."

"Wrong! Not true! I *can* change what's around me! I'm doing it right now! I *have* done it! The pastel smoothness of the creamy streets and their speckless delusions – Damnation on it! Hell and fire! They must not persist unharmed! They – all of them! – living in their gel-wrapped, plastic, pink and sweet lives. They've never known pain! They know nothing of real sorrow! They have no understanding! They *can't* understand!"

So furious was his ranting that red lines slid from his stretched and mulched face. Drops of blood slipped away to strike the dry earth underfoot like pittances tossed to a beggar.

Something in his features … the way the cool, luminous moonlight bounced off the patch of skin near his undamaged eye, caught Elara's attention and coaxed out some forgotten memory.

"Do you have any idea what it feels like to see what I see, Ascendant Aeve? To feel the world like a net, strung tight over you?"

Instead of being molded from scars, Elara saw his face as a mask, tumorous, engulfing him in malignancy. He continued speaking – either to himself or her, she wasn't sure.

"…Barbed with teeth, woes lashing you like a whip, ripping muscle from bone carelessly, heartlessly…"

The mask could be plucked off, one scabby portion at a time. Underneath, the real man of the past existed without wrinkle or blemish.

"…To be so well-acquainted with sorrow that nothing else is commonplace, and all else is imagination? Hm? Do you know, Ascendant Aeve?!"

She filled the air with a whisper. "Of course I know."

His face retracted like the jaws of a shark. "Lies! No one knows! No one cares! No one feels how I do! No one understands! They will all burn! All of them!!"

"You were sitting in the back."

"What?!"

Elara's mind started reconstructing his features.

...Tanned, earthen skin. Strong nose and wide lips. Eyes – two of them –deep, dark brown nearly black, staring out, anxious, unsure. Dark enough to nearly match the tone of the thick, wavy hair that framed his face...

"I recognize you, Adherent ... Fallow? That's not your real name."

"Adherent?! Don't call me that! I am not even an ascendant!"

"What did you do to yourself...?" Elara saw her memory of the man side by side with the creature in front of her.

"I am not an adherent. I am not an ascendant! I am the true Transcendent! I require no evidence of it! I require no Stabat! No strictures! Nothing to control me!! I've seen it!"

"There is no Transcendence, Fallow." Elara spoke in a trance, caught in her thoughts. "It's an idea. An allegory, maybe. The Stabat ascend us, one circle at a time, and then it ends. *Death* is Transcendence. Life to death, death to life."

"No!! I will break it! I've seen it! The place of fire! The burning sky! The gods will know my name! I will pry their realm open, and obliterate the cycle! I will transcend death! I will *not* die! I won't! I can't!"

"Selenist... That's where it was. Several years back. I remember. The time when we congregate. During the demonstration of kanas. The 72 hand positions. You were sitting in the back. An adherent of Mors. Whether or not anyone else remembers, I do. I remember what you look like under those scars. I've seen your true face, the one you so desperately tried to destroy ... or conceal."

Silence. Fallow became as still as an untouched puppet. It was several minutes before he spoke again. When he did, his once-handsome face split like broken glass running red with the blood of pried fibers.

"It doesn't matter anymore – what you remember, or who I was. I see a world, Elara Aeve... I have scoured the landscape of the future, seen the horror, seen Illusion stripped, seen the cratered wound that will leave a permanent rift in the realms. I have plans. No sight left unseen! Nothing denied!

"We must be as inviolate as Logic believes they and their god are. And when the creation becomes the creator, the creator becomes the one trodden on like a broken light! New Corinth will sink into darkness, and we will rise beyond our sunken catacombs to take our rightful place as heirs of Earth! And, it will happen in a way no one thinks possible! Advent is nigh!"

In his grin Elara saw the reddened, destroyed realm of skyfire she saw her visions. Countless dead. Fields of bodies, spread towards the horizon. The Veneerians on the walls, splayed in gristly arrangements... They had, in the end, met their prophet.

Fallow had gripped who he was and held it high as an object of contempt. He'd decimated himself and rejected the form he'd been given. He'd taken the chisel of Creation and drove it again and again to rend all majesty from the sculpture of his life.

No... No... This man was no Kali'ka. He never had been.

"If you reject the world I offer, Ascendant Aeve, then you – the Great Mistress' greatest proponent – will not live to see it! You don't deserve to! You're no better than the scions!"

At that moment, Elara saw herself as a third entity, transfixed by Fallow's appearance. Her feet stopped. She screamed at herself to move.

"You'll see," Fallow mused. "I won't fail. My actions will mark the rebirth. Trust them. Trust *me*. There is no doubt. They will understand, all of them. You must be made to understand, too, ascendant. You must be released. Awoken, just like New Corinth."

Fallow's body shifted. His posture sunk. Before Elara could react, his fluttering gray robe was all she saw. Quicker than a slip of air, he was next to her. Her left side. Her blind side.

She gasped as pain exploded under her ribs. Her respiration caught. Her lungs couldn't move.

The pain in her side welled like a pocket of acid. It pounded like the beat of the sun. A presence – foreign and edged – lodged itself in her kidney. The acrid swell of Fallow's breath drifted across her as he whispered.

"The renal artery is particularly devious, you know. So much pain for such a small area. Such a concentrated source of blood, flooding through a narrow tube."

She felt his wrist rotate. Pressure like a mountain bore down on her side. Agony, sharp like shrapnel, tore through her body.

"Pain is a threshold system, you see. You would have witnessed that if you were here for Ashram's creation. Nothing is registered up to a point, and then pulse, pulse, pain! All or nothing, in spurted waves, just like the Spirit of Logos itself. I have only to push hard enough, and you react. And you *did* react, like an organism of reflex.

"You and all those in Cloister Sangra – your old advocate, too; I know you're looking for her – you've been funneled into a narrow tube. The dredges of you Unchanged are shuffling along to Ignis, are they not? Drawn out, then packed into one spot, ready and waiting for *me*.

"I only regret that I couldn't get my hands on that sweet little sister of yours. In a less well-composed state … of course."

Charlotte?! Elara could say nothing. She could do nothing but stay unmoved, paralyzed, unable to even gasp for air. Any attempt to draw breath sent excruciating agony lancing through her body. Her consciousness flickered in and out of wakefulness.

"We are the gods we've always invented, Ascendant Aeve. Why not embrace that role? The realm of dominion is ours. It's not the realm of Illusion. It's *this* one. We need not wait till death. That's what you've never understood."

A shuck of flesh, a tear of cloth, a blaze of anguish, and Elara dropped to the ground. Through teary, hazy vision, she saw nothing but whirls of dust rising from where she'd struck the dirt.

"I was going to string you up on one of these crosses, like the offering you are … but no matter. We can let the Veneer to do what it does best: forget those it never noticed lived."

What? What was he talking about? The words made no sense. They slipped away like water through a grasping hand. Like the red of life steaming hot and thick, soaking through her robe to pour into the dirt of the Veneer.

"You've fulfilled your role, Ascendant Aeve. Your sacrifice will not matter, just like all the other idols throughout history. In the Eternal Darkness to come, no one will know what happened here, today."

Memories swelled inside like choppy waves. Odd bits of frothy images, of Charlotte, of Cloister Sangra, of Inos, all swirled together, leaping, crashing into themselves.

"Goodbye, daughter of Aeve. You carry her name well. Failure defines you. Shame describes you. Your cursed lineage has ended."

She saw his clenched fist hang in the air to her side, squeezing, trembling.

"Your future is alone. Your myth has ended. Creation would have it no other way."

Great Mistress! Deliver me! Deliver your Vessel from this place!

His fist sped towards the gash in her side. The world exploded in pain.

CHAPTER 27
A LIFE TAKEN

Jacobs lurched through the desecrated roads of the Veneer, weeping, wailing, stumbling. He sidestepped steaming refuse, bloated corpses, jabbering lunatics, and rotten animal carcasses. The scene in front of him swayed and leapt like a drunken beggar. His cassock, the last remaining stitch of his vestment, was rimmed in grime and ruined beyond repair, and his palms were torn from the sheering force of slamming into wall after wall in a stupor. Never before had his heart strained so hard to keep up with the relentless skittering of his legs.

No one paid him any mind in the least. No one turned to look as he passed. He, the High Devotee of the entirety of Logic, and no one recognized him. No one cared. No one here could associate him with what he'd done.

It felt good.

But the darkness... Oh Logos! The darkness. How could they live like this! He couldn't see anything. There were no details except near the red glow of the occasional fire, illuminating the patchwork, stained rags of people huddled around it.

And the moon... He'd seen vocodor footage, sure, and he had his imagination to aid him, besides. But nothing could've convinced him of its ethereal ... *beauty*. Billions worldwide, not subject to the Eternal Day, could see the clear night sky as it truly was... But did they? Did they look up and really, *really* see her?

Here in the Veneer, the only things the moon's face could highlight were horrors of decay and indigence. The only people left to witness her striking features were the forgotten, the lost, those who had been forcibly conjured from the remnants of a pre-Logic socioeconomic system that shoved the indigent into one walled extrusion bubbling out from New Corinth proper like a cyst steeping in its own rot.

If only the rest of the scions could come here, and see, feel, hear, smell with their own bodies... If only they could perceive with their own intelligence. Would they pay attention, then? Would they understand? Without the head-wrapped bandana of light and Logical blindness, would they see what Jacobs now did?

Hegil! This is where I sent you...? Oh Logos, I'm sorry! Please! Please forgive me! Jacobs knew better, though... It would take far more than a silent plea to set right those things which had gone manically, inconceivably wrong.

He understood now. There was no Path of Gold, only a path of dirt. No Eternal Day, only an eternal farce. Levitant didn't eradicate anything, didn't extract anything, didn't even gloss over anything. There was no purity, no cleansing, no sanctity.

There was nothing. Only lies. A sham, all of it. The entire world, one sacred pile of dung. The entirety of Logical formulas and plots and stability was one giant fragile shell encasing blathering madness and absurd nonsense.

Their society was not at the apex of history, but the summit of self-deception. All of them, sitting in the golden spires of the Uppers, attending galas and Penance, cleansing each other day and night, lost to their sensations, unaware of their inner motivations, reveling in their tangible abundance... They would be pouring wine down their gullets and declaring their sovereign insolvency even as their mansion of glass collapsed onto its foundation of vapor.

With the next turn, Jacobs tripped and righted his balance. His eyes landed on a spot down the road.

Some misshapen lump laid in the road. Darkly gray in the moonlight. A rock? No, the texture was wrong.

A pale patch stuck out from beneath it, near its bottom edge. Skin? A light shade, matching the ghostly moonlight. A person? Crumpled in a heap. Was that a foot sticking out? Sticking out of … clothes, then?

His eyes were snared by some trick of moon and shadow. A glimmer on the clothes, faintly metallic. Folds and flats of fabric came into focus, thick and coarse, swirled in an unflattering cut. An unadorned, untreated material.

It took several moments to make the final connection that slipped from of his mind like beaded mercury over glass.

Kali'ka!

His body coiled, ready to spring him away, demanding that he respond. Hegil *had* indeed tracked their nest here, after all! But in the middle of the street? Not hiding? There didn't seem to be any apparent threat.

Half-curious, half-instinctive, Jacobs headed straight towards the only person he'd seen since arriving who was familiar in any way. Softly, he swept to one knee in front of the motionless clutter of twisted cloth.

"Um … excuse me." His tentative whisper became a strained whisper-shout as he tapped the cloth. "Excuse me!"

Delicately, gingerly at first, his hands fumbled over the person, seeking something solid to clutch. Grasping something thick enough to be a shoulder, he pulled, and a face rolled over towards him.

Jacobs gasped and stifled a cry.

It was a woman, horribly scarred down one half of her face. Dirt and gravel clung to bruises and scrapes across her cheekbones and eyebrows. A gash across one her temples cut through what looked like strange decorative facial paint. Her chest rose and fell, shallow, irregular, sticking and releasing. Her fingernails were split and shattered, her fingertips bloody.

Her hood lay under her head like a pillow. The thick wool must've cushioned her skull and maybe bought her a few more minutes.

Jacobs' fumbling hands pushed aside the tangled strands of her thick, darkish hair in an attempt at gentleness. Her features were oddly peaceful, serene as though she was happily asleep.

The hair, something in the face… She reminded him of Lucrece Dagon, daughter of the Aeve family. Except, this woman was … harder. Rawer. Bolder. Untamed, like a savage fox. A sleeping fox. Made of steel, but wrapped in velvet. Most dangerous when cornered. Lethal when left with no options.

When he lifted his hand to wipe sweat from his face, it looked near-black in the moonlight. He rubbed his fingers together and nearly choked at the sticky wetness.

Blood. Fresh and thick. Coating. Saturating. He looked down to see an ever-widening pool growing under the woman, soaking into the hem of his cassock.

"Oh Logos, no, no… What happened?"

It didn't matter what she was or what she believed, Kali'ka or not – she was just a person, not a crazed cultist or a roving monster. He was here, and he had the capability to help her. He *had* to help her.

He could never banish the image of the woman in Pantheon. He could never erase the deed, never make it right … but he could at least emulate what he'd do if he *could*. One life taken for one life saved.

In that moment, it didn't matter that a Kali'ka had maimed and killed Scion Driscoll in his booth. One Kali'ka was not *all* Kali'ka. In seeking to destroy them all – in clustering them together, perceiving them as one group – he'd indirectly sought to destroy this one woman in front of him, who now bled and died in the filth of the Veneer.

Grabbing an arm, he hoisted her dead weight up into a sitting position, cradling her head to avoid lolling or jostling. He grunted as he shoved her onto his shoulder, and roared as he pushed himself to standing. His legs trembled, and he nearly buckled under the weight. Through her robes, he felt her firm, dense, muscular frame.

He managed two staggered steps before his knees locked and he nearly collapsed. He thought his spine would snap in half. His squishy limbs, weak from a lifetime of reports, meetings, paperwork, and discussions, simply didn't have the strength.

Huffing, head filling with blood, he swung his gaze left, right, peering, squinting through the darkness. Nothing. Nothing but empty streets.

Over there! Crossing an adjacent avenue. A tall figure with broad shoulders next to a smaller, diminutive silhouette that drifted like a delicate shadow.

It didn't matter if they ignored him. It didn't matter if they tried to kill him. The only way for nothing to happen was for him to *do* nothing.

Jacobs inhaled sharply and compressed his gut with more savage force than he thought possible. "YOU!! You there!! There's as much Levitant as you want if you help me!"

***

At full sprint, Inos sliced into a narrow alleyway, bashing into the far wall in a spray of synthstone chips. He skipped off of it and using the momentum to propel himself forward, legs tearing in front and vaulting behind, face pressed to the wind, air rushing into his ears. The cool night air frosted his closely shaven scalp. The alleyway's compressed, single-file lane lead to a two-way fork. The small mendicant hobbled ahead as quickly as possible, leaving a hovering trail of dust behind him.

Nowhere left to run, you bastard!

Lowering his shoulder, Inos smashed into the mendicant, ripping them both off their feet and sending them slamming into the packed dirt in a tumbling slide.

Before the mendicant could recover, Inos grabbed his vestments and hurled him onto his back, clamping him in place, forearm under jaw.

The scrawny, haggard man shrieked hysterically and exploded in a frenzy of pell-mell punches, bucking and writhing, shredding gouges in the dirt with his feet. His wide, slathering mouth chomped and his bulbous eyes darted and rolled.

It was pathetic, amidst all that fury, how little strength he actually had.

Inos felt pity rise to constrict his heart. He felt as though he'd seized an abused child. The little man was so frail and wispy, he could have vanished and no one would have noticed.

Inos couldn't allow himself to forget his purpose, though. There was too much at risk. Mercy was a luxury of time. Temperance was the handmaiden of goodwill. He couldn't afford to have either.

Into a small kennel he dove, into a place in his spirit where hibernated a host of ruthless feelings. It thrummed with power, this secret, screaming place where the cruelty of the past still flourished, the place inside where he housed the essence of the Veneer and the youth he used to be.

In the cool night air, puffs of white blew from Inos' mouth to roll over his quarry's face. "What would it take to coax a mendicant of Logos into the Veneer? To draw you into darkness, so far from the Eternal Day? Your master must want something very, very important."

"I – I wasn't trying to escape!! I swear! He made me do it! He made me! I had no choice! You have to understand! I was just doing what he told me to!"

"Who? Who *he*? Who made you do what?"

"He… He just told me that you'd angered him somehow." A toothless gap in the top row of his teeth whistled. "He wants to talk to the other one, the one you were with! Have an audience with her. I'm fully aware of the procedures necessary for audiences, and this is far, *far* from the mark!"

"Who? Who coaxed you here, and who wants an audience?"

"I have two masters now! I dealt with him. I talked to him, like I was asked! I worked with him, and he took me in! I had no choice! He'll be so upset with me! I can't serve them both! I can't be here and also there. I'll never make it back! Never!" His babbling speech digressed into a deluge of rambling incoherency.

Make it back… Inos followed the words to their rational conclusion. Time to gamble on what he surmised was true.

"His name is Fallow, isn't it? Your second master."

All of the mendicant's movement ceased except for little facial twitches. His bulging eyes locked onto Inos like a magnet.

"You were with Fallow," Inos reiterated.

"Y – Yes."

"In the Veneer."

"Yes."

"Then where were you leading me?"

"Th-Th-That's the point! I'm not supposed to *lead* you anywhere. I'm just supposed to steer you away!"

"To leave Elara by herself. The 'other one.'"

"I wasn't supposed to get caught! He'll kill me! He's crazy! And he –

my teeth – oh Logos! Why! Why!! He hurt me! I did nothing to him! Why??" His baggy face scrunched up and he broke down into tiny sobs. "Y – Your... your friend! She's go – going to be alone. With him. In Ashram."

Ashram...? A place of peace. Fallow's warped truth, no doubt. A stronghold, most likely. Him, alone with Elara. Inos would've given up on anyone else's survival.

Kali's Eyes... Elara, I'm going to keep my promise, I swear. I'll find you.

"Then what are you doing here? Why is a mendicant in the Veneer?"

"The High Devotee. He sent me here to make a deal with Fallow."

"The – what? The High Devotee?" Inos pried at creaky memories, "Jacobs Osgood? Reaching out to the Kali'ka? That's mad!"

"It's true!"

"Mendicant, I know Logic cares about its public image more than anything. I understand the lack of a response to our presence – publically. But if you had the opportunity to make contact with our order, why not just send in a squadron of magisters? Or re-route the comeyes for reconnaissance? Doesn't the High Devotee command such power? Doesn't he represent the totality of Logic, aside from His Holiness?"

The mendicant adopted his best attempt at grinning slyly while lying on his back. His scattered, yellowish teeth glinted in the pale moonlight.

"Listen, Kali cultist... The inner workings of scions and the Logical elite are far less interesting to you than other, more – shall we say – delectable things, I'm sure. Living underground for years and years has most certainly sullied your palette and dulled your enjoyment of pleasurable activities. At the very least, it must be hard to keep in sundries.

"Fallow has a supply chain here in the Veneer, you know. Plastein, Levitant, new mixtures of neurophages – the kind they brew here in the Veneer. I could waylay a courier, redirect a shipment, divert attention... It's what I do best! That's why the High Devotee trusts me so much. Acquiring information is – "

The mendicant gurgled as Inos drove his weight down through his throat. "Do you think an ascendant of the Goddess can be *bribed* like the rest of New Corinth? No, mendicant! We make ourselves *hard*. We ready ourselves for life *and* death, unlike your citizens. This is not the time to bet your well-being on the patience of someone who can, and will, break your body into fragments! You'd better tell me direct, precise answers before a far less indulgent *Kali cultist* comes along!"

"Please! P-Please!! G-ah! Let me go! It hurts!"

"Tell me! Clearly! What do you want?!"

"Yes! Yes! Ok! I will! I will!" One of his bloodshot eyes twitched like a bug flipped on its back. Spurts of spit blew through his purplish lips.

Inos eased up on his throat. "Is Jacobs Osgood acting alone?"

The mendicant nodded, his bottom lip quivering.

"Mendicant, we have no part in the dealings of Logic. You know nothing about us. You've denied our existence for centuries!"

"Only to New Corinth! We've left you alone intentionally! You, the enemy! The *only* enemy! You defiled Advent Square! You murdered one of our scions in the Cusp. You castrated him, even! Severed the Godhead! That was what triggered the High Devotee's response! You struck first! Your crazy cult is a breeding ground for insanity!"

"We – what?! You mean – Fallow…? Kali's Eyes! Mendicant, even your leaders aren't that blind. Why would we keep completely to ourselves for centuries, and then deliberately incite fear? Fallow's acting alone! He has none of our support, except those he's managed to deceive. He's a danger to *our* order as well as to yours!"

"You're a threat! All of you are a threat! No one knows any difference! The High Devotee just wants to use you as leverage to make a point. He wants to be the Lion of Logos. He – I've seen him. Something inside him is… It's like he's forgotten about the unity of Logos!"

"The unity of Logos…" Inos stamped down a humorless puff of laughter. "Osgood's deal. What did he want? Tell me!"

The mendicant glanced down and wriggled a hand free to pluck at Inos' robe. "One of these. He wanted one of your robes."

"What?" Inos blurt. Anyone could wear their robes, but only a Kali'ka could deceive another Kali'ka. Dread swelled in his heart.

"And … what did Fallow ask for in return?"

"The trees... He wanted to know where all the trees in New Corinth are."

The trees. Inos' mind raced, leaping, backtracking on the mendicant's words, plucking phrases here and there, sifting through patterns of speech.

The mendicant burst out in terror. "Please, please, it's so dark! I – I can't stay here! Help me out of here! Help me!! I need to be in the Eternal Day! The light! The white of Logos!!"

"Fallow keeps babbling about gods and fire and how blind Corinthians are. About wanting to destroy the Eternal Day! About wanting to kill His Holiness! But you – you don't really feel that way, right?! What have we ever done to you? What does he really want??"

What does he want? The question repeated inside Inos again and again. One by one, he felt his mind travel through conclusion after postulation after deduction...

Incite prejudice and fear.

Instigate events that validate the incited fear.

Employ the outcome as evidence.

Exacerbate through recrimination and reactionary behavior.

No truth besides subsequence. Post hoc ergo propter hoc.

We can't be recognized for who we are.

Only we can recognize each other.

Appearance used as the garment of identity.

Inos vibrated in a suspended segment of time. He stared at the ground, feeling nothing, seeing nothing but the expanding vision inside.

"It's literal... Fallow's plan is *literal.* Don't you see? None of you have ever been in the dark – literally – not even with your eyes closed. Not you, either – not until you came here to the Veneer. He *literally* wants to destroy the Eternal Day. The Eternal Day refracts from those synthstone walls of yours, doesn't it? If the architecture of Advent Square is destroyed ... Kali! He wants to bring darkness back to New Corinth, physically! Advent... His Holiness... everyone will be there, misting on Levitant, their minds lost. Creatures ... ready to be butchered."

The decrepit mendicant's eyes grew wider. His jaundiced skin paled, and his lips flapped as if he was trying to make noise.

Inos stared into the man's face, weighing, judging, slicing to his core.

"What's your name, mendicant?"

"H -Hegil." At the sound of his own name in his ears, he visibly calmed.

Inos saw Hegill for who he was, dormant but alive, sleeping within himself like a lukewarm fire. His indignation and pride persisted. In his own way, Hegil had fought back to survive. He'd persisted through the disgrace and trauma he'd suffered since arriving in the Veneer. Inos could only imagine what it would have been like to live in the Eternal Day his whole life, then to suddenly be sunk into the darkness and decay of the Veneer.

In that moment, ascendant of Kali and mendicant of Logos co-existed, face to face, unconflicted, unconvinced by the misconceptions they'd come to believe as fact.

"Hegil, even though I wear the same robes as the ones who hurt you … you can see the difference?"

Composed and surprisingly sober, Hegil nodded.

Moments later, Inos released Hegil's neck, grabbed the man by the shoulders and lifted him to his feet. He couldn't have been much heavier than the bones in his body.

Hegil stood knock-kneed like a hunched bird, sheltering his torso with twig-like arms thin enough to encircle with a fist. The tufts of hair on his knobby skull wafted in the chill, night breeze.

Inos laid a hand on one of his arms and held it firmly, warmly.

"Hegil… We can work together to fight against Fallow. You're not alone. None of us are. Take me there, please. I need to find the person I was with. Take me to his stronghold. Take me to this … *Ashram.*"

CHAPTER 28
VANGUARD

Elara gasped awake. Her eyes darted around and her blurry mind reoriented itself. Alive... She was alive. Both hands. Both feet. Muscles worked, but weakly. Lying down. In her robes. Bed? No, just a clump of random fabrics. Small rocks jabbed her back.

Slowly, her vision came into focus. Some half-demolished building. Synthstone, rubble everywhere in heaps. The ceiling to the second floor was gaping open, its edges dripping some backlogged moisture. No furniture. Several exits to other rooms. Dank, cool. Light. Genuine light. Austere, washed-out and chill. The Veneer, then. Morning, post-dawn.

Advent. The Pageant of Miracles. She'd slept through the night?

It was then that she saw them.

Children. Teenagers, at the oldest. Earlobes, skulls, lips, scapulae, punctured by chains, rods, and spikes. They lurked around her in a milieu of prowling forms, pacing, crouching in corners, clinging to edges of the ceiling above, peering around doorways. All of them eyed her with the same insatiable intensity.

Elara scrambled to her feet, sliding through gravel. Pain lanced into her side like glass. She cried out and stepped backwards, heart racing, head swooning, trying to keep her observers in sight. They didn't react at all.

"Who are you?! Why am I here? What's going on?!"

Across the room, a shadowy figure leaned against a rotten, decrepit doorframe. A young man, muscular for his age with a mammoth bone structure not yet filled out. His flesh was run through with the same piercings as the rest.

He was clearly their leader. He had the most space around him, and he was the most at ease. Latent intelligence gleamed in his chill eyes, frigid like the forthcoming winter. Even only standing, doing nothing else, it was though all the champions of ages past had poured their essences into him. Once born, he now had to await a second birth – maturation – for his body to be fully capable of representing his ancestors.

He stepped forward and settled his feet. "We couldn't find enough plastein to fully heal the cut in your side. You should be careful, Red."

"Red?" Elara growled, huffing from the exertion of pushing herself too fast, too soon. A delirious haze of memories raced within.

...Hobbled by agony, lurching around the Veneer. Stumbling, falling, fading from the world of life, of heat. Face grinding in the gritty ground. Gripping with her fingernails and pulling, tugging forward. The last of her blood spilling onto the cold, hard earth...

The young people continued milling. They all stared out of hardened sockets from a distance that should not belong even to the oldest man or woman.

"You... You're the Errati. The children of the Veneer."

Their leader frowned and nodded. "Innocence. That was the name he took. Has to be him. He told you about us. He left to join the grays when I was a child. We've all heard the stories. I'm Devin. That's the name I chose. I took over for him."

Innocence...?

Inos Noscent. A Veneerian name... Shaped into the sounds of a first and family Corinthian name.

Elara clamped her mouth shut, refusing to show her surprise. Devin's insight was uncanny, his revelation unnerving. But she couldn't reveal anything, couldn't get careless.

Inos ... *Innocence* ... was out there, listening, hunting, pursuing the same goal as her. She couldn't compromise him, couldn't hinder their shared goal, no matter how much she wanted to sprint away, scan, search, scour the streets for him – to know that he was safe, and let him know that she was safe.

"How did I get here? What do you want from me?"

Devin flexed fists that were too large for his adolescent body. A rusted, metal hoop in his forearm twitched. "Nyx said you could help us. She said that you could get rid of them, for good."

"Nyx," Elara said flatly.

"Your sister."

"My ... sister? Charlotte??" Elara swung her head around, looking for the smallest glimpse – the big, emerald eyes, the hair like a cloak of amber, the sole fragment of beauty lifted from a horrible, decaying world of refuse and malice. "Charlotte's here?"

"Charlotte. Hm... So that's what it is," Devin murmured to himself. "She never told me."

Clutching her side, Elara stormed towards him. All of the Errati around the room jumped into defensive postures, poised to strike.

The young man didn't budge. He just sized her up with eyes like twin, frosted mirrors.

"Damn you, child – I swear, if you did anything to harm my sister..."

He frowned as though offended at the suggestion. "Nyx and I brought you here. A scion found you in the road."

Elara scanned his face. Only one possibility seemed true. It seemed fitting, somehow: Charlotte, skulking in and out of their family loft in the Uppers, making her way here, befriending these people – her peers, age-wise. Elara herself had slunk away to ... how many places?

Rather than be upset that Charlotte didn't tell her about her visits to the Veneer, or be concerned for Charlotte's well-being, Elara felt strangely relieved. Vindicated, almost. Best to let Charlotte have something that belonged to *just* her. Best to let her develop the nerve to forge out on her own.

Devin, the way he spoke about Charlotte... He was a worthy companion, at least. An ideal compliment for her sister, and she for him. Protectors of each other, in completely different ways.

"She's safe, then?" Elara asked.

Devin nodded, fingering the metal loop in his forearm. The flesh above it, hardened into solid scar tissue, didn't budge.

"Fallow," she said. It was not a question.

"He went out there." Devin pointed towards the Eternal Day. From where Elara stood, she could see the tips of the Uppers piercing the arc of perpetual light across the horizon. "Most of his men went with him. We can take care of the ones who stayed. We're going to burn their fucking hideout to the ground."

The timbre of his words, matter-of-fact and offhandedly harsh, resonated in Elara's heart. They were relatable. Soothing.

"He invaded our home," he continued. "Attacked us. Kidnapped people. Tortured them. We've heard the screams night after night. We've seen it first-hand. Nothing but the Veneer claims a Veneerian, not some ... *intruder*."

Elara found herself nodding, remembering the Chamber of Sarcophagi, reliving the screams of the Kali'ka who were butchered there, the Kachina among them, by Fallow's murderous throng.

"The Errati will guard you, Red. Protect you. A tenth of our number. Hundreds. They all volunteered. You can get close enough. You kill him, and we're even."

Elara looked around at the Errati in the broken down building. They screamed absolute defiance without breathing a word, like an endless dare. Defiance of what they hated, of what hated them. Defiance of anything that sought to manipulate or control.

They wanted to help her? Fine. These young adults were the purest manifestation of Kali, here in the Veneer. Without cloisters, without kanas, without meditation or rituals, without tales or parables, they were primed to burst. Ever-ready. Fully acceptant of the strength that crowns through agony.

They were capable, more than most, of choosing how they would live and die. Life to death. Death to life.

Elara leaned in towards their metal-lanced leader, Devin. With her lips curled back, she breathed the promise of smoking vengeance into his face. "You make sure my sister is safe, child ... and *then* we're even."

Devin nodded briskly, straining to maintain eye contact.

Without another word, Elara bolted away over pockmarked floors and past hollowed-out walls. Some of the Errati trailed out after her, in a loose line, keeping low. The pain in her side, from the dagger, cut into her with each step. Like so many times before, though, she clutched the pain and harnessed it, leveraging it to propel herself onward.

Errati dropped from eaves or dashed out from alleyways as Elara snaked through the Veneer, matching her gait, merging into one body of enforcers. Before long, hundreds of hard-eyed warrior-children, forged of bonded muscle and metal, formed up into a phalanx of bodies with her in the middle.

She kept her eyes on the other side of the Tame River, towards New Corinth proper, following clues left in the memory of Fallow's words, ringing with venom, smothered by the memory of his dagger lodged in her side.

...The Eternal Darkness to come... The broken light... Awoken, like New Corinth... A use for their lives... Funneled into a narrow tube... The place of fire... Obliterate the cycle... The Goddess made conscious...

What was it Inos had said? 'His actions will reveal themselves'? So they would, it seemed. A grand gesture, no doubt. Something 'worthy' of an heir of Earth.

She knew exactly where to lead the Errati. She knew exactly where Fallow would be.

With the drum of their feet in her ears, and a renewed purpose roaring inside, Elara, like a furnace-blown blade – leader, survivor, kindling for the Errati's fire – marched on the Eternal Day.

CHAPTER 29
TO LEAVE A SCAR

Kneeling in his old chambers in Mors, Fallow quested in his mind for that other place, the world of flame and shadow, of a red sky and a blood-soaked earth. His true home; the one he would *make* real. No one was left to stop him. The champion of the Kali'ka had fallen – to *him* – and was likely rotting in the Veneer at that very moment.

He could hear Oren's shallow, shuddering breath behind him. The man's jittering was starting to grate. He'd put on a good show in Ashram, but Fallow knew exactly how weak and cowardly the man was.

"Transcendent Fallow, everyone is in place."

"Make sure that the robes remain off until His Holiness has arrived, Oren. And remember – it must be past sunfall! Keep an eye on the moon in the west."

"Yes, Transcendent."

"Make sure the ones you brought from Sangra play their parts. They must know the fullness of their betrayal."

"Yes, Transcendent… Of course."

Fallow rose and started pacing, stepping in and out of pools of light from torches near the entrance to the chamber. He mulled over timetables, dispositions of his brood, tasks yet to do, tasks completed.

"The transceivers are functioning as intended?"

"All of them are hooked up to your switch. I have the box ready." Oren's hands were pulled into his sleeves. Through the wool, Fallow could see the man nervously fidgeting.

Feeling your use reaching an end, my disposable provocateur?

"And the Magistrate, Oren? Not that it matters. Their comeyes are useless. They can't tell us apart from the stupidest, most light-blinded Corinthian."

"Distributed as expected, Transcendent. Not a single more, also as expected. Within the immediate radius of the trees in the square, more often than not. Unless they leave their posts, they'll be among the first to fall."

Fallow chuckled and starting tugging at his cheeks, exploring for congealment or rot. The texture felt like tenderized and braised meat, with little cavities and ridges.

In the corner, his newest toy didn't make a sound. She must have fallen asleep somehow. Otherwise, he was sure he'd hear the same muffled screaming and flurry of scuffles interspersed within a dull clank of heavy chains.

No matter how often he heard it, her sounds tickled his spine and soothed his belly like cuddles from a favorite pet – a fact she strangely seemed to not understand.

"Oren ... what do you ... *feel* when you look at your once-cohort, there in the corner?"

"I..." Oren swallowed and blinked away sweat that slid down to his eyes. "Nothing. I feel nothing."

Fallow studied him a moment, scrutinizing. "Then there is a place for you in the world to come. Since you are no longer needed in your ... former capacity, I had my doubts. Compliance is an admirable attribute in lesser creatures."

Oren did nothing, said nothing. Fallow snickered at him.

When you were born, I knew you not, fool... In death, no one will know you still.

"Hmm... Definitely," Fallow growled, as though answering a suggestion that had just occurred to him. He turned towards his toy in the corner, feeling heat pump through his swiftly engorging penis.

"Oren, wait for me outside. Put out the lights on your way."

In overly hasty, jerking motions, Oren bowed and turned to the torches on the wall. One, then the other, he snuffed them, sinking the room in perfect darkness, and exited to wait at the door. He wisely said nothing. The man knew about Fallow's *tastes* by now.

Fallow softly scrunched his way over the gritty floor. Scuffing came from the corner. Chains clanged. She must have woken up. He felt a sharp bubble of excitement rise in his chest.

"Ssshhhhh, Ascendant Marin. Life's eye gazes indiscriminately on horrors and beauties alike. That's the credo of the Kali'ka, right? Hm? One interpretation, at least."

The rustling sound in the corner became a frantic scramble. Throaty screams strained against thick gags. It made him chuckle.

"I know why you're upset, Marin. It has nothing to do with your stupidity in bringing Elara Aeve into the fold. It's because you're still too well-composed. But you mustn't blame yourself. Most Corinthian women are distressingly well-composed."

The insane scrambling continued. Chains bashed into the wall.

"I will guide us to an era where the Eternal Day of New Corinth has no meaning, you see. Where no one can notice the minute flaws you've obsessed over for years, both physical and of character." He started gathering his robe at the hem. Throbbing and stretched to burst, he craved release.

Mere feet away, he could feel the heat of her body, the kinetics of her limbs, the energy of her frame.

"Fear is the lie of false expectations. But once you accept the reality of what you expect, fear vanishes. You should be happy. You're one of the first to come to understand. A vanguard for the lightless nightmare to come."

He lifted his robes over his head, tossed them aside, and settled himself into place, on his knees. She couldn't see him, right? No one could see him naked. No one! What was that scratching sound? She might be clawing at the floor.

"Just let it pass over you. Hush, now. Through you and over. Let it pass, let it pass…"

He whipped his arm at her, again, again, again, bludgeoning her jaw until he heard it crack. She made no sound aside from strained breathing.

Take away their ability to flee, and they fight. Take away their ability to fight, and they protest. But take away their ability to protest ... and you've broken them. No one is anything without a voice.

While she lay there, dazed, groaning groggily, he began – with a single, violent thrust.

She gasped, howling, beating him in whatever pathetically weak way she could. She clawed his face in gouges that tickled and ran like riverbeds into the cracks of his teeth, sliding over his tongue, coating his throat in his own warm stickiness. Her legs hung uselessly, forever severed from her spine.

He made no attempt to push her away. These fresh wounds he wouldn't treat. They would remain with the rest, just like they had so many years ago, rending the face of the powerful, potent man who raised him.

...Penance! Father couldn't live with the rage. He'd looked through all the volumes he could in Reliquary, for an historical precedent that committed one person to only one other. Their mother was supposed to belong to him, and him alone! She didn't have to do it. None of them did! They wouldn't listen, though. They had their comforts, their constancy, the evidence of their feelings to guide them. At worst, they didn't care. At most, they were fully aware.

Fallow still remembered waking up that morning, following the trail of tiny red droplets on the floor that led from his parents' bedroom to a woman's slender finger limply crooked under the table in the dining area. Father was sitting in a chair nearby, hunched over, dry-heaving. He was soaked in dark blood, both skin and clothing. The Eternal Day shone brightly as always, catching the scarlet fluid in glistening twinkles.

Father turned towards him, face ragged with open rips, one eye shredded from its socket. Eye jelly smattered his cheek and hung limply from its hole. A heavy jaw and forehead of granite framed the iron tendons and muscles that comprised his body.

Since having his mendicant status revoked, Father had worked fourteen to eighteen hour days in the Cusp of the Veneer, in its pitiful excuse for an economy, to keep their household afloat. Fashioning metal brackets to support synthstone molds used as bedrock for the climbing golden spires of the Uppers. At least they hadn't Excised him.

In his spare time, he'd relearned the ancient art metallurgy, splicing metal and fire, forging tools and eventually blades like the one he gripped in his hands, slathered in sticky red... An art he would pass along to his son.

His deep baritone mumbled through tattered, blood-caked lips. Little flaps of skin waved around as his remaining eye fixed itself unblinkingly on his son.

"Alastor ... Look what your mother did to me. All I wanted to do was make love to her one last time. That's what it is, you know! It's not just an animal act! All I wanted to do was take care of her. Now no one will know about her infidelity. Remember that word, Alastor: infidelity. No one will know about her Penance. No one will know how she shamed us. No one will know how much of our time she wasted. Never again will we have to be reminded of what Logic did to our family."

As he spoke, a pile of bones and mismatched reddish-pinkish things seeped watery red onto the floor.

Fallow's father was a scholar, an exemplar to be admired and exalted! Overlooked because of borderline Nihil Obstat accusations like "non-compliant," "distressing," or "overreaching." Forced out of even such a menial role as slopping Penance booths. Mendicant ... a term the scions used to dump all of their scorn.

Weren't all parts of the body of Logic necessary? Was a toe more valued than an eye? Other scions never made use of the knowledge at their fingertips. But Fallow's father delved into tomes, learned of the past, and used words belonging to a true purveyor of lore long forgotten: "infidelity," "make love." Fallow had learned well, to learn from his father how to investigate the past.

His father had been a strong, profound man. For him to have been able to brutalize and destroy the one he loved, who had created his reason for living... The *will* required was marvelous!

Smiling in the dark, Fallow wondered how long he should let Marin enjoy herself. This was what she wanted. It was what they all wanted. It was either this, or they would betray him. Force them to stay, or watch them leave.

He kept his rhythm steady. No need to rush. He was certain that his father would have done the same.

Not too long, though… Advent Square was waiting for him.

Somehow, someway though, like the slow creep of hot breath on the back of his neck, he sensed Elara Aeve still hunting him, prowling the realms in life or death, to find, dismember, and demolish his existence.

ACT III

EMBERS

CHAPTER 30
ADVENT

Jacobs squished his way through the Corinthian throng standing shoulder to shoulder across Advent Square. Millions of Corinthians stood compressed in the multi-tiered levels of the square, like a single, swollen body ready to burst.

He kept his eyes out Grand Magister Hammar and the rest of the Magistrate. Wherever they were, their signature scarlet tabards were lost in the milieu of Corinthian clothing. Thankfully though, the massiveness of the crowd swallowed Jacobs face and transformed him into an anonymous citizen.

The towering construct at the lowest level of Advent Square, where the Pageant of Miracles took place, resembled a symbolic representation of the heavens. It shifted shape, form and color, in time with perfectly programmed holos portraying backgrounds for the phases of Logos' life: the Virginal Union, the White Halo, the Mystery of the Lion, and ultimately the Ascension.

Against the holo-shifting backdrop, the pageant's players strode and gestured. Their words rose to soar over the crowd, trumpeted through static speakers positioned near viewscreens around the square. Most in attendance relied on the viewscreens for the merest glimpse of their god in flesh – His Holiness himself, emerged from the Tabernacle to play the role of Logos. Scores of flo-globes whooshed through the sky, morphing and shifting like darting clouds, filling gaps in sound. Triumphant music rolled over the square in blaring torrents during choral interludes interspersed though the pageant's exposition.

The crowd inhaled and exhaled in awe. Squeals of delight or gasps of pleasure arose on all sides. Misters decompressed and scores of women cried, 'Compel me! Compel me!' The broadcast was flooding the world, where billions of glassy eyed Logicians sat glassy-eyed in their lofts, misting, cheering at precisely timed moments in roaring unanimity.

"...The Advent of Days is upon us, we who have labored to make ourselves presentable to our Lord and Master, to be pure through Penance, to exalt in the riches He has bestowed upon us, never turning an ungrateful eye, a sneering lip, or a closed heart by allowing anything but His perfect bliss to penetrate the holy temples of our bodies..."

Even under the possibility of being once again pinned under the paw of the Lion of Logos, Jacobs had had to reenter the very heart of the Logical machine, the soul of its organism, at least one last time to witness the spectacle of Advent.

After years of fretting, of tapping away at his armrests in boredom, cowering at the copy of the Crystal Throne in his residence, it had been shockingly easy to escape. Run. Just run. At his lowest point, Jacobs had leveraged the one power still afforded him: the power to *leave*; the power of refusal.

Now, he'd rescinded that right – or used it *again* – and turned around to come right back, the prodigal son returned to the heart of Logic, willingly.

There was one final thing he needed to see – one more piece to the puzzle locking into shape in the foundation of his soul. He had no idea what it was, but he could see the patterns, now. He perceived the flow of events as they conspired within the foothills of Advent. New Corinth and the rest of the world flowed toward Advent's divine peak, and Jacobs had but to follow his awakening internal compass to catch their current and flow with them.

"...If you are hungry, hunger for Me. If you are thirsty, thirst for Me... For I have hungered as no man has, thirsted as no man has, and I tell you,

you will not receive your fill unless you sup of the flesh of the earth and sip of the river of life. For as long as you seek to slake your hunger and thirst with bread and water, your belly will remain forever empty, your throat forever parched, your womb forever barren..."

Jacobs saw Advent Square as a single pattern, lifted into sight, welded to the white of the Eternal Day. One tapestry. The whole image of Logic, taken one apparatus composed of countless, seamlessly fused sprockets and widgets.

All around him, every man, every woman bowed and capitulated to mysticism blended with mechanized faith in an intoxicating brew. Anesthetizing, tranquilizing, taming. Logos and Levitant, two halves of the same deception. The sickness and the cure, bundled into one poisoned inoculant.

It was there in the endless plastic faces, like clay gauzed with transparent film, molded into the shape of rapture: the unblinking eyes, staring like painted glass; the smiles of pearly white, sparkling aside flashes of faceted lights – blue, yellow, green, bright.

Overstimulation. A plateau disallowing sensitivity, fine sensation, and critical thought. Disallowing the eye to focus by presenting a constricted field. Distilling the breadth of human experience through a hair-narrow filter. Denying tragedy. Revoking the means to step boldly, to know how to choose freely.

It seemed impossible that no one saw what Jacobs did. Absolutely, unfathomably, terribly impossible ... just like how he'd used to be.

But in truth, some did see – the Kali'ka. Like the woman he'd rescued in the Veneer. Like the brutish adolescent and the delicate child who swept the Kali'ka away, swearing her safety, vowing their indebtedness. They were his kin now, the hidden, the maligned.

"...Know that it was not I who healed you today, but you. I am merely the representative of your own faith, the resolute choice of your own heart, the mirror outside..."

Keeping his arms clutched close to himself, Jacobs bumped into someone and muttered "excuse me" with his head firmly planted down.

At that same moment, a few nearby people side gasped. Jacobs' head jerked to the sound, fearing that someone recognize him, only to see their own heads turned away towards another location. The ocean of bodies shifted slightly, enough for Jacobs to see the target of their stares.

Kali'ka gray, winding through the crowd with serpentine grace in plain sight of everyone, like a smear of darkness on the brilliance of the Eternal Day. The sight stabbed him with fear. He felt as though by seeing their gray robes, his secret connection to the cultists was bared to everyone.

Someone shouted. The crowd bulged and opened in the direction the Kali'ka went. A shout, then shout. Jacobs could see nothing except a crush of bodies rustling around some core. Screams from several directions. Something slammed into his back. He stepped on something that gave. More screams.

Everything was turning to mayhem.

"...All who believe are due the same bounty, the same fullness of peace is theirs if they but claim it as their own..."

Jacobs tried to run, but was lodged in place like a peg of wood. There was a struggle between two Corinthians. He could see fists, blows exchanged. Faces, contorted into savagery. Others, into fear. Eyes, lost to something primal. Pockets of violence erupted all around. Blood. It flew through the air. Some splashed across him like speckled dots of red rain. He shouted in horror, and his shouts merged with the cries of others.

People tried to flee, shoving in different directions, but like him they were trapped by the sheer volume of humanity. They pushed, pushed, and failing that, hit, howled and raged as the shouts of many became cry of one.

Between the jostles and knocks and shoves, Jacobs saw patches of Advent Square below. All levels, all ramps, all arches, all platforms, the same thing was happening, at one time.

The datacast could barely be heard above the bedlam.

"...For those who were sick and are healed, you are blessed. But those who were healthy and never sick, you have been doubly blessed..."

The players in the pageant started to notice what was happening. On the viewscreens throughout the square, they looked out in confusion and disbelief.

His Holiness stepped forward from the center of the pageant, out of his field of holo-projectors, out of his globe of overflowing white light, out of the role of Logos.

For one glimpse before being rammed in the chest by someone's stray elbow, Jacobs saw not an imposing, nigh-omnipotent god ... but the face of a wrinkled old man, unprotected in the light of the Eternal Day. Powerless to help. Powerless to intervene. Powerless because no one was listening.

Powerless.

Logos! Preserve me!

In Logos' holy city, lighthouse of Earth, kept spotless for centuries, the High Devotee Jacobs Osgood was caught at the epicenter of a full-blown riot of millions.

***

Elara sprinted through the last few blocks leading up to Advent Square. In comparison, her pack of Errati looked like they were loping, slicing back and forth, staying in formation like a flock of birds, compressing, expanding to suit the shape of the roads. Their wild, frenzied eyes incessantly scanned the environment – odd corners, errant pathways, roofs. They squinted as they searched, eyes watering – the Eternal Day was as foreign to them as they were to it.

The few Corinthian stranglers they swept by – not packing Advent Square, and not at home watching datacast – dashed here, there, lost to some unknown terror. Their faces told the story of true, ragged, unstilted emotions pulled from tactile experience that flattened the paltry peaks of Levitant and faith.

Those who saw Elara and her troupe screamed and bolted in another direction.

As Elara and the Errati ran, a great roar expanded ahead, like an ocean in continual surge. It distended, growing wider, stuffing the air like water rushing into a citywide jar. Within it, she heard an undertone of clanging, harsh and concussive.

They rounded one last corner and came to a halt at the edge of Advent Square, along a landing connected to the highest tier of the square. Elara stood there huffing, staring numbly at the impossible horror spread in front of them.

"Goddess…." She gripped a nearby guardrail for support.

The sound she'd heard was *people*. The singular swell of countless layered shouts, screams, and raging snarls. Brutality and murder. Every level of Advent Square, roiled with human spillage and overflowed with the maniac rage of one storm. The Pageant of Miracles had devolved to a singular mass of crude, flailing appendages and graceless chaos.

On the spot stained by Fallow weeks prior, crushed skulls poured, limbs were torn from sockets, and toothless faces wailed for the grace of death to take them. The balmy white of the Eternal Day soaked in their screams as readily as it had the adulation of their god.

Hundreds of robes stood interlaced among the Corinthians like dark specks of dirt. Spaced apart in a deliberate pattern. Gray. Kali'ka. Each of them whirled and spun, slicing with copies of the same dagger that had slipped into Elara's flesh in Fallow's stronghold. The same ones wielded in Mors, in Sangra, and by the assassin in the Codex.

On the holy day of Advent, Kali'ka were no longer a myth, no longer out of reach … but also not quite human. They were impossible to ignore, but impossible to understand. They were an *appearance*. A concept. A concept built from pressurized fear, steeped in a now-undammed reservoir. A concept, fit to destroy with the weapons of human birth: teeth, fists, and nails.

The acrid tang of Levitant hung heavy in the air. In the throes of artificial passion, adrift on a delirious, ravening sea of psychochemical mind-froth, Corinthians were lost to whatever was pleasurable, whatever felt right… For whatever felt right was *good*.

This was the ravening beast sleeping in the belly of New Corinth. Kali's face, if unacknowledged. The true lusts, the true needs masked by

Levitant and faith: the death-drive, the craving for self-obliteration. All Fallow had done was nudge it awake. Prime it, then give a target. Be both the arrow and the bullseye, and fuse them as one.

To strike out...

Self-awareness wasn't the goal of the Kali'ka, Fallow said. Self-control wasn't enough, he'd exhorted. They must extend outside of the sphere of their own body. They must influence and direct. That was the basis of his argument: the need to change *others*; to mimic cloister life, except without the inclination, without the guidance, without the sundering of Logical programming; to simulate initiation; to force the hand of an otherwise voluntary choice.

If Inos was there next to her, Elara would've slipped her hand into his, pivoted away on the spot and ran away, dragging him to whatever life they could muster, in whatever fractured future had burrowed into their realm of razed hope and impossible sanctuary. Him, the other part who made her stronger.

Charlotte, at least, was safe ... in the Veneer, of all places. With Devin, she was far safer than she would be, anywhere else.

The rotating viewscreens overhead sparked and flickering, displaying the bottom level of Advent square crisply, sharply. The magnified view panned across the players in Advent Pageant as they screaming on the ground. It passed over rampaging bodies and snarling faces, and came to settle on a horrible, impossible sight.

Is that...?

Her heart nearly stopped when her eyes confirmed what she feared.

Marin. It was Marin.

Elara's eyes flew to square, back to the viewscreen, back to the square. Marin! Bloodied, nearly unrecognizable. Strung up on the mechanical construct in the lowest level of Advent Square, head lolling. Her advocate and mentor, beaten, tried and resigned. Hopeless and alone.

Next to her, a form stood with his arms outstretched to the chaos of the square.

Fallow... It had to be him. There. Right there, in the eye of the storm.

Damnation and fury swelled in Elara's heart. A potent need groaned alive inside of her, the one who had embodied the identity of the

Goddess, worn Her mask, wielded Her blade, invited Her in, been seen by Her exact eyes, and touched Her mind. Her, who had branched the gap between Creation and Illusion, and been marked for her actions.

Elara would match it. She *could* match it. All of it! The earth was hers. Kali was hers, and Kali belonged to Earth. The power of earth and sky rested within, in the space where the living walked. And where the living walked, gods required their hands.

The remainder – the final piece – would fall to the survivors.

Behind Elara, the Errati stood strangely calm yet bristling with need. It was there in their eyes, skimming the bedlam with lust. It was there in the edges, points and chains of their willingly metal-skewered flesh. To them, more than anyone else, she entrusted the future. To Charlotte, to Devin.

All Elara did was nod to the Errati, and they – acceptant, unquestioning, comprehending her intent – descended piece by piece like human droplets falling into the ocean of Advent Square.

Elara pressed her palms onto the guardrail and hoisted herself over it into the square, landing in the Errati's midst as they formed ranks and engaged Corinthians at their perimeter. She waded into the fray in a singular series of unbroken, cleaving motions, joining its carnal rhythm, lending her flame to the great conflagration.

Slowly, they inched forward, fighting and moving as one. Like planets to the sun, the Errati drew power from Elara in their center – the caretaker to the motherless, surrogate for the unwanted, champion of the despised.

In the battleground of blood where no one won, the bottom level of Advent Square loomed closer. There: Fallow, Marin, and the final leg of the great, horrible path of tooth and claw.

From Elara to Kali, daughter to mother, progeny to forebear, Elara cast a silent plea into the realm of Illusion. To the Great Mistress it flew – an intent of the heart, heard by no one, evaporated like mist, carried along the dying screams and steaming blood striking the sun-blanched air.

Goddess ... I am Your one. Fill me! Let me be the Vessel for Your power! Let me be Your will on Earth!

***

Square and direct, employing only minimal movements, Inos darted through Advent Square, shaking Corinthian assailants, scanning the crowd, trying to regain his direction and relocate Elara.

There, in the lowest level! The crowd bulged around her. How the Errati were there, with her, he had no idea – but they were buckling. His brothers and sisters of the Veneer gave up their own bodies, grappling inch by inch. It was only because their group drew so much attention that Inos had managed to get as close as he did.

Elara had given herself over to a fugue of passion and would discard her own life to murder him – he could see it from where he was. Barring that, she would simply take down as many enemies as possible.

But even she could not overwhelm them all.

Inos had to reach her, he had to get back to her. He had to intervene. Always behind ... he'd always been a step behind. A step behind their enemy, a step behind Elara, a step behind an abandoned Ashram. No longer!

How they would escape after reaching the center of this menace was utterly beyond him, though. Maybe ... maybe it didn't matter, anyway.

His decision had been made at the Gehana, when he'd seen the edge of Kali's blade glinting in firelight, when he'd stared into Elara's untamable eyes, so similar to Kali's mask. It had loomed from that moment onward, a pregnant awareness, bloating in his heart like a portent, cooling towards a defined end. Collapse and supernova, right then, in Advent Square.

This was his duty, his right, his *purpose.*

Welding his eyes to Elara, he tore towards her, ripping through the throng, battering Corinthians aside with elbows, fists, knees, whatever he could. No deviation. Just a straight line. Cut, cut, cut. They snatched at his clothing, tugging and yanking, pounding and beating, scratching and biting, slowing him down however they could.

Fatigue clotted his clarity. His breath labored. The precision of his kanas began to slip. Small blows began nicking his body. He was weary ... so, so weary. But if he altered his forward-pushing momentum at all, it would mean annihilation at the hands of a crazed mob.

Several hundred meters away, the great trees spread across Advent Square, tall and swaying. Everblooms. *The trees,* Hegil had said... *The trees.*

Amidst the fury of survival, Inos noticed the trees' green leaves, the sturdy branches, completely oblivious of the gouts of blood, the crushed bodies, the fear, the chaos. Unresponsive or perfectly acceptant, Inos couldn't tell. The trees simply existed, separate, apart from the rage of men and their schemes of self-destruction.

Elara's back was right in front of him. Around her, the last of the Errati fell to the crowd as Corinthians dove towards her, seeing only one target and one target only: a gray robe, a cultist, an *other.*

Elara stopped moving. She screamed and raised an arm towards something in the distance. Some deep rumbling rocked the earth. A snap and flash. The great trees all across Advent Square erupted in balls of fire. The ground ruptured in a deafening cataclysm of white and orange, tearing the sky in explosions of stone and flame and flesh and gold and marble. Air pressure slipped, and Inos' ears popped as shock waves carried racing fire to vaporize all the screaming Corinthians in little silhouetted effigies of agony.

Inos thought of nothing. There were no last ideas, no hesitations. He only knew he had to preserve Elara. His borrowed time had run out. He could bargain no more.

Then he was there, leaping over the slain, slamming into her, enfolding her body with his own. His energy became hers, a blanket of protection. She was their shield – all of them – and he was hers, as he knew he would be. They flew hard to the ground, one entity, indivisible.

Amidst sulfur and heat and chemical tang, the last thing Inos' smiling face smelled was the sweet caress of Kali's own hair tickling his nose.

***

Elara moved from point to point, ceaseless, kinetic, flowing like skinless water, undivided from the air. By never planting her weight, never pausing, never fixing her position, there was only motion. She entered her own space, blank and empty.

The Errati encircled her like armor that crushed what it couldn't deflect. With them, Elara carved a path through the horde like a cleaver of the gods scraping along the marble stone of Advent Square.

Bit by bit, though, they were being eroded under the sheer mass of wave after wave of Corinthians, as they gave up their lives for a chance to strike back at the one who'd invaded their home.

They stayed loose, giving each other room to pivot and shift. Anything that made it past them, Elara touched. Anything she touched, broke. Necks and fingers twisted till they popped. Faces wept blood as she beat them. She felt no impulse towards restraint, no mercy. The full measure of kana after kana had found their final master – High Ascendant of the Kali'ka.

Her yantra – fresh and newly inscribed in an emergent ritual of Brae's – seared in her skin, radiating, actuating her inertia, their curled, slashing emblems linking one to the other, conducting energy, enmeshing her in a cocoon of turbulent power. Like trade winds, she felt their lines of force race across the canvas of her skin, digging out energy she didn't know she had, strengthening and enveloping her, foot to spine to center to hand.

Lost to the fullness of fury and the unity of emptiness, elevated by her chain linked suit of inscriptions, her consciousness accelerated up, up, beyond the limits of skill and body. She saw the Corinthians not all at once, but *one at a time*. And paired with any one opponent, she was unstoppable.

The entire time, Marin and Fallow grew in her sight. She was nearly there. Just a little more. Just a little more!

"Errati! Stay with me! Forward! Forward!!" The few who heard her – the few left – clung to her, their barrier dwindling.

At ground zero, Fallow scanned the crowd as though searching for something. He seemed nervous.

His gaze settled on Elara, and his one eye erupted in shock. Immediately, he pointed in Elara's direction and turned his head to yell to someone. She was close now – so close! – no more than fifty feet.

Marin raised her eyes, her expression completely lost, broken, demolished. Her limp, aged body barely fit her robes. Gashes streaked her chin, bruises mottled her cheekbones, and spatters of blood dotted her forehead. Elara saw her as clearly as if they were standing face to face.

Fallow lifted some kind of small metal box into the air and cradled his thumb on what looked like a switch. His head was faced towards the sky as his lips screamed unheard words.

"NO!!" Elara flung a hand towards Marin, towards their break, towards the root of words unspoken, towards an empty spot of blood and pain.

But Elara's voice wouldn't carry, wouldn't reach its target. It was too late. Around her, the final remains of the Errati fell one by one, leaving her purely, completely alone as the crush of Corinthians closed in.

Fallow's thumb flipped the switch.

For one single moment, Marin's eyes widened in recognition of the woman who she'd advocated for years ago, a young person dying from the hate inside, dying from her own awareness, ready to bloom, ready to thrive, ready to destroy.

Elara screamed, mind lost to horror, and as she screamed, explosions shattered the ground around her. The earth trembled. Heat raced. Fire shrieked. Pain tore into one thigh.

Something slammed into her back, flattening itself against her, molding around her as she and it were taken to the ground, knocking air and consciousness away in one lost breath.

CHAPTER 31
TRANSCENDENCE

Groggily, blearily, dark shapes began to impress themselves on Elara's vision. They swished and flit into little sparks of color that shattered into multihued sunbursts. Some pungent vapor rankled her nose and lodged itself in her throat. Corrosive. Crisped. Sulfuric.

A groan pressed from her lungs as she rolled onto her stomach. Bits of dust and rubble fell from her to clack on the ground. Her palms slid on a gritty smear of soot and soil. Singed edges of her robe curled into her field of vision. Dust smoked off of her.

She tried to stand – a natural instinct – and immediately collapsed, gasping, paralyzed by agonizing jolts of pain forking through her thigh.

Her hand leapt to the area. Warm stickiness soaked through her robe and slicked her fingers. Hard, sharp edges were sticking out of flesh too tender to touch. Shrapnel. Metal, rock, wood, some foreign body. It embedded itself in her flesh, filling space that never asked to be filled.

Leaning into her one good leg, teetering like a pendulum, she shouted herself to her feet. Her head beat in throbs of thunder. Sound swooned in and out, compressing to a pinpoint, expanding to a shrill whistle. Muscles screamed in soreness. Every segment of her skin felt abused, flagellated by some grinding scourge. All energy was stripped away, drained to a null point. She stood half-contorted, letting the pain pass through her, curled in the shell of her own torn robes, with all her weight resting on her good leg.

Beyond lay only darkness. A quiet darkness. Darkness that shifted and blurred at the edges. She blinked once, twice, trying to rattle her eyes awake. They were open, though – fully open, and there was no light. No Eternal Day. It was gone.

There were only vague orange patches, twitching here and there. Fires. Wavering, simmering. There was no glowing sky, no burnished paths. Her single living eye drank only the night – utter, impenetrable– while her other eye found a matching shade to its onyx sheen.

Once Elara realized what she was looking at, her jaw fell and her strength nearly gave out. She steadied her balance and squelched nausea that rose in her belly, sharp and acrid. Her head swam and reeled. Breath would not come.

Great Mistress, no!

Surely this could not be the same place, not Advent Square. It was some duped reality. Some trick or imitation.

All was decimation. Everywhere, the dead lay, indivisible from blasted bricks of gold and blocks of marble. Soaked in a single layer of blood-drenched dirt and grit.

Whole patches of unscarred skin lay strapped in forked patterns over bloody husks. Scorched clothing smoked and wafted, melted onto bodies. Here and there, by some fluke of blast pattern or trajectory of debris, some people were still standing, teetering back and forth in the dark like animated corpses, skin blackened with cracks of red like canyons. Others rolled back and forth on the ground in final, lingering agony, calling to Logos through raspy throats or sputters of sound that passed for words. They, like the crackling fires of the square, refused to die.

Their moaning laments of anguish rose to soar into the clear night air, a requiem of mourning for the offerings below. Above, the stars bore silent witness to the open-air sepulcher of Advent Square – stewards for a folding age, dispassionately observing the precession of time. This link was no different than any other they'd seen. From fist to tool, from bone to fire to metal, again and again. Endless, perpetual.

The never-ending brilliance of New Corinth, the lighthouse of the world, had had its spine broken. The artificial light of the Eternal Day, bouncing from wall to wall, magnified and enhanced by synthorganic materials, had winked away with the destruction of the square.

A chill wind buffeted the torn plain and cut through Elara's robes, freezing her skin. The wind of winter's first night was settling into the marrow of the city, without the veil of warmth from the Eternal Day, to guide New Corinth towards a long hibernation. A night that saw them for the first time, without the haze of perfect white.

Nearby, the remnants of the Pageant of Miracles smoldered. Its broken pyre of metal and holo projectors rose in the night like a memorial. His Holiness – who sought to embody Logos – the players who'd pretended to be his retinue and counselors, now lie in a pile of unrecognizable, saturated red, having gripped each other close as they burned.

Marin! Compulsively, mind tattered, Elara started to lurch towards the center of square on her one good leg. After a couple steps, her strength caved and she collapsed to her knees.

She knew what she would find there, at the center of the cataclysm. There was nothing to see. Nothing there. Nothing left but the promise of death. She was not driven by the hope of finding anyone alive, but by the need to disprove hopelessness.

Inos? She spun left, right, searching for any sign of him. "Inos! INOS!!"

Nothing. The only reply she heard was the echo of her own voice, mingled with the moans of the near-dead. She knelt there, alone. Spent and empty, like a vented furnace.

Inos wasn't by her feet. He wasn't in the distance. He wasn't close by, nor anywhere else. He wasn't anywhere else because he'd been right by her side. The armor. The shield and standard-bearer.

That had been him, enfolding her from behind. She knew it. Saving her. Giving back the life she'd refused to take.

"NO!!" Elara shrieked. She wailed and pounded her fist into the bloodied, scorched earth again and again. A bone in her hand popped like fractured glass. She didn't feel it at all. It couldn't crack her shell of grief. Nothing could, ever again.

"Kali ... Great Mistress ... no, no – why?! WHY?!"

Nothing answered her. Nothing but the utter totality of failure and

the completeness of loss. There was nothing left to reclaim. Nothing …
nothing at all. Her tears soaked into the ground, diluting the dirt,
watering the blood.

From the void of the night a sound arose, echoing clear and constant.
Scrunch, scrunch. Drawing closer. Regular, resolute.

Smoke coiled and writhed, its edges rushing away from a shape that
pushed outward from the darkness. Shoulders, head, and robes a mere
tone's difference from the blackness they dwelt in. Then, the face.

Fallow. Fresh, fleshy gouges ran like red tributaries across his smile.

Debris crunched underfoot as he stepped firmly, holding his head
high like a warlord surveying the field, casting his unconcerned features
this way and that way.

"This is what I always wanted, Ascendant Aeve. Do you understand
now?" He kicked an arm out of the way. "A *scar*. Like these." He pointed
to his face, then hers. "Like those. Simple."

Elara knelt there, utterly still except for silent sobs that shuddered her
chest. The sheer *waste* … the lost potential … it beat at her mind,
battering her spirit, hammering her again and again till she was sure she
would erupt.

Marin, disintegrated. Inos, discarded. So much potential. A future –
their future – erased before it could be sketched. Hopes, wishes, vanished
to the will of the fiend who circled her like a sliding snake. Life,
evaporated. Kali'ka against Corinthian, Corinthian against Errati, man
against woman, child against child, brethren against brethren – all
obliterated with the selfsame indiscretion, slaughtered at the spout of
excitation.

When the hundreds turned thousands turned millions cried in one
voice of agony, engulfed in a convective rush of flame, consumed by
tendrils and curls of tongued fire, Elara had become one with them. The
same unbearable pain that had consumed her in the Well had consumed
them all.

Fallow kept talking. His voice clawed through her skull, scraping and
digging. "I wanted a tear deep enough to not heal over in the exact
flatness of its predecessor. A mar on the face of a pristine lie. Something,
finally, that Logic can't ignore. Not by the participants of this pageant,

no. But by those who *survive them*. There is no plastein for the mind. No plastein for the soul. No plastein to coat memories and make them whole."

Elara closed her eyes. They could have left, she and Inos. She'd wanted to help, wanted to salvage their order. But nothing was worth this price! It was too great! Too great! Why hadn't she just left? Why?? Kali take it! Kali take it *all*!

"This was always present, under the surface, Ascendant Aeve. Finally, they've seen what we've always seen. They saw it until their screens grew dark and the datacast stopped transmitting. Now, they sit and wonder, knowing nothing but the lack of knowing. Nothing but fear. The fools at home, the ones overseas. They now hold this memory inside ... forever!"

Like stones from slings, his words struck her, again and again, until she stopped feeling them. Past the words, past the meaning, they became only sound. Sound that tapped her mind and passed straight through.

"This is how you win wars, Ascendant Aeve. You *demoralize*. That has always been the strategy. Victory is an act of *will*. It is a choice. So is defeat."

She dove with his sounds, probing past her body and into her spirit, feeling its shape and boundaries. Heat was there, held inside. The fire within, safe in a small, untouchable pocket. The fire of life, of muscles and cells that burned with an electric surge. Fire was around her, in the air. The air flit the hair on her brow, cool against the wetness upon her cheeks. The wetness of spilled blood, soaking into the earth under her knees. Blood was within, where flesh still beat.

All was in everything, and everything was one, harnessed in elemental unity.

"Logic has to be destroyed, Ascendant Aeve, not bargained with. This is the beginning of their end! You know that! They are a *blight*. A sickness of history, and Kali is the Goddess of Time. She wipes the slate clean. We are her Hands. What more is there to consider?"

Elara's blood snarled, smoking in the cold of the night. Time was smoke, and it curled its tendrils tightly, squeezing, choking, streaming from burned corpses into the night of the new moon.

Even though Elara couldn't see the moon above, she knew her face beamed constant, cloaked behind darkness, her chill circle full and completely round under a cover of black, hidden from the tortured plane below. A perfect circle. A perfect circle of time and gray light. Complete. Unified, with comparatives. Without contrast. Without boundaries.

Emptiness.

"Instead of working with me, *Elara...*" He sneered her name. "...You worked against me! You didn't trust me. You fought me. You tried to stop me. You deepened the division. I could have led all of us, if you'd just given in! If you'd just let me!" His face twisted in scorn. "Foolishness! It happened anyway!"

Kali was in the moon. The emptiness of her face projected itself into the mirrors of Earth, the vessels below. In Elara, the moon saw only its own image, pristine and in absolute clarity. Elara was emptiness itself, acceptant of what shone into her, a direct reflection unable to filter unwanted feelings, unwilling to distort the image within. She was the form for the shape a new moon.

Through her, Kali became the heat below.

Elara's tempest of all-consuming despair – her regret, her anguish – turned *outside*, into a storm of wrath and energy. Her outer form – hollow and frozen – turned *inside*, becoming a void of nothing, blank and glacial.

For a being of limitless internal fire, her outer motion had no end. Her energy soaked to the brim and filled high enough to shatter the sky, swathing her in colorless, distant starlight.

This is what they always truly lusted for," Fallow hissed, eye constricting, "...Death."

Yes, she thought. *And you, as well ... Nightwalker.*

From one instant to the next, Elara erupted. She howled in violent rapture, a hell-screech of all spirits brutally ripped from their resting. It was a howl wrenched from memories of the earliest times, of plains of ash and fire like the square she now tread. It beckoned the hearer to join and descend into unabated carnal suffering. The entire aspect of the heavens seemed to shrink, and all light dimmed in cowering terror.

Never had she screamed so. Never in argumentation, anger, or lust. Her primal core ruptured. And like a twitching infant convulsing its first breath, the universe seemed cold and spasmodic and cruel.

Turning on Fallow the usurper, Fallow the daemon, she covered the distance between them in an instant.

His one eye widened, and it was finished before it began. One strike, and it was done. So she had decided, and so it was.

His body surged to the ground in a disheveled heap, chest caved in at the sternum. Tips of ribs were sticking out of his sides. His lungs and heart were skewered. He had only a few moments of wide-eyed, wordless rattles before blood vomited from his lips like an overflowing cistern. Then, he was dead.

Elara stared at him, hollow. Her hair floated in front of her face. Somewhere, something told her it tickled her eyebrow and nose.

There was no victory, no satisfaction. Nothing was inside. Nothing but emptiness. Emptiness, as a bounded volume. Emptiness, forever and eternal.

She'd felt nothing when her head made contact. No force. No force at all. No force… the force of eternity. Containing nothing, and so from it could come everything.

Ascendant.

Elara turned towards the voice amidst smoke and fire and rage, all cooling. Tiny embers floated amidst red sparks and blackened motes, lingering indecisively.

Flapping within the fumes and vapors of Advent Square was a Stabat, wrapped in Kali'ka gray. Its third eye hovered in the darkness, a solid white orb with a dilated pupil, locked on Elara. Its putty-white face sunk into the night.

In a small, closed part of herself, Elara thought it a curious sight. A Stabat, outside of a cloister? Strange.

Yes, she thought in reply.

You have Transcended. The illusory realm awaits. The Great Mistress beckons. Come.

Transcendence … The word should've provoked shock and incredulity, but it didn't. The sooty air should've also coaxed a cough, but it didn't. The sulfuric sting should've baited a blink, but it didn't. The tongues of fires should've cause her to shield herself, but they didn't. The pain in her thigh should've inhibited her movement, but it didn't.

There was nothing inside to provoke or invoke. Nothing to push against. Nothing to weigh against.

Fallow lie on the ground, his blood leaking out to choke the earth along with the mingled blood of all the shattered bodies around him. Bodies of his own making. It all poured so easily, as if fleeing imprisonment.

Now he could dream all he wanted. The other place had consumed him – not the illusory realm of Kali, but the place of his own design. A place of never-ending torment, a place he couldn't escape, not in life, and now not in death. His one eye bulged as if in sudden horror at the sight he'd forever be left with.

Empty, void, Elara glided straight-backed after the Stabat, her windswept, auburn hair waving with the rhythm of flames, as she was slowly swallowed by the darkness of New Corinth's first true night.

**

Ascendant Oren sprinted along the highest edge of Advent Square, shrouded in darkness. Cloaked within black air, he raced, leaping over charred bodies and stony rubble, gaping holes and scattered fires.

Dead. Advent Square was dead. Slain in a hurricane of blood and fire. All of the Kali'ka of Mors, inciting violence amongst Corinthians, dead. All the defectors from Sangra, dead. All of it, gone. New Corinth would follow suit; it was only a matter of time.

Advent was the only eulogy Fallow's minions would receive. Those posing as Corinthians, Magistrate, whomever could get close enough to plant the bombs – they'd done their jobs perfectly.

Never would Oren have suspected that success felt so much like failure.

Fallow was dead. Dead, by *her* hand. And her… *alive.* Elara Aeve was alive, impossibly. After all their efforts, after everything she'd suffered, she was the last one standing.

While Oren had watched, crouching behind rubble, she'd stood up to Fallow. She'd refused to give up, no matter that they'd already succeeded in destroying the Eternal Day, no matter that she'd lost everything.

With the barest effort, she'd obliterated Fallow's body, without a word turning to trail after the Stabat who'd shown up from nowhere.

They were never a match for her. Never.

He should have known better: talking with her, living near her, looking directly into those jade eyes, burning like lances of flame. The instinct, Kali, was alive and flourishing, embedded in her, in the essence of genes and life. Such will … it resonated in both Creation and Illusion, forever.

She would destroy him without prejudice, on sight. He knew his mistake, but he wasn't foolish enough to stay. "Making due" was a moot concept he would not test by approaching her.

It was to the survivors he looked, searching for signs. Some shining glint, some tone of fabric. There was nothing left for him.

Was there enough plastein in existence to restore the remainder of Fallow's brood? They'd be soulless. Leaderless. Lost without their leader, the slave-master whom Oren feared would haunt him and control him even in death; the one-eyed fiend of blood and nightmares, greedy for the lack of anything not his own.

Oren had witnessed it all, from the man's first fervent words uttered in secret covens. He'd watched it escalate, watched Fallow argue with ascendants in Mors, watched him pore through ancient tomes, assault other Kali'ka, let them brutalize his face, take a new name, and then grow into a monster of hubris and murderous whims.

Oren had been there, right next to him, afraid until the end.

He could have done something. He could've intervened. Completely and truly, he knew the totality of his betrayal. It had all been there in Marin's face, in Ashram, as she hung on the cross.

But death didn't want him for his crimes. Not even the flaring trees of Advent Square had touched him. Him, the one person who deserved it the most – deserved to be sprayed with fragments of whizzing stone and consumed by rolling flames.

There! He stumbled on a set of clothing he recognized. One of hundreds planted as instigators in the populace. One of those he'd coerced in Sangra. Fallow would have never trusted them to hold the daggers he personally forged; only those from Mors were allowed that responsibility.

The person was mutilated, barely breathing, shredded like tenderized meat, oblivious even of his – her? – own pain. A small grace, one soon to abscond to the greater grace of death.

Oren had completely forgotten that death was the favor granted them by the Goddess. She ferried them across the ocean of life and death. Life to death, death to life. They'd all forgotten, wooed by charismatic words and passionate speeches bundled in the guise of euphemisms, aphoristic speech, and self-sustaining pathos.

There could be no comfort, no truth in circles and ascendancy now. All was tainted, so all must be new.

Weeping, he knelt to lift the cindered form he'd found, whispering words of sorrowful comfort and hollow reassurance. He had no idea if the person even heard him.

There must be more. There must be! For whatever life they could have, whatever home they could muster.

Home, home… Is that what we've been searching for all along? A true Ashram? A new Ashram? A place of peace? Were the cloisters not that place…?

Time to rest, time to sleep, and in waking, forget their dreams. Here at the great awakening, conceived and consecrated in a fertile womb of Logical misery and suffering, childish notions of peace were abandoned to the blackest night.

Leaving, cradling the broken person on his shoulders, Oren diminished into the dark horizon of New Corinth's scarred face. Along the way, he gathered whomever he could, like pebbles scattered to the ocean, to go, search, and find their one final place of rest.

They couldn't go to Mors. They couldn't go to Sangra, nor to Ignis. They couldn't go to the Veneer, and they couldn't stay in New Corinth proper. They couldn't go to any known place. But where, then…?

Where else but New Corinth have they not beaten their plowshares into spears?

CHAPTER 32
MARBLE AND BLOOD

Jacobs sprinted through the darkness engulfing New Corinth, staying out of sight, running across avenues only when necessary, crisscrossing along minor causeways between buildings. The swell of the swarm grew behind him. Corinthians. Lone stragglers, small pockets or massive mobs, fleeing, pouring through the streets as though they were aisles leading to Penance.

If their rabid hysteria didn't engulf him, then the bombs would. *Bombs.* The word jangled in his head like a lone coin, impossible to grasp. Bombs ... *under trees.* All across New Corinth. Starting in Advent Square, growing, spreading. Crippling the architecture of the city that supported the Eternal Day.

He'd colluded with them. He'd been the crack through which a madman seeped. All of it, his fault. All the plastic faces, melted, ruined into an abominable gallery of wrecked and fractured forms.

Millions of lips cried his damnation, millions of scorched eye sockets demanded reasons. They chewed at his brain like a parasite. They painted his inner eye red with the chasm of a newly rendered, bloody history, piercing his mind with slivers of stained-glass, corrupting and tainting all he saw and would ever see.

There was not enough plastein in existence to wash over Advent Square and reform all the missing tissue. Replace all the missing *soul.* In the land of bounty, milk and honey had finally run dry.

While others slaughtered, struggled, and died, his childishly soft skin escaped with only scratches and bruises. His survival made his role clear. His duty was obvious. He was Jacobs the Coward. Jacobs the Destroyer. Jacobs the Inveigler. There was nothing left to do but follow his role through to its final conclusion. Nothing to do but run. Nothing to do but *erase*.

On the other side of the Elysian Plazas, the meters-thick synthstone of the Basilica Formata glowed dim in the starlight. The Mausoleum wasn't in use during the Pageant of Miracles, and would provide the perfect point of entrance.

Passing through the Atrium of Bane's Lack, leaping up the Steps to Glory two at a time, he circumvented the main entrance of the Basilica to a nondescript, single red door meant for seminarians, scions, and magisters only. Huffing, legs quivering, feet throbbing, he placed his palm on the entry pad, and with a beep and click, the door was open.

His access wouldn't be revoked until he was legally Excised. As expected, Grand Magister Hammar would follow even such obscure, fringe security protocols to the letter. Jacobs hoped he never saw the man again.

As he pattered though the massive, domed interior of the Mausoleum, his shambling amble was the only sound he heard. With a seating capacity in the hundreds of thousands, now completely empty, Jacobs felt overwhelmed by empty space. Lumensrods and lumenspanels filled the superstructure like tiny indoor stars, illuminating the creamy white architecture in a ghostly blur.

The moment he crooked into the left-hand path past the great, twin alabaster statues of Logos, a figure stepped out from behind a nearby column.

Jacobs stumbled to a halt, his feet preparing to dart this way, that way.

Out from the still and stark shadows of the Mausoleum stepped the desiccated, decrepit figure of Hegil. Cassock torn to rags, body slicked in as much refuse and feces as it was abrasions and blood.

Jacobs felt his hand fly to his mouth as he gasped. Disbelief flooded his brain. "Hegil! By Logos … what… what are you doing here?!"

Breath heaving, his voice trailed to nothing, It was simply too much to believe, too much to process. His hands gripped his hair, white-knuckled. Tears streamed from his face.

He stumbled towards his friend, "Hegil! Oh no, it was so… I'm so glad to see you! Oh Logos, the pageant… It … You …"

Hegil took a couple steps backwards.

Jacobs stuttering through a clogged nose and mucous mouth. "What – Hegil… W-what are you doing?"

"It's your fault." The words cut the air coldly. The voice didn't sound like Hegil at all.

Jacobs blinked, not comprehending. "What?"

"You sent me there." Baleful eyes glared at him, inset within flaps of sallow skin. By Logos … his face was pulverized and terribly beaten. Were some of his front teeth missing??

"Hegil, what…" Jacobs' mind dashed over facts, fumbling and losing its grip. Surely he'd misheard. "Hegil … do you know what's going on? Out there? Advent!"

"You…" Hegil held back tears that welled into eyes so bloodshot, they were nearly totally red. "You sent me to talk to that man. To Fallow. He… He … Why?! Why did you do it!?"

Terror stabbed Jacobs' heart. Electric panic coursed through him, scorching, freezing. "Hegil, there's – what do you – have you seen…"

Hegil didn't wait for him to finish. "Shut up!! Do you know what he did to me?! That place, those people … Oh Logos, you can't know! You can't!"

The grace and prowess of Jacobs' speech slipped away. He couldn't speak, couldn't process. "Hegil, I was… Oh no … I'm so sorry! Please! Please!"

The emaciated man surged forward like an unchained cadaver, forcing Jacobs to dance out of the way. "Sorry!? There's no one left to absolve you, High Devotee! There's nothing left! This is your fault! All of it! You bargained with them! And for what?! His Holiness…" A squeak of despair came from his throat. "I heard the explosions. That's what Fallow did with the information you gave him. *You!* You used me, just like always! Did you give me even one thought while I was gone??"

Jacobs could barely formulate a response. Dozens of potential replies swept through his brain. There was simply too much to say at once.

"Hegil ... listen. This was the only secure place I could get to. Millions of them, Corinthians – so many. Oh Logos ... The people, all the people! They're, they're *gone*. The city is gone! Look around you! The Eternal Day is no more!"

"I'm well acquainted with darkness, now, *Your Grace*. The Veneer has a way of forcing the hand of choice."

"I know! I was there, Hegil. I was there. I saw it. I saw it, too."

"Is that where you ran to? I watched the comeye footage from your Parish – the Breaching with Lucrece Dagon and her daughter. What were you trying to do? What did you think would happen? Did you think you could just *escape*? You're the High Devotee!!"

"Hegil, that girl ..." Jacobs shook his head, waving his hands as though to clear a passageway for coherent thought. His lungs felt trapped. "It's not that simple. There are other reasons."

"Reasons? What reason could there possibly be in denying a little girl her natural birthright, in denying her the gift of her heritage, in denying her union with our Lord Logos?"

Jacobs rushed forward, words flowing freely in a passionate lack of restraint.

"Union with Logos? Union?? Rape!! Rape, Hegil! That's what it used to be called! Check the Reliquary! Abuse! *Theft!*" Jacobs heard his voice crack, felt his chest sob as tears slipped down his face. "Taking advantage of a person – a child! – before she's possibly ready to make such decisions! Before she's ready to understand its complexity! Its magnitude! Glossing over the intricacies of emotion and handing her theological tenets, instead! Setting the rudder to the course of her life, defining what she must do and think before she's even done anything! *That* is the true crime, Hegil! *That* is the true lie! That's all we've ever done!!"

Hegil's glower deepened, like the patch of black after lightning's crack. A sneer pulled his loose lips back.

"You were the model for us all! The greatest under the His Holiness! Your devotion has waned to nothing, High Devotee! Is that why you're here, now? To spout Nihil Obstat at me?!"

"No, no, Hegil! That doesn't even matter anymore! Nihil Obstat, none of it! You have to listen to me! It's not like that! I … This place…" He lifted his hands to the Mausoleum, to the sprawling streets beyond. "This place isn't real! It's stone and words *only*! I can't deny what I've seen! I can't lie to myself!"

Hegil scuttled forward, features grossly expanded and stretched. Rabid breathing vented from his shattered teeth as his hunched back swelled. "Traitor!"

"What?! There's nothing to betray, Hegil! There's no loyalty to be given to a fraud! It's over! Finished!"

"A fraud?? We had paradise, Jacobs! What role did you play in its undoing? What right did you have to choose for the rest of us?!"

Flashes of images flit within, jabbing Jacobs' mind like skewers. The citizen in Pantheon, begging for her life, proclaiming her innocence, clothed in the garb of someone else who may or may not have died in the same ignominious, agonizing way.

What right did he have to choose for anyone else…? None. None at all. That was exactly the point.

Hegil pressed. "I knew you were acting strangely, even before Advent Sermon! Even before you asked me to go that horrible place!"

"Hegil, I'm sorry! Listen to me!"

"Listen to you?! Listen to you?! I don't have to listen to you anymore! *'The words of a liar have no meaning! They are as a barren harvest…'*"

Jacobs finished the verse along with Hegil, their voices overlapping. "*'…Sowing nothing but unfulfilled promises!* First Partite, Book of Pericles, Cadence 7, Dram 23, The Abridged Version. I know, Hegil! I can quote it, too! We learned those words together! Side by side, in estuary!"

"From you, they're curses and deception! Traitor! Traitor!"

Jacobs grasped for Hegil's shoulders, stretching, reaching. "Please, listen to me… Please."

Hegil recoiled, speaking over Jacobs' mumbles, trying to back away. "No! Don't touch me, don't touch me!"

He raised his arms in defense and made contact with Jacobs. Jacobs reflexively gripped his friend's arms – some gene-deep, raw reaction he'd never tapped.

Both men froze, arms locked, twins to each other, High Devotee and mendicant.

Hegil's face took on a bubbled, warped perspective. His pupils seemed to constrict, his mouth seemed to inflate like a predator diving to kill. "Let me go, Jacobs! Let me go, damn you! Too long! Too long!"

Hegil pushed and Jacobs braced himself. The next moment they were diving to the floor, smashing into pews, tumbling, grappling, shouting at each other through grit teeth and sprays of spittle, knocking over lumensrods with uncontrolled legs and the crude combat of bare survival.

Jacobs begged the entire time. "Stop! Stop!"

In reply, Hegil howled and shoved him against a column. Jacobs' head knocked against the marble. His vision dimmed.

Hegil lunged at him and lashed his fingers around Jacobs' neck, squeezing, twisting. Air stopped entering Jacobs' throat. He felt his tongue whip around uncontrollably. Blood was puffing up his face.

Through a strained, compressed throat, he pleaded. "He ... gil! What... are you...?!"

Only snarls and bestial grunts answered him. Only the maniacal glare of rolling eyeballs, grimy flesh, clamped teeth and slathering lips. It was all there in the portrait of Hegil's face, painted with the nuances of long, hardened, darkened years, scoring through to a venomous underbelly.

How long have you hated me, my old friend?

Hegil wanted him dead. He *would* kill him.

In a detached part of himself, Jacobs started to float, strangely calm, without resistance. In no way did Jacobs want to fight or harm Hegil.

But even though he doubted his right to live, he didn't doubt his right to protect himself.

A cutting wail burst from his lips, and in one clean motion he bashed Hegil's arms away and tackled him hard and flat to the floor. Jacobs, unleashed, fought for the first time. The fury of his life – the same forgotten wrath that was scouring the streets of New Corinth – poured from him in tidal waves.

Jacobs jammed his thumbs into Hegil's knobby Adam's apple and snared his unshaven, oily neck with interlocked fingers. He braced himself over his friend's body, knee to sternum, sharp and ruthless, driving all of his weight, every last ounce, down through his thumbs, torquing, crushing Hegil's throat like a wet towel. He bashed the back of Hegil's head into the stone floor, again and again, hearing it slowly crack open.

Hegil beat, kicked and clawed blindly, at whatever he could reach – stomach, ribcage, thigh, arm – the stringy ligaments of his neck writhing in a feeble attempt at escape. Blood started to spit from his lips and streak the tiles under his head. His gaze began to faze and roll around. His eyelids grew heavy and his face grew purple. Amidst little coughs, his attempts to fend off Jacobs began to weaken.

For one clear moment, before his eyes faded to emptiness, shock and the bitterness of betrayal peered into Jacobs' face, the face of his one and only friend.

But Hegil said nothing. He *could* say nothing, ever again.

His bloodshot, disbelieving eyes rolled to the back of his head and the breath of his life ceased in final rattles and jerks. One moment alive, one moment dead, easy as a slip of wind, blithe as the turn of a page.

All was still except the strained quivering of Jacobs' muscles clenched around his friend's crushed throat. He knelt there, staring at the virulent red staining the floor under Hegil's head, seeing nothing but the white-wash of permanence, crisp and damning.

Anguish exploded from his throat like a cannon. He wept and howled like a newborn.

"Why?! Why, Hegil... Why... Did it really matter that much? Enough to do this? Enough... for this...?"

Above, an alabaster statue of Logos towered, watching dutifully with a fixed smile, ever unchanging, shaded by night.

Under the gaze of New Corinth's god, tears and phlegm and sweat and wailing cries of remorse were Jacobs' baptismal bath, on an altar of hard marble. He and the Basilica both, shrouded in the cleansing force of blood, dirt and death.

Even as his chest pumped in sobs, Jacobs stood, muscles weak and trembling, to fumble over a nearby lumensrod and lift it to the air for light. He clasped one of Hegil's still-warm hands, encompassing he and his friend in the fuzzy sphere of the lumensrod's light. Everything around them seemed dimmer for the difference.

Blinking through the blur of tears, he gazed up at the alabaster statue of Logos.

Its eyes held nothing – nothing at all. There was nothing in their depthless gaze but shallow shadows. It was a blind witness to a crime between brothers, capable of nothing but reflecting the white of the artificial lumensrod in dull tones. Between it and Jacobs, air passed crisp and moist, inhaled and exhaled in moments of corrupted purity, bruised stillness, and battered solace.

You were a man too, once ... before we traded ourselves for your divinity.

With the lumensrod held aloft and Hegil's hand in his, Jacobs turned without a single look back, as he dragged Hegil's body behind him.

He struggled up the four-story marble stairs one at a time. He lurched past his plush, purple seat in the Reserved Cove of the Chosen, past His Holiness' pulpit, to the rear of the altar, past the Sacristy and down the hallway to the Conclave Wing.

He wept the entire way with no one to hear, no companion except the echoes of his own cries, the slide of his friend on the floor behind him, and the crackle of flames growing in his mind.

Hegil would be consumed in the same blaze as the rest. Just like Advent Square.

We don't need it anymore, my friend... We don't need any of it. Let's start again. Let's make a paradise that accepts us the way we are.

CHAPTER 33
THE SOURCE

Elara floated, a mirage in the form of a woman, head lowered in the exact pose of the Stabat leading the way in front of her, staring into the darkness of time. She was a mere shadow of her companion, and of herself, alone along the last length of the long procession to her own memorial service.

She hefted a small, cylindrical lumensrod that illuminated a small sphere of Cloister Sangra around them, taken from the house that held the pore they'd used to enter the cloister. Only a few solitary torches popped here and there along Sangra's walls, like final outposts on the edge of an abandoned wasteland.

Elara strained to catch the shapes around her, cast from the slant shadow of the lumensrod. The hematite, the yantra carved into the stone. Her core of cores stretched to grasp their depth and stuff them into her bosom, to fathom the meaning and flavor of a breathing universe.

Instead, apprehension, grief, hatred – all of them sparked and died. Sensations struck on the flint of her will and instantly fizzled. She was empty. A sleeping walker. A walking sleeper. Down, down, her solitary slippers stepped, echoing the emptiness within.

She was absent, like the cloister. Without people, without their words and energy. She tread deep inside a deceased stone titan, creeping around the bloodless vessels of its gargantuan body, seeing where rites used to take place, people used to be. Remnants of fighting abounded – blood, snatches of cloth, scuffed up stone, upturned firepots, cooled to blackness.

The Stabat said nothing as it led the way. It merely glided in its sinuous way, the back of its ashen head hovering atop robes that hung like free-flowing water.

What other choice was there? There was no one left. No one to care for. Maybe this was her secret desire, all along… To have no one to love. No obligations to others. No demands. No potential for pain. Charlotte, at least, was safe, wandering somewhere above….

Some part of Elara had died in Advent Square, along with Inos, along with Marin, along with the Errati, in the field of reaped lives. Some part of *all of them* had died – Kali'ka, Corinthian, Veneerian. The rest of her, the part left behind and walking, was now just a house of dampened flesh.

Just like the Stabat.

She'd known their destination the moment they entered the cloister. They spiraled down the 144 steps of the Seventh Arteriole, through its emblematic stretch to the Chamber of Sarcophagi.

It wasn't surprising at all. No matter how she struggled to avoid the inevitable, she kept coming back. Since visiting the Well of Kali, she'd known she would wind up here, carried out on a bier of fingers and palms in a funereal imitation.

For a moment, she wondered how they'd get through the swirling, shifting darkness of the pore at the end of the hallway. The Undying Firepyres had to have gone out by now. The Kachina were likely as cold as the stone of the floor they lied on.

Before she could wonder aloud, the Stabat lifted a palm towards the pore, made some slashing motions in the air, and mumbled something that sounded like cracked kamisheet sliding over itself.

As though carried away in a puff of wind, the blackness of the pore dissipated in tiny swirls of black like smoke. The entryway to the Chamber of Sarcophagi opened wide, like any other doorway.

The Stabat lowered its arm and entered. Elara followed, detached but still disturbed at how easily the Stabat had extinguished the cloister's best-kept wards.

Inside the Chamber of Sarcophagi, the rest of the Stabat waited. They encircled the vacant, black opening to the Well of Kali. The eleven remaining sarcophagi stood undisturbed. There were no bodies in the chamber, though plenty of blood remained, in pools and smears. Fallow's followers must have taken those they'd murdered, like in Mors.

Elara heard her feet slide over the grit and rubble from the shattered sarcophagi, and come to a halt.

In unison, all the Stabat lifted their left arms and pointed at the entrance to the Well. Their intent was clear.

Unconsciously, Elara found her eyes tracking along them, ticking off one at a time. One, two, three, four…

Eleven. No twelfth one. As she thought.

She looked from the empty spot in the Stabat's ring to the empty spot on the floor of the chamber, where the twelfth sarcophagus had inexplicably exploded.

In absence, the lost sarcophagus told what it knew. It cried secrets, the spinebacks on the floor of her room, untouched and unanswered.

The Stabat next to her, her guide… Was it one of the same ones as before? The one in the Codex? The one in Mors? The one who stood over her as she lie burned and charred?

Elara's eyes tightened, and through the half-moon eclipse cloaking her field of vision, she stared directly into the Stabat's unshrinking iris. Subtly, nervously, its eye twitched like an insect leg.

"You… You're the Aegis Council, aren't you? You're the ones named in the spineback I found in the Codex."

None of the Stabat budged. Their eyes stayed fixed on her. Not one of them breathed. No metabolic processes, no respiration, no digestion, no endocrine secretions, no temperature regulation. Still flesh, to the last.

"You were there, at the beginning. You're our progenitors. You built this place. The cloisters, this chamber, the Well. You made these devices … these sarcophagi, to keep yourselves alive? Or, bring yourselves back?"

The Stabat said nothing, did nothing.

"Why do this? So you could stay with us, watch over us, lead us towards … here? Right here and now? This time? This place? Why? Transcendence? Have you been leading me here, one Circle of Ascendancy after the other?"

No response, still. Elara spoke at their unfeeling flesh. Their hands remained outstretched towards the Well.

"The thirteenth sarcophagus is down there, with the mask and blade. A shrine. But there's never been a physical Goddess ... right? There can't be anything inside of the sarcophagi. There's never ... there's never been a Kali on Earth. She's not... She exists in the illusory realm. In Illusion. She can't be here, alive, in this place. You..."

Their pale, putty-like skin emanated like dull chalk. It was a creature not quite alive.

"These things." She lashed out and gripped the arm of her guide. It didn't react. The toughness of muscle lay atop bone, the cords of sinew ran beneath. Like a person, but unwarm and uncold. "These are your bodies. This is what you look like, here. This is your projection, from the other place. From Illusion."

Its third eye stared unblinkingly, as though blinded by what it saw.

"You've awoken. The sarcophagi bridge the gap. They cross the planes. Illusion and Creation."

Its eye jittered briefly. Its lips – gray and frozen – stayed shut.

"Kali's Eyes ... how deep did your knowledge go? How much have we lost? Why did we lose it? What could be so important that you ... you wouldn't cut yourself loose after all this time? Let yourself die?? Why won't you let yourself die? The Goddess grants us all the grace of death! Accept it!"

All the Stabat stood in place. Sentinels, dead as stone. Remnants and shadows of what was – *who* was. Not the omnipotent creatures they were believed to be, but something far more piteous and ... *meager.*

Ahead, the black chasm of the Well of Kali gaped, awaiting Elara's presence, peering at her like a sister to her left eye. Inside, at the bottom, lie the mask and blade of Kali, lashed by silver chains to the thirteenth sarcophagus – message to the living, ark for the Goddess – waiting for her still.

"Fine, Stabat... I'll do it. But not for you. Not for anyone else. For *me.* I want – I want..." The vision of an ashen Kali blew across Elara's sight. In the land of red sand, in the place where time stopped, Her black hair whipped in the wind as She stood staring over the edge of a broken cliff, gazing on fields of dead.

"I want to know. What's inside, what's out there… All of it. I want to know why. I want a *reason*." The Stabat didn't answer her. She didn't expect them to.

If she didn't emerge, no one would know. Beyond the desolate remains of the uncounted dead, there was only memory, and memory vanished over time. She would simply be gone, swept off the pages of this age, without a reference, without possessions for executorship, nor even a trail of clues that spoke her name.

Maybe it would be for the best – history left alone without the mark of her existence. All she'd done was toss kindling on the flames of their collective bier. Maybe *that* was Transcendence: to act, knowing the repercussions, but not needing to live to see them.

Elara held up the lumensrod and stepped to the Well, staring face to face into a blackness without depth or direction.

Would she be a just Goddess, she wondered…? Would she crush the survivors of the cataclysm above? Would she brutalize the world under her cruelty?

Would the Stabat, one day, become afraid of what they'd helped make?

"Great Mistress…" Elara breathed. "I commit my body to You."

Inhaling one final breath, she lifted a foot and descended into an impenetrable, eternal darkness.

CHAPTER 34
REBIRTH

*H*and over hand, she gripped and hoisted, higher and higher, her *robes flapping wildly in the harsh, arid wind. The enflamed, turbulent atmosphere swirled with yellow and orange fibers of light and dust. The plains and their scarlet dunes below spread wider and wider, erupting in gouts of flame and rock, saturated with the heaped dead.*

How long had she been here? How long before her body quit? She had no memory of arriving, and could foresee no end to her staying. There was only constancy, persistent as a wheel. A perfect circle of endless, boundless time. Only the climb. Only the top. She must get there. She must!

If she didn't, she would break on the peak's lifeless face, erode with the scarlet stone, dissolve into the air like a fine powder.

Maybe then, though ... maybe then she could catch on the swirling updraft surrounding her, and be carried high, bodiless, to mingle with the sky above in streaks quick as lightning. To leave, to fly and forget the suffering below.

Screaming, she reeled a hand out and clasped a stony outcrop. No, it would not claim her, this place – not now, not ever! Nails torn, palms bloody, she reached, tightening her grip, locking her muscles, refusing to relent.

One final pull, and she mounted the cliff edge.

With both feet planted, she was home, standing firmly at the apex of the mountain, encased by an endlessly racing cocoon of sky-fire, scrunching her toes in the dirt.

...Toes? Bare feet?

She looked down at her body. No slippers. No robes. Skin was a dusty gray-white, like tinted ivory. Hands were whole, untorn. Nude? No... Covered in jewels, bangles, bracelets. Long necklaces of burnished gold looped to her stomach, between her breasts. Her waist was enchased by a white fur skirt, cinched in place by a sash of pearls from which tiny daggers dangled.

She felt neither cold nor hot, nor tired nor alert. She just ... was. Full and complete, with no comparatives.

Her hand idly lifted a lock of hair to her face. She pinched it and rolled it between her fingers. Jet black. Long, nearly waist-length, billowing in the wind. Atop it, she felt some kind of ... diadem? Smooth, metal and gems, intricately adorned, cradling her head like a crescent moon atop the clouds.

How...? Why...?

The moment she questioned, her wonder vanished. Her confusion wouldn't hold, wouldn't stick. It poured away like water. Normalcy settled onto her like a descending bedsheet. Doubt dissolved into resolve, which transformed into bemusement.

Yes, of course. Who else would she be? This was who she was. Transfigured. Unified. Returned to the source. Returned to herself.

Ahead she looked to where she knew he would be. There, at the edge of the cliff, the place where she surveyed the land below for endless hours on end.

He stood like a monument of Creation. Stone without earth, flesh without error, indivisible from the ground he stood on. Silhouetted against the fiery sky.

His smile drew her nearer.

She closed the distance, and placed her hands on his blue-skinned shoulders. Heat radiated from his flesh.

"I'm sorry you had to wait," she murmured.

He took her hands, gently, and slowly ran his thumbs across them, smiling. "I knew you would come here."

"And I knew you would be here. You are always here. You're the only one who stays ... the only one I know."

"Until forever ends." His voice rolled over her soothing, imbuing her

with fortitude and clarity.

"*Until forever ends,*" *she whispered.*

He looked out towards the scarlet, windswept sky of flame and grit. "*This place … it reflects dimly, more and more. Our brothers, our sisters, our wars, our follies … they are shadows, empty and gray.*"

"*There is still one who remembers … all of it.*" *She lifted a hand to the fields below, where body upon slain body lie unremoved from the same spot they fell.* "*She remembers even the daemons and their kin. She has reached the same place that I did.*"

"*She has seen herself?*"

"*And so disappeared. My face shown, for my presence here. She is me. Her will reflects my intention.*"

"*So they require us, still.*"

"*So long as there is the heat that grants life, I will be needed. I go when summoned, and then return to this point, the navel of my birth. There is no other way.*"

He nodded softly. "*Theirs is the place of mirrors, where the substance, the origin, lies beyond. We slip in between, again and again, to live. But time … time grows long. Ages fold. Soon, what we unwittingly set into motion, here on this battlefield, will become all of our futures.*"

"*What of the rest?*"

"*Think not of them, love, or let the attachment grow too fond. They are false gods. When they die, it is complete. They do not return here.*"

The wind rushed past her, carrying red dust with it. She watched the dust vanish against the background of the blood-toned sky. "*They brought this on themselves. By need, I was summoned, and by need, they were destroyed. But you … you were the only one who calmed me. The only one left.*"

He ran his hands through her long, black hair, letting time linger, refusing to speak, letting her say what she must say.

"*I don't want to forget. Every time, forget only to remember. Not again.*"

At her words, a great sigh released from his chest, and his fathomless, bottomless eyes drank in her face. "*Worry not. When you die, you will return here, and you will remember everything forgotten. We are never apart, in this place … in the memory of the past."*

True, she thought. True.

She breathed in his scent, light on the wind. It flowed into her, becoming one with her form. He and she were joined, now and forever.

They slipped into each other's arms, embracing, letting one long kiss linger for time uncounted.

Parting, he lifted an arm to the side.

She smiled only for him. "Soon."

"There is no length of time I would not wait."

"And there is no distance I would not travel."

With that, she leapt off the mountaintop, surging to the ground below. She landed weightlessly, the barest touch, and loped away on bare feet, vaulting kilometers at a time. The barren heath spread to the line of the horizon, becoming one with the undivided sky.

Along that horizon, directly in front, her goal rose steadily in size. From roots to trunk, the giant tree of life – manifest, incarnate – reared taller than sight could follow, broad as an entire world.

In one bound, she soared halfway up its height, clutching bark and pulling, from branch to crumpled seam, to leaf, to trunk. Upwards, upwards, forever upwards.

There overhead, an ocean of clouds spread puffy and white, billowing on the winds of time and space between two planes. Guardian and entrance to Creation.

Closing her eyes, she inhaled a breath and held it firmly. She pushed off one final time and punctured the cloud layer. Moisture enveloped her.

Emerging in an eruption of water, she blast downwards towards the oceans of Earth.

Arms wide in acceptance, she fell, fell, to the ground and oceans expanding below.

In one vision it spanned before her: grassy plains, windswept mountains, verdant forests, vast deserts, snow plains… A place of life and so, so much beauty.

And her, the heat below.

Details in the landscape began to impress themselves on her sight. Rapidly she plummeted, as though the air itself held no friction … at least for her.

She was one with the elements. She was the elements themselves, in one form.

Opening her mouth wide, she prepared to consume Earth and its firmament.

CHAPTER 35
TRUE NIGHT

Jacobs raced through the crystal and silver corridors of the Conclave Wing of the Basilica Formata in a stuttered hobble-jog, exhausted, wincing at the pain in his knee, staying ahead of the blaze roaring behind him. He clutched his chest, coughing, while fumes of smoke curled around him, rising from the spiral staircases leading out of the Reliquary.

I did it! I did it... Paradise – lost. Gone ... forever!

All it had taken was disabling the Basilica's fire suppression systems and a flicker of sparking light from the end of the broken lumensrod he'd taken with him from the Mausoleum.

In his mind, he saw the Reliquary as it just was, row upon row of handwritten parchments, forgotten artifacts, sacred paintings, sculptures, in room after room, blackening, smoking as snaps of sparks ignited into waves of fire, gnawing deeper and deeper into furling edges, singeing wood and melting busts.

Every last scrap, incinerated. The sickness of Logic – their shared delusion – seared away, lifted off the pages of history as easy as dabbing a blot of ink.

Jacobs' past, immolated in the crucible. His complicity, incinerated with the metal rack he'd used in Pantheon, along with Hegil's body ... just one of many holy relics reduced to empty, charred molds, preserved in ash for the forthcoming age.

From the Reliquary, the fire would grow to a colossus of flame, devouring the Basilica and the surrounding, central hive of New Corinth. In the dusk of Logical civilization, fire was needed to destroy the old life. All things must be made new, or else all things would come to pass once again.

He made one final turn, headlong down the path he'd taken in from the Mausoleum, and the hallway in front of him exploded in flames.

Blistering heat blasted him off his feet. Glass along the windows and ceiling shattered, and the floor rocked as though smashed by the fist of a titan.

As quick as it came, the inferno vanished. In its place was a hovering, wavering core of heat and light that boiled in the hallway like the surface of a simmering sun.

Jacobs pushed himself up to his knees, trembling, whimpering, shielding himself with his hands. Another bomb? He was unable to cast his gaze directly on the source of the light in the hallway – so bright, so absolute.

Gingerly, he peaked through a crack in his fingers.

A moment later, he howled in terror. He could do nothing but kneel there, staring at an incomprehensible sight. Unable to tear his eyes away, unable to reconcile what he saw with what he knew couldn't possibly be real. He tried to turn and flee, but fear – perfect, primitive and uncontrollable – paralyzed him utterly.

There, in the stillness of the night, stood a being in the shape of a woman, blazing like a supernova in mid-eruption. Flames coiled and swam around Her ivory body like liquid fire curving across the haloed edge of the sun's corona. They slid across Her skin in undulant waves, rippling like tongues desperate for taste, clinging to her waist-long, obsidian hair, searing the air but leaving Her body unburned.

It – *She* – was the radiance of the cosmos itself, in an incarnate, physical form. The nuclear fire of stars, the core of cores flipped outward and condensed to a single source.

Jacobs covered his face with one hand and clutched his chest with the other. "No!! Oh Logos! No, no, no ... please, please, don't hurt me!! Logos, help! Help!!" Terror shattered his reason and rent his comprehension. His heart rocked his ribcage like a raging animal trying to escape.

By contrast, Her chest rose and fell softly, slowly. Her black lips were a vent in the mantle of Earth, a crevice to the molten, blood-red pit of her mouth. At Her side, in Her right hand, hung a single-edged, curved sword.

"Please, please, I didn't, I didn't know. I didn't know! Please, please, no – don't!" There was no way he was awake. No way he was *alive*. It wasn't real... It *couldn't* be!

She just tilted Her head to the side as though confused by his babbling. Eyes black like onyx globes stared at him, polished and glistening in the light – in *Her* light. A quick blink, and Her eyelids slipped down and up. The act was impossibly, imperfectly, human.

She opened her mouth to speak, and her words shredded the air like a shockwave. They pummeled Jacobs' body, splitting his ears, squeezing his brain and his guts till he swore they would pop.

"Statues don't speak, Jacobs Osgood. Nor do they listen."

His name ... She knew his *name*?! His sundered mind couldn't stop producing blurts of sound. Sounds that didn't make sense. Words that couldn't be formed. Intent that wouldn't be words.

"P-P-Please, please, forgive me! Please! I – I – I'm sorry! Forgive me! Forgive me!! I didn't know! I *couldn't* have!"

Her upper lip curled in a something approaching disgust, and the grip on Her sword tightened. Those horrible black eyes, like twin, starless skies, never stopped peering into him.

"I will not forgive you, child, because I have no power to do so. Will, though originating elsewhere, belongs to the created. Choice is the power of the living."

Jacobs tried to speak, tried to construct words and sentences, but his mind was locked. Nothing could make him comprehend what was happening.

A god...?! It had to be! Not Logos. Another one. A real one. Some other kind of being. Jacobs had spent his life advocating belief in a deity, and now ... when one was real, in front of him, all he could do was beg for mercy.

She could end his life away as easy as blowing out a candle, he had no doubt. She was *real*. A physical goddess, right there in front of him. Visiting Earth, exhumed from the realms, appearing to *him*. Why? Why him? Why now??

"Yes! Yes, great one … of course, of course! Please, please don't hurt me! I didn't know… I didn't know! I – I…"

She frowned as though his words were confusing.

"Hurt you… No. It's your abuses that have brought Me back, once more, to dwell in this plane for a time. You should have no reason for regret." Her black lips curved into a grin. "You made Me."

Jacobs wailed, hugging his own chest, barely understanding Her words. She adjusted her grip on her blade and pounded the air with her voice.

"I return now, at the turning of the age, in the waning warmth of winter, in the late hour, as the clock moves to strip light, and all dims to a closed, chill center. Sword and moon will rise in their time, and My face will be known to all, yet again. All things will become new. My counterpart will carry on in my stead, until the time is fit that I continue what has happened today.

"Those who have dedicated themselves to Me – to be My hands when I was submerged in the haze of the past, to be My adopted children in this life and the next – belong to a fate different from those of this city. Damned are those who do not see and cannot act, but damned more are those who *do* see, and still do not act."

Subtly, the flames around Her shifted, deepening, thickening into a turbulent roil. Her wild face, shrouded in fire that flowed like enflamed magma, hardened into pure stone.

"But listen carefully, High Devotee … With each woman touched, with each instance of abuse, with each of your brothers who thought himself a god, with each injustice at each moment, you have sunk your blade deeper into your own throat. You have choked on your own blood. You have reaped your own crisis, at the hands of the living, the created, and now the solemn grace of death will not be yours. That choice *does* belong to Me."

Her mouth twisted and retracted over curled, pointed fangs.

"Life is *your* Penance, scion of Logos."

Jacobs sobbed. All his frustration, all his grief, all his denied shame, smothering and squelching his soul – decades and decades of anger, all of it – poured out like a waterfall.

What other choice was there? What other choice had he but to admit what lay within? Nothing could be hidden from Her – nothing!

She lifted Her swordless hand into the air and twisted it this way, that way, tilting Her head to peer at it. The flames along Her ivory skin rolled and wafted like streamers of smoke, curling, coiling, shifting from white to blue to orange. They were part of Her, fused with Her essence, merged and joined like water to water.

Her lips puckered into an 'o' shape, and with one tiny puff of air, the flames on Her hand whisked away. "Yes … it is fitting that the disciples of a dead god belong to the one they cry for."

She stepped forward, once, twice, three times, and the entire Conclave Wing lurched as though hammered by a barrage of crushing ballistics. Whole segments of stone architecture – statues, friezes, support structures – cascaded to the ground. Columns collapsed to crack and burst on the floor, and the remaining fragments of the glass ceiling plummeted in shimmering sheets that blasted apart on impact.

Jacobs wailed, face slick with drool and tears. He couldn't pull his eyes from the floor behind Her. Tiles – pure, creamy marble – smoked with Her imprinted footprints. Their scorched edges hissed and glowed red. Every slope of the toe, every contour of the skin, preserved in an unmoving freeze.

She bent over and leaned directly towards his face. The heat – oh Logos, the sheer heat! – bore down on Jacobs' skin like an iron weight, filling his flesh. His mind blanked, and into its place stormed an intimate understanding of death.

Surely, he would not survive. Surely, this was it!

"But you, High Devotee … you belong to *Me*."

She lifted one of Her extinguished fingers and delicately, tactfully, depressed it onto Jacobs' forehead, right on the browline, between his eyebrows.

Pain lanced straight through Jacobs' brain, pinning itself to the back of his skull. His skin seared and hissed and his mind peeled back like a sheath, exposing a weightless, levitating crux atop his crown that expanded upwards, upwards, outwards, infinitely.

His once-blind consciousness filled to overflowing with the liquid light of Her fire, connecting him to himself, at one point of a circle, the circle never-ending, but unlatched and viewed as a loop entire – past, present, future – all perspectives at once, all as one. Himself, an infinite mote, indistinguishable from its whole, traveling circuitously, bound but moving.

And Her, the center. The focus. The pivot around which he moved. The center around which all life moved, since time's inception, from Whom the blood of generations siphoned their resolve.

When She lifted her finger off of his forehead, Jacobs' senses smashed into his body and he gasped awake. His lungs drank the sooty air blissfully, greedily.

On his forehead, between his eyes, was a perfectly ovular, red welt where her finger had been. The curves of her fingerprint curled within it.

"By this mark, I will know you. I will peer out into the realm of Creation, and you will breathe in My sight. Your third eye is open. Creation and Illusion are one."

Wide-eyed, jaw agape, Jacobs stared upwards. Awe filled him, like Her flames, like the light within and the light without; the light that existed with or without darkness, with or without the sun above.

"You have seen My face, Jacobs Osgood, both when I was alive, and now when I am not. You know Me in your heart. You are the seed of change."

For the first time, Jacobs saw past his fears and adulation, and found himself drawn to Her features. So human, so ... real. The rosebud lips, the vulpine jaw – they flitted through his mind like a specter, snagging memories, tugging him to a dark, vile, fetid place ... where he knelt on the cold dirt, cradling the head of a woman in Kali'ka robes, her scarred face and mane of auburn fire faint in the dim light of a near-new moon.

"You!! It was you in the Veneer! I – I saved you! I carried you out! You were – you were almost dead! What... H-How is this possible? How??"

She said and did nothing. It was impossible to tell if her eyes were moving, or if they were even pointed in his direction.

"No, scion of Logos ... I saved *you*."

Kneeling in wonder, Jacobs lifted his upraised palms, hoping, craving, desiring just a single touch!

"Remember this day, Jacobs Osgood, when I, the Goddess of Time, Kali, bound you to Me ... forever."

As soon as the words left Her mouth, an eruption of fire and light consumed Her. It compressed into a ball of flame, hovering, swirling, tumbling over itself and sucking in all heat. A flash, and the flame burst in a detonation that raced through the Conclave Wing in streaks and strands before evaporating into nothing.

With Her presence gone, with her fire absent, the Conclave Wing was immediately plunged into the frigid darkness of night.

Jacobs' body gave way and he collapsed to the floor, bawling, begging for Her warmth, curled like a discarded newborn ripped from the womb in a fresh, agonizing birth.

He didn't notice Grand Magister Hammer and a small band of battered magisters sweeping in to hoist him to his feet and pull him away from the smoke creeping out of the Reliquary. He didn't notice being carried towards the Oculus and into the barracks and headquarters of the Magistrate, where the other surviving scions and seminarians hid.

Once the fires of Advent died down, when it was time to emerge and rummage through the embers, picking out the salvageable spots of their faith and fanning them back to health with the labor of their own hands ... they would need him again, Hammar knew, no matter what had happened before, no matter what had to be erased.

They would need him, and only him – the fractured High Devotee. Him, the successor to His Holiness. Him ... the legal Godhead of the entirety of Logic.

As they trotted, Jacobs mumbled to himself, oblivious of the dark world around him, mind ablaze with the purification of inner light.

"...I see Her. Oh Goddess, I see Her! The darkness ... I admit it! Take me ... to shadow. I must go! To shadow ... I must go, to shadow..."

***

Huddled in the Central Conflux of Cloister Ignis, Oyame sat with her knees pulled to her chest, one of hundreds of Kali'ka who knelt to tend wounds, whisper in hushed tones, argue in strident voices, cry and comfort, meditate with their hands in their laps, or practice kanas in small clusters.

The cold was sinking into her limbs and the light from scattered torchlight and firepots shrunk into the darkness.

It was all so impossible. So quickly, from New Corinth to Mors, from Mors to Sangra, then leaving to race through the Eternal Day to arrive at Ignis. And the stragglers since then … Kali'ka from aboveground, seeking refuge, not dressed in their robes, shell-shocked and manic. At least, those who knew the pores to Ignis. Those not left wandering without a home, abandoned in the mayhem above.

The stories they brought with them were as unbelievable as the rest. The Eternal Day, destroyed. Riots in the millions. Death and destruction, never before seen in New Corinth. Once the Corinthians had glimpsed it, they'd gorged on it like just another covetous obsession.

And Oyame's parents, her family … she had no idea of where they were or what they were doing. They'd always attended Advent in person.

She admitted how she felt about them and their wanton, unthinking indulgence in Logical values and customs. But … she didn't hate them *only*. No. She didn't believe that hate and love couldn't co-exist. She thought them ill, their illness being the symptom of a more ineffable, uneasily quantified context of causes.

If Oyame tore into her inner self to find what lay there, to find the face of Kali, and then just built another immutable, fixed identity … how was she any different from her parents? Perception was a state of mind, and her mind was *hers* to define.

Oyame wiped the back of her hand across the underside of her eyes, wiping away dirt, sweat and tears in one streak. Nearby, she caught the eye of Ascendant Brae – the burly, bull-shouldered man whose presence was oddly comforting. He was so gentle. So unflappable and constant. It was no wonder Elara had trusted him to ferry them all to safety.

Even worried and fearful, eyes haggard, Brae's cheeks widened as he smiled at her from underneath his thick, frizzy beard. A second later, he turned to someone – Adherent … Cassandra, was it? – who caught his attention and bowed to him before speaking.

Oyame was like Brae, she felt. He had some inner core that couldn't be touched.

Somehow, all of the trials the Kali'ka had endured, all of Oyame's personal strife and hardships … they hadn't hardened her. She felt imbued with the heat of insight and determination – the Goddess' own gifts – not ruthlessness and an acceptance of inevitable suffering. She didn't consider herself a blade to cleave, or a hammer to bludgeon. She thought herself a person, simply, rationally, trying to better herself. Able to do what her two hands could, ready to say what her lips and tongue would.

Circles, ascendancies, rote and ritual … it all seemed wrong. Even though she'd just finished her initiation a short time ago – and would never say so aloud – she sensed an indefinable defect in the heart of their order, aside from the conspiracies in Mors. A puncture that had nothing to do with lunatics like those who killed Ascendant Cyrus, butchering him like an animal.

No … *that* defect was something else entirely. Something as hidden as bone, as deep as genes, as primitive as fear and anger themselves. Something in their collective memory, unlearned and therefore resurgent, again and again. Something having nothing to do, intrinsically, with the Kali'ka.

Elara could help them. Elara could save them. She *would* save them. She'd survived; Oyame knew it. Oyame *believed* it, without seeing, in the innermost root of her being. Oyame had seen Elara's will, her discipline, her unparalleled willingness to throw herself at hazards.

Elara and Kali were one, and together they could bring the Kali'ka back to themselves. To shatter the shackles of a less free future. To bring themselves back from a tattered, beaten group of worn and disheartened disciples.

The moment this thought passed through Oyame's mind, a flare of light, blaring like a trumpet, stormed through the Central Conflux. Heat, pure and potent, evaporated the moist, frozen chill from Oyame's flesh. The ground quaked, the walls trembled, and tiny bits of dust fell from the ceiling.

When all of their eyes adjusted to the sight standing in front of them, body after body fell prostrate to the ground. Their weeping rose like an offering to echo through the earth above them, ringing the air and striking on the drum of the cosmos. For any being who would listen, for the evidence of sight, for the confirmation of belief, for the ardor of knowledge.

For the Goddess. For Elara Aeve, daughter of the Great Mistress Herself, in whom the face of her Mother shone so, so brightly....

CHAPTER 36
PASSING OF AGE

Sophia sat on the floor of the parlor in the Dagon loft, indivisible from the empty darkness of the air, her tiny hands motionless as she stared into the family viewscreen. Its hissing blackness stared at her like a great, all-seeing monocle, dead and broadcasting the stupid noise of the afterlife.

She knew better. She'd seen him – Logos, the dead god. Melted from his bones in a glorious, pyrotechnic blood display. Huddled and trembling in the lowest level of Advent Square. The men and women in gray – such a calming shade. The tenor of Corinthian screams. All of it, blown wide and winking away. Color, light, heat, flashing. Gone. Her, Sophia, a happy shadow, giggling in the corner while rapping her little plastic toys on the floor, just one of the nuances and gradations of a fallen darkness, content to be alone.

No, mommy had said. There was no need to go in person! They could change their mind, couldn't they? Of course they could! The Dresdons and the Carthags might be there, all resplendent, and they might ask about Sophia's Breaching – sneer sneer, finger point, daddy's rolling eyes. The expense for tickets, and the indulgence it represented, were more than enough. Then there was wine, Levitant and squishy sounds for hours.

Then, they'd all watched. Mommy, daddy, her in the corner. Shouting along with the people in the viewscreen who tore at each others' faces, all jumbled up into funny poses.

When it all went away and the bright sky shut off and the evercracks near the ceiling showed only darkness ... Sophia had understood. She knew what must be done. She knew the solution to the plague festering in her heart. The response she'd been waiting to give, for all the contradictions presented her, all the laughs and cajoling between all the upturned lips and frowns.

A fire poker wasn't the same as what the gray people in the viewscreen used, but it was similar enough. Almost anything could be used for the same purpose. The gray ones had provided the model. It was her first time, but she knew how to do it. It was easy. Go for the spots that looked soft. Be quick, and strike hard.

The poker was less bloody than she would've imagined. Most of it was on her hands, on her clothes, on her skin. Or the floor. It was sticky and smelled strangely sweet.

Since then, the walls of the loft vibrated with thuds of explosions. The floor rumbled with ceaseless yelling and tromping of feet. Stories below, doors' widths away.

She realized that she was still sitting there because she was waiting for an answer.

She had to find him, the man who left her untouched, who left her uncleansed. The High Devotee, dressed so lovely in purples and whites, just like in the lithograph on the fireplace mantle.

Really, she hadn't cared either way. It wouldn't have changed anything. She would have had to come back to the same house, walked down the same streets, and felt the same way. The root blemish would have persisted.

But now, staring at mommy and daddy, she wanted to be touched. She wanted to be penetrated. She wanted to receive the Spirit of the dead god. To let the white flow and receive her fill. She wanted to feel ... *something*. The thrill of darkness was already wearing off.

It must be by him, though! He was the only one she wanted. All the rest were liars, but he could be trusted. Yes. Trusted to make her his bride. He was kind. So very kind.

Crinkling her nose at a little tickle from her wispy hair, Sophia turned her head to the kitchen. Her brow pinched into a quizzical frown, and the scar across her eyebrow crooked like a crack in a mirror. She was starting to get hungry, but she was tired. Usually mommy made food.

But mommy just laid there in the dark. Her budded lips, painted dark red, hung open. Blood dribbled out of them, congealing and starting to cool.

Mommy's hair was so beautiful, like straw dyed with persimmons. So soft and luscious. It always was, because she went through great lengths to take care of it. She always went through great lengths to take care of things she cared about. Sophia always thought her own hair – dirty blonde, a tinge coppery – looked like a cheap facsimile in comparison.

Now mommy's hair lay draped across her olive-hued eyes, wide with eternal shock, brushing the length of the neck to her bosom, down to the viscera below as it slopped out to run across the floor in rivulets of red, pooling and filling the synthetic, violet carpet flush with scarlet.

Maybe Sophia needn't go to the kitchen at all. Mommy could provide for her still, like always.

***

Devin stood along the Cusp of the Veneer, at one of the Bridges to Paradise arching over the Tame River, staring out into New Corinth.

There was more light behind him in the Veneer than in front of him in New Corinth proper. More light from natural fires and scavenged lumensrods than from operable standlamps and clusters of glo-globes dotting the cityscape.

Veneerians were starting to trickle out into the city, creeping across the Bridges to Paradise. Slowly, tentatively at first. Their reserve wouldn't last, though, not when they saw no resistance. He'd heard stories about what the Corinthians called the 'Hale Riots', from the few in the Veneer who lived into their 40's or 50's.

As soon as the great arc of light to the east, beaming along the sky, had fallen, and they were left with a clear, black sky, Devin and the rest of them had known that the world they knew was gone.

Explosion after explosion had shattered the air, the thrum of shockwaves and the roar of flames echoing out to the Veneer. Logic relied so heavily on artificial light... Could they really have expected anything differently? Did they really believe their society would just persist endlessly, day to day to Eternal Day?

The Veneer would grow bold enough to diverge and spread, splitting to cover and consume the entirety of the city like a blanket. Ravaging and washing every surface bare from the force of their collective motion, sheering New Corinth of its own populace, the parasitic bumblers of a Logical Earth.

No strength in this world, nor any other, could stop the wrath of the survivors. Nothing could dissuade it. Nothing could erase the memory of whatever cataclysm had happened. Nothing could abate it, could deflect or even slow it. Soon, no place would be safe, no place untouched.

He doubted that the Corinthians really grasped the import of what had happened. In paradise, where there was no murder, no assault, not even the concept of *lack*, their citizens did only what *felt good*. That meant, therefore, that violence *felt good*. They were simply acting on the same modality of impulses that defined every one of their actions. Logic had leashed them along to that exact outcome.

Devin looked down to the rusted hoop in his forearm, remembering the chain that used to snake through it and yank him around from place to place, while his father laughed and laughed and pointed at him to passersby.

Until he grew large. Until he grew stronger than the one who sired him.

Yes, he would personally attest to the bliss of violent conflict. All the Errati would. It was, in essence, what defined them. They knew far better than anyone. Far, far better than those among the Veneerian population who just moped and stared at nothing until dead, having simply given up.

That was why the Errati had to be the force that guided the city. They had to be the will to chaos. They needed to steer the headless beast and focus its drives. They would lead by example, and he, Devin, would be their chieftain.

He had no idea if Nyx's sister, Elara, had succeeded in killing Fallow. But if she was the vanguard, the Errati were the phalanx. They were her guardians, and her deeds were their protectorate, going before them.

Devin knew that Elara was the same as the Errati, from the first time he saw her and that jittery scion, his face torn in anguish, his fingers lingering on her robes as Devin hefted her on his shoulders to trek across byways, through back alleys, over trash heaps and through broad lanes with Nyx trotting as his side.

Now he knew why Nyx – *Charlotte* – was who she was. Charlotte had been personally warmed by her sister, heated by the molten core of Earth itself, incarnate in the body of a woman. Imbued with rushing fire, a dauntless, steadfast courage, and a carriage of fluid grace. Charlotte was just as indomitable as her sister, in a completely different way.

That was why he tried so desperately to understand her decision. Not using rationale, no. Not in words, no. Devin's understanding was a wordless pool of intuitive insight. Nyx had helped him bring more of his intellect to the forefront, but not anymore. Maybe, never again.

He would wait, though. No matter that she might have believed his words only gallant declarations of immature emotion, or that she told him not to, or she might forget him far before he forgot her.

Facing the Tame River, hiding Nyx in a safe place in his heart, Devin raised his voice to his legion of Errati.

"We run!"

Behind him, glimmering in the pale light of the stars above, the Errati stood amassed in the thousands. Every single one of them. Blended creatures of rods and muscles, bolts and skin, hooks and bones. Some were gangly, some were short, some were lanky, some were horrifically malformed, but they were all the same.

They were the unseen world of New Corinth come to life. The unconscious made visible, ready to surge.

"If they touch us, they die. Street by street, alley by alley. Otherwise, leave them alone. There's no other way to make them learn. This is *our* city, now. Our denied birthright. Our new home."

All of them howled with bared teeth, hefting crude bladed and blunt weapons, shaking them high overhead in the night of the new moon, implements designed for one purpose only.

Slaughter.

Devin raised his fist and they charged forward, feet pounding the earth, spearheading the way with an ocean of warcries, discordant, savage, magnificent. The sound called to Devin's blood, drawing it forth like a razor biting down on the artery of his soul.

As the mass of flesh and metal surged towards the dying heart of New Corinth, Devin started to laugh.

***

With a small satchel of supplies pressed to her hip and her shinsen slung on her back, Charlotte flit along the edge of the Tame River, the Bridges to Paradise arching overhead, connecting the Veneer and New Corinth like the arms of conjoined twins trying vainly to push each other apart.

She ran through an internal checklist while there was still a chance: toiletries, dry food, changes of clothes – all packed to economize space and minimize the weight her shoulders and spine would bear.

As she moved, things she'd always wanted to say filled the full scope of her thoughts. Things she would likely never say, at least to the people she wanted.

They never got me, El ... the scions. Thank you.

Since Elara left the Aeve family loft years ago, Charlotte had felt them splitting like a reed torn in half. As time went on and that reed grew taller, its split tip grew further apart. The stress on the base of such a fragile plant tore it further and further, down to its roots, undoing the past as it tore. Undoing their shared memories.

Charlotte loved her sisters, both of them – even Lucrece, confused and lost as she was – but she felt like her memory of Elara was more real than the person she'd seen last, in the Errati's hideout, disfigured, wounded, careless with herself, transformed from a sensitive young woman – her caretaker – into something Charlotte didn't understand. Something she'd made herself into, by need or otherwise.

That lack of understanding hurt more than believing that Elara had died out there in New Corinth.

The distance between them brought attention to unspoken words, deepening their silent pact of mutual understanding. Charlotte would never break that pact with her tongue, if only to preserve the fragile, brittle sanctity of their shared past.

That was why Charlotte never believed in the Kali'ka, or any other doctrine. Lucrece's life had folded to Elara's, and Elara's to Charlotte's. Their family was a chain of sacrifices, cascading through generations, from one sister to the next. She owed them more than repetition of the same.

And Sophia ... Charlotte mourned her little cousin. She mourned her in the way she could only mourn the living. Alone in the world back there, truly apart, a victim without any support.

In some way, Charlotte believed that Elara had construed events to lead towards a final vie for absolute, condition-less freedom. The freedom of not remembering. The freedom granted only in death.

Elara belonged to the realm of Illusion, as she had called it ... forever and always.

And now, Charlotte would belong to the realm of Creation.

She had to leave. She *must* leave. It didn't matter where she went, or how. She couldn't stay in New Corinth, not so close to the past. Not in the family loft, with so many reminders. Not in the light or the dark, in peace or in conflict, not with the people called mother and father.

They weren't her parents, not really. They weren't *parents*, period. They were barely strangers. They were nothing. They treated her like nothing, and so were undeserved of anything. And in the land of Logic, nothing was worth her time, not anymore.

Except Devin.

Charlotte stopped in a patch of shadow, crouching, quickly wiping tears from her eyes, trying to steady her breathing. Ahead, the Tame River broke free of the city walls and curved its way into the countryside. She brushed her amber hair from her face and retied it behind her head, finding her eyes drawn upwards to the endless, starry sky.

He had to understand, out of all people. He *had* to. But even if he never did, he would accept her decision, someday. She didn't think she could leave him behind believing otherwise. But she also couldn't leave, not fully, not like she needed to, believing that it was the last time she'd see him. He would wait there, stuck in the moment of their parting, even though she had no other choice but to move on.

They were all so alike, the three of them ... the sisters of Aeve. Convinced they were doing what they had to, convinced that their choices were forced, but ultimately only hiding like the new moon above, sheltered in a sea of darkness. Protected in shadow.

And on the shortest day of the year, New Corinth began its own Eternal Night.

In night, they all existed under the shelter of the moon. Lies had been put to the senses, and reality could not be ignored – not for Corinthians, not for Veneerians, not for the rest of the watching world. It was not the same moon that slipped its eyelid – *her* eyelid – shut, to sleep for a single night ... but a moon shrouded in blood. A moon shadowed by the sky she beamed behind.

A new moon ... and Charlotte was among its first descendants, a true child of darkness, birthed in light.

Charlotte tugged the straps of her pack and examined the buckles and notches. She scanned the river ahead. The sweetness of damp soil and robust vegetation wafted in from the landscape, penetrating her chest, passing into mist as she exhaled into the chill air.

Her mind felt shapeless, like the vapor she exhaled, free of form and able to ape the aspect of obscure forms. In that formless state, in the colorless gray of a moonless night, the stillness of the moment engraved itself into permanent and emblazoned imagery.

This exact instant had never existed, and would never, again. Neither had today. Neither would tomorrow.

Where her legs traveled, she would be taken, and where she was, she would be. That was all, and nothing more. A future unrestricted, unpredicted, unknown and endowed with mystique. That was the place she would reside, and she herself would make it.

The path walked is what I do, and what I do creates it.

Smiling a small, nearly imperceptible smile, Charlotte Aeve darted off along the edge of the Tame River, humming a tune of brightness, a melody of restoration that rose spontaneously to guide her exodus into the free night.

EPILOGUE

Kali, the Goddess of Time, took the last final steps leading up to Her throne, chiseled into the lonely dark of its cavernous underground home. Blazing like a star in the frozen void, Her flames engulfed Her, curling and sliding, swimming in a dream of stellar flames.

She was all the light needed. She was the heat below.

Sunk in a nigh inaccessible cistern of Earth, resting in its bowels, this chamber was not a place that the eyes of Her life – Her most recent life – had ever seen. That life was already fading to the greater fraction of Her identity.

The past dangled in the back of Her mind like a muffled echo. The present was a fragmented swatch of chaotic noise. So many things, now, were hazy. Time itself, though Hers, unwound.

"You have performed admirably … Aegis Council."

Thank You, Great Mistress. She felt, rather than heard, Her council's answer, rasping in a single voice. Spread in a semicircle around Her throne, they stood with heads lowered and hands clasped, the hoods of their robes pulled forward. Their sallow, waxen skin glowed luminescent in Her light. They stood in the same spots they once occupied in life – the original twelve, last of the first Kali'ka who once walked the catacombs of this bygone cloister with Her.

"I know what you want, old ones. The present we foresaw has come to pass. My face has been kept safe, like an unspoken secret, in the hearts of My followers. Our purpose has ended. There is no more need for ascendancy, no more need for any of the old rites. Your stewardship is finished. I have returned. We are one, the Vessel and I. Creation and Illusion, made undivided."

They stood unmoved – eleven of them. The Nightwalker had already unbound one of their number in a crude, forced manner.

He was a clever creature, the Nightwalker, but filled with futile ambition. Artificially induced Transcendence... What a fool. He only knew how to take what he couldn't have, and how to poorly imitate what came naturally for Her Vessel.

Now he was cast adrift on the ocean of life and death, hovering aimlessly in the void, never to return, never to leave, never reborn, never unborn, never remembered.

Kali lifted Her blade high above Her head, letting Her power flow into it, letting it fill to burst till it glowed white hot and its flames overflowed and dripped to the ground in tumbling, crackling tongues.

Fangs bore, She turned Her face – rapturous and savage – towards Her council, peering through the veil of waking memories and the skin of cosmic fury.

"Are you prepared?"

Yes, Great Mistress.

She crooked Her arm, and in a single, vicious lunge, cleaved the air. An arc of surging flame tore from Her blade and through Her council like the lash of a solar flare. The flames shredded their matter to nothing, disintegrating their bodies in a flash of red dust that singed and vanished.

Finally, She was alone. Utterly, truly, alone.

Far away and high above, She felt Her council's sarcophagi rupture in a detonation of force and stone, collapsing the backbone of Cloister Sangra and caving in whole faces of earth into its vast, empty pit – burying the thirteenth sarcophagus, cutting the cord, and obliterating the chance for future generations to speak to Her through the mirror of Her Well.

Her blade was Hers once again, and Her mask was no longer a mask. Her mask was *Her*.

Turning, the Goddess lowered Herself onto Her throne and in a single thrust, drove Her blade into the stone underfoot. A cascade of fractures splintered from its edge and raced across the floor.

There She sat, in the core of Her keep, sliding Her fingers along the black basalt of Her throne's armrests, with her sword driven into stone next to Her.

The imprint of the Great Divide was keener there, in the original cloister, than elsewhere. That and … pain. So much sorrow, so much regret, as though the stones themselves soaked it in. The time before the Burning, well before the current age, reverberated all the way to the present through the smallest of ripples.

Her fingertips sensed granular inconsistencies and subtle, coarse imperfections in Her stony armrest. This small, delicate act of the body – the focus on detail, the connection with something tangible, something elemental – breathed a whisper of Her earthly form into Her body, pushing to the forefront like the silhouette of a lone woman hung in the sky, practicing kanas against a backdrop of fused nebulae.

Soon. I'll see you again, soon, little one… Be safe.

Thinking of those She once loved, the Great Mistress smiled and passed from the world of Creation, enveloped in the fusion of starfire, taken back home in a chariot of atomic brilliance.

Left in Her place was a body of fine, milk-gray ash – sitting in the form of woman on a throne of vitrified glass – fused into place by a heat that did not cool, *would* not cool, bonded by the glow of furious cells of embers, white and pulsing. A monument to one who once walked amongst the living with a passion so deep, it left a physical mark on a physical reality.

In this way, Kali would never leave Creation again.

From Her central point, heat radiated in a perfect sphere, at all points, along all axes, equidistant from Her origin. Within Her flawless circumference did all things shimmer and burn and silently seethe in the stillness of an endless, underground night.

So the altar was laid. The nascent womb. A new skin for the living Goddess.

ABOUT THE AUTHOR

Richard Milner is an author; the founder of The Writer's Kiln, an online discussion and consultation group for writers; a former English teacher, both in the U.S. and abroad; and a narrative designer in the video game industry. He is also the creator and moderator of Sit Down, Shut Up & Write (Orange County), a productivity-focused writer's group on meetup.com.

He thrives on fringe and speculative subject matter, and takes strong influence from music and visual arts. With a background in Psychology, he finds particular joy in merging character-driven stories with elements of genre fiction, especially within a mythological or metaphysical context.

Richard currently lives in southern California with his uncommonly patient wife, his distractingly cute cat, and his jarringly energetic dog. He ranks soup and coffee among mankind's greatest accomplishments.

Stay connected:
facebook.com/richardmilnerauthor
twitter.com/AuthorMilner
authormilner.tumblr.com

Visit his website:
richardmilnerauthor.com

37417092R00225

Made in the USA
Charleston, SC
06 January 2015